FOR BUTTER OR WORSE

FOR BUTTER OR WORSE

ERIN LA ROSA

THORNDIKE PRESS
A part of Gale, a Cengage Company

LIBRARY OF CONGRESS CIP DATA ON FILE.
CATALOGUING IN PUBLICATION FOR THIS BOOK
IS AVAILABLE FROM THE LIBRARY OF CONGRESS.

ISBN-13: 979-8-88579-938-6 (softcover alk. paper)

Published in 2024 by arrangement with Harlequin Enterprises ULC.

For Eoghan (my Devil)

1

NINA

Nina Lyon stared into her dressing room's vanity mirror. Her palms were planted firmly against the table, but she bounced on the balls of her feet — the same way she did whenever she was nervous. And she was borderline vibrating with unease.

The average at-home viewer would never notice, because her glam team, who'd become experts at giving her the "natural" look — despite the false lashes, bronzer and endless eyebrow filler — had done a superb job. Her stylist had zipped her into a classic black jumpsuit accessorized with a gold statement necklace and slim python belt that cinched her waist and showed off the roundness of her hips. Even if she didn't feel confident, she looked as flawless as a mirror-glazed cake. She was iced perfection.

"I can do this. I. Can. Do. *This,*" she said out loud.

"Hell yes, you fucking can!" Her sister Sophie's voice burst through the phone. "Hell yes, you fucking can!"

Nina looked down at her best friend, Jasmine, and her sister on FaceTime. If anyone could pump her up, it was her minihype team.

"Repeat after me," Jasmine commanded. "I will not fall in my heels."

"Now that you've cursed her by saying it out loud, she's definitely going to fall," Sophie chided.

"On this very helpful note, I should probably go." Nina raised a playful eyebrow.

"Nothing, and I mean *nothing* is going to go wrong!" Sophie said.

"Just remember these words — do not fall —"

Nina interrupted her bestie, "Okay, 'bye!" Then she ended the video chat.

She exhaled sharply. Normally, she wouldn't give Jasmine's comment more than a passing thought. But tonight was deeply important, and something as innocuous as tripping could actually be a problem.

I can do this, Nina reminded herself. It was the taping of the finale of the third season of *The Next Cooking Champ!* and she'd worked her entire career to get to this point. While most chefs cooked in obscurity,

8

people knew her name. She was also a female chef, a minority in the restaurant world, and the producers had taken a chance on her. But she'd earned her spot. She'd built Lyon — a successful restaurant — on her own, and had won awards while growing a loyal clientele. To her, food was more than a meal. Food was *everything.*

"We need a hair-and-makeup check on Nina," Tiffany, a producer on the show, said quickly into her headset. She had one of those inscrutable faces that meant getting a read on how she was feeling was nearly impossible until she actually spoke.

"What do you think?" Nina cautiously spun to show the full effect of the costume designer's wardrobe choice.

"You're sweating." Tiffany stared at Nina's hairline.

Okay, well, that wasn't the answer she'd hoped for. "Wait, I'm what —"

"Walk with me," Tiffany said, cutting her off, then turned on her Converse-sneakered heel. Nina trailed after her.

They left the cocoon of Nina's dressing room and made their way to the soundstage, which was outfitted with cooking stations, KitchenAid mixers, multiple burners, mixing bowls, measuring cups and an alphabetized spice rack. The setup wasn't dissimilar from her own restaurant's kitchen . . . except for the reality-show part.

Nina carefully ran a finger along the top of her forehead. She *was* sweating, and not just because of the bright, overhead lights or the row of cameras that would soon be trained on her.

Sharp footsteps approached the sound-stage, and Nina turned to see the real source of her jitters: Leo O'Donnell.

Her cohost on the show was as annoying as a piece of spinach lodged in between her front teeth. He wasn't a chef. He was a businessman, and his only accomplishment was turning his father's charming Italian restaurant, Vinny's, into a bland chain. Unlike Nina, he wasn't passionate about food — all he cared about was the bottom line.

She just needed to make it through this taping, ideally without screaming at him. If she accomplished that, then they could go back to doing what they did best: hating each other.

However, not yelling would be difficult, because Leo — aka the person whose face she pictured when she needed to pound out some dough — always knew how to provoke the worst in her.

After tonight, though, the show would wrap for the season. She'd return to the day-to-day running of her restaurant, and trade in bowls of prop food for the real thing. Instead of working with Leo, where she had to control her gag reflex, she'd be in the kitchen with Jasmine. Just the thought of her old routine was like a warm cup of cocoa — comforting and extremely necessary. As much as Nina loved mentoring the budding chefs and working with the insanely talented behind-the-scenes crew . . . she needed the time off. From Leo the man-child, to be more specific.

A stylist soundlessly appeared at Nina's side and worked on the unruly flyaways that always erupted from her head under the heat of the on-camera lighting, while a man with a compact dabbed over her forehead.

"How's *my* hair and makeup?" Leo stopped and cocked his chin at the exact angle for the overhead light to accentuate his immaculate swoop of dark hair. It was as if someone had marked, with an *X,* the exact spot for him to stand so he'd look his absolute best. He was close to being six feet tall and carried himself in an overly confident way that gave him even more height. He wore a crisp white shirt, unbuttoned just enough to reveal the faintest whiff of his chest hair — a touch she'd bet a hundred bucks that *he'd* made, and not the stylist.

As he came to stand next to her, he studied her face.

"Are you sweating?" he finally asked.

"What?" *Of course, he'd noticed.* "No." She self-consciously touched her hairline again.

The makeup person gave him a once-over, then smiled. "You're set."

Nina rolled her eyes. One of his many flaws was that he was physically flawless. The kind of man who only got right swipes and never had to pay for a drink in his life. And if anyone claimed they weren't attracted to him, well . . . they'd be lying. Like people who said they hated cake. *Liars.* Even Nina would never deny that he was handsome, in a certain light, if you squinted hard enough. Luckily, his habit of "playfully" undercutting her canceled out any urges she might have toward him.

"It's a good thing they can get your hair big enough to hide the witch hat." Leo absentmindedly rolled up the cuff of his shirt, like he hadn't even noticed she was there.

Nina ignored how seeing a hint of his skin made her mouth twitch, just slightly. *Stop drooling.*

"Don't you want to use a little powder to take the shine off his cloven hooves?" Nina

12

asked the makeup person, but she couldn't help but notice that Leo's lips twinged at her comment.

"We're back in sixty!" Tiffany called out loudly to the crew, then turned to Nina. "Should I be worried?"

"If he can play nice, I will, too." Nina eyed Leo, who either didn't hear her or, more likely, chose to tune her out.

She understood why Tiffany was twitching, just like everyone else on set. For the first time in the history of the show's three seasons, they were taping *live*. A ploy to boost the ratings, which had been steadily declining thanks to all the new reality shows cropping up . . . or so the network executives had explained. They needed to attract viewers to remain on the air, and stay relevant, even if it meant entering dangerous territory by taping live.

Which meant there were no editors to cut around the indignant stink eye Leo made every time Nina gave a food critique. The director couldn't call "Cut!" so the audience wouldn't hear the fake retching sounds Nina made when Leo attempted a lame dad joke. While nuanced editing created the illusion that Leo and Nina were occasionally cheeky toward each other, rather than mortal enemies, this time they wouldn't have that luxury. They had to pretend to be absolutely delightful together — two sublime cake toppers for their audience at home. The stakes were high, and it was Tiffany's job to keep them both in line.

"Don't worry. I'm channeling Betty White." Nina squeezed Tiffany's shoulder.

In classic Tiffany fashion, she returned the gesture with a blank look.

"We both know I'm not the problem. Only one of us has an official nickname," Leo said offhandedly, like he hadn't just turned the stove up to high.

And now Nina was truly about to boil over, but instead she bit the inside of her cheek to keep what little cool she had.

Even after years of having "Nasty Nina" trend on Twitter, be used in tabloid articles and left in comments on her IG posts, the fact that she had *that* as a nickname genuinely hurt her feelings. She was Nasty Nina, and the word *nasty* was definitely not a compliment. Especially not when trolls on Twitter lobbed it at her any time she so much as forgot to smile as the end credits rolled.

"I guess I should thank you for coining the nickname?" He was the reason she had one, after all.

"It was a joke. How was I supposed to

14

know people would run with it?" He shrugged off her annoyance, like he couldn't understand why she'd even be bothered.

That moment, captured in the holiday special during the show's second season, was one she'd never forget. She could replay the clip on YouTube — it had over three million views and counting — whenever she wanted. His comment had caused their relationship as coworkers to turn from placid to a raging hellfire.

A contestant had baked a cake into the shape of Santa's naughty-or-nice list. Unfortunately, the iced cursive letters weren't easy to read. So when Leo bent down, he'd said, "Nasty or nice? We all know I'm on the nice list, but Nina . . ."

In response, she'd made a face. More specifically, her nostrils flared, her eyebrows raised nearly up to her scalp and her mouth had twisted open into a horrified grimace as if trying to swallow Leo whole.

The Nasty Nina meme soon followed. His offhand "joke" resulted in #NastyNina trending on Twitter for a whole weekend. And the nickname had stuck, further adding to her current reputation problem.

Well, "problem" was more of a euphemism for "nightmare." When the show first started, patrons had flocked to her restaurants in San Francisco, Napa and Los Angeles. But after multiple seasons in which she'd been the harsh judge, the crowds had waned. As it turned out, people didn't want to give money to a chef who made everyone cry. Nina was never proud when one of her comments hit a nerve, but she didn't want to sugarcoat her reactions, either. She knew women were expected to be nurturing and sweet, but that just wasn't her style. While she liked to think of herself as a mentor, ultimately, she preferred to give honest critiques that would help the contestants improve their craft. Was being candid really so wrong?

The novelty of her being a celebrity had worn off, too, and as of last month she'd quietly closed her Napa location. Her San Francisco spot had closed the year prior. All she had left was her Los Angeles restaurant — the first one she'd opened. At this point, using the show's platform to turn her reputation around was critical.

And going down as the female Gordon Ramsay had never been part of the plan. She was ambitious, worked hard and saw this as a massive opportunity. She'd signed on to the show with the hope that she could become a household name and brand herself so she'd be in every living room in

America. Eventually, she'd get her own show and open more restaurants. Maybe even bring her food to the east coast. A chef could dream!

But how could she accomplish any of that with Leo by her side? The truth was, he wanted her to be seen as the mean judge. From day one, he'd taken advantage of the fact that she was blunt, so he'd cranked up his own charm. When asked about how he "managed" working with Nasty Nina in interviews, he never came to her defense. And while she couldn't completely prove it, she was fairly certain he'd even talked a producer into giving her the smaller dressing room. How else to explain that she got ready in a broom closet while he had enough space to fit a sectional sofa?

"We're back in thirty!" Tiffany shouted to the set. Then added to Nina and Leo, "Remember, don't step on each other's lines. That last rehearsal was a disaster."

"I'm happy to deliver Nina's lines, since she seems incapable of reading off a monitor." Leo glanced beyond her and directly at Tiffany, just as easily as discarding a wilted garnish.

Whatever — she wasn't going to let his petty antics distract her from fixing how the viewers perceived her. Well, maybe she was . . . "The real problem is that you think your voice is the only one worth hearing." Nina enunciated every word, and he finally looked at her. She glared back.

"My voice is preferable to the screeching banshee noise that comes out whenever you open your mouth." He smiled widely, his teeth as white and sparkling as a clean countertop.

"I use a pitch only dogs can hear, so no surprise that includes you." Nina squeezed her arms tightly across her chest to keep from lunging for his throat.

"Children, this is *live.* And you promised to behave." Tiffany listened to her headset. "Back in fifteen!" Tiffany walked away from them, disappearing behind the wall of cameras pointed their way.

"Did you miss a Botox session? I see a line." She reached up to touch a finger to an imaginary spot on his forehead, and he swatted her hand away.

Her breath caught in her throat at the unexpected warmth of his skin against hers. But she immediately shook it off.

"Back in ten!"

"Why don't you take your broom and ride off to the local coven meeting?" He ran a hand through his unfairly thick hair.

"Back in five!"

"That would be great for the show's ratings. All alone, you'd rock that demo of viewers who love watching paint dry." Nina smirked, happy to have the last dig before they went on-air.

"Three, two . . ." Tiffany's voice faded and the red light on camera C blinked back to life.

"Welcome to the finale of *The Next Cooking Champ!*" Leo said in his fake, shellacked-on TV voice, which was smooth and measured in a way his natural one wasn't.

The first time she'd heard that tone was the day they met, in a truly unglamorous casting office. When he'd walked in she'd assumed he was in the building for a different audition — leading man in an upcoming rom-com or handsome doctor in a future Shonda Rhimes drama. He had the good looks of an actor, and the arrogance of someone who wasn't used to being told no. But, incredibly, he was there for the cooking show. He was in tailored, dark-wash jeans and a snug black shirt that fit him like poured chocolate ganache. He had thick chestnut waves, well-groomed facial hair and a distinguished nose that bent ever so slightly at the top. He was lean and defined, like he put in effort, but wasn't about to say

19

no to a slice of pizza. Or three. Which Nina preferred. She couldn't get involved with someone who didn't eat. Of course, now that she knew him, she would never ever, ever, *ever* consider being with someone like Leo.

Not that she dated. She didn't have the time, unless you asked her sister, who thought it was more that Nina didn't *make* time. Most men were intimidated by someone on television who had a reputation for being "difficult," and her last relationship had been, well, an absolute failure.

"For those just tuning in, I'm Leo O'Donnell."

"And I'm Nina Lyon. We have two contestants competing for the prize of two hundred thousand dollars, a cookbook deal and the title of *The Next Cooking Champ,*" she said, reading off the teleprompter.

She smiled for the cameras, but a big shot of genuine dopamine hit her at the same time. This was the *finale* of the third season. Her job was hosting a beloved cooking show, and she had the privilege of helping to change someone's life for the better. She was damn lucky to be in this position. And she was a good mentor and chef. She wasn't going to let the fact that Leo was standing next to her diminish any of what she'd

20

achieved.

"That's right," Leo chimed in. "Our contestants have one hour remaining to present us with their appetizer, entrée and dessert courses. They're cooking live so you can really get a sense of the pressure they're currently under."

She would definitely get through the taping. Why had she been so stressed about being with Leo? The night wasn't about him, or her, really. She was just excited to see the dishes the chefs made for them. She could do *this.*

"Let's check in on our two finalists!" As she turned to move toward a cooking station, she caught Leo's eye. He winked at her, a move so subtle she wasn't even sure if the cameras caught it. But she did, and a quick flutter rose in her belly that then caused her to blink rapidly. A move she was absolutely sure the cameras *did* catch. *He is so irritating,* she told herself.

"Tell us about your entrée, Samantha." Leo leaned across the counter, something he always did to endear himself to the contestants. "It looks like a dish I'd want to eat with a tall pint of beer."

Samantha visibly relaxed at the comment. For all of Leo's faults, Nina couldn't deny how quickly he made the contestants feel at ease. He wanted them to succeed just as much as she did. Maybe she could remember that one positive trait whenever she wanted to stab daggers at him with her eyes.

Then he tap-tap-tapped his foot at Nina. He'd started this "fun" new tapping code during dress rehearsals. His way of signaling that he was waiting for her to speak. As if she couldn't do her job fast enough for his liking. He'd found a secret way to irritate her, even though she'd asked him repeatedly to stop during rehearsals.

The response flowed out of her as if the tapping from his foot had turned on the faucet in the sink. "Speak slowly and simply so Leo can understand what you're saying."

She instantly regretted the dig. Hadn't she just talked herself into trying to be nice to him? Being rude wasn't who she was, not really. Only Leo brought out this side of her. When she watched clips from the show, she sometimes barely knew whom she was watching. She just couldn't fake being polite with him, no matter how hard she tried. Still, this version of herself wasn't who she wanted to be, or what she wanted the fans to witness.

He raised one thick eyebrow at her, a challenge. She'd tossed out the first grenade,

22

and now he'd probably return with a cannon.

Shit. So much for not reacting to him. Being enemies was their dynamic — it was how they were. She just hoped they could make it through this live taping without destroying each other, and the show, in the process.

2

LEO

"Don't look Nina directly in the eye or you'll turn to dust," Leo fired back. He relished getting under her skin. Seeing her cool, calm demeanor crack, even slightly, gave him a thrill. *He,* lowly Leo, had an effect on *her,* the unmovable Nina.

Then he remembered the cameras were rolling. People were watching at home, including his mother. *Ah, shit.* His mom was the head of their household, and she was going to give him hell for being rude. He clenched his jaw.

He shouldn't have done the tapping thing. He knew it annoyed her. He just couldn't help himself.

"Leo . . ." Nina's voice was thick with condescension and her lips formed an *O* that seemed poised to suck out his soul. "Look at you with a little joke. You are *hilarious.*" Weirdly, the low hum of her voice settled in his brain and made the hairs on the back of his neck stand up. A primal defense mechanism telling him to flee before he was eaten alive.

He didn't think of himself as someone who could ever be disliked . . . until he'd met Nina. He was *extremely* likable, in large part thanks to his dad. When Leo had worked at the family restaurant during summer vacations in high school, his father said that every customer who walked through the door should be treated as family. That everyone-is-family-here attitude eventually became the slogan for their business when they opened a second location. *Everyone is family here* was printed on the menus, and written in each new employee handbook.

And Leo had taken the motto to heart, even outside of work. He wanted to make his father proud, which is why in college he'd been homecoming king — his peers had voted. Votes don't lie! When he first took over his dad's business, he became President of the Small Business Association of Southern California and had been honored with an award for Restaurant Philanthropist of the Year . . . twice. Not a brag, per se, but worth noting. He'd been asked to host the Pasadena Culinary Cup Awards four years in a row — back by popular demand. And women, in particular, loved him. He'd made it onto a list of BuzzFeed's 27 Hottest Reality Stars — number fifteen was a coveted spot! He'd never had an enemy, until now.

So he was bothered by the idea that Nina genuinely hated him. Well, more than bothered. Just that morning, he'd had a massage, stress-eaten a Double-Double from In-N-Out and listened to one of those ridiculous meditation apps. The massage was soothing, the burger delicious and the meditation app surprisingly relaxing, but still . . . not his usual filming day routine, and all because he couldn't handle not knowing what mood she'd be in on set.

The truth, which he planned to take to his grave, was that he was insecure about his position on the show. He'd never attended culinary school. He had an MBA and had inherited his dad's successful restaurant. Nina was a celebrated chef known for being innovative with food, and he'd created a chain of profitable eateries that served traditional Italian fare. He'd foolishly hoped that he and Nina would be friends when he initially came on the show, but that dream disappeared the moment she'd decided he didn't belong there in the first place.

Leo clenched then unclenched his fists, the way his former therapist taught him. His pulse was faster than normal, and he had to get his anxiety under control. He couldn't take a break, or retreat to his dressing room to regain his composure. They were live.

"Should I tell you about my main?" Samantha, the first contestant, asked hesitantly. "I'm making pan-seared scallops, seaweed salad and a squid-ink-infused black bun."

That snapped Leo right back to the present. *Stop fixating on Nina.* He was representing the Vinny's name, and he had a role to play — wholesome, warm, friendly. Being passive-aggressive on-air wouldn't accomplish that.

Doing his job wasn't much help, either, though, because the overall look of Samantha's dish was Halloween on a plate; the black bun, green of the seaweed and orange seared tops of the scallops weren't exactly making his mouth water. Vinny's wasn't a gourmet eatery, as Nina liked to remind him — "endless breadsticks aren't something to brag about" — but his father always emphasized the importance of bringing out a good-looking plate of food to customers. Presentation mattered, but just as he always

27

did, he'd dig deep and find some encouraging words to highlight his nice-guy persona.

"It's a very *spoo-o-o-ky* sight!" Leo elongated the word *spooky* in what he hoped was a comical way. Nina cleared her throat beside him, as if holding back judgment. If this was a normal taping, she'd groan in pain, like she always did at his jokes. Then he'd clench his jaw, and the director would tell everyone to cut.

"There you go with that Leo wit again . . ."

He glanced at Nina and swore she rolled her eyes at him.

"Nina, we're all dying to know what a James Beard Award winner thinks. Why don't you start?" He arched an eyebrow. *Come on, insult me back.*

Her nostrils flared at him before she said, "Chef Gontran Cherrier does a similar bun at his bakery in France, but it's sweet and chocolaty. This is a unique spin on it."

Interesting. If he didn't know her as well as he did, he'd almost think Nina's comment sounded like praise. But she was never generous with compliments. He, of all people, knew that.

"Chef Gon . . . ?" Samantha began. She clearly didn't know who Chef Cherrier was. Leo saw an opportunity to save Samantha. And, yes, he could've done it without throw-

28

ing Nina under the bus. But where would the fun be in that? He stepped in and said, "We all know Nasty Nina likes to name-drop."

Shit. He was aiming to poke, not tackle her. But the nickname had just slipped out, which was a surprise even to him.

Nina opened her mouth to respond, but he caught sight of Tiffany's flailing arms out of the corner of his eye. The teleprompter lit up, and he quickly said, "We will check in with Freddie once we come back from the commercial break with our special live finale of *The Next Cooking Champ!*"

The red light of the camera went black.

Nina whipped around to face him. Her cheeks were flushed, and her eyebrows pinched together. He hadn't realized steam could actually come out of someone's ears, but he was fairly certain he spotted some wafting out of hers. "Did you seriously just call me that? On-air? *Live?*"

He could feel the heat of her breath on his skin. Goose bumps prickled up his arms and neck. He was . . . inexplicably excited.

Even though Nina was arrogant and a know-it-all, that didn't stop the way his body responded to her. While — logically — he knew to keep as far away as possible, illogically, he was drawn to her. Despite her personality, she was still gorgeous — all wavy dark hair and curves that made looking away difficult. Not to mention that sometimes when she got mad, he seemed to get . . . *more* turned on. So, yeah, he had some weird fetish for opinionated women, or something, and she happened to be exactly that. The fact that her hair always smelled like cinnamon, which made his treacherous, double-crossing impulses want to lean closer to catch a whiff, didn't help, either . . .

His phone vibrated with a text from his twin brother, Gavin. Dude . . . chill.

Leo blinked. *Right.* His family was watching the show, and he clearly looked like an asshole. His brother wouldn't have sent him a warning text otherwise.

"Nina." His mouth went dry when he saw the hurt expression on her face, and her sagging shoulders. He'd made her feel this way, because he was a total idiot, apparently. "I shouldn't have used your nickname, that was wrong of me. Let's just pretend I never said anything."

"So I should also pretend you didn't bring up my James Beard Award, like it's something to be ashamed of?" She narrowed her eyes at him. "Sorry you run a conveyor-belt restaurant." Her voice was full of acid, but

30

she blinked, then quickly looked down.

A conveyor-belt restaurant? He deserved her rage, but he'd offered an olive branch and she'd snapped it in half.

"I know what you think of me, Nina. The only food worth eating costs a month's rent, right? How's that going for you? I heard the LA location is in trouble now, too." He flinched as he said the words. He wanted to take them back, but couldn't. Her Napa location had just closed, and her San Fran restaurant had long been shuttered. Being pompous wasn't what the masses wanted, and foodies didn't love that she'd "sold out" and joined a TV show rather than focusing on her craft.

"We're back in sixty," Tiffany shouted across the soundstage. "Can't I trust you to act like you're the luckiest fucks in the world because you're getting paid to eat food? Do *not* get me fired," she added to Nina and Leo.

Nina didn't say a word in response, which was rare. She bit her full bottom lip and kept her gaze focused on a spot beyond Leo, refusing to meet his eyes.

If they had been friends, he would have told her that he'd had to quietly close one of his locations this year as well. He'd made a poor business decision and overextended himself. Though, maybe she already knew about his failure and had chosen not to mention it. For as brutal as she could be toward him, she only lashed out when he did. Why couldn't he just keep his damn mouth shut? But he didn't have the time to fix what he'd said, because Tiffany was counting down from ten, nine, eight . . .

"I'm sorry, seriously. The taping is almost over," Leo offered as the countdown continued. "In an hour you can take out the cauldron and cast a hex on me. Then I'll either be dead, or we'll have hiatus and you won't have to see me for months."

"I don't plan to see you ever again after this." Nina didn't look at him, and instead smiled as the red dot of the camera lit up and they came back from the commercial break.

Didn't plan to see him again? *So dramatic,* he thought. He squared his shoulders and smiled alongside Nina as they both read from the teleprompter.

Nina was eerily calm as Freddie, the next contestant, described her entrée of tamarind-and-balsamic-braised beef short ribs, sunchoke-and-truffle puree and sautéed chanterelle mushrooms. The kind of calm in a horror film that serves as the buildup to the first kill. Leo was starting to sweat under the jacket. She was definitely hiding something from him, and he knew it wouldn't end well.

When they called time on the contestants, Nina and Leo moved into the separate judging room, which was really just a different part of the soundstage with plaster walls. They ate appetizers of seared duck liver and coconut shrimp, the two entrées and basil panna cotta with tomato jam and deconstructed pecan pie for dessert. There were flaws with the dishes, for sure, but overall, each piece was restaurant-quality. Freddie and Samantha would do well beyond the soundstage, and Leo was jealous of their talent.

Taking over his dad's restaurant had never been a question. Vinny's was a family business, and his mom wanted to keep it that way, especially after his dad passed. But while hanging around the kitchen made him capable of cooking the recipes, so long as he followed them, he was never inventive enough to craft his own. Gavin had been gifted all the talent for cooking. So Leo had over-indexed on the congeniality, and studied hard in school so that he could master the business portion of running a restaurant. Still, he wished he'd inherited some of his dad's talent, or any of it, really.

"Freddie's short ribs were just how I like them, tender and smoky." Nina's eyes closed, as if she were savoring the dish all over again.

Leo swallowed. Had the words *tender* and *smoky* ever sounded so . . . explicit?

When she opened her eyes, he realized he'd been staring. He cleared his throat and looked away.

"Well . . ." He searched for a question that didn't involve asking her to repeat *smoky* on a loop. Seriously, why had that sounded so hot? "What about Sam's panna cotta?"

"The tomato jam overpowered the basil for me," she said matter-of-factly. "Which is a shame, because she's usually such an expert with pulling together unusual flavors."

He let out a big breath, which he hadn't realized he'd been holding. He knew they were back on track. They'd announce the winner, wrap the season and go on hiatus. The show was nearing the end, and they'd managed to put his Nasty Nina comment behind them. Why the hell had he gone and used that in the first place? He wanted to shake his head at himself, but the cameras were still rolling.

"That was a heck of a sigh!" She laughed. "What? You disagree?" She crossed her arms, almost playfully.

He cocked his head. He knew he shouldn't get his hopes up, but her smile seemed like a win. Getting to look at her directly in the eyes without feeling her bore a hole through his skull also felt good. He decided to roll with the new and improved mood she appeared to be in.

"No, not at all." He crossed his arms to mirror her. "If I've learned anything over the last few years, it's that in the end, you're always right."

"So are we agreed? We know who *The Next Cooking Champ!* will be?" She practically beamed.

A deciding vote had never come this easily before. They usually spent a solid half hour playing "toss the snarky comment" when it came to judging dishes. He would lob a "You would say that . . ." and she'd snap back with an "I know you don't cook, but . . ." Eventually, they'd land on a decision, but this one was easy. Maybe she'd more than forgiven him. Maybe by mentioning her nickname on-air, he'd somehow released the demon that had followed them around since the second season of the show. Was it possible they could actually be on set and . . . just be normal?

"We're agreed."

■ ■ ■ ■

Freddie wept when her name was announced. Leo let Nina have the honor of presenting her with *The Next Cooking Champ!* chef's hat, hoping the gesture might alleviate any residual tension.

Then Tiffany signaled for them to wrap the show. They'd practiced the ending and it was going to be a straightforward see-you-next-season spiel.

Only, instead of walking over to Leo, Nina approached the stage. He frowned. Had he misremembered the order of events?

Nina stood in the spot Freddie had occupied moments earlier when giving her acceptance speech. She straightened her shoulders, then leveled Leo with one direct and unwavering look.

A knot formed in his stomach. He should've sensed a shift in the air.

Without having said a word, he already knew that Nina hadn't forgiven him. They weren't on good terms. Nothing had changed and, in fact, things were about to get significantly worse. This was the part of the horror film where he met his untimely fate.

"Before we end this season, I have an announcement to make." Her voice boomed across the soundstage, steadfast and resolute in a way that made him nauseous with anticipation of what she was about to say. "I had a realization tonight, thanks to our *friend,* Leo O'Donnell, who reminded me of what's important."

Leo twitched. Did she call him a "friend"? And what on earth had he said that remotely stuck with her?

She let out an audible breath, then shook her hands, like she was brushing off some nervous energy. "This will be my final season of *The Next Cooking Champ!*" She smiled tightly, but Leo's mouth fell open. Was this really happening?

"As you all know, I'm a chef first and foremost. The food is what's important," she continued, sure of herself. "So that's what I'm going to get back to — focusing on the food. And maybe in the future, you'll see me on a different show. I'd absolutely love nothing more than to come back when the time is right. But for now, if you need to see *Nasty Nina,* come to Lyon. Thank you so much for the advice, Leo."

She looked directly at him then, and he tensed under her gaze. This was happening. They were broadcasting live, and Nina had just essentially dropped the mic.

He took a few steps toward her as she continued to walk past the cameras, away from the producers, and toward the exit.

"Nina?" he croaked. She didn't turn back, but the red light on the camera pointing at him turned on. *That's just great.* The GIFs that would quickly follow of him looking like a sad puppy were going to be the icing on this clusterfuck cake. If she wasn't going to come back, he'd have to go to her. He shook his head and started to sprint until he caught up with her. She turned and a thick, wavy strand of hair fell in front of her eyes. They burned amber back at him — danger.

"You've made your point." He leaned closer and put a hand on her shoulder, feeling an unexpected jolt of static electricity. She glanced down, then shrugged him off.

"If you haven't noticed, I was on my way out. What do you want?" She crossed her arms and looked away. For a split second she seemed bored, just like the first time he'd met her.

"If you're going to quit then you have to at least make fun of me on camera. It can't just be that you're gone." He was trying to joke. He wanted desperately to turn back the dial and return to the beginning of the taping, before he'd pissed her off to the point of leaving.

But she wasn't laughing, smirking, or even so much as giving him room to breathe. Instead, she slowly shifted her focus back to him, as if just noticing he was standing there. Then her gaze intensified and Leo took in a deep breath from the force of it. "Good luck," she said. "You'll need it." Then she broke eye contact and continued to walk toward the glowing neon exit sign at the corner of the stage. She grew smaller until he could no longer see her at all.

He turned around to face the soundstage. There was a camera in his face and the red light glowed back at him. *Fuck.*

@mrsleotoyou mom and dad are fight-ingggg

@doughb4ho is this real????

@thankunxtbaker Leo ur so hot. I would never walk out on you. DM me, please!!!

@le0snumber1 knew this was coming. #NastyNina strikes again

@nuts4nina hello!!! He was being a dick-head!

@bakingchmp99 this is why we can't have nice things.

@bbqbrother GOOD 4 U! Nina always seems like she's perpetually on her period. Time 2 get RID

@rollingpindiva never used to respect Nina. Seemed like a bitch. but I think I might just marry her now?

@LeoFan03 same ^^^

@rollingpindiva your profile pic is kinda cute

@LeoFan03 ☺

3

NINA

Charlie: At least I know our relationship isn't the only thing you left unfinished.

Nina had reread the text from her ex many, many, *many* times. They hadn't spoken since she'd left him after joining the show. So the passive-aggressive message was a surprise. She couldn't exactly blame him for being hurt — no one wants to be dumped — but she *had* left for a reason, and he knew why.

Leo probably didn't even have relationships long enough to keep women's numbers in his phone. She'd seen enough tweets from gossip columnists to know he always had a new date, and never anyone steady. Not that she should be thinking about Leo, or his dating habits, anyway . . .

"Are we adding fish sticks to the menu?"

Jasmine — her sous chef, business partner and best friend — snapped her back to the present. To stop spiraling into an existential crisis, she'd come into work three hours early. Since she'd left the show for the restaurant, she might as well get back to it. And if she stayed home any longer she would've been forever sucked into the void of checking the mentions on her phone. Which there were plenty of — fans asking if she was really leaving the show FOR REAL, THOUGH? Trolls telling her that #Nasty-Nina should've left a long time ago, the standard comments of "you're ugly" and worse.

"It's a no to fish sticks. We don't have a kids' menu," Nina said.

"Then what are your plans for that poor fish?" Jasmine nodded to Nina's prep station, where a beautiful piece of sole had been cut into finger-size pieces.

Nina was supposed to be trimming flyaway edges from the fillet, but instead she'd nearly shredded it into oblivion. She hadn't been paying attention, like, at all. Her thoughts were a bowl of eggs she'd meant to cook into a perfect omelet, but had ended up scrambling instead.

"Can I play the I-just-quit-my-job-on-live-TV-and-life-is-hard card?" she said, then told herself, *Also, I'm sure Leo is over the moon that he'll never have to work with me again.*

"Lucky for you, I happen to love fish sticks. They're an underrated option. I'll make the waitstaff a snack out of this." Jasmine quickly swept the limp hunks onto a clean plate, and put it off to the side. Then she turned to study Nina.

The thing about having friends who know you *really* well is that you can't hide anything from them. So Nina stood, hands at her sides, and waited for Jasmine to just say what a pathetic human she looked like. Or, at least, that's how Nina pictured herself in that moment — not showered and only awake because she'd had multiple lattes.

"I know you're not sad about leaving the show." She squinted at Nina. "You said the only thing more satisfying than taking off your bra would be if Leo got permanently trapped in quicksand."

She had said that. And, now that Jas had mentioned it, just the thought of Leo's hair ruined by sand while he tried in vain to get out made her smile.

"He deserves many things, that's true. But the show wasn't all bad," Nina argued. There was the crew and getting to mentor the chefs — she loved those parts of the job.

44

And, of course, getting to be on TV had perks, including the bottle of homemade hot sauce Padma Lakshmi sent just that morning with the note "You're my new lady crush."

"Oh, Nina, my sweet summer child." Jasmine's fiery orange eye shadow seemed to sizzle back in a challenge. Nina had no idea how she kept her makeup so flawless while working around hot stoves all day, but Jasmine wasn't like any chef she'd ever met. She dressed like a sorority girl whose extracurricular activity was being part of a biker gang, and she actually did ride a motorcycle to work. "Nina . . ." she repeated.

"Ugh, I mean, obviously Leo is the worst bro to ever bro in the whole bro world."

"That's right. Not today, bro." Jasmine squeezed Nina's hand, then returned her focus to the prep work.

Nina should have done the same. She was tired of thinking about Leo. She needed a healthy reminder that quitting was the right choice. Being in a kitchen was her happy place; surrounded by yummy food, making a meal look like art and zoning out to the hum of the restaurant. So standing in her crisp apron and prepping sole meunière for the nightly special should've been invigorating. No blinding lights from being on set, no nervousness about saying the wrong thing on camera and, most importantly, no Leo. But she'd been in the kitchen for a few hours and all she felt was numb.

She absentmindedly rubbed at the long scar that ran across her thumb — her hands were covered in marks from years of accidentally touching a hot lid or nearly slicing off a finger while dicing.

She wanted to focus on the food, but . . . Would the crew and Tiffany ever be able to forgive her for walking off the show? Did leaving permanently seal her fate as Nasty Nina?

"You look like you're about five seconds away from muttering to yourself. So let's talk about *what you did last night.*" Jasmine's natural hair was tied up in a bun with a little gold skull pinned to the front. It bobbed slightly as she leaned across the prep counter. "Just know I'm biased, and selfishly very glad to have my best friend back."

Over the years they'd become codependent. Like cheese and bread, they were fine apart but always much better together. Being on the show meant less time for Nina in the kitchen, and less time to be with her best friend. "We both know I'm impulsive."

"Not a bad thing. In fact, some — me — might say it's one of your best qualities."

Nina hesitated, then asked, "Did I do the right thing by leaving?"

In the moment, leaving seemed like the only option. The food world was dominated by men. Only seven percent of kitchens in America were run by women. Which meant she'd spent the bulk of her career relying on men to help her move up, and actively avoiding the ones who wanted to keep her down. And there were plenty of men who had tried to keep her in the place they thought she belonged — beneath them. She just wouldn't allow another man — Leo — to control the narrative of her career. Even if he might think it was "just a nickname."

"Has Leo given you Stockholm syndrome?" Jasmine stirred the boiling pot of potatoes in front of her. She was prepping a potato-foam-and-onion confit. "Reminder — he called you nasty. Nas-ty." Her mouth opened in an expression of both rage and disgust. "You had to quit Twitter for a month after he gave you that nickname. Remember what he did to your mental health? Not okay!"

"Definitely not." Nina straightened. Leo didn't know the extent of what she'd seen over the years in her comments — name-calling, constant critiques of how she looked . . . and then there were the death threats. The nickname just added fuel to the pile-on-to-Nina fire. But when they'd started working together, she never would've imagined their relationship would devolve into . . . this. Sure, they had very different ideas of what fine dining looked like, but she hadn't despised him, not at first, anyway.

In fact, she appreciated what places like Vinny's provided — comfort, consistency and an easy meal, particularly for families. Nina and Sophie had relied on cheaper meals when they were kids being raised by a single mom. So despite what Leo might think, she wasn't anti-Vinny's. She just wasn't interested in befriending a man who clearly didn't respect her, or even try to.

"We're booked solid tonight." Nina deftly changed the subject. Lyon hadn't had a fully booked night in over a year. The food was award-winning. The location was prime. She was a celebrity chef. So a line out the door should've been a given, and tonight there would be one, but for all the wrong reasons.

"You should quit TV shows more often." Jasmine smiled tightly. "Kidding . . . sort of."

Nina was well aware that her "dramatic" — as her publicist had called it — exit had caused a stir. #NastyNinaMeltdown trended on Twitter for a few hours, and her

48

publicist had been bombarded with requests from journalists who wanted to know more about exactly *why* she'd left.

Because I was tired of being slowly driven insane by a man who cares more about hair product than my feelings.

Weirdly, her publicist hadn't found the response funny in the slightest. What he did agree to do was steer the reporters to Lyon, where they might be able to get a quote. Bribing people to come wasn't exactly glamorous, but she saw a fully booked restaurant as an opportunity. If she could remind people of the experience of eating at Lyon, then maybe she could salvage her business. Reputation meant everything in the food world, and if she couldn't keep at least one restaurant afloat then she'd officially be losing hers.

Slowly, and out of the public eye, she would build her reputation back to where it used to be in the foodie world and then, maybe, just maybe, she could revisit her goal of being on a show. Only this time, she'd make sure she didn't have a cohost.

There was a loud knocking at the restaurant's back door. Nina didn't know who it could be, because service didn't start for another few hours. The pastry chef, bartender, bussers, servers, manager, host, dishwasher and line cooks wouldn't be in for a while longer.

"That's a superhuman knock." Nina started to take off her apron.

"If it's Thor, then let me answer," Jasmine said. "Chris Hemsworth needs to rescue me from my pants."

Nina guffawed in response. The only reason Jasmine was single was because she worked restaurant hours. Which meant prime date-night times were out of the question. She hoped Thor was waiting, for Jasmine's sake.

Nina pushed open the kitchen door and made her way into the dining room. She gave a quick glance to the thick wood trim around the windows, the boxed beams along the ceiling and the woodburning fireplace. Little slivers of golden light pierced through and highlighted the deep mahogany floors. Her restaurant was gorgeous, cozy and impossible not to love.

Growing up, Nina's mother wouldn't have been able to afford a glass of wine at Lyon. Now Nina owned the place and their last name was embossed above the front door. Her mother had been so proud of what she'd built. The LA spot was the only location she'd lived to see, so letting her down wasn't an option.

Don't worry, she thought as she patted the side of a wall, *I won't let us close.*

She sighed, then turned and headed down the hallway, past her office, bathrooms and supply closet, toward the back loading door.

Nina peered out the window — no one there. She opened the door to see if a package had been dropped off, but there was nothing. Just an electric fall breeze, the kind that buzzed with anticipation. September in LA could be hit-or-miss. Sometimes the days were as hot as summer and other times you could grab a gingerbread latte and feel like you were somewhere with distinct seasons. Today was the latter.

"Nina," a hushed voice said.

She exhaled sharply. Of course, he was there, ruining an otherwise perfect moment.

She slowly turned to face Leo. Even with enormous sunglasses and a hoodie pulled over his head, she'd recognize that swoop of dark hair anywhere. And he'd either had time for a spray tan, or the warmth from the sun was hitting him just right to make his skin look as golden as the top of a crème brûlée.

She squinted, and he had the nerve to smile back.

She wasn't going to let him get her flustered, especially not at her own restaurant.

Though how was it possible that he managed to fill out a hoodie this well? Like, who has muscles underneath bulky fabric? Leo did, because, of course, he'd be *that* guy.

"I know you're not familiar with what a *real* restaurant is like, but the front door isn't usually located in the alley," she snapped.

He clicked his tongue before responding. "See, for a moment I was wondering if I'd made a mistake coming here. But I'd hate to miss this witty repartee."

"It's not repartee if I'm the only one with wit." She straightened, like one of those exotic birds she'd seen in an episode of *Planet Earth* when they wanted to intimidate predators. "Why do you look like an extra from *SVU*?"

Leo pulled down the hood and took off his sunglasses. "Did you know there are paparazzi outside your restaurant? I'm surprised they're willing to drive this far east." He shook his head to himself. "Why have a restaurant in Silver Lake? It's like the Brooklyn of LA. Shouldn't you be in West Hollywood, where the real money is?"

"If I'd known there was a portal from hell located so close by I would've reconsidered the location." Less than a minute in Leo's presence, and she'd slipped back into insult mode as easily as popping dark chocolate into her mouth. The taste of knocking him down a peg was as sweet as always. *This* was why quitting the show was the right move — she didn't like the version of herself he brought out.

"Can I come in?" He ignored her comment and started to walk toward her, as if she'd already answered.

But she wasn't going to let the bad egg back in the carton. She took a step forward, blocking his path. "What about anything I've said makes you think I'd want to see you in this alley, let alone my restaurant?"

"We need to talk." His jaw flexed, revealing just how square it was. "You owe me an explanation."

Of all the things Leo could've said, expecting more from her was definitely rich. "I don't owe you anything." She didn't notice him move closer until they were standing on the same step, inches apart.

"If you're still mad about the nickname thing, I'm sorry. Okay?" He looked up at her through lowered lashes. The vulnerability in his creamy brown eyes was unnerving, which must have been why her heart seemed to stop, then thudded wildly.

Leo closed the space between them. They weren't touching, exactly, but she could feel warmth coming off him. If she so much as breathed harder, her chest might brush his. He'd grown stubble overnight, and his lips parted slightly to reveal the wedge between his front teeth. She didn't like the way her mind lingered on what his stubble might feel like against her mouth. She had to go.

"Forget it." She turned to head back inside, but Leo gently caught her wrist and held on to it.

"What I did was wrong. I messed up. I really am sorry." His expression was genuine, a trait she rarely, if ever, saw from him.

But Nina knew Leo well, and she'd watched him charm his way out of every uncomfortable situation she'd ever seen him in. *Not this time.*

She shook her hand free from Leo's. But as she did, she inadvertently pulled him forward, and he tripped. All six foot whatever of him *tripped* and fell forward. She had to lean into him just to keep them both from falling. Their bodies pressed together and she immediately felt a surge of pain. Her nose smashed awkwardly against his solid chest, his chin knocked against the top of her head and his designer shoe stepped on one of her purple sneakers.

"You clumsy, big-footed demon." She spit out the string of his hoodie, which was stuck in her mouth.

"Don't act like you aren't enjoying my pecs. I pay a trainer good money to get them that firm."

She rolled her eyes and shoved Leo forward and off her. But as she did, shouting erupted from farther down the alley.

A man was running toward them, a camera pointed. "Leo! How long have you and Nina been dating? Nina! Is Leo a good kisser?"

Nina frowned before her brain could catch up. There was a reporter, with a camera, who'd just seen Leo on top of her — not good.

"You really are very talented at ruining my life, you know that?" Nina hissed at Leo.

"You think I'm talented?" He smirked.

If they waited any longer, the photographer would be right in front of them, just close enough for her to grab the camera and throw it to the ground. Which is exactly what he'd want her to do — then he'd have a real Nasty Nina headline, plus a reason to file a lawsuit. She needed to do immediate damage control.

Without hesitating, she grabbed Leo's hand and led him to the door. His grip tightened, and his fingers wound through hers until their palms fit perfectly together.

He'd probably learned how to rub his thumb as lightly as possible across a woman's hand just to disarm her, and disarmed was exactly how Nina felt.

He's such a jerk, she told herself, but that small reminder didn't stick the way it normally would.

4

LEO

"I just realized that we didn't answer that poor man's questions. Do you think we should pop back out?" Leo joked, but there was a touch of bile rising that reminded him this wasn't at all funny.

Nina locked the door behind them. When she turned to face him, the way she crossed her arms suggested she wasn't amused, either. In fact, she looked downright pissed off.

"Actually, I don't think he captured my best side. Let's ask if he'll do a reshoot." Why was he still jabbering on? Oh, right, because he talked a lot when he was nervous, and his heart was racing. No one liked surprises. Though that didn't feel like the reason his hand was shaking. Of course, there was also the fact that he'd fallen on top of Nina . . .

They'd worked together for three years,

and in that time they'd never once so much as hugged. At the start and end of each season, they greeted each other with wary glances — not even handshakes were exchanged. So hurling their bodies against each other was certainly a new experience. Which must explain why being entangled with her limbs had been so confusing, and why his dick had, well . . . responded. It was clearly an uncontrollable reaction from the total and utter shock of his body colliding with hers.

"You really do make terrible jokes," she said in the flat, snobbish way she'd perfected.

Being somewhere with Nina other than on set was as bewildering as waking up from a too-long nap and not knowing the day or time. Only, he'd made the decision to track her down at her restaurant. So he should've been more prepared to see her, but he was completely off-kilter. He was standing in her space — her restaurant — and that made him feel even more on the defensive.

His eyes darted around the hallway, across the woven blue rug and up to the framed photos of baguettes and cheese wedges that covered the walls. His skin warmed from the heat coming out of the nearby kitchen. The smell of butter and cream mingled together like the tastiest candle you could ever light. He'd never had the food at Lyon, but he already knew what he was missing.

He wasn't there to admire the decor or wonder what the menu offered, though. His life had been completely and utterly turned upside down, all because of *her.* It'd been less than twenty-four hours and already there was a petition circulating online for the production to launch an investigation into why Nina quit. He'd thought she was the judge everyone loved to hate, but it turned out she had a secret and rabid army in the waiting. Most of the tweets centered around Leo, and the fact that he'd used her nickname. He'd never actually called her Nasty Nina out loud — not even the first time, when he insinuated she'd be on Santa's nasty list. But this time he had, and the fans saw his action as sexist. Not that he disagreed with them — he'd made a stupid slip, and what he'd said was wrong — but now there were questions as to whether he should be "canceled" as a human. His PR team was in full-on crisis mode, and they anticipated that the speculation around his involvement would only get worse.

And it wasn't just his character that was taking a beating. The lunchtime rush that typically flooded Vinny's restaurants — all located in areas heavily populated by office buildings — had been more of a trickle today, according to his managers.

Not to mention that his agent had received a call from Tiffany, where she informed him that without Nina, there may not be a show. Well, there would be a show, but they'd recast both Nina and Leo so as not to leave a "bad taste" in fans' mouths. Even though Leo had built the show just as much as Nina had, that didn't matter. Leo was starting to look like the *real* bad guy, a twist he never anticipated.

He couldn't afford to close another location, and neither could the employees who relied on the success of Vinny's for their livelihoods. The mere thought of having to let more people go from their jobs wasn't one he was even willing, or emotionally able, to entertain.

So it was clear that the fans preferred Nina and Leo together, getting along, rather than apart. Like in the stock market, uncertainty led to volatility, but how was it fair for his restaurants to suffer just because of some misunderstanding?

"Why are you making that face?" He was referring to her mouth opening and closing, like a goldfish who'd accidentally flung itself out of the bowl.

"Ugh, I think I got your body spray in my mouth." She gagged for added effect.

"Makes sense." He nodded. "I felt you licking my arm."

"I know better than to eat poisonous objects," she responded with a tight smile.

Footsteps approached and Leo straightened. He'd learned to always be *on* when he was in a room with Nina. People expected them to act a certain way because of the show, and he'd perfected the art of playing the nice guy who always had an easy smile, even if he was losing his mind from all of the anxiety of the last twenty-four hours.

A Black woman with hot-pink lipstick and visible tattoos approached them. She clocked Leo, then Nina. "Am I in the Upside Down?"

"I'm Leo." He stepped past Nina and held out his hand.

"I know who you are," she said with a frown, not about to shake his hand.

"It's the craziest thing — but were you ever a model? I swear I've seen you in a billboard campaign." He wasn't above cheap flattery to try and get on someone's good side. Especially if that person seemed to be Nina's bodyguard. And he had to

61

make sure Nina had been bluffing last night. If she didn't plan to return next season, then Leo wouldn't be able to return, either.

"Nice try." Her tone had a mocking *there, there* energy.

"Don't worry, Jasmine," Nina said to her friend. "There's nothing going on here. Other than Leo insisting on destroying my life. Again." Nina turned to Leo and coldly pursed her lips.

He ran a hand through his hair. It wasn't every day that he was accused of destroying a person's life. He had a regular at the restaurant who always said that the complimentary breadbasket refills were "destroying his thighs," but that wasn't quite the same as what Nina was talking about here.

"Sounds like I'm about to get the Mace from my bag." Jasmine cocked her head and gave Leo a look that suggested she could crush him with very little effort.

"Garlic and holy water would be better. Could you give us a minute?" Nina said to Jasmine. "I'll handle this." She waved her hand at Leo. He was the *this*.

Jasmine took in a deep breath, then added, "Leo? If you hurt my friend again, I'll use our cooking torch on your hair. Nice meeting you!" She smiled widely before heading back down the hall and turning into the kitchen.

"She seems . . ." Leo searched for an adjective that would describe a metal band Barbie, but came up blank. "Like she has a very fascinating Instagram account."

"She is my best friend, and you're lucky to have breathed the same air as her," Nina said protectively.

Seeing her attached to someone, and vice versa, was certainly a glimpse into her life he hadn't anticipated.

There was a loud banging on the back door, followed by banging on the front door — they were surrounded by the paparazzi.

Maybe coming here hadn't been the best idea, but he'd genuinely thought they could just talk things out. There was always someone else lingering nearby — a producer, an agent, a makeup artist. Why not try a conversation, just the two of them?

"What are you actually doing here, Leo? If you're trying to show me what I'm missing, it's not working." She leaned as far away from him as possible.

He mimicked her movements and let his back rest against the wall of the hallway. If he wanted to dominate the conversation, he'd take on a power pose. Hands behind his head, legs open and wide — a classic negotiation move. But he didn't have the upper hand here — he was seeking answers only she had — so he crossed his arms and made himself small. He was willing to acquiesce if it meant getting what he wanted — her to come back to the show.

"People are saying you left because of me." He paused to let the comment sink in. While Nina clearly thought Leo was selfish and only cared about himself, he really did want to know what had pushed her to leave. Maybe making sure he wasn't the reason she'd left *was* selfish, but . . . oh, well.

She didn't say a word back. Instead, her sharp gaze burrowed a hole straight through the core of him, her lava meeting his earth. Message received: Nina was pissed.

He straightened and cleared his throat. They both had business to lose and gain, so he just had to make sure he didn't end up on the losing side. He decided to take a gamble, the way she had last night.

"Okay, I can take a hint. I may have been part of the reason why you left the show. But I also know that your business is in trouble, to put it lightly," he said. "You took a risk and blamed me. Let me guess, your reservations have spiked today, right?"

"What's your point?" She'd never been one to shrink away from a challenge, so he wasn't surprised to see a burst of energy infuse her. She leaned forward.

Annoyingly, her chef's apron didn't seem to hide the cleavage poking out of her V-neck sweater, though. Not that he was staring, or anything. He dusted those thoughts away as soon as they showed up.

"Here's the thing, Nina — people have sympathy for you temporarily. But in the long run? You'll still have a perception problem." He was winging this impromptu TED talk, but everything he said was true. And, feeling himself gain some traction, he uncrossed his arms — confident leaders made their body language open, just like the books had taught him.

"They're mad at me now. It's affecting my business, absolutely. But how do you think they're going to feel when I put out an interview explaining that I'm the victim in all of this?" He eyed her, but she wasn't budging from her new identity as "woman with flames for eyes." "When I explain that I've had to fire my employees, hardworking people, because of the bad press? They'll turn on you just as quickly. And then, instead of being Nasty Nina, you'll also be 'selfish,' 'manipulative' and 'entitled.' "

She looked down and licked her lips, considering. Good, maybe she would finally see the big picture instead of fixating on their present issues.

"If you think you can scare me with any of that, I'm sorry to say that you're mistaken." She smirked and planted her hands firmly on her hips, the alpha woman asserting her dominance. He couldn't say it wasn't sexy to watch. "Believe it or not, I've dealt with bigger assholes than you."

"Give me a chance. I'll try harder," he replied, attempting a joke.

But her jaw clenched and he swore he heard her growl. So he took a deep breath, from the bottom of his belly, the same way he did whenever he sensed a panic attack coming on.

"I'll walk you out." She turned so fiercely that even her hair swung with her as she headed toward the door.

How had all of this gone so horribly wrong? He was supposed to come here and convince her, with his unshakable charm, that she should return to the show. But he'd lost sight of everything he was supposed to be focused on and made this about him. He'd questioned her business, and now she was unceremoniously kicking him out. Maybe he could salvage . . . something.

"Not a good idea." He subtly wiped his sweaty hands on his pants. "We haven't strategized. People will see me leaving. What am I supposed to say?"

He tried to turn on his biggest and purest look of helplessness, which he hoped would have some effect on Nina. Not that he ever had an effect on her, even when he worked for it.

"You went to business school. I'm sure they taught you about diplomacy." Nina's hand found his, and she squeezed it, then added, "Don't feel too badly, Leo. At least you have those nice pecs."

She held his gaze for a beat, then winked. Before he could respond, she'd opened the back door and shoved him out. When he turned around to make sure he'd heard her correctly, the door closed behind him. The place where her hand had been was suddenly cold, and when he looked ahead, there were several people pointing cameras and phones toward him.

Normally, the stress of a situation like this could bring on that head-spinning shortness of breath he knew all too well. He'd never had a panic attack on set, or in front of a crowd, and he didn't want to start now. So he swallowed down his nerves as he tried to block out the questions being shouted at him from the paparazzi.

Which, actually, wasn't as hard to do as it normally would've been. Because his thoughts kept running back to the interaction he'd just had with Nina . . .

She said I have nice pecs.

5

NINA

Sophie: I'm still confused as to how you kissed Leo?? You hate him??

Jasmine: Ditto ^^^

Sophie: I did have a sex dream once about this guy who worked at a sandwich shop who I absolutely despised.

Jasmine: . . .

Sophie: We had amazing sex. In the dream. The size of his salami was really disturbing.

Jasmine: Nina, please tell us you're alive so Sophie shuts the hell up about her sex dreams.

Sophie: And he kept saying he was going to "slam-a-me" with his salami. Isn't that gross?

Jasmine: Do I need to hear this? At 9 in the morning?

Sophie: But it was also kinda hot . . . right?

Nina: Alive.

Nina leaned across the long, granite kitchen island. She wasn't about to tell her sister and best friend that while she hadn't made out with Leo, she *had* complimented his pecs. That, plus quitting the show, would likely put her at intervention status. And while she would've loved to see them both show up on her doorstep with wine, she already had a packed day ahead of her.

Her head felt like it had been placed in a mixer with the setting on high. She hadn't slept at all, really. It was impossible to sleep when what she'd said to Leo played on an endless loop: *at least you have those nice pecs.* She cringed each time she remembered. In what world would she pay him a compliment at all, let alone about his body? While he *did* have an objectively firm chest,

70

judging from how solid of a landing she'd had, that didn't mean she needed to comment on it. He was smarmy, and self-absorbed, and had been slowly destroying her career for the last three years. And knowing Leo, he probably just *loved* that she'd said anything kind to him.

Clearly, she was sleep-deprived and reeling from taking one of the biggest risks of her life. She was just embarrassed that in her stupor, she'd accidentally flirted with Leo. She pulled at the end of one of her wavy curls, feeling drained. Out of all the feelings she'd wanted to leave him with, cockiness wasn't one of them. He already had enough of that.

She'd made a cappuccino, and she took a much-needed sip. She scratched her eyebrow in irritation because, annoyingly, the scent reminded her of him. He didn't smell like bad body spray, as she'd claimed. He smelled like espresso. The last thing she wanted was to associate her favorite morning beverage with him, so she'd made herself a cup just to try and reclaim it. She took another sip. Still smelled like Leo, but she'd keep drinking to try and change the narrative.

The doorbell rang, interrupting her progress. She knew who it was, but they'd have to wait because she needed the cappuccino more. She took one more satisfying gulp before the doorbell rang again.

She padded down the warm terra-cotta floor, through her 1940s two-bedroom Craftsman bungalow that was turning into a de facto war room. Her team all planned to arrive shortly — agent, manager, lawyer and publicist — and were going to fix what had happened between her and Leo. She hoped one of them had a time machine so she could take back the pecs comment.

As she approached the door, she spied Tom. He tapped an imaginary watch on his wrist.

"As your publicist, it would've been helpful to know you two were dating," he said as he walked in.

"We're not dating," she replied emphatically.

He grabbed her cappuccino and took a long sip. "Oh, that's good, make me one of those. Actually, I'll keep this. Make yourself a new one."

Nina reached to get her cup back, but Tom held on to it. "You're my publicist. Aren't you supposed to bring me a latte?"

He followed her back into the kitchen. "Well, I would've, but I've had quite the night. You see, one of my clients quit her job, then made out with a coworker. Which wouldn't be a big deal, except she's famous and people love nothing more than to talk about famous people's sex lives. So while she was making out with Jamie Dornan's look-alike, I had to stay up all night fielding press inquiries." He finally took a breath.

Nina hit the Start button on the espresso machine to drown out whatever else Tom had to say. Since Tom's frantic call yesterday, she was aware that the photos of her and Leo had been published. And while they hadn't kissed, it definitely looked that way. Her name and Leo's had trended separately, along with #TheNextMakeout-Champ. She also had fielded several impromptu questions from last night's customers, many of whom were reporters, and she didn't exactly have a great canned response to "Have you and Leo been dating this whole time?"

No comment became her go-to response. Which hadn't impressed anyone, especially not Tom.

"You're early, you know. I could've been showering. Or eating. Or . . ." Nina ran out of things she usually did in the morning and instead took a sip of her new drink. She closed her eyes as she savored the flavors. "Lord, I am good at making these. Should I

73

open a coffee shop?"

"Focus," Tom said through gritted teeth.

She led them out the back door and onto the porch. There was a round table, and they both sat down. Her backyard had two fat sycamore trees that blocked out any view of her neighbors. The leaves had turned a golden yellow with the slight change in temperature, and brown, furry seeds the size and shape of gumballs littered the lawn. The kitchen was her happy place, but her backyard was where she came to relax. She knew Tom wasn't about to let her, though.

Tom tightly smiled and drummed his fingers against the mug. She'd been working with him since joining the show. She hadn't needed a publicist before, but as her personality began to dominate more than her food, he'd become necessary, and she hadn't exactly made his life easy. She'd forget most of his media training when the cameras turned on. When he'd secure her a magazine interview to soften her image, she'd unknowingly say something else that would get twisted into an even bigger problem — who knew that "our show changes people's lives" could be turned into the headline Nina Lyon Takes Credit for Success of Cooking Show. Tom was good at his job — he wasn't the problem. The problem was that Nina wasn't all that savvy about being famous. That, and some people apparently wanted to watch her fail.

"I came early so I could lay things out for you before the vultures arrive." He straightened in the chair and pulled on the ends of his jacket before looking back at her. "Your manager and agent are going to want you to go back to the show. It's a moneymaker for them. Your lawyer is going to inform you that the photos taken yesterday were legal to use and we can't remove them — that's true. And he's also going to tell you that you have to re-sign with the show soon, or you're officially out."

"And what are you going to tell me?" She raised her eyebrows. A whole team of people weighing in on her career decisions took some getting used to. It was their job to voice concerns — like having her own inner monologue amplified times ten. *Quitting the show was the biggest mistake of your life. The fans are right about you being #NastyNina. Leo thinks you're obsessed with him now . . .*

"I was going to ask what you want from all this." Tom's expression was neutral, which was annoying. Out of all of her people's opinions, she needed his the most. Mainly because he was the only one who told her the honest truth, not the sugar-coated, dipped-in-chocolate one her agent liked to serve up.

"I want to be taken seriously again." Her voice was so low she barely recognized it, but she was expressing her deepest, truest desire. Being on the show had caused her reputation to crumble instead of soar. She'd been left in the oven too long and burned to a blackened crisp. "This show was supposed to give me a platform, and now people just think I'm a joke. That's not what I want for my life."

She'd wanted to be a chef that little girls could look up to — a role model. Empowering other women was where she wanted to be, because she'd never seen a woman with the career she now had when she was coming up in the industry. And after landing a spot on the show, she thought she could be that person for aspiring chefs.

And, maybe more importantly, her brand was different from other female chefs who flourished on TV. She wasn't like Giada or the Barefoot Contessa, with slick, ocean-front homes that made wealthy people feel seen. Or Rachael Ray, who made meals in fifteen minutes using canned ingredients. Nina wanted to show that food could be an experience. The same way that she and her mom used to cook together. All her childhood memories were tied in to their tiny kitchen. Nina could just as easily pull up the smell of her mother blending flour and rosemary in the mixer as she could breathe.

Through cooking, feelings and emotions could be expressed in complex ways. How many male chefs had been able to show the art of food on TV? She didn't see the same for women. Female chefs were expected to be nurturing and wholesome — two things Nina definitely wasn't. She'd thought that hosting *The Next Cooking Champ!* might lead to her own cooking show — where she could control the content, the message and her image — but she felt so far from that dream that she wasn't sure there was any way back.

"Have you had enough caffeine to hear my honest opinion?" Tom bent forward, elbows on his knees. "Fake it 'til you make it. You need to stay relevant if you ever want to get the one-woman show you've been working toward. You're a celebrity chef, so people will come to the restaurant to see you, but they won't do that if you're a has-been. Leaving the show the way you did definitely got people intrigued. You have their attention, especially after yesterday with Leo. You want a second chance? You have to stay in the public eye, at least for now. Use this moment to your advantage, because if you just disappear off the face of the earth then so will your chance to actually alter how people see you. No one will care that you've changed if they have no idea it's happening."

"I've already quit the show. I can't go back." She just couldn't imagine how doing the same thing — struggling to stay sane with Leo — would help to change anything. A large cloud blocked out the sun and turned the porch cool. She pulled her sweater tighter around her arms.

"I wasn't talking about the show." He smirked. "I was talking about you dating Leo."

"We're not dating, and we didn't kiss. He nearly broke my nose . . ." Ugh, could her final encounter with him have been any more awkward? Sometimes she felt like the universe intentionally put her in situations where she'd look bad in front of Leo. If so, the score was Universe one million, Nina zero.

Tom allowed an extra beat of silence as he grinned knowingly. "Fine, you're not, but it sure did look like it, and that's all that matters. People were afraid of you when you were the mean, terrifying judge who made people cry."

"I didn't make people cry." *Not on purpose, anyway.* Nina whacked his shoulder. Which was surprisingly toned. That was the problem with some LA people: they worked out too much and didn't eat enough.

"People are sexist assholes and don't believe women are allowed to be tough. I don't make the rules! But now they think you and Leo have been dating this whole time. It gives every moment together on-screen a totally different meaning. You should see some of the articles and tweets about you. People have totally forgotten they hated you."

"Aren't you supposed to be making me feel better?" Nina asked defensively.

Tom turned his phone screen to face her. "My assistant put together a deck of the top tweets and headlines in the last twelve hours. Look at these."

Could Leo O'Donnell Be Taming the Nina Shrew?

Opposites Attract? Leo O'Donnell and Nina Lyon Spotted Making Out

Did Nina Lyon Quit TV to Save Her Relationship with Leo O'Donnell?

"I never liked Nina before, but I definitely ship this pairing." — **@NxtCookChmpFan**

"Yessssss I've been waiting for this moment since I started reading the Nina/Leo fanfic" — **@Nina4President**

"Is that a rolling pin in Leo's pocket? Lol" — **@FoodPornOrBust**

Nina sighed out what seemed like every last breath she had in her body, feeling as deflated as a cake that had failed to rise. If she stepped back a bit, she could see that Tom was presenting her with ingredients for a recipe: an increase in approval from the fans, needing to get her career back on track . . . and Leo. She just wasn't sure how they all would blend together.

"You should try to make things work with him," Tom said, cutting through her confusion.

"Tom, you cannot be serious. You're my *publicist,* which is French for 'find a way to fix this.' " She was kidding, but also absolutely not kidding.

"I don't speak French." He stared her down. Took a sip of his cappuccino. Then leaned back in the chair. Okay, so he definitely was *not* joking about the Leo idea.

"You can't be telling me that trying to 'make things work with Leo' would actually help my career."

"You and Leo can both get good press out of this," Tom said. "He's a well-liked hunk of man meat, and the fans want to see you two together — it's that simple. Being with him will keep you in the public eye, with a platform, and buy time to focus on the food and your own goals. And for Leo, being near you elevates the status of his chain of restaurants. That's why he signed on for the show in the first place. He's looking for legitimacy, you need a comeback — it's a win-win."

The *bing-bong* of the doorbell startled Nina. The "vultures" had arrived. And like Tom said, she knew they'd try to sway her to simply go back to the show, but she couldn't. How would that make her look to her fans? Like she was just letting Leo get away with calling her nasty? She'd never forgive him for that. Yes, she wanted to have an audience, but not if it was at the expense of her pride.

"I don't want Leo's help," she finally said.

"Celebrities fake relationships all the time for their careers." He shrugged. "Wake up! There's a bigger game going on around you. It's all about whether or not you're going to be part of it or fade into oblivion."

"There has to be another way." Nina eyed the fence surrounding the lawn. It was a solid ten feet high, but maybe she could jump it, disappear and create a new identity. Wigs, fake teeth — she'd don whatever disguise necessary to avoid her fate.

"For the next month or so, while we put your career back together, all you'd have to do is kiss a hot man. Go to events and do just enough that the public's appetite is fed." Tom snatched his phone off the table. "I'm going to get the door, and you're going to think about what I said."

She buried her face in her hands and let Tom's words wash over her. The thought that Leo could be the answer hadn't even crossed her mind, but now that it had, she wanted to erase it.

6

NINA

Nina took the glittery hot-pink helmet and gloves that Jasmine handed her.

"Put that on and tighten the strap," Jasmine instructed.

"I should probably be more nervous about this death trap." The engine of the bike purred calmly back at Nina. She'd never ridden a motorcycle. But working in restaurants at a nonstop pace for years had turned her into something of an adrenaline junkie. "But I'm actually excited."

It was their day off — Lyon was closed on Mondays — and it was also the day of the week when they went to have lunch at a new restaurant they'd never been to. They did this because eating was important, as was keeping up with the LA food scene. Usually they met up at a spot, but today, Nina had agreed to try the bike. She was ready for anything that could speed her as fast as possible away from the harsh realities she was facing. Some people had comfort animals — maybe she'd have comfort motorcycles.

"You're gonna love this." Jasmine kicked her leg over the bike and settled onto the seat. Her hands met the handlebars and she ran her palms over them. "Then we can get you lessons. And you can get your own bike."

"The only thing I know how to do is cook," Nina said. "And eat. Speaking of, we better get going before my stomach starts consuming itself."

She approached the bike, but felt as clueless as if she was trying to get into the saddle of a horse. How was she supposed to sit on this thing? There seemed to be almost no room left for her. Surely Jasmine had miscalculated the bike's ability to fit two people. "I can just follow you in my car?" Nina asked.

"No way, you're going to sit right behind me," Jasmine said.

"But, how . . . ?"

"Trust me, you'll fit." Jasmine waved over Nina with her hand. "Okay, now hop on, and hold on tight."

"There's not, like, a seat belt?" Nina circled the bike looking for any kind of safety measure that would keep her from flying to her death. She found none.

"No. Hence the hold-on-real-tight advice." Jasmine smiled beneath the plastic visor of the helmet. "You're my best friend. You know I won't kill you," she said reassuringly. "Probably not, at least."

"If you do, I will come back and haunt you." Nina swung her leg over the bike's seat and situated herself as firmly as she could behind her friend. "And I won't be a nice ghost, either. I'll break shit."

"Ain't that the truth," Jasmine said as she revved the engine.

Nina wrapped her arms around Jasmine's waist and threaded her fingers together so tightly she was sure her knuckles had already turned white.

"Tap me on the shoulder if something is wrong," Jasmine called back to her. "And when I move, you move — mimic what I do when we take any turns."

"Okay." Nina blinked rapidly. Was she going to remember any of those instructions?

When Jasmine flicked up the kickstand, the motorcycle shot forward, as did Nina. And she couldn't help herself — she squealed, either from pure fright or exhilaration. The weirdest part was that as they zoomed out of her driveway, her thoughts traveled to Leo. What would he say if he saw her on a motorcycle?

After ten minutes on the bike, Nina was ready for a break. And luckily, they'd arrived at their destination. They parked on a residential side street, just off the main drag. Her legs and fingers and arms and — well, entire body — had gone stiff from being wrapped around Jasmine with the force of a pair of Spanx. Nina stepped off the bike, stumbling slightly as she readjusted to standing.

"You stayed on!" Jasmine shouted. She unclasped her helmet, took Nina's and locked up the bike.

"I'm not buying my own any time soon, but I can see why you like yours." There were moments when Nina had felt like she was for sure going to fly off and become roadkill. But then, she hadn't. And they'd arrived in one piece. And the smile that crossed her face was because even though she'd been scared for a good sixty percent of the ride, the other forty percent was joy from moving fast and feeling the air spin around her.

Of course, she wouldn't count the time she'd spent wondering what Leo would think of her in a sparkly pink helmet . . .

"You ready for the best donut of your

life?" Jasmine rubbed her hands together.

"I'm ready for at least three of the best donuts of my life, thank you." Being a bike associate, or partner, or sister, or whatever phrase wasn't "bike bitch," had made her hungrier than she was before they'd started.

"Do your parents know you're here?" Nina asked. The *here* being Highland Park, an LA neighborhood where Jasmine grew up and her parents still lived.

They walked across the sidewalk and the rubber soles of Jasmine's Doc Martens groaned with each step. "Yeah, I told them we were coming. But they're working on the Valentine's Day gala plans — they strategize this shit so far in advance. They want me to swing by next week, though. Would you . . . ?"

"You want me to come with?" Nina had played buffer for Jasmine on many occasions. Her parents could be . . . intense. They'd not only been married for thirty years — Nina had attended their pearl wedding anniversary party that summer — but they also worked together at the botanical gardens as codirectors. They were one of those couples who dressed alike without realizing it and spoke a shared language that only required looks and head nods. They were inseparable, and Jasmine was the only thing they were more passionate about than gardening. And with that passion, came the real problem — they loved to micromanage their daughter. As Jasmine had once told Nina, "I'm a Sagittarius and we cannot be tamed."

"You know it." Jasmine made prayer hands in front of her chest.

"Always down to see Dori and Cory." Even their names sounded fake when spoken out loud.

"They won't shut up about you, so I know the feeling is mutual," Jasmine said.

Nina smiled softly. Unlike Jasmine, Nina liked hearing Cory and Dori's opinions about her life. Their nosiness reminded her of her mom. At the end of the day, though, they weren't her parents. She didn't have to hear them harp on her regularly, just when she came for the occasional visit. So she could completely understand where Jasmine and her annoyance came from. And she tried to deflect for her friend as much as she could when she was around them.

They turned onto the main street and Jasmine pointed at a chalkboard sign that read, High Tea is SERVED in elaborate cursive scrawl.

"You do know scones are not donuts, right?" Nina wasn't one to pass up any baked goods, but a donut was a donut. No scone would do.

"This is not your white, British-royals high tea, my friend. This is Highland Park high tea. It opened a month ago, and I think we're about to have our whole world rocked."

The Jam's exterior was black-and-white — if you blinked you'd miss it. But when they went inside Nina immediately spotted a colorful mural of dinosaurs seated on velvet cushions, eating donuts and drinking out of porcelain cups. A pristine glass display case on the opposite wall featured rows and rows of endless donuts — a happy welcoming committee of frosting and dough.

"We'll be having tea for two," Jasmine said at the counter. "And for my donut, could I get the Swirly Rosewater, please?"

As soon as she saw the names and flavors of the donuts, she instantly knew two things: one, she was going to love these, and two, Leo would absolutely hate them. Nina suddenly felt sympathy for Leo any time a contestant created a unique flavor pairing on the show. She raced to find the donut her friend had ordered in the case, and landed on a frosted pink cake donut that had a lemon rosewater glaze topped with roasted pistachios. "You live your life in pink, Jas."

"No better color. So from what I read online, the deal is that instead of scones, they do vegan donuts —"

Nina's eyes narrowed, and Jasmine glared right back. "Don't judge. What are you going to get?"

"I need chocolate," Nina said. She scanned the rows in search of the perfect solution.

"May I recommend our Chocolate from the Crypt donut?" the saleswoman suggested from behind the display. Her sharp bangs and blunt ponytail bobbed as she explained, "It's our fall-themed donut — chocolate cake with a chocolate glaze, and it's got a kick from the cayenne pepper and cinnamon we add in."

"Oh, my donut," Nina said. In the case was an absolutely gorgeous chocolate confection — the cayenne and cinnamon flakes on the outside created a black-and-orange effect. "I am sold."

"You got it." The saleswoman nodded and rang them up.

A narrow hallway covered in murals of cartoon animals drinking tea led them to the official tearoom. Soaring ceilings revealed exposed beams and brick walls, signaling that the building was likely older and newly restored. Modern, barrel-back walnut chairs were clustered around ultra-sleek Scandinavian round tables. Nina felt like she'd followed Jasmine down a rabbit hole and emerged into the modern interpretation of the Mad Hatter's tea party.

"This is like . . ." Nina began. "It's a fun aesthetic."

"I know, right?" Jasmine replied as they sat down.

"It makes me feel like I'm not cool enough to be here, but glad I got invited." Nina picked up the prix fixe high tea menu on the table. The Jam's version of finger sandwiches were crispy "chicken" sliders, potato-hash tacos and mini banh mi, and in lieu of scones, they offered cornbread with raspberry jam and their signature donuts. "And it's all vegan . . . ?"

"Yes, my friendly carnivore, and hopefully delicious."

Two stainless-steel tea trays arrived at their table, piled high with the food and topped with their donuts of choice. The server dropped off matching stainless-steel teapots, along with three different kinds of nondairy milk.

"I am very into all of this." Nina started with the donut, because why the hell not?

And she was going to have to give some vegan recipes a chance after tasting what was a seriously delicious donut. "Damn, this is so annoying. Am I going to turn vegan now?"

"I'm not going to fuck with nonvegan donuts anymore. Not after these." Jasmine bit into her pink donut and moaned.

Nina poured herself some tea and added oat milk in. "Have you been thinking more about opening up your own spot?"

Jasmine had worked alongside Nina for years at Lyon, but she'd also been talking about starting a restaurant. While Jasmine may have had the ability to quickly master any DIY skill she tried, she'd been stuck on exactly what direction to take her most personal project.

"Honestly, no." Jasmine popped a fallen piece of donut into her mouth. "The problem is, I like too many things. How can I start a restaurant when I can't even decide what the menu will be?"

Nina nodded. She hadn't considered that Jasmine's hobbies, which were many, might not just be things she was interested in — they might also be superproductive ways to procrastinate on building her own restaurant.

"Do you want me to give you a spiel, or

are you just venting?" They gave each other advice on everything, but Nina didn't want to be pushy.

"I tend to like your spiels. Spiel away." Jasmine leaned back in her chair and nibbled on the end of a "chicken" slider.

"Okay, when I opened Lyon, I started by thinking about what experience I wanted to create." Nina had talked to Jasmine about this part of the process, but not in great detail. "I wanted people to walk in and know that they were in my home. Like they'd been invited to my house for the first time, and every detail would bring them into my world. Through the environment, and the furniture, and the little messages I scribble on each day's menu — everything is personal, because Lyon is me. Which, now that I'm saying it out loud, sounds incredibly narcissistic. But I have a point of view, and I express that through my food. I needed my restaurant to tell the story of my life and childhood. I wanted it to feel the way my mother made me feel every day. So maybe think about your aesthetic, and the rest will come."

"You like that word. *Aesthetic.* You've used it a lot today."

"Word of the day." Nina shrugged and picked up her tea. "Bottom line, I'd eat anything you cook. You're the most incredible human in the world, and other people need to know that, too."

Jasmine traced a finger along her jaw, finishing a bite of cornbread. "To use your word, I like the *aesthetic* of this neighborhood. Even though I grew up here, every time I come back, there's a new store or bar — more people wanting to move here. I know it's complicated — gentrification is changing this place. But it's an old neighborhood, and this feels like a part of LA that a lot of people don't get to see. It's so diverse. And when I come here . . . I feel like I'm invited, in a way. Maybe it's just because my actual childhood home is here? I don't know."

Nina nodded. She wasn't about to pretend like she would ever be able to grasp what it was like to be a Black female chef — a minority within a minority. But she did understand the importance of feeling accepted, and maybe that was what this area did for Jasmine.

"You might have to build a kitchen from scratch," Nina said. The buildings had clearly been on this street for decades — heavy brickwork and intricately designed storefronts that just weren't around in busier parts of the city. Which might mean they weren't built for the full-size kitchen Jasmine would need. "But I bet they have some gorgeous spots with options for outdoor dining. You could do those hanging bistro lights and cover the walls with ivy." Nina's hands flew as she spoke, as she painted herself a picture of what Jasmine's future could look like.

"Maybe this neighborhood could work." Jasmine's eyebrows raised.

"Dori and Cory would be thrilled." Nina swallowed a bite of her potato-hash taco and was delighted to find that the "cream" drizzled across the top tasted remarkably like cheese.

Jasmine smiled at her, and Nina felt a rush of the energy she always had when they were together, inspiring each other.

"Do you think you'll be able to get on the bike again, or should we call you an Uber?" Jasmine asked.

"Actually, I'm going to get another donut and do some work." Nina needed to respond to some emails. And she also needed another donut, no doubt about that.

"Proud of your choices." Jasmine leaned down and kissed Nina on the cheek. "Especially if you order a pink donut."

"Love you," Nina replied.

She leaned back in her chair and reached

for her phone. She wasn't interested in whatever nonsense was waiting for her there, but she couldn't avoid her situation forever.

No pressure, babe! Tom had texted. But your moment with Leo is now!

She stuffed her phone back in the bag. She should've tossed it off the side of the bike and into the road when she'd had the chance. Because she knew in her bones that Tom was right. For better or worse, she'd made her bed, and Leo was already sleeping in it.

7

LEO

Leo sat across from his brother, Gavin. He made direct eye contact and nodded his head, checking off all the boxes for being an attentive, loving sibling. But he hadn't heard a word of what was being said, seeing as he was distracted by a text from Nina that really had his head spinning.

"Bridget Jones's Diary." Gavin's sharp voice snapped Leo back to the room.

"Is the greatest love story of all time. What about it?" Leo looked around the restaurant, which was currently empty after a particularly busy night. The press coverage from his and Nina's nonkiss seemed to have piqued people's interest, or appetite, or both. Either way, Leo was pleased with the results over the last few days.

The unexpected uptick in business had energized him. Or maybe, more accurately, he was just excited to have something else to focus on that didn't involve Nina. So, the night before, he'd come into the restaurant and pulled an all-nighter, working on the bookkeeping. After all, if business continued to improve like this, maybe things could turn around for Vinny's.

His family knew he was a workaholic by nature, but his mom and brother definitely wouldn't be okay with him skipping sleep to crunch numbers. Especially if they had any clue about his history of panic attacks . . .

"So you approve of the new appetizers for the holiday season?" Gavin closed the binder he'd laid out — their dad's old recipe book. Gavin, as the head chef, had updated it throughout the years.

"No, not approved. I wasn't paying attention." Okay, so he'd slipped, lost focus, and now his brother knew. Whatever.

"I know. I'm your twin brother. I was making fun of you." Gavin smirked. Every time he looked mischievous, he reminded Leo so much of their dad.

"Not identical."

"Lucky for me." Gavin grinned widely. As twins, they shared the same dark hair, eyes and gap between their teeth, but that was about all when it came to similarities. Leo was tall and lean, while Gavin had the thicker build of their dad. His brother actually looked like he owned a restaurant that served pasta, whereas Leo took great pains to get in a daily morning run. Still, you'd know they were brothers . . . or long-lost cousins.

"Gavino, give it a rest with the recipes," their mother said as she approached the table. Whenever she entered a room, she owned it immediately with her height, her angular nose and her long, sleek gray hair. Their dad always said she should've been a movie star, and she certainly carried herself in a way that made Leo feel like she belonged in front of the camera instead of him.

She was also the only one who used Gavin's full name, refusing to shorten it by dropping the *o*.

"And *you*." She leaned over Leo and wrapped her arms around his neck. She was a shark when it came to sniffing out issues. "Ma knows when something's wrong. Too many espressos again?"

In Leo's experience there were few things more terrifying than an Italian mother who knew something was off with her son. They were impossible to lie to, difficult to calm down and wouldn't settle for the answer of "nothing."

His mom slid her glasses off her face. They hung around her neck on a slim gold chain, and her curious fingers wove around it. She squinted, as if that would squeeze the truth out of him. "It's your new girlfriend."

Gavin covered his mouth to stifle laughter. Leo pursed his lips. *Here we go.*

"Leo has a girlfriend?" Maria, who'd been a server at the restaurant since his dad opened it, chimed in. She laid out her receipts on the table and winked at Leo. "Does this one know she's your girlfriend?"

"That was a one-time thing." Leo was thankful his stubble hid the flush rushing to his face. He dated a lot, but contrary to what clickbait headlines claimed, he wasn't a playboy. He just really wanted to settle down at some point, and he hadn't found *the one* yet.

Especially because he'd been searching for the love of his life since . . . well, at least since the third grade, when he'd asked Racheline Bradford to be his Valentine. She'd said no — they were clearly not meant to be. But he was undeniably a hopeless romantic, which he blamed on his parents' perfect marriage. And sometimes he made rookie errors, like calling a woman with whom he'd gone on two dates his girlfriend. Which apparently made him "clingy," ac-

100

cording to the woman in question. That second date had also, unsurprisingly, been their last.

"Come on, you know I don't talk about my personal life at work." He tried to sound authoritative, but it was clear from the blank stares they weren't buying it.

"This is my cue to head out." Gavin stood, and was instantly met with a kiss from their ma.

"Don't leave me here with *them*," Leo pleaded.

"You did this to yourself, bro." Gavin gave a salute before turning to make his way to the exit.

Leo sighed.

"But this time I get to meet the girl *before* you call her your girlfriend, eh?" Maria tilted up his chin so he could look at her. "If I don't approve, then she's no good for you."

"You and everyone else here will want to approve," Leo snorted, but there was comfort in knowing that the people in this place really did care about him. The flagship restaurant didn't have turnover. Maria had been with them for thirty years, as had Hector, Sal and Ramon. The newest hire, an extra weekend host, had been with Vinny's for two years. They were a kind of family, but still, Leo tried to keep his private and personal lives separate, which was the professional thing to do. Even if his dad, who had never stopped talking about family while at work, would have disagreed.

They were in the restaurant's dining room, and Leo should've been going through the night's receipts. On a normal night he'd be able to go home, shower off the kitchen smells of garlic and fried oil, and fall into the comfort of his overly fluffy down comforter.

But not tonight, because Nina had texted and asked to meet.

Of course, his brother, mom and the wait-staff didn't know anything about that. They would be gone and in bed before Nina showed up, and he wanted to keep it that way.

"And for the record, Nina isn't my girl-friend, Ma," he protested.

"Yeah? Maybe she would be if you got a life." His mom stood up. She then straightened the collar of his shirt and added, "Stop spending Friday nights with your mother. I'm taking the paperwork home, and you should go home, too. Get on an app or go to a bar — just don't call me."

"Love you, Ma."

"Love you, figlio." She kissed the top of

his head and left him sitting alone at the table.

Would she still love him if she knew he was having covert, late-night meetings with the woman who'd once called him "duller than a butter knife"?

The restaurant had cleared out. He'd turned off all the lights except for a few in the dining room and the entrance. Nina didn't need to see the back-room addition they'd built a few years ago to accommodate corporate lunches and holiday parties, or the second dining room he'd added for lunchtime overflow. He'd show her what he wanted her to see — the original Vinny's space, as his dad had envisioned it.

When he'd gone to Nina's restaurant, he could feel the differences between what they'd each created. Linen tablecloths versus disposable, a small vase of freshly cut flowers versus a plastic cup filled with crayons and reservations versus a last-minute decision.

He wasn't embarrassed by Vinny's. He just didn't feel like validating everything Nina likely thought about what a restaurant like his had to offer — that Vinny's wasn't good enough, and *he* wasn't good enough.

His cell phone vibrated.

It was Nina: Knock knock.

There was an antique mirror his dad had tacked onto the wall near the server's station, so the waitstaff could check their appearance before seeing customers. Leo eyed himself. He'd gotten a fresh haircut, not because of Nina — well, a little because of her, but he was also due for one. He'd trimmed his stubble, as well as the stray eyebrow hair that always stood straight up. He looked good. Not that he was trying to look good, exactly.

He unlocked the front door and looked out. Nina wasn't there. He didn't see anything until a movement in the parking lot caught his eye. She was in skintight black pants, a black, V-neck T-shirt and a black leather jacket. She wore sunglasses — even though it was the middle of the night — and her hair was pulled into a tight ponytail.

She was like a sexy assassin coming to make her kill. At least he'd go out with a nice view. He needed to speak so he'd stop staring. "You know, you made fun of me the other day for trying to look incognito. I think you've taken it to a new level."

"I wore my best I-don't-want-to-be-here outfit." She ducked under Leo's arm, which was holding the door, and took off her sunglasses.

104

"Believe it or not, you texted me." He closed and locked the door behind him. The waiting area, where they were standing, was wide and lined with chairs, but they were only a few inches apart. He didn't move. Vinny's was his home base, after all.

"You didn't give me much of a choice now that everyone thinks we're dating." She cocked her head at him.

Oh, so now this was his fault?

"It wasn't all bad. I seem to remember you saying I had amazing pecs." Seeing as this was the only nice thing Nina had ever said to him, he planned to remind her of it as much as possible.

"You're exaggerating." She crossed her arms and shot him a warning look. "I did *not* say that."

He smirked, pleased at her discomfort. They both knew what she'd said.

"So this is what a Vinny's looks like, huh?" She'd changed the subject and turned to eye the space.

He held his breath. He was, in theory, fine with Nina insulting him, but he wasn't sure how he'd react if she started to lay in on his dad's restaurant.

"This is the original Vinny's my dad opened thirty years ago." Leo gestured to the photo wall: his dad smiling in a chef's apron, a picture of his dad, mom and babies Leo and Gavin outside of the front of the restaurant, seven-year-old Leo twirling spaghetti on a fork, Gavin holding a meatball the size of his head. They'd replicated that wall in every single Vinny's Ristorante, but these were the original photographs.

"Cute kid." She turned to him. "It was thoughtful of your parents to hire a child actor, knowing these would be hanging up for everyone to see."

"That is the nice thing about living so close to LA." He surprised himself by playing along with the joke, instead of taking the bait.

Nina didn't notice, though. She was busy staring at a photo of his dad, who was smiling widely in an apron that read, I'm Not Yelling, I'm Italian! "So, your dad's an Irish guy who opened an Italian restaurant."

Leo was acutely aware of the fact that a popular Italian chain being founded by a non-Italian wasn't traditional, but his dad had never been conventional. When he was passionate about something, he just went for it.

"He opened Vinny's for my mom. He met her in Rome, where she was from, while he was studying abroad. He fell in love with my mom, and the city. She agreed to marry him so long as he never asked her to cook." Leo paused, remembering the way his father loved telling people this story, and how most people laughed at that line. When he looked over at Nina, he couldn't tell what she was thinking, but he knew she was paying attention.

"He'd been studying business, but switched to culinary school when he came back home. Everyone apparently thought he was crazy, except for my mom. He sent my mom his first report card, where he had straight A's, and she agreed to marry him. My dad opened Vinny's, because his name is Vincent. Then he named me Leonardo, and my brother Gavino. Dad always said he was Italian in spirit."

"Wow." She licked her lips.

He'd been listening so intently for her reaction that he heard her swallow.

"That might just be the grandest romantic gesture I've ever heard," she added.

He blinked. There wasn't even a trace of sarcasm in her voice. That was . . . different.

"So-o-o-o-o-o," she said, elongating the word as she spun around the room. "Where should we talk?"

Leo set Nina at a booth while he went to the kitchen to get an espresso for himself, a sparkling water for her and a slice of tiramisu. When he came back, she looked at him cautiously.

This was foreign territory for both of them. He'd sat next to her at the judges' table for dozens of episodes of their show, but this was the first time they were sitting down to eat together without the presence of camera operators.

His leg jiggled under the table. Maybe he was just hungry, and the lack of sleep was getting to him, too.

He handed a spoon to Nina and she took it. "I know what you think of Vinny's, but there's no way you won't like this. It's my dad's recipe, the most perfect tiramisu you'll ever have. It's won actual awards." That wasn't a lie. His restaurant was a chain, but that tiramisu never tasted like it came out of a "vending machine," as she liked to say.

She stared icily at him before taking the smallest possible amount of tiramisu from the plate. He leaned back. *Just you wait.*

She took a bite and looked away. Then her eyes closed and her mouth curled up in satisfaction, which she tried to hide with the palm of a hand. He was having a hard time taking his gaze from her mouth as she licked a speck of dessert from her upper lip. For a moment, he understood how the chefs on their show felt when they presented a dish, and how rewarding it was to impress someone like Nina.

"Your dad was a very talented man" was all she said as she took a much bigger spoonful.

His dad would've been supremely happy about this review. "I assume you didn't come here to taste-test the food."

"No." She put down the spoon. Her expression hardened slightly. "My place is booked solid for the next two weeks. That hasn't happened in over a year. How is business here?"

"A bit more foot traffic." That was an understatement. They'd had to call in servers on their days off to see if they could come in to work extra shifts.

"Clearly, you falling on me was good for business." Her cheeks flushed a crimson that matched the red of the checkered tablecloth. "My team thinks this could be a beneficial arrangement for both of us. If we pretend to be . . . dating."

"Dating?" He'd heard her, of course, but . . . what was she talking about?

"Please don't make me say it again." Her face fell in her hands. "Do you know how humiliating this is for me?"

He blinked, hard. Did he know that ask-

ing him to date her was humiliating be-
cause . . . she was embarrassed of him?
"You're the one who asked to meet. Now
I'm not good enough to fake-date you?"

He couldn't believe how weird this situation was. The two of them in his dad's
restaurant, all because of a nonkiss, and now
she wanted to date him? Maybe she was
actually a hallucination and the lack of sleep
had finally caught up to him . . .

"No, I'm not —" She sighed, clearly
exasperated. "I'm not saying I'm humiliated
by you. I mean, your dad jokes are embarrassing, obviously —"

"Graceful as ever," he said, interrupting
her rant.

"I don't want to have to ask someone to
pretend to be my boyfriend so my restaurant
won't close. That's humiliating. To me." She
was looking directly at him, and her hand
clutched her chest. "But I don't have any
other choice. I'm desperate here. Your dad
built this place from scratch, right? I did the
same with Lyon. Imagine how he'd feel if
you had to close this. That's how I'm feeling, too."

Vinny's would never close. Leo wouldn't
let that happen. And, more critically, her
restaurant wasn't his problem. He did
understand where she was coming from,

110

though. He wasn't the total monster she always assumed he was.

"I'm happy to brainstorm other ideas. I could make some calls to investors, see if there's someone —"

"You need me, too, Leo," she said briskly. "I know about the contract. Without me, there's no *you* on the show."

He clenched his jaw. He should've guessed that if Tiffany had reached out to him, she'd reached out to Nina, too. He didn't want Nina to know that without her, he really was exactly what she thought — nothing.

"So the quid pro quo you're offering is that in exchange for me being your arm candy, you'll come back to the show? Do you actually think that will work?" He stood, leaning a hand against the tabletop. They couldn't date indefinitely. At some point they'd either get caught or try to murder each other with sharp kitchen objects.

"I'm not coming back to the show," she said emphatically.

"Just because I'm this attractive doesn't mean I'm an idiot. There's nothing in it for me if you don't return as cohost." Without the publicity the show brought, he'd have to continue closing restaurants. There was no reason for him to help if she wasn't willing

111

to do the same.

"We can't survive filming another season together. I nearly burned the place down on my way out. Dating would be temporary until I solve the reputation problem *you* helped give me."

Nasty Nina. He couldn't deny the hand he'd played in that.

"We could try it for a month — a few dates each week — see how it goes," she continued. "And in return, I'll be by your side. People will continue to come to Vinny's. And all the press we get will help to ensure the show wants you back, even without me."

"You can't guarantee that," he said.

"No, I can't." She sipped her water. "But I can bring you into the food world."

"You're in my restaurant. I *am* in the food world."

"I don't want to be mean, but you're not in *my* food world." She shook her head. "I'm sorry, that sounded obnoxious."

He chuckled bitterly because, annoyingly, what she'd said was true. He did need her in some way, because the public liked seeing them together and the increased restaurant traffic proved it. A month together would mean a month with great sales. "But what you're offering me is a month, and what I need is a permanent solution," he hedged.

"The only reason the network wants me back is because I'm respected in the food world. I know every chef in LA. I can help you cultivate something better than just working with me — I'm giving you all of the connections I have."

Leo looked away as he considered what she was saying. In many ways, the entertainment world was all about who you knew. And he didn't know any chefs beyond the ones who worked for Vinny's. So what could be better than giving him clout? Having friends in food would mean he wouldn't have to prop himself up on another person's platform, least of all Nina's.

"To be honest, Leo, you don't have any better offers. We can buy each other time, which we both need." She locked her jaw, then said, "Take the night to think it over."

Nina stood and looked around the room, then knocked on the wooden table. "This is a really special place. I can feel that. Mine means just as much to me, you know?"

She searched his eyes, almost pleading. He couldn't help feel a pang of guilt as her eyelashes fell, and she shook her head in resignation. What would his dad do in this situation?

His dad wouldn't be in this situation, of course. And even though Leo didn't owe her anything, he *was* in the unfortunate position of being up a creek with Nina handing out the last remaining paddle on earth. He would either have to swallow his pride and accept his fate, or continue to close down his restaurants and force people out of jobs. He had to try and save what his father had built. If not for himself, then for everyone who depended on him.

And there were plenty of people who needed him to succeed, his mom and brother included. Where would it leave his family if Vinny's went under? His pulse ticked up at the mere thought of having to shutter their restaurant.

He knew what he had to do, whether he wanted to or not, so he stopped Nina before she reached the front door. "We have a deal," he called out.

She turned to eye him. She didn't have a maniacal, cartoon-villain grin, the way he assumed she would. She looked stoic as she nodded back, binding her success to his.

He swallowed hard. This was either the best or the worst decision he'd ever made in his life. And he genuinely didn't know if he'd survive whatever Nina had planned.

8

NINA

"Sophie, I can't do this. I'm a terrible liar. People will know we're faking everything," Nina said. "I think my elbows are sweating."

She gripped then released the steering wheel, pretty certain that if she squeezed any harder it'd break in half. And maybe she deserved a broken car. After all, she'd somehow wandered into an alternate dimension where she and Leo were in a relationship, they had to trust each other and, worst of all, her career depended on all those things. So, apparently, she was experiencing some kind of cosmic punishment for being mean to Leo. Why not add broken car to the trash fire of her life?

" 'Kim, there's people that are dying.' " Sophie's stern voice boomed over the Bluetooth speakers in the car. "And, yes, you just made me quote the Kardashians, so you know you're being a brat."

Nina had called her sister for a pep talk. It wasn't going well. "Why do I keep calling you when I'm in crisis mode?"

"I have no idea, you know I don't do self-loathing well." Sophie sighed, loudly. "And stop complaining about going on a date with Leo O'Donnell. Do you know how many times I've imagined covering that man in caramel and licking it off?"

"Come on, Soph." Her sister had always loved talking about sex. She was also pansexual, and always said she was attracted to people, not gender. Which Nina admired in many ways, because for all the openness Sophie had about sex and love, Nina was the opposite. She had a hard time opening up about her feelings, even to her own sister.

Which probably explained why Nina was irked by the idea of Sophie thinking about Leo in a way that was R-rated.

Then she spotted him in her rearview mirror. Nina nervously shook out her shoulders. "He's here. I've gotta go."

"Love you. Stop being such a Kim."

"You always know what to say. I still love you," Nina said as she hung up.

She nibbled her bottom lip. Her car windows were tinted just enough that he wasn't able to see her staring at him from the mirror. He looked casual, in jeans and a navy sweater with his hands in his pockets — almost as if he was just a regular dude, and not the man who had been slowly draining her of her will to live. As he looked around the parking lot, his eyes landed on her car.

She slid down in her seat, as if that would save her from his laser-beam eyes. He likely knew the make and model from their parking spots being next to each other on set. Why hadn't she ever bothered to "accidentally" open her car door into his? A missed opportunity.

He walked toward her, trying to squint through the windows, and when he got to the driver's side door, he looked at her with something akin to concern.

She didn't immediately move, as her body felt like a Popsicle that was stuck to the inside of the freezer. But then he tapped on the window with his knuckle, and she quickly sat up. She realized that she probably looked a bit unhinged — her face was practically smashed against the steering wheel. But she also felt like she had lost a piece of her mind by agreeing to this, so there was that.

When she opened her door, he immediately said, "Glad we're both thrilled to be here."

"Surely I can't be the first woman to try and hide from you?" She got out, grateful she'd worn her heavy boots, which always made her feel a bit like Lara Croft.

"Oh, is that what you were doing? You're so short, I just assumed you were normally eye-level with the steering wheel." He gave a little shrug.

She rolled out her shoulders. "Charming, as always."

"Remember to tell the reporters that when they ask how our date went!" He gave an exaggerated thumbs-up, then turned and walked toward the ice-cream-shop entrance.

This was already the worst date she'd ever been on, and it had barely started. Yeah, she was definitely going to need to channel Lara Croft to get through the evening. "What do you usually get here?" Leo asked, when she finally caught up to him.

There was a small and steady line outside of Magpie's Soft-serve, Nina's favorite neighborhood spot. For their first date, a trip for ice cream seemed like a quick and easy way for them to be spotted. And if she was going to be stuck out with *him,* at least she'd have something sweet to make everything better.

"The corn is a classic, but they also have horchata, which is really excellent." Maybe she could talk about ice-cream flavors for the entirety of the date — at least that was something to take her mind off whom she was standing next to.

"Those are not ice-cream flavors. One is a vegetable and the other is a drink." He stared down at her, a slight frown crossing his mouth.

Ah, so he was trying to annoy her and prove a point about the place she'd chosen for them. But she wasn't about to stand back and just let him shovel out his standard level of bullshit. Especially not when he was openly mocking ice cream — that just wouldn't be allowed.

"Actually, it depends on when the corn is harvested." She crossed her arms, really digging in. "It's a vegetable when it's fresh, like corn on the cob, but when it's fully mature it's actually considered a grain."

"Wow," he finally said. "You are a total fucking nerd."

She blinked back at him. He studied her with an intense look and her chest tightened at the attention for some reason.

"What can I get for you?" The man behind the counter clasped his hands.

"Well, I've never tried your ice cream

before." Leo leaned his palms into the counter. He wore a mischievous grin she really didn't care for.

"Our menu is on the back wall, and we can give you samples of anything that intrigues you. We make it all fresh, including the hot-fudge toppings."

Nina raised an eyebrow at Leo. He could say whatever he wanted about the names of the flavors, but this was a small business that made everything from scratch. His dad had started a small business once upon a time, so surely he could appreciate that.

"Would it be possible to sample one of each? I'm told it's a very creative menu, and I'd love to get a new vendor into my restaurants." He scrutinized the menu again, placing a finger to his lips as if deep in thought.

What kind of monster . . . ? She'd wanted this to be quick. Was he intentionally prolonging their stay? Maybe he really did want to bring in a new vendor, but they could send samples to Vinny's, which he damn well knew.

"Oh, I'm sure the owner would be thrilled to have you test the flavors." The staffer leaned in closer to them. "We're all big fans of the show. It's good to see you two back together."

"We're happy to be together, too." Leo

placed a hand on Nina's shoulder and gave her a peck on the top of her head.

Her mouth opened, and she said, "Ah," in a way that made it sound like air was being squeezed out of a deflating balloon. She wished she had a pair of tongs to pry off his hand. But they were in public, so she forced her mouth into a friendly smile. She was going to get even with him for this one.

"Nina, you're okay if we stay a bit longer, right?"

"Leo, we don't want to take up too much of anyone's time, especially with this long line." Nina nodded behind them, where there was a line, albeit a short one. Her jaw clenched at the slight misfire.

"Oh, it's really no problem. Go find a bench outside, and I'll set you all up with samples!"

She blinked back. "Great." She tried to be enthused but was sure she sounded as disturbed as she felt at the idea of having to watch Leo eat lots of dairy.

If she was going to survive the rest of this minidate, she'd need more carbs. "Could you also bring us waffle cones to try?" she asked the staffer.

"Cup is fine for me, please," he added.

Ugh, unreal. Now he was also one of those people who ate their ice cream in cups to try and avoid more calories, or whatever?

This was going to be the longest nondate of her life.

9

LEO

Leo took a lick of his sample. Roasted strawberry sounded like pretentious foodie nonsense, but it did somehow taste like a creamy milkshake. He didn't exactly know what part of the soft serve was "roasted," or why anyone would want to do that to a strawberry, but it was all kinds of tasty. He wasn't planning to admit that to Nina, though.

"Well?" She raised an expectant eyebrow. She dipped a piece of waffle cone into her sample, but her lip stayed curved up in a know-it-all grin.

He knew she'd nearly lost her cool when he suggested they try all the ice cream, but now that they were actually eating, she seemed to accept that they were stuck together. Which was a shame, as he'd hoped to annoy her for a bit longer.

"I've had better." Leo settled more firmly

on the bench. He took in the little plaza where the shop was — twinkle lights above the awning, bright, sunflower-yellow benches lining the sidewalk.

"Oh, please, you practically moaned when you took a bite of the matcha." She snapped a piece of waffle cone in her mouth, then stretched her legs out and leaned back into the bench.

"I had a brain freeze, and that was moaning in pain." *Lies.* The matcha had made him moan.

"Oh, so you hate it? I'll just go ahead and eat what's left then." She reached for his cup, but he pulled away from her.

Well, he hadn't considered she'd take the damn thing from him. He wasn't about to give up ice cream easily.

"No, no. They say too much dairy can be a bad thing. I'd hate for you to get sick." He took a too-big spoonful and swallowed. An instant brain freeze followed, and he cupped his forehead in his hands.

When the splitting pain ceased, he looked up. Nina smiled widely back at him.

"Yikes." She took a bite of waffle cone. "Another brain freeze, huh?"

What had he done wrong in a past life to be totally reliant on Nina to help his career? And why did that have to involve one-on-

one dates with her? They'd been alone together a couple of times, and their interactions seemed to be getting worse instead of better. At what point would they both realize this charade wasn't worth the hassle of having to play nice with each other?

Not that they were being kind now, even though they should be. For appearances, if nothing else.

"Maybe we should . . . call a truce? At least until we're done having to work together." They had to come up with a new plan or try something different.

She licked a bit of ice cream off her bottom lip and studied him. "When you say, 'a truce,' you mean . . ."

He knew Nina well enough to know when she was trying to push his buttons, so he pushed right back. "I mean that while we're together, I will forget the fact that you're a massive snob."

Her gaze slowly shifted to him and she pursed her lips.

Damn it. Well, he couldn't help himself. "Sorry, I will stop saying things like what I just said," he added.

"Okay, and I guess I'll pretend that you aren't a sexist asshole." She closed her mouth in a tight smile, blinking.

He ran his tongue across his teeth as he

took in her statement. The truth was that they'd both done shitty things to each other, enough to fill multiple tell-all books that would hit the bestseller list. But if they actually wanted their arrangement to work, they'd have to at least try to be better. He needed to do better by her.

"You're right, what I did was wrong." He turned to face her to show that he meant what he was saying. He couldn't deny that he'd used "Nasty Nina" to intentionally hurt her, and what he'd done was plain old sexist — would anyone ever use that term against a man? He knew the answer was no, and he shouldn't have used it to provoke Nina. So now he had to put on the big-boy pants, eat shit and be a better person. "I deserve all of the hate I'm getting right now, because using your nickname was a massively bad move. And you may not believe me, but I never knew that it would become a whole thing when I first said it. I didn't mean to repeat it, but I was on edge at the finale. Not that that's any excuse. It was wrong of me to say, period."

His chest filled with a huge breath as he waited for her to respond. She straightened and took a painstakingly long time dabbing a napkin to the corners of her mouth, a pause that he deserved.

126

"I don't forgive you," she finally said.

"I don't expect you to," he said.

"A truce. We'll call a truce."

"Okay." A little smile tugged at the corners of his lips. "A truce."

They locked eyes, and she gave the hint of a smile back. Not exactly a handshake, but he'd take whatever bread crumbs of friendliness he could get. That was the people pleaser in him, after all.

"We should head out." She clapped her hands on her thighs, signaling their time was officially up. "We've been successfully spotted."

He looked around and saw a few small clusters of people staring at them. One woman caught his eye, waved and then immediately rushed over.

"Could I get a photo?" she said breathlessly. "My mom is gonna flip!"

Nina elbowed him and raised her brow as if to say "See? People!" She looked so proud of herself that he nearly chuckled. Instead, he raised an eyebrow back in acknowledgement — showtime.

They stood and posed with the fan as an onlooker took the photo.

"Can I get one, too?" the person who took the photo asked.

"Sure!" Leo smiled. There wasn't a massive crowd; it was a Monday night, after all. But since they'd agreed to do one photo, that meant they'd be taking photos for a bit longer. Which meant more uploads from fans, which meant more exposure and, ultimately, feeding the lie that was their cursed love story.

Hell, at least standing to pose with other people meant he'd have a guaranteed physical buffer between him and Nina.

The crowd had thinned. Their date had turned into a successful photo op, which was exactly what they were aiming for. And the night had been successful in other ways, too, like getting to eat ten flavors of ice cream. And, of course, Nina agreeing to call a truce so they could work toward their common goal as a "couple."

"Well, my little sugar plum, that was fruitful," he said to Nina. "Can I call you 'sugar plum'?"

"Does it look like you can call me that?" He knew she wanted to look intimidating in that moment, but the sun had completely set, and her face was lit from the neon of the storefront. She looked . . . almost like someone he might consider kissing, if this had been an actual date.

He brushed away the thought. "I'll see you

later this week." He rocked back on his heels. "Should we hug? Not sure what's appropriate here."

"Maybe next time. Baby steps, Leo." She turned to head toward her car.

He smiled back. "Baby steps for my honey bear."

As he watched her, she stopped and looked back at him. "Oh, and Leo? Since we're calling a truce and all, I should tell you that your fly has been down this whole time. Sorry, I probably should've told you sooner. Must be that nasty side coming out."

She shrugged her shoulders in an overly cutesy way, smiled and then walked off.

He fumbled for the zipper on his jeans and quickly pulled it back up. Was she for real? *I probably should've told you sooner?* Had she really just let him take all those photos with his pants unzipped?

All right, now things were definitely going to be interesting.

GOOGLE NEWS SEARCH FOR NINA LYON AND LEO O'DONNELL

Battle of the Bulge! These 11 Celebs Can't Stop Flaunting Their Jewels

Leo O'Donnell Fans Drool Over Unzipped Pants Pic!

Thirst Trap o' the Day: Leo O'Donnell's Pants Are Unzipped While He Licks an Ice-Cream Cone

We Zoomed In On Leo O'Donnell's Unzipped Sitch So You Don't Have To!

Forgot to Zip Up? Leo and Nina Spotted Post-Coitus

The Photo You Didn't Ask For: Leo O'Donnell with his Pants Unzipped

Nina Lyon, Watch Out! Leo O'Donnell's Bulge Is On the Loose

Former *Next Cooking Champ!* Contestant Has "No Complaints" About Leo's Unzipped Pic

From: Tom
To: NinaLyon; LeoODonnell
Subj: Moving forward . . .

Okay, I think we can ALL agree that the headlines coming out now are helping no one. Leo's bulge puts the spotlight on Leo instead of on both of you as a couple. And, Leo, well, if you want to become one massive thirst trap . . . let me know, because I represent those kinds of IG clients and would be happy to help.

But moving forward, how about you both follow a script? No more games.

We're going to do a big reset here. I'll arrange the dates. You do as I say. Your careers will be fixed. Call me Tommy fucking Poppins.

Obviously, all of this only works if you both start trusting each other. And pretend — CONVINCINGLY — that you're in a real relationship. Bottom line: Do. Your. Job.

Sound good? Great. Itinerary for this next date attached. No changes or requests.

Byeeeee
Tom

131

10

NINA

As Leo walked down the driveway toward Nina's car, she placed her forehead in her hands and repeated the mantra she'd told herself since getting Tom's email:

Do your job. Do your job. Do your job.

But, as usual, Leo made her job feel like a Herculean effort. Because as he smiled that smug smirk of his, she realized that almost every part of him irritated her. He made terrible dad jokes, though he clearly thought they were funny. He put on a phony smile for everyone, just showing how disingenuous he really was. And he'd apologized to her for using her nickname only after she called him out.

On top of all that, his annoyingly dark and thick hair did this perfect wave thing that she had a gut feeling was natural with no product involved. Ugh, even the way his pants fit as snugly against his thighs as a smooth demi-glace was obnoxious.

But she had to try because, as Tom said, she had no other choice.

Leo slowly opened the passenger-side door. He ducked his head in. "Aren't you supposed to come around and open the car door for me? What kind of date is this?"

"Fake date," she corrected.

"Chivalry is clearly dead." He got in. "Swanky ride."

"It's not the latest Tesla model," she said, deflecting. Even though she hadn't been able to afford her own car until she turned thirty, she was still self-conscious about having spent as much money as she had. She'd saved up and bought the BMW with cash. She should have been proud. She *was* proud. "She does have heated seats, though."

"Oh, I can definitely feel that." Leo wiggled in his seat, emphasizing how delighted he was. "I'd ask where to, but I got the itinerary. Nice to have someone else plan a date for a change."

"Oh, Leo, dates with blow-up dolls don't count." She smiled tightly.

"You clearly haven't met the right dolls, then," he countered.

And she laughed, which horrified her. Since when did she indulge his corny jokes?

Judging by the pleased look crossing his lips, he'd just gotten exactly what he wanted. But Nina had a job to do, and she wasn't about to let him forget that. "Look, this may all be some joke to you, but I'm not good at pretending. I mean, you've seen me on the show — our poor contestants! My face says it all."

"If you want, I can guide us through this." His voice was gentle and even, like a scam artist trying to convince her that she should wire money to a downtrodden prince in exchange for a royal title.

"Like you did at the ice-cream shop?" She needed to *try* and trust him, like Tom said. But that was proving to be hard already.

"That date doesn't count. It was a trial run. This is the real thing, a redo. And not for nothing, but I happen to be great at first dates."

She still felt on edge, despite Leo's nice-guy act. Probably because she knew him, and his tricks, all too well. "Is that so?"

"By the end of this fake date you'll be begging me for a second." He grinned, momentarily exposing the gap between his front teeth. She had to stop herself from staring at the pink of his tongue, which was only slightly visible. "Worst case, we cut the date short, right? Not that scary."

Fine. The day was high stakes — if the public believed they were together, this could be the beginning of turning her career around, and if they didn't . . . people would have another reason to rejoice in her demise. So if she was going to play make-believe all day, she'd need to just embrace the fact that she was on a date with Leo, in all of his smug glory. She'd pretend she was someone else — someone going out with a hot but heartless cardboard cutout of a man.

"There's going to be photographers crawling around this place," she said. In general, she didn't love having her photo taken. She "had a knack for finding bad angles," as Tom liked to say.

"Oh, I'm well aware." He fastened his seat belt. "That's why I dressed so sharply."

"It all makes sense now." She rolled her eyes before moving the gear into Drive — partly so they could get this over with and partly so she'd stop staring at how his arms looked in the jacket. It occurred to her that she hadn't noticed how thick his arms were before, not that she cared. A half hour later and they'd arrived. Tom knew how much Nina loved Halloween season, which is why he must've thought visiting a pumpkin patch a few weeks before the actual holiday would be a good idea. Mr. Bones was known as a place where you might see real-life celebrities walking among the rows of curated pumpkins. There was even a small, roped-off area for any paparazzi who wanted to catch a glimpse of someone famous coming in or out at the entrance. In other words, this was the perfect place to be spotted.

Which was exactly what they all wanted, right? At least that's what Nina reminded herself of when she parked the car. Her thoughts were interrupted by Leo taking a very loud and intentional deep breath. She looked over — his eyes were closed, and he was slowly blowing air out of his mouth.

If she didn't know better, she'd guess he was meditating . . . in her car? She really didn't want to get into whatever weird shit this was, but she had to interrupt him. They couldn't just sit there forever while he found his third eye. "I don't know whether to buy you a yoga mat or burn some sage to get the memory of whatever this is out of the car."

A sheepish expression crossed his face. "This may be hard to believe, but you aren't the only one who gets nervous."

She watched him drop the visor and examine his hair in the mirror. "Yeah, but you get nervous about your hair," she quipped. "I'm nervous about losing my career."

Leo flipped the mirror back up, then turned and leveled her with an unwavering glare. "My business is at stake, too, Nina. Not only do people think *I'm* the bad guy now, but if I lose the show? There goes my platform to sell the restaurants. People depend on me the same way they depend on you, so don't act like you're on an island."

Her eyes flickered down to where Leo's hand was clenched. She swallowed. He was right — they *were* in this fake relationship together. And she'd brought the idea to him, not the other way around. Leo was doing this for himself, but also to help her. When she looked back up, his expression softened.

"Whether we like it or not," he said, "you're stuck with me."

She definitely did not like it, but he wasn't wrong. She needed to get the pretend date over with.

She got out of the car, and the slightly cooler October temperature — well, seventy in Los Angeles was cool by their standards — sent a buzz through her. She'd take any little bit of extra energy she could get.

"Remember, we're just two very attractive

people going to pick out festive gourds," Leo said as they walked through the parking lot.

Okay, so he could occasionally crack a non-corny joke and she'd never noticed before — big deal.

As they approached the entrance it was hard to ignore the two bulky cameras pointed their way. Nina tensed. These were professional celebrity stalkers who'd probably seen every variation of a relationship in Hollywood. What if they could instantly sense the lack of connection between her and Leo?

Then, as if detecting her fight-or-flight response, Leo unexpectedly reached for her hand. She pulled back in surprise, but he held her steady there.

"What are you doing?" she hissed. His grip remained confident, while her hand felt as stiff as a week-old bagel.

"Dating you," he said through a smile so wide and fake it may as well have been painted on.

She took in a deep breath and blew back out as she nodded at him. Okay, she was going to follow Leo's lead because she was working on trusting him. Baby steps.

They paid the entrance fee and walked into the pumpkin patch. Well, "pumpkin patch" was a stretch. They were in the middle of a city, and nowhere near farmland, so Mr. Bones took over a parking lot every year. The lot was covered in hay and decorated with cobwebs and orange twinkle lights to set the fall mood. Every style of pumpkin imaginable was placed on top of neat rows of hay bales, and a Dolly Parton scarecrow, complete with pumpkins for boobs and an impressive blond wig, greeted them as they walked in. This was Hollywood, after all.

"Halloween is weird, isn't it?" Leo released her hand so he could pick up a pumpkin.

She should've been relieved to not have to touch him anymore, but Nina fidgeted. Her mind went blank with what to do with her free hand, as if she hadn't been single for years. It was unnerving how easily her body could fall back into the habit of having someone to lean on, and how good the human contact — even from Leo — had felt. She picked up a pumpkin of her own, white and speckled with green, to keep her hands occupied.

"A whole holiday built around begging for candy." He inspected his classic orange pumpkin for flaws.

"What are you going on about? Candy is what makes it the best holiday," Nina responded. "But I guess demons don't eat candy?"

"Not if I want to keep these pecs in shape." He winked at her.

The mention of his pecs sent her thoughts back to how she'd fallen against them. She could almost feel the warmth of his shirt along her cheek. Why did he have to go and mention his pecs?

She glanced around to keep herself from eyeing his chest. There were plenty of people nearby, but were any of them buying that she and Leo were a couple? They'd walked in together, held hands, were shopping for festive gourds . . . all things that could happen if they were on a real date.

"Should we do it?" Leo's low voice hummed in her ear.

When she turned toward him, very much confused, he nodded at a towering inflatable slide just behind them, a doublewide made for people to slide down two-by-two. The slide was Halloween-themed: it had a looming jack-o'-lantern fixed to the top, with multiple spooky ghosts at the bottom. A father and son slid down, screaming with glee, just as she turned back to face Leo.

"You spent all that time on your hair — aren't you afraid you'll mess it up?" The truth was, she would absolutely go down that slide, any day and anytime. She just didn't think Leo would be game to do an activity that might make him look less than perfect.

"Quit stalling." He walked past her and toward the ride. "Come on. Last one up there has to ride down face-first."

She wasn't about to lose that bet, and she'd pay all the money she had left to watch him do a belly flop on a slide. She started to sprint. She went right past him, and then felt him immediately nipping at her heels.

"You're cheating!" he shouted as they ran.

And she laughed as she beat him to the entrance because, really, beating Leo at anything, even if it was a silly bet, was extremely satisfying.

They went down twice. The first time, Leo had accepted his fate and gone face-first. When he reached the bottom, his swoop of hair looked more like the flat top of an eraser. She'd laughed so hard she'd nearly peed. The second time was just fun. Why not go again?

"I'm not going again." Leo shook his head.

"Third time's the charm." She smiled wistfully up at the slide.

"I feel like I'm going to be sick, and I have

a wedgie that I can't do anything about because . . . camera phones."

She gave him a good once-over. He did look a bit green, admittedly. She could've guilted him, but she was feeling generous since she was actually . . . enjoying herself. The realization that she was having a good time while in the same vicinity as Leo was startling.

"I'm coming for you next year," she said as she pointed to the slide.

"Are you talking to inanimate objects now?" He perked up.

But she ignored him, because she spied a costume tent against the fence and beelined for it. She examined the masks and hats for sale. Dressing up was her third favorite part of Halloween. The first being the candy, then the decorations and then donning a disguise for the night. As much as being in front of the camera was important for her career, when she was out in the world Nina didn't love being recognized. So when she was in a mask, she didn't worry about being spotted by a fan or having her photo snapped by a stranger's iPhone.

"Want to take the photos?" Leo said as he came up next to her. He picked up a pair of googly-eye glasses and put them on. One bloody eyeball bounced around on a curly wire and down toward Nina.

Taking photos was the whole point of their itinerary. Starred, underlined and printed in big, bold letters for them. Before they could leave the fake date, they needed to pose for festive photos. Then they were supposed to upload those to their respective IG accounts and leave comments on each others' posts. Get the fans talking, Tom had explained. Once they'd accomplished that, their work would be done for the day.

So the fact that Leo wanted to take photos clearly indicated his desire for the date to be done. Which was fine; she wanted that, too. And they'd managed to make it through an afternoon without completely snapping at each other, which was more than she'd expected.

Leo cocked his head toward a pile of stacked hay bales, topped with strategically placed baby pumpkins — a clear photo op.

"Sure, let's get this over with." How long could they stay at a pumpkin patch, anyhow? She shrugged and started walking toward it.

He took off the googly-eye glasses and scowled.

"What?" she asked, partly annoyed, partly curious.

"Just trying to get the witch hat and pointy shoes in frame." He moved slightly

143

to his left, then right.

She channeled her most intense withering gaze, then said, "How are you still single?"

"I'm not, remember?" He pointed at her. "Seriously, though. You need to look like you're having a good time." He put down the phone, then gnawed on his lips, deep in thought. "Oh, I know! Imagine I've stubbed my toe in an extremely painful way."

Now *that* really did make her smile.

"Excellent, excellent," he said as he reviewed the photo.

They switched places, and Leo arranged himself as she raised the phone for his photo. "Want to know why I'm smiling?" he asked.

"Absolutely not." She started to snap pictures. No denying he was all kinds of photogenic — not a bad angle to be found.

"I'm imagining you —" he began.

"Half-eaten by wild dogs?" She cocked an eyebrow his way, channeling Bridget Jones for the sake of her sanity.

His mouth opened, then closed. Then he said, "Did you just quote Bridget Jones?"

She squinted back in confusion. "You know that movie?"

He blinked rapidly as he straightened his shirt. Then brushed invisible dust off the pumpkin in his hands. "I've seen it."

The scowl crossing her face was impossible to hide. He'd seen one of her favorite films? And a rom-com, no less? And he'd liked it enough to remember lines from the movie?

He walked past her and toward the checkout line without so much as meeting her eyes. She watched him, so shocked that they actually had something in common that she nearly fell face-first into the haystacks.

@**NinaLyon**'s Instagram Comments

@**NinaLyon** caption: Meet my gourd-geous new friend.

@**LeoODonnell** This is a very gourd pun.

@**NinaLyon** 😉

@**lyonessa** omg omg omg you twoooooo

@**ninaleostandom** holy flaming cheetos, they are totally dating

@**leosmooshme** you owe me $20

@**ninamazzze** COME TO MY HOUSE, WE LOVE YOU

@**marrymeleo4ever** He's mine, bish!

@**pizzaratizme** hot pumpkins . . . (o)(o) . . .

@**karensimmons** With all due respect, not a flattering outfit or color on you.

@**doughnotcare** ur bio says, "Love God, thy neighbor, and tacos"

@karensimmons yeah

@doughnotcare . . .

@karensimmons ?

@doughnotcare annndddd we're done here

11

LEO

"Don't overthink this," Gavin warned. "Just go with your gut. What do you want? What would make you happy?"

Leo clicked his tongue against the roof of his mouth. The sun was beating down on them, and he pulled his baseball cap lower. How to even begin to answer those questions?

Then what he wanted — no, needed — came to him as clear as the crack of the bat meeting the ball.

"A pretzel. Lots of salt. Cheese dip." Leo didn't take his eyes off the field. The Dodgers' left fielder scrambled to the outfield wall, but the ball hit by the opposing team was out of there. Worse, the bases had been loaded — a grand slam. The game was not going well.

"Okay, I'll get that. Plus the ice cream that comes in the hat." His brother paused thoughtfully, then added, "And a Dodger dog." Gavin stood up and made the awkward shimmy down the row of seats toward the stairs.

One of the best parts of coming to a game was the food. That, and spending time outside of the restaurant with his brother. They'd grown up coming to games with their dad. Making the pilgrimage to Dodger Stadium for a few games every year was necessary.

Leo took a sip of his lukewarm beer. The Dodgers were behind by five. It was the top of the sixth. A kid behind him gently kicked the back of his chair. This was his day off. He was supposed to be relaxing. He should relax.

And even though he was in a mostly full stadium, surrounded by people yelling at the players, and the blare of the announcer's voice, without Gavin next to him the place felt very quiet. So quiet that Leo's anxiety started to go from a low hum in the back of his mind to front and center.

He needed distractions. Like his brother's rambling. Or food so crunchy, salted and fried that it would overload his senses. Hell, he'd even settle for one of those stadium waves that required his full attention so he'd be in sync with everyone else standing up and throwing their hands in the air. Because when he was alone with his thoughts, they inevitably wandered back to Nina. Specifically, he wanted to know what she'd thought of their day together.

Because for him, he couldn't shake the feeling that something was deeply, deeply wrong. He hadn't left their date fuming, or on edge. They'd spent time alone together, and it had gone . . . fine. Better than fine, actually, because he hadn't minded being with her at all. They'd made the occasional dig at each other, but beyond that, no major fights. If the outing had been with anyone other than her, he might even have thought they'd had fun.

Which was why he needed a reality check from Nina. He'd feel so much better if she just texted him a message that said something like "by the way, I still hate you and your stupid face" to snap him out of thinking that everything had gone well.

He checked his phone just in case, but there were no new messages from Nina. Just a selfie of Gavin with his tongue out and dangerously close to Leo's soft pretzel. As he pocketed his cell, his sunglasses slid down his nose from the thin layer of sweat on his face. Gavin never remembered to get them seats in the shaded part of the stadium, which meant Leo always ended up sweating buckets through every game.

"Hello!" a pointed voice called out. "Could I get a picture with you?"

He looked to his right and saw a middle-aged woman grinning back at him, a cell phone in her palm. Her husband pretended to fiddle with the zipper on his jacket, his cheeks so red he was either sunburned or mortified.

"Of course." Leo smiled kindly. He always took photos when people asked, because coming up to someone took guts. Plus, he could use the diversion, and, if he was really being honest, the ego boost.

"Visiting from Michigan. Thought we'd spot celebrities all over the city." The way she said "city" sounded more like "ciddy," her Michigan accent coming through. "But you're the first we've met!"

"You clearly saved the best for first." A little dad joke was his signature move. So why did it make him wonder what Nina would think of it? He had to stop wanting to know what she'd think — he could guess, and it involved the words *please* and *stop.* Which meant he was back to trying to distract himself, so he stood and came to the aisle to meet the woman for the photo. "Fan of the show?"

Small talk was easy, he'd never had a problem there. His dad had taught him the art of making people feel seen. When he'd walk around the restaurant, he went out of his way to have quick chats with the customers. Going beyond, though, was where Leo had never felt quite comfortable. Because any time he did open up to someone, the relationship inevitably fizzled. So he'd learned to try and stay surface level for as long as possible. But he was hopeful that someday he'd meet *the* person with whom he could be vulnerable without scaring them off.

"I've actually never seen the show." She giggled behind her hand.

"Is that so?" He feigned amusement. He was used to being approached by people who actually watched him on TV. This was . . . different.

"But your face is all over the internet." She handed her phone to her husband. "Bill, stand up there. You want to angle the camera down." Then she looked at Leo. "Ready?"

"All over the internet?" he repeated. He and Nina were making headlines and trending, and he didn't know if that kind of recognition was at all a good thing, but there wasn't much he could do at this point.

"You and that lady, the real bossy one? You're all my friends talk about right now. They love that she's this sassy chef, and they say you're real funny. You're a comedian, is that right?" Her eyes twinkled, as she was just trying to be friendly.

Leo's smile temporarily faded, and he forced a grin. Even though she'd asked an innocuous question, he suddenly felt like a guy who'd never graduated high school being compared to a PhD from Harvard. Regardless of whether Nina was in the same room, he would always pale in comparison.

"Bro, someone mistake you for that TV chef dude?" Gavin said as he came down the stairs and slung an arm around Leo. "Happens all the time." Gavin winked at the woman.

She looked between them, and a frown crossed her lips. Then she clasped her hands at her chest, gripping a strand of invisible pearls. "You mean, you're not —"

Gavin interrupted, "I hear that guy's brother is even better looking than the famous one. Crazy, huh?"

The woman's mouth formed a tight and accusatory little line. She grabbed her phone angrily from her husband. Then, without another word, walked down the stairs.

"Thanks for the save," Leo said. They maneuvered back to their seats.

"What are twins for?"

Leo tried to smile, but felt a grimace fighting through. He didn't want to tell his brother *why* he'd needed a save. "A woman I don't know hurt my feelings" would require further explanation. Was his ego really so fragile that a single question would send him into a shame spiral?

Yes, Leo realized, it was.

They sat, and Leo grabbed the pretzel from his brother. He ripped off a chunk, then dipped it in the cheese before taking a bite. He chewed, trying to focus on the taste of all that salt and dough. But the woman's words swirled in his head: *you're a comedian, is that right?*

Is that what people thought of him? That he was just a joke? Sure, in a sense he was a form of comic relief on the show. When Nina cranked up the tension with a scathing critique, he took things down a notch with a lighthearted remark. But were his job and Vinny's really so unimportant that people couldn't recall what he did? Nina had built a business all on her own. She'd carved out an identity for herself. People would remember her as a chef, but how were they going to remember him?

"If you don't take this from me, I'm going to finish it," Gavin said through a mouthful of chocolate ice cream with sprinkles.

"All yours," Leo replied. He rested what was left of the pretzel on his knee. He suddenly didn't feel hungry anymore.

He was being childish and ridiculous — logically, he knew that. And why did he care what a random stranger thought? But he was a successful restaurateur, a businessman. Not to nitpick, but he had an MBA — which some people might find impressive.

And he'd agreed to a fake relationship to try and save his family's legacy, not have Vinny's pushed to the side. Chain restaurants were a precarious business. If he messed up, he'd make his father's restaurant seem like a second-rate Olive Garden. But if he worked hard to get ingratiated more into the world of food, there was a chance that Vinny's could be a destination, not a last-ditch option.

"I'm gonna need another Dodger dog if the score doesn't turn around soon. You?" Gavin popped the last of his hot dog into his mouth.

"Nah, gotta save room for tonight," Leo replied.

"Ah, your date."

Yes, he had another date with Nina. And this one wasn't a fluffy photo op like the pumpkin patch had been. They were going to dinner, and she'd agreed to introduce him to the restaurant's chef. If he was going to make the best out of the situation, this could be his opportunity.

So he had to stop fixating on how well their first "date" had gone. The fact that they hadn't bit off each other's heads was a sign that their arrangement might actually work in his favor. He wasn't in this to be Nina's friend. And tonight would be all business. He needed to be more than just the guy standing next to Nina Lyon.

12

NINA

Nina poured a pile of flour onto the counter and formed a nest with her fingers — first flattening down the flour, then digging out a hole in the middle. She cracked an egg and poured it into the opening. Then she grabbed a fork and quickly whisked.

"Watching you do this is quite soothing." Sophie sat on a stool at the kitchen island and took slow sips from her glass of rosé.

Nina smiled. They used to watch their mom cook every Sunday — the one day she always had off. Being in the kitchen had become their weekend tradition — make a lot of food in the morning, watch a movie in their pajamas and have a massive brunch with enough leftovers for dinner.

"I'm glad," Nina said. "And you look very chic right now. It's inspiring me."

Sophie had embraced the bohemian style of LA. She wore a cream linen skirt, a marigold-yellow silk tank and a floral scarf around the topknot on her head — like a well-decorated cupcake in a hipster bakery.

"Tell me, sis, what's happening with the icing?" Nina nodded at the counter, where she'd laid out a bowl, mixer, cream cheese and sugar.

"Oh, maybe you forgot, but I have a heart condition." Sophie tapped on her chest, where her heart — and her pacemaker — was.

Nina guffawed. Her sister had been born with a condition that had been monitored. But when she passed out at the age of five due to a low heart rate, the doctors decided she needed a backup option — hence the pacemaker. It certainly wasn't keeping her from stirring up icing, though.

"Nice try, but you have a robot keeping you alive, so you're technically stronger than all of us," Nina said.

"Mom never made me cook." Sophie raised an eyebrow and took another sip of wine.

"That's because she had me to help her." Nina met Sophie's eyes. They were both silent for a beat.

Nina looked down at the pasta dough and licked her lips. Their mother had passed away six years ago from breast cancer, but

Nina still had moments where she forgot that she wasn't there anymore.

Sophie swallowed the last of her wine. Then wordlessly walked over to make the icing for the Funfetti cake — their mom's favorite.

Nina watched her, unsure of what to say. They were both sad. Their mom's birthday had gone from being fun to a day of remembering what they'd lost. But Nina's mom had always told her to be strong for her little sister. When her mom went to work, it was Nina who made sure both sisters got to the bus stop. And when they came home after school, Nina got dinner started and had Sophie doing her homework. Nina had been not only a sister, but also Sophie's guardian. And she didn't regret the role she'd been given — she'd brought so much of her experience being responsible for Sophie into overseeing her own kitchens — but being "strong" had also translated, at least for Nina, to not showing every single emotion she'd had. So when she was in situations like this, where she and her sister were both on the verge of tears, she didn't always know how to respond.

Her mom had never been cold with them. Always warm and loving — giving them hugs and kisses the minute she stepped in the door. So what would their mom do? Nina walked over to Sophie and hugged her from behind.

"This sucks," Sophie sniffled.

"Yeah." Nina rested her cheek on her sister's shoulder. "We don't have to celebrate her birthday. We could just drink wine and be sad, like normal people."

"Mom wasn't normal people," her sister said quietly.

Nina nodded into her sister's shoulder. Their mom was their sunshine, their everything, and they'd been happiest when they were all together. Her mom had been Nina's best friend, until she couldn't be.

For her funeral, their mother had requested that they take her ashes to the ocean, listen to Prince, drink a bottle of wine and watch the sunset with her one last time before letting her go into the waves. Letting her go, though, had never fully happened. There wasn't a day that went by where Nina didn't want to talk to her mom. She still had her number saved. For the first few months after she died, she'd call her mom's cell and let it go to voice mail, just to hear her voice recorded. "This is Sheila Lyon, leave me something happy" had brought her to tears more than once. But her mom didn't want them sad about her life being over. She only wanted her girls to remember the good. Sophie was right: their mom was not normal people.

Still, her eyes welled as she stood with her sister on a day when their mom should be right there in the kitchen with them. She couldn't help but be sad that Sheila wasn't there, no matter how much light she'd brought.

"Okay, I'm not your personal Kleenex, though." Sophie nudged her with an elbow.

Nina wiped her nose on her sister's sleeve for good measure.

Sophie turned and they full-body-hugged. Today would be sad, period.

She wasn't sure how long they stood locked together, but eventually they both went back to cooking. Sophie turned on a Prince playlist from her phone as a breeze from the open kitchen window brushed through Nina's hair.

"What are you gonna wear tonight?" Sophie's words broke through her thoughts.

Her third date with Leo. Maybe she should've rescheduled, but she wanted to take her mind off what day this was and who was absent from it. Plus, Leo was safe — he wouldn't know it was her mom's birthday. He wouldn't ask if she was okay or hug her in an overly meaningful way that then made her cry.

And their last date hadn't been as awful as she'd expected. Pretending to be in a relationship wasn't ideal, and neither was acting like she couldn't see the photographers who took their photos. But they hadn't had a blow-out fight. He'd even made her laugh, which was a real shock. So maybe this date would surprise her in a good way, too. They'd have dinner, some wine, and then she could go home and fall asleep and this whole awful day would be over and done with.

Nina's eyes went wide. "What's tonight?"

Sophie shot her a look. She'd asked Nina about the date every single day for the last three days.

"Excuse me if I want to live vicariously through my sister who is going on a *Bachelor*-style prearranged date with a very, very, very sexy man." Sophie turned on the mixer and the hum of metal meeting the glass bowl filled the room.

The other part of the date that Nina was trying very hard to not think about was the suggestion Tom had left at the bottom of his emailed itinerary.

Try to look like you're dating this time. Please and thank you.

Photos of them holding hands at Mr.

162

Bones had made the rounds on Twitter, IG fan pages and celebrity-gossip websites. The articles, paired with a "no comment" statement from Tom, had sufficiently caused a lot of speculation as to their relationship status. But as Tom had put it, "I hold hands with my grandma — anyone can do that." If holding hands with Leo wasn't enough for him, she didn't love the alternatives that popped into her head.

"Let me lick the spoon." Stress-eating was the answer to most problems, anyway.

"That's what you're gonna be saying to Leo later tonight." Sophie gave her an exaggerated wink.

"How did you get to be like this?" Nina dislodged a wire beater from the mixer and took a luxurious lick of the cream-cheese frosting. "We have the same mom, grew up in the same house, shared a bedroom . . ."

"I'm just lucky." Sophie removed the other beater. "Are you gonna tell me you didn't have fun on your last date? I saw the photos — you were both smiling and laughing like crazy. And you can't act for shit."

"We were zipping down a slide — of course, we were smiling," Nina hedged.

"Exactly, you did something silly with him. You don't normally let yourself be vulnerable like that." Sophie took a lick of icing.

"What are you talking about?" Did Sophie actually think Nina was so stuffy that she never had any fun? "I went on Jasmine's motorcycle the other day."

"Yeah, and that's your best friend who's had that bike for five years — it took you that long to loosen up." Sophie leaned back into the countertop. "So all I'm saying is, whether fake or whatever, dating Leo might actually be good for you."

"Is your pacemaker short-circuiting? Sounds like you might need another jolt." Nina flicked her sister's chest.

"Ow!" Sophie yelped. "Just kidding. I'm part robot. I feel nothing." She licked the wire beater again and shook her head. "When will the pasta be done?"

Nina was cooking a French pasta called pâtes aux lardons. Curly tagliatelle noodles with Gruyère cheese, bacon and loads of butter — creamy perfection on a plate. Their mom had kept the recipe in heavy rotation because it was simple, delicious and within the budget of a single, working mother.

And being around Leo had given her a craving for that pasta. Something about the way his meaty arms filled out the jacket . . .

okay, stop thinking about Leo's arms.

"Thirty minutes," Nina answered, shaking away the thought of Leo.

"And you still want to watch *Bridget Jones*?"

She had not told Sophie that it was a movie Leo had seen. Or that she'd quoted it to him on their last date. Or that Leo did this lip-curl thing that reminded Nina of the smoldering glare Mark Darcy did at the end of the movie.

"Yes, if that sounds good to you?" She felt like she was hiding a secret from her little sister. But Sophie was a romantic, and after calling out Nina for actually enjoying her last date, this would just about send her into a glittery explosion of hope. The last thing she needed was to leave little bread crumbs that would lead to a happily-ever-after house in Sophie's mind.

And besides, this was their mom's birthday. Maybe she had Leo on the brain because of their date later, but she wasn't counting on him for anything other than taking her mind off what day it was.

After Nina plated the pasta, and Sophie iced the cake and cut them slices, they moved into the living room.

"Do you not have a cleaning person or something?"

Nina did not have a cleaning person, especially now that any extra money she had was being poured back into Lyon and paying the staff. "I am the cleaning person." She carefully curtsied so as not to spill the nearly full wineglasses in her hands. "But I see your point."

The coffee table was cluttered with cookbooks and recipe cards, a spillover from the office at Lyon, where she'd run out of room completely for her food research. There was also a butcher knife on top of one pile of books, and she honestly wasn't sure what it was doing there. She placed the wineglasses on the hardwood floor, and gently carried her piles of papers to sit on top of . . . more piles of papers.

"This is bad." Sophie cringed as she looked around the living room. "Not *Hoarders*-level bad, but you're not far from it, either."

"I don't spend much time at home," Nina hedged. Which was true: these days she was either at the restaurant, digging through farmers' market produce for something inspiring, or working on her image problem with Leo.

"I don't blame you. I wouldn't want to die in a cookbook avalanche, either." Sophie placed the plates on the newly cleared coffee table. Then sat on the couch. She immediately bounced back up in surprise, turned and picked up a heel Nina had left in between the couch cushions. "And I hadn't considered death by stiletto, but let's add that in there."

Nina grabbed the shoe. The one she'd taken off and thrown — apparently on the couch — the night she quit the show. "I keep the kitchen clean. Doesn't that count for something?"

"Is that what you tell yourself?" Sophie lifted the couch cushions, checking for more unintentional weaponry. When she came up empty, she brushed off the seat with her palm, then sat down. She grabbed the plate and took a bite of cake, finally relaxing. "Mom would never believe that I've somehow become the tidy daughter by default."

Nina smirked. She hadn't spent enough time with Sophie in the last year — had been too consumed with work. She'd missed having her under the same roof. "Why don't we hang out more?"

Nina discreetly nudged a rogue bra under the couch with her big toe.

Sophie spooned in a big mouthful of cake. "Are you asking or requesting?"

"Both, I guess."

"I don't know." Sophie shrugged. "We're

both busy? Life? Stuff?"

Nina gave a wry smile back. "Too busy taking care of Rain Boots?"

"My pet goldfish is not to be mocked." Sophie pointed her fork at Nina.

"It is when you've had the same one for eight years. You're a record holder."

Sophie put down her plate. "The longest goldfish lifespan on record is forty-three years. I plan to beat that."

"I have no doubt you will." Nina hit Play on the TV, and the opening credits began. "Sophie?"

"Yeah?"

"I love you."

"Okay." Sophie swiped her finger into Nina's frosting. "I'm not used to you being sappy. You're freaking me out."

Sophie took Nina's plate of cake and scooted over to the opposite end of the sofa.

"It's freaking me out, too," Nina said.

13

LEO

"I'm not going to puke, I promise." Leo looked over at his driver, Ashley. He had a *driver.* And that driver glared back at him.

"You better not, because I'm one of those people who can't handle someone else barfing. Like, I end up vomiting, too. Just the thought of it . . ." Ashley cupped a hand to her mouth and gagged. "Oh, shit. Seriously, do *not* do the thing you keep talking about not doing."

The network hadn't splurged on car service for Leo, ever — even to LAX, when he needed to hop on flights to promote the show across the country. But Nina's publicist clearly wanted them to have a good and safe night, hence the built-in designated driver.

He thought they'd arrive together, but as Tom had said, "We want glamour. Mystery. Romance. Fantasy." As a final touch, he'd added, "We don't want Ralph from Uber."

So Leo, prone to being carsick, sat up front and watched as the iconic Sunset Grande came into view. Set deep into the Hollywood people thought of when they pictured Los Angeles, the hotel and restaurant was right off Sunset Boulevard. The looming, castle-like exterior, complete with turrets and towers, was impossible to miss. Like the pumpkin patch, famous people were known to frequent it, and paparazzi loved to wait nearby.

Ashley pulled up to a valet stand, handed Leo her card and said, "Just text when you're ready."

So he put the card in his pocket and got out.

He was going to meet an important chef, and he wanted to make the best possible impression. It was a lot of pressure. The chances of him having a full-blown panic attack felt slim — he'd gone to the baseball game to distract himself from fixating, and none of the usual warning signs had popped up. But now that he was in front of the Sunset Grande, a ball of nervous energy hit him. His foot manically tapped the literal red carpet that led from the curb to the inside.

Nina hadn't arrived, but the paparazzi had

— two men with long-lens cameras stood across the street, their shots trained on him. He tried to channel his best I-don't-see-you-and-am-casually-handsome look. Though, judging by the concerned glance the valet attendant gave him, he probably appeared more nauseous from the car ride than anything.

His stomach knotted as a town car, identical to the one he'd arrived in, pulled up to the curb.

Leo straightened, trying not to look at the car too intently. And besides, he couldn't see through the tinted windows. But he wondered . . . was she watching him?

The driver got out and opened the back door.

He saw her legs first. Ankle boots met her bare calves, and the tops of her knees were hidden under a maroon, long-sleeved body-con dress. His gaze momentarily flitted to her breasts, which were pushed up and toward him. He was only human, after all, and they were really amazing breasts. He was used to seeing her in conservative wardrobe choices for the show, or the casual-date look she'd had at the pumpkin patch and ice-cream shop. In this fitted, sleek dress that showed off every one of her curves, though, she looked . . .

This is work. She is your coworker.

He walked toward her, but when he reached her side, he wasn't sure what to do. Should they hug? Hold hands? Kiss each other on the cheek? Or . . . ?

Tom neglected to leave instructions in his email as to this part of the night. But the paparazzi were watching, so he had to act fast. He wrapped an arm around her shoulder protectively, bringing her into his side.

"I'm shorter than you, but using me as an armrest is a little offensive," she said through gritted teeth.

He had to admit that she fit perfectly under the crook of his arm, armrest or not. He leaned down until they were so close that her wavy hair brushed against his cheek. He blinked away the cinnamon smell of her, not about to get distracted.

"Go on," he said in a hushed tone. "Wrap your arm around my waist. I assure you it's quite trim."

Her fingertips grazed the side of his torso. He unexpectedly stiffened. Her touch was so light that it was difficult not to think of what her hands could do if they trailed their way down the rest of his body.

Think of church, clipping toenails, people who say the movie is better than the book, cold showers, Nina undressed in a shower and . . . No.

He didn't want to think about her naked, but the dress and her arm around him had short-circuited his brain. He just needed to keep reminding himself that this was Nina and she didn't even want to be here with him.

As if to prove him right, when they got inside the Sunset Grande, she pulled back. The cameras were gone and they were away from the photo op. Clearly, she knew what they were here for — business — and *he* was the one who had to keep his thoughts in check.

They sat at an outdoor table, under a crisp, white umbrella by the edge of creeping green vines. The space was outfitted with woven Parisian chairs, cream tablecloths and enough potted plants to create the illusion of a secret garden in the middle of Hollywood.

But he wasn't there to enjoy the ambiance, even if the twinkly lights above his head were undeniably whimsical. His mission was to make a valuable connection for Vinny's.

As they sat down, he looked at her. She glanced at him. They both licked their lips at the same time. Their dates always seemed to have their share of awkwardness, but for some reason, this one felt even thicker with tension.

"How was your . . . day?" Leo's voice shot up an octave at the end, like even he didn't know why he was asking this. But, hell, they had to start somewhere.

"My day was . . ." She stopped herself. Then drummed her fingers on the table and nibbled at her bottom lip. "Fine."

Nina had been short with him plenty of times in the past, but her response felt different from when she was trying to exit a conversation. Something was off . . . and judging by the way she was avoiding his eyes, she couldn't stop thinking about it. He wasn't going to assume she'd open up to him, but he at least wanted to give her the opportunity.

"*Fine* is one of those words that usually means not fine," he hedged.

Nina opened her mouth slightly, as if considering this. But then the waiter approached the table, looking bored.

"All set to order?" he asked.

Leo wondered if he'd been trained not to react to anyone — including celebrities — with any kind of emotion. "We haven't seen the menu." He picked up the menu in front of him and scanned the page.

"Mind if I order for us?" Nina asked. "I'm

craving comfort food. And I know what I want."

He looked up from the menu. The flickering candlelight on the table cast a warm glow on her face. He'd never noticed how long and thick her eyelashes were.

"Go for it." He leaned back in his chair. Why not? He was curious to hear what a food snob ordered for dinner.

"We'll have the beet salad, linguine and clams, and the burger. But give us an extra side of fries," she said without so much as taking a breath. Then she glanced at him, checking to see if he wanted to add anything.

Leo waved a hand to say he was all set, but he was admittedly shocked she'd ordered a burger — a rather normal menu item. It was as odd as the video Gavin had sent of his cat riding around on a Roomba.

The waiter looked past them as he asked, "Anything to drink?"

"We'll take the 2014 Corton-Charlemagne, please." She gave him a friendly but fake smile.

As the waiter turned away from the table, Nina exhaled. And she seemed relieved to be alone with Leo, which was new.

"You ordered without seeing the menu," Leo said.

"I always check out menus before I go somewhere. And I've watched you eat food for the last three years." She sipped her water before launching in. "We both know you give extra points when people cook with beets, and they happen to be in season. Linguine and clams will be a light and salty middle course. I don't know if you like burgers, but I do. Like I said, I need comfort food."

So she'd been studying him. Cataloguing what he liked and disliked. Making mental notes of his actions on set. Which was probably just her way of sizing him up, right?

She placed her napkin on her lap and slightly rearranged the silverware. Then carefully inspected the breadbasket before grabbing a roll covered in seeds and smearing it with warm butter.

She chewed, swallowed, then took another sip of water. Finally, she looked at Leo. "What? Are you too vain to eat bread?"

"I run an Italian restaurant. We practically invented it." Leo reached into the breadbasket without looking, and then took an enormous bite of the dinner roll he pulled out of it.

"The Egyptians invented bread, you know." She licked butter from the corner of her mouth.

"Know-it-all," he said, shoving a bite of bread in his mouth.

The wine arrived, and the waiter opened the bottle and poured them two generous glasses.

They drank in silence, both chewing bread, then sipping their wine.

"Do you want to talk about it?" Leo took another sip. The wine was crisp and light, with a buttery finish. Not something he would've known to order, but he already knew it would perfectly complement the meal. "Seems like maybe you didn't have a great day."

Her eyes flitted down, and she fingered the wineglass stem. Her mouth turned into a concerned frown.

He'd never seen her look sad, had he? He'd assumed she was incapable of feelings, judging by her harsh reviews to the contestants, but ever since the pumpkin patch, his perspective had shifted. She was guarded, and very careful about whom she let see beyond the walls she'd so carefully built up.

She studied him for a few seconds, then grabbed another roll. "How is it fair that you eat an entire breadbasket and still have abs, but I just get rounder?"

"Then keep eating, because you're round

in all the right places." He froze. *Holy shit.* He really had been single for too long, and now he was letting his cock do the talking.

She stopped chewing and quirked an eyebrow at him.

He was pretty sure his eyebrows had run so far up his head that they were no longer visible. He tried to keep breathing and not let on that he was freaking the fuck out. Yes, she looked amazing in the dress, but that didn't mean he had a right to comment on her body. And now she likely thought he was some desperate, pathetic loser who'd always had a crush on her. When really, he was just hoping they could get through this date without arguing.

"Sorry to interrupt." A woman stood in front of their table.

Thank the gods of well-timed interruptions, he thought.

"Chef!" Nina stood and hugged the woman.

"It's a little hard for the executive chef not to notice when Nina Lyon walks into their restaurant!"

Leo adjusted the cuffs of his shirt. This was *his* moment. The one that would make the charade of dating Nina worth the hassle. If he wanted to make his own mark on the food world and have any chance at working in TV without Nina, then he had to look alive.

The distraction of meeting the chef was almost enough to help him forget what he'd just accidentally said to Nina. He'd made a little slipup. Not a big deal, but he couldn't help sneaking glances at her out of the corner of his eye. Was she going to let this go?

"I'm being rude." Nina turned her focus to him. They locked eyes, and she gave him an encouraging look. "Leo, this is Chef Rhoda Spence. Chef Rhoda, this is Leo O'Donnell," she said.

He smiled widely and got to his feet, trying not to show so much teeth that he reeked of desperation. He'd meant to say hello, but instead said, "I'm her date."

He needed help. Professional help, so he wouldn't sound like a complete doofus. This was a work connection he was making; Rhoda wasn't a writer for *People* magazine. She wouldn't report back on what she'd seen at their dinner. But the words had flown off his tongue as easily as the compliment to Nina had.

If Nina was bothered, she didn't show it, as she quickly said, "Leo is also in food."

"Really?" Chef Rhoda crossed her arms and smiled. "Food people are my kind of people. What do you do?"

Okay, now here was his in. The chef had no clue who he was. She didn't watch the show. She assumed Leo was important because he was here with Nina. He wasn't the comedian sidekick — he was whoever he sold himself to be.

"I'm a restaurant owner." He stood a little straighter with pride.

"It takes money to run a restaurant," Chef Rhoda said. "You're a friend to chefs everywhere."

"His family started the original Vinny's in Pasadena." Nina nodded to Leo, and he nodded back. Sharing a little moment with her was surprisingly comforting. "I'm sure you know it?"

The chef's brow furrowed and she nodded. "Yes, who doesn't know Vinny's?"

"It's an institution!" Nina smiled broadly.

He wasn't sure if Nina was being genuine, but she was doing him an incredible favor. If you'd told him a month ago that he'd be out to dinner with Nina, and she'd call Vinny's an institution . . . he never would've bought that. But here they were, helping each other.

So maybe things *had* changed between them, and they'd come to some sort of friendly understanding. Whatever the case, a rush of enthusiasm shot through him. Buoyed by Nina's confidence in him, he knew he could navigate the conversation with this chef. But then . . .

"I think I ate at one in the Dallas airport." The chef scratched the side of her chin. "Or maybe that was an Applebee's?"

All the confidence Leo had felt drained out of him as a beat of silence stretched between them, across the restaurant and maybe all of Hollywood. Leo was on a date with one of the most well-respected chefs on the planet, talking to a chef who cooked for celebrities every single day and he . . . ran a chain of family restaurants.

There were a dozen things he could've said in response: "Hope you liked the service!" or "Wait 'til you see what we have planned for LAX." But his mouth went dry. How could he convince the chef that he was a serious force in the food world when she'd knocked him down to size without even trying?

"This meal is on the house," she said to Nina. "We're honored to have you."

As if on cue, the waiter appeared with their meal and set it on the table.

Nina elbowed him in the ribs. He looked at her, and she nodded toward the chef. Her expression basically said, "Say something,

181

you unbelievable moron." He should at least thank Rhoda for the meal, but his anxiety had finally caught up and taken every possible word from his mouth.

So without so much as saying goodbye, the chef walked away from the table.

They sat back down.

He hadn't realized how quiet he'd become until the sound of Nina's finger tapping against the water glass forced him to look up. She was staring back.

"Leo," she said gently.

"Nina," he said curtly.

First the woman at Dodger Stadium, and now the chef at the Sunset Grande. Two people from very different worlds who had both found him unremarkable in comparison to Nina, all within less than twenty-four hours. Could he feel any smaller?

"I'm sorry." Her eyebrows formed a worried line.

"Why are you sorry?" he asked.

"That wasn't how I wanted the conversation to go. Let me ask her to come back —"

He stopped her. "I own restaurants that exist in airports. That's a fact."

Why did this bother him so much? Oh, right, because his business was always second-rate in comparison to Nina's, and nothing he did would ever be good enough.

"Okay. I just feel . . ." She shook her head and looked down at the table.

"Pleased? I'm sure that was fun for you to watch." Wow, he did *not* intend to sound as bitter as he did, but he couldn't stop the words, or the tone, from spilling out.

"I knew you didn't like me, just didn't realize you think I'm a terrible person." She rubbed her temples.

He didn't think she was a terrible person — not really. Especially not after she'd tried to help him with the introduction and supporting Vinny's. He'd just . . . choked, and completely blown the opportunity that was right in front of him. He'd been lost in his own insecurities, so when it came time to speak . . . he'd frozen. His anxiety was to blame, not Nina. How other people reacted to his business was out of her hands. The least he could do was be friendly back to her, the way she'd attempted to be to him.

"I don't think you're terrible, Nina." He was an idiot, is what he should've said. He was aware that his pride often got the best of him. What would his mom say if she saw how Leo had acted? How he'd made Nina feel? "You tried to help me big-time, and I'm just disappointed in myself. I took that out on you. I'm sorry for saying that. If my mom were here, she'd smack me on the head."

A barely perceptible sniffle came out of Nina. When he looked at her, really took a moment, he could see that her eyes had welled up. She wiped at the corners with her napkin.

"Oh, shit, Nina . . ." *Goddamn it.* Had he seriously made her cry? He shifted in his chair. What should he do in this situation? Should he go to her side? Give her a hug?

"Calm down," she said as she dabbed away more tears. "Not everything is about you. Today is just tough for me. It's my mom's birthday."

Leo straightened. She'd never mentioned her mother, and he had no idea why her birthday would cause Nina to cry. But he sensed there was more she was about to share, so he waited.

"She died, a while back. When you mentioned your mom, it just made me think of her. Sorry." She nervously laughed and wiped tears from her eyes. "I don't usually cry."

"I cry during those Sarah McLachlan ASPCA commercials, if it makes you feel better." He didn't cry about the loss of his dad. He didn't allow himself to go there, which is why things like rom-coms, or sappy movies, were of special interest. They gave him an excuse to cry, not that he was about to tell Nina all of that. "I'm sorry about your mom."

"I thought coming out would distract me." She sniffled and ate a handful of the fries. "Fuck, how are these still so good when they're cold?"

He didn't know exactly what she was going through, but he could relate. He'd lost his father, and every holiday, birthday, or day without him was painful. The fact that she'd been willing to spend time with him on her mom's birthday spoke to who she was as a person. She could've rescheduled, but she'd come out, anyway, and tried to help Leo, all while she was suffering inside.

He leaned across the table and whispered, "I know what will make you feel better."

She sniffed. "Chocolate?"

"More satisfying than sugar." He sighed. Was he really going to tell her the story? Yes, he was, because he'd been passive-aggressive and he never wanted to see her cry ever again. "When I was out with my brother today, a woman recognized me."

"So far this is not doing the trick." She took a big gulp of wine.

"Just wait for the punch line." He cracked his neck. He wasn't going to enjoy revealing how embarrassing of an afternoon he'd had, but making Nina smile would be worth the humiliation.

"She wanted a photo together. I mean, obviously, who wouldn't want their photo taken with someone as good-looking as me?"

Nina rolled her eyes and shoved another handful of fries in her mouth, but he noticed the hint of a smile cross her lips before she did.

"When I asked her if she was a fan of the show, she said she knew who you were — a famous and classy chef." Okay, so the woman had said sassy, not classy, but Nina didn't need to know that part.

Nina cut the burger in half, then cocked an eyebrow. "Okay, can you get to the point?"

"She asked if I was . . ."

Nina leaned across the table. He was going to have to just say the words.

"She hadn't watched the show. So she asked if I was a sidekick comedian. For my job. Like a clown."

Nina pursed her lips to keep from smiling. "Does she know you have to be funny in order to make it in comedy?"

He smiled back. She was teasing him, and he weirdly liked it. "That's not true. Good looks can get you far in life."

"That did make me feel better, thank you." Nina looked up at him from under her thick lashes. Her eyes were red from crying, but in the candlelight her skin had a golden glow. "I'm sorry the chef was dismissive. Next time I'll make sure the interaction goes well."

He couldn't believe he'd gone out of his way to be rude. He had to be better to her. He would never hurt her again.

"No, I need to be prepared." What he said was true — he could research the chefs more, do the homework he needed to come in swinging. Running the restaurant was his full-time job, but he needed to treat this as his part-time one.

"So we both had a bad day," she added. "Should we cheers to that?"

She picked up her glass, and so did he. Her fingers lightly brushed against his as their glasses clinked. A little tingle ran across his skin, and he didn't want to pull away.

"I'll 'cheers' to drinking a bad day away." *With you.*

The thought entered his head and he let it linger there. The realization that he was having a decent night with Nina, while unsettling, felt oddly calming. Being on her good side was so much better than being on her bad one. And now that he'd seen how well they could work together, he was going to do everything he could to keep it that way. Which also meant he'd have to keep his thoughts in check — they weren't friends. Nina was business, and she couldn't be anything more than that.

NINA'S TEXTS

Tom: Did you make her cry?

Leo: What?

Tom: Nina, did this man make you cry?

Nina: No.

Tom: THERE IS NO CRYING IN THE SUNSET GRANDE.

Tom: [Tom Hanks *League of Their Own* GIF]

Tom: There are photos of you crying into a wineglass with a fistful of French fries in your hand.

Nina: ????WHAT????

Leo: Oh

Leo: Fuck

Leo: Shit

Tom: Yeah, you're oh fucking shitting right.

Nina: The restaurant has a no-photo policy???

Tom: I have a no-crying-in-public-while-you're-supposed-to-be-looking-in-love policy.

Tom: FIX. THIS. Act like you're fucking each other's brains out.

Nina: ::: typing :::

Leo: 👀

GOOGLE NEWS SEARCH FOR NINA LYON AND LEO O'DONNELL

Nasty Leo? Nina in Tears After "Romantic" Dinner

Sweet & Sour: Leo Leaves Smiling, Nina Leaves Crying

Desperate Nina Begs Leo to Stay: Waiter Tells All

Nina and Leo Over? Another Food Couple Bites the Crust

They're Hot, Then They're Cold — The Complete Nina-and-Leo Relationship Timeline

17 Men in Food Nina Should Rebound With

Are Nina and Leo a Recipe for Heartbreak?

Table for One: Nina's Newly Single Life

Body Language Expert Reveals That Leo O'Donnell Is Definitely Cheating on Nina Lyon

QUIZ: Which Nina Lyon Cry-Face Are You?

14

LEO

Leo had called in sick to work. He wasn't actually sick, but he was having one of his . . . moods, as he called them. So the lights in his living room were dimmed, and he'd kept the curtains drawn.

He wasn't sure if it had been the chef's comments at the Sunset Grande or seeing himself in the news being blamed for Nina crying . . . but one or all of those things had triggered him.

So his laptop was open and glowing back at him with work he could be doing. He had unanswered emails, the continual pileup of bookkeeping and a strategy doc he'd started working on for Tiffany to try and convince her to bring him back onto the show without Nina. All of those tasks were waiting, and he should've started in on them, but . . .

He just stared at the screen, unable to. Working had never been a problem for Leo

— it was what kept him motivated. But when he fell into this mood, or funk, or whatever it was, it was like he could barely find the energy to stand, let alone be productive. Instead, he became frozen by the avalanche of his thoughts. Swirling, spinning and absolutely all-consuming words falling over him, as sharp and violent as a hailstorm.

You will never fix this mess.
You are a failure.
Everyone hates you.
No one will ever love you.
You're not good enough.

The words were what he heard before his panic attacks, too. Only now, and whenever he found himself in this self-loathing, unable-to-function place, he was buried alive by them. Versus when a panic attack came on, and the sensation was more like drowning and trying to frantically swim to the surface. He didn't want to leave the cave his mind had crawled into — he just had to wait until a light shone through to lead him out.

Leo's phone vibrated. He exhaled heavily and checked the screen. His mom was calling. Not unusual. They talked every day. He just didn't know if he was up for pretending like everything was okay, when he felt anything but. If he didn't answer, though, she'd just call back, over and over, until he picked up. Then, if he didn't pick up, she'd drive the five minutes it took to reach his house and open the front door with her key. And he didn't want his ma to see him . . . like this.

"Hey, Ma," he answered.

"Where are you?" If she'd picked up on his tone, she didn't call it out.

"At home."

"There's a rerun of *You've Got Mail* playing on channel sixty-four. Do you get that channel?"

This was something his mom loved to do — call him and tell him what to watch on cable TV. He would've switched to streaming services years ago, but he didn't have the heart to not indulge her favorite pastime. "I don't know — what's it called?"

"What do you mean, 'what's it called?' It's channel sixty-four."

He sighed. He hadn't had much life in him before the call, but he could feel his heart rate ticking up at the anticipation of fighting over technology with her. "Is it TBS or ABC or one of those?"

"Just turn on the TV to channel sixty-four, like I said." She was shouting for no reason now — she wasn't angry; this was just her way. "You love that movie."

He did love a Tom Hanks/Meg Ryan combo . . . but he'd been settling into his day of sitting in the dark, waiting for the hail to clear from his mind. He wasn't sure he could stomach a rom-com.

"We can watch it together," she continued. "And you can tell me all about your date with Nina."

Ugh, no. He wasn't in the mood to talk to his mom about Nina. Because he'd have to lie about dating her, and then tell her the truth he'd barely been able to wrap his head around — they had a connection. Not just from knowing and working with each other, but there was a spark of something between them. Even if it was just a friendship spark.

"You go to dinner with a woman, and then she ends up crying? Did you break up with her?"

He rubbed his forehead. This was not going to be a short call, as he'd hoped. "No, Ma, I didn't break up with her."

"Because for some reason, you always get dumped. I don't understand why. You're handsome, smart and on TV. How could these idiots break up with you?"

He hadn't told his mom that he may not be on TV for much longer, thanks to how he'd treated Nina. She loved bragging about how her son was a celebrity. When she introduced herself to a new person, she always started with "My son is Leo O'Donnell, you know, the famous man?"

"But then I see photos of Nina crying," his mom continued. "And I'm wondering — did my Leo break up with someone this time? He didn't get dumped, like all those other times?"

"This is not making me feel great, by the way —" he said.

But his mom cut him off, maybe not even hearing him. "I also know that you want to get married to someone special. Give me grandchildren. So I'm wondering, what is going on here? What could possibly make this woman cry? And then I realized the answer — you must have proposed to her. She's got tears of happiness."

Leo guffawed. His mom could not be more off, though he was pretty sure she knew that, too.

"I barely know Nina," he said.

Except now he knew about her mom, and he'd hinted to her about his anxiety. Which was more than he'd revealed to any woman he was dating in a very long time . . . maybe ever. Leo had relationships, but he had a hard time getting them past a few dates. He was never willing or able to reveal the parts of himself that he was sure he'd be judged on. With Nina, he hadn't expected to feel anything for her beyond his usual remorse at being paired with her. Which is why he'd felt comfortable opening up — she already hated him, so what was another pour of alcohol on the flames? But something small had shifted with them, and now he *did* care what she thought.

"I did not propose to her," he clarified.

"I don't know what you're waiting for." His ma tsked. "When you know, you know. Just like Tom Hanks knows he's meant to be with Meg Ryan."

"That's not actually how the movie goes, though. They hate each other at first, re-member? And then he pretends he doesn't know who she is, and is kind of catfishing her." He paused. "As I'm saying this out loud, it's not actually the healthiest start to a relationship."

"My Tom would never catfish anyone. They're in love. They are together."

"Okay, okay," he chuckled.

Leo grabbed the remote from his coffee table and turned on the TV. He did get channel sixty-four, but it was the Home Shopping Network, and most definitely not a rom-com. He scanned the listings to see where his mom's movie was until he found *You've Got Mail.* It was the dinner party scene, where Tom Hanks scoops up a caviar garnish, and Meg Ryan says, "What are you doing? That caviar is a garnish!" And he goes ahead and scoops more.

"Okay, I found the movie." Leo settled back into the easy give of his couch cushions. There was something soothing about watching with his mom, even if he could hear the slight delay between their TVs.

"Caviar is not a garnish," his mom said, almost disgusted. "It's delicious. Why wouldn't someone want to eat it?"

"Parsley is a garnish," Leo said.

"Nothing is a garnish," she corrected. "If it's food, it should be edible and not decorative. That's what your father always said."

"That's true."

Growing up, his dad and Gavin cooked together, while Leo and his mom watched movies. And while Gavin was never interested in anything sappy — and later revealed that "watching straight people kiss was never my idea of a good time" — Leo loved his mom's romance-skewing choices. When he was old enough, he got to occasionally pick one, too. They watched everything — from *Moonstruck* to *10 Things I Hate About You.* He was a sucker for a happily-ever-after, so movies like *Casablanca* were out.

"You know I just want to see you happy,

right?" his mom said.

Leo licked his lips. This was one of those moments where he really felt like he could tell her exactly how he was feeling. She'd given him this little bridge that he could walk across, into her arms, and tell her that he was going through some shit, and needed help figuring it out. There had been plenty of times like this — where he was hurting, or his anxiety was overwhelming — but he'd never taken the opportunity to tell her the truth. He'd always been too aware that he was supposed to be the strong one for his family. And what he was going through wasn't what they needed or wanted from him.

"Leo?" she persisted.

"I know," he told his mom.

He had to be strong for his ma. So he'd give himself today to wade through the hailstorm, but tomorrow he'd have to snap himself out of this . . . something.

"That's my good boy." He heard her let out what sounded like a sigh of relief. And before she hung up, she said, "Ciao, baby."

Leo held the phone to his ear and listened to the nothingness. He stayed like that — watching the movie play out and wondering what the hell he was going to do about the mess he'd gotten himself into.

From: Tom
To: NinaLyon; LeoODonnell
Subj: FIX. THIS.

Attached you will find your itinerary for tomorrow's outing. But here are some helpful tips:

1. Do not cry. Do not make each other cry. Don't so much as wipe the dust from your eye, because someone will take your photo with their phone at that exact moment and, to be honest, I don't have the strength to spin another sob session.

2. Leo, people now think you've made your girlfriend cry. Remember that if you feel the urge to actually make her cry.

3. Nina, people feel sorry for you ☹. No one wants to eat at the sad lady's restaurant!

4. Please try hard to look your best on this date so that when people see photos of you together . . . they think sex.

5. Kiss. Do it in front of people. Out in the open. Look like you're enjoying it. Details

in the itinerary.

Best,
Tom

PS — Do not fire me for suggesting #5, I'm just DOING MY JOB, UNLIKE YOU TWO.

15

NINA

Don't text him. Don't text him.

Leo was officially seven minutes late to their fourth non-date. Maybe he had the wrong address or time, Nina thought as she sat in her car. But she couldn't text to ask those things, because Leo hadn't reached out. And she could be petty about things like that.

She was embarrassed about spilling her guts to him at dinner. And crying. Then being photographed while crying.

She never would've told him about her mom — she couldn't believe she'd done that. But she'd had wine and was feeling vulnerable. She thought going out with Leo would help her forget about how much she missed her mother. But instead, she'd opened up. And to Leo, of all people. What had she been thinking? Now she couldn't even look him in the eye, because he'd give her that oh-you're-sad-and-motherless look back. The same reaction she got any time she told a guy about her mom. Although he hadn't actually given her the pity eyes. So maybe Leo was different, in that respect.

Still, not reaching out, even to see if he was planning to show up, felt like the safer option. And she was used to not talking to Leo. His muteness shouldn't have bothered her, but there was no denying the fact that she had checked her phone a lot more since their last date. Roughly ten thousand times more, if she had to guess. Wasn't he going to at least comment on Tom's insane email?

And then she'd "accidentally" wandered over to his Instagram to see if he'd posted anything new — he hadn't. Even when she wasn't checking his page, she couldn't get rid of him in her own feed. All of Nina's mentions were about him.

@MsNinaIfUrNasty He's hot, but you're hotter. THANK U, NXT

@CookieBrooke r u and **@LeoODonnell** really broken up??

@LitAsAnOven best part of breaking up is making up amiriteeee

This is all a sham. I don't know what I'm doing with my life, she'd almost replied, then stopped herself.

Tom made sure to tell her that he'd been fielding mountains of press inquiries from reporters wanting to confirm whether or not she and Leo were dating. Of course, a few discerning Twitter users had assessed the situation and surmised that their relationship was all for show. But the overwhelming majority — 150,000 organic tweets and counting — had taken the bait. People thought that LeNi — their new couple-ship name — were the real deal.

Nina's IG post of her holding a pumpkin from Mr. Bones, where Leo had commented, was her most-liked post of all time. The comments were overwhelmingly positive, which was a change from people discussing how mean she was to contestants. And magically, the photo had added an additional 200,000 followers to her account.

So the charade seemed to be working. Or, rather, it was working to boost their social media profiles. Reservations at the restaurant had steadily increased since starting this new "relationship," but she wanted them to skyrocket so she could feel at least a glimmer of hope that she wouldn't have to close Lyon. In Tom's estimation, the best way to do that was to push harder . . . and kiss Leo.

A tentative knock on her car window startled her. She clutched her chest and turned to see Leo. His face was way too close to the glass as he smiled a big, goofy grin.

But when she waved him away with her hand, he took the hint by backing up slightly. Her eyes focused as his arm flexed against the hood of her car. He wore a fitted, sky-blue shirt with a slight V-neck, and it was impossible not to notice his well-defined tricep along with a few other muscles she didn't know existed.

Tom had asked them to look sexy, and Leo had clearly delivered. Not that she was attracted to him, or anything, but he did objectively have a nice body . . .

"Do you plan to pay for a car wash so I can get that handprint off?" she joked as she got out of the car.

"That handprint will be worth a lot of money someday. I recommend encasing it in plaster so it doesn't lose any details."

"You mean so I can lift your fingerprints and report you to the authorities when they eventually figure out you're an axe murderer?"

He smirked back, then kicked up his leg

behind him and held on to his ankle as he stretched out his upper thigh.

If they stayed here any longer, she was in serious danger of lingering on how his thigh was straining against the fabric of his workout pants.

"Should we hike?" she squeaked before turning away from him. Climbing up a mountain wasn't her idea of a good time, but it was Tom's. And at a particular lookout outlined in Tom's email, there would be a waiting paparazzi, in case they wanted to . . .

Nina couldn't think about kissing Leo. That just wasn't going to happen.

They started up a residential street that wound its way toward the mouth of the park entrance. They walked under enormous fig trees, the seeds smashed and sticky sweet on the sidewalk.

"This is a terrible idea for a date." She was already breathing heavily.

"Oh, I don't know. It's refreshing to see you actually be bad at something."

She not-so-gently punched his arm, which was as thick and muscled as a juicy cut of meat.

"That was sort of a compliment, you know. I was saying you're not bad at anything." He rubbed the spot she'd whacked.

"Including punching?" She squinted as she looked up at him.

"You're quite good at that, too, yes." He smiled back at her.

The smile sent a flutter through her, and she shoved down the feeling.

"I'm guessing you hike regularly?" she asked, changing the subject.

"I'm more of a runner. But my dad took my brother and me on a hike every Monday when the restaurant was closed. We'd see the sun coming up and we'd spot lots of coyotes and deer. I think it's peaceful." A car blasting EDM whizzed past them. "As peaceful as LA can get, anyway."

By the time they made it to the mountain and began to climb, Nina knew she'd made a huge mistake in agreeing to this. She was on her feet a lot for work, but hiking exercised a new group of muscles.

Leo wiped the back of his hand across his brow, so she must not be *that* out of shape if even he was feeling the burn. Then he peeled his shirt off and over his head.

She did a double take. If she'd had a mouthful of water, it would've been a spit take. Leo was shirtless. She stopped moving. She couldn't tell if she was horrified or mesmerized by the sight of his abs, which looked like a waffle iron, minus the syrup.

She'd imagined that underneath the starched and boring button-downs was a stack of white dinner plates in the shape of a human form.

But there he was, half-naked and absolutely real. "Everything okay?" He turned to look back at her. "Has my Adonis-like physique stunned you speechless?"

She wasn't going to let him get away with a compliment to himself. "I'm just a bit dumbfounded. I didn't realize people are still doing spray-on abs." She couldn't not acknowledge the abs. She didn't want to be rude to them just because they were attached to Leo.

"I sure hope that's what the man in the van was doing when he told me to close my eyes." He stretched his arms above his head, which made his chest look even broader and trimmer than before.

Show-off. Though, she admittedly did not mind watching the show. "Didn't anyone ever teach you not to take spray tans from strangers?"

"I must've missed that class in business school. Now come on, it's not much farther to the top."

He waved for her to follow, and she moved surprisingly quickly. The draw of those abs was powerful.

Hours had passed. Okay, probably more like five minutes had gone by, but Nina had had just about enough of climbing up mountains.

"Are we there yet?" Her breathing was ragged, and she could barely complete a sentence.

"Actually, yes." He handed her his water bottle, which she eagerly gulped from.

They slowed and stood at the lookout. The sun was beginning to drift lower in the sky, the colors fading to a golden hue. The air was cool against her hot skin, and downtown LA was in the distance, the soaring sky-scrapers clustered together like a cup filled with knives.

And then she noticed a man leaning against a tall tree. He was dressed inconspic-uously, but the long-lens camera he held told her exactly who he was and the mo-ment he was waiting for.

She looked down. Her sneakers were firmly planted to the earth, but her body swayed slightly. When she looked up, the trees were fuzzy, like a film had been placed in front of her eyes. She tripped, and Leo caught her by the elbow.

"Whoa, you okay?" He sounded like he was talking through water.

Her hand trembled. Maybe she was dehydrated, or the long hike had exhausted her. She hadn't eaten a proper lunch. Did she need to sit?

She blinked, trying to stop the skyline from vibrating. She wasn't going to faint — right? — but she didn't feel steady on her feet, either.

"I'm *not* going to faint," she said out loud, and mainly to herself.

His grip tightened on her elbow, while his other hand held her waist steady. "People who have to say that are usually about to faint."

"Tom said there's no crying at the Sunset Grande." She didn't want to cause another scene. First, she'd been photographed crying, next she'd be photographed fainting when they were supposed to be looking sexy together. This wasn't good for her or for Lyon. If customers didn't want to eat at a sad lady's restaurant, the fainting lady wasn't going to be reeling them in, either.

"Trust me?" He spoke low into her ear, the hum of his voice like a soothing sip of tea.

She nodded, surprised to realize that she really did trust him. Because she'd felt a kind of shift in their dynamic. She hadn't opened up to anyone other than Sophie and Jasmine about her mom. And, for some reason, she felt safe in revealing part of herself to Leo. Maybe because he'd lost his dad, too, or perhaps the combo of wine and fries had played a role. Either way, their relationship had changed. And apparently, she now trusted him.

Leo brought Nina's back against his chest, holding her from behind, his arms securely under hers, keeping her steady against him. "Take slow sips of this water and lean against me. I've got you."

Nina took a slow sip, then a deep breath.

"Good, more deep breaths," he encouraged.

"This is why I don't hike," she joked.

He breathed in slowly, then out slowly. And she mimicked his breaths, in and out. They breathed together, and then she relaxed, letting her body fall back against his. He was solid and she was shaky, but he held her so tight that the weak feeling melted away.

"Let's focus on something to help with the dizziness. Did you always want to be a chef? Come on, tell me a story," he added.

She'd been asked this question countless times in dozens of interviews. People were usually curious about how her career began. Her mom was why she'd wanted to be a chef. She loved telling this story.

This was a happy memory. Why not share it with Leo?

She kicked at a rock under her foot and it skipped along the road, stopping short before tumbling off the side of the mountain. "When I was a kid, I used to eat cubes of butter covered in sugar . . . as a snack."

She hesitantly looked up at Leo. If he hadn't judged her for crying while eating, she was giving him another opportunity to show his true colors.

"Impressive," was all he said in return.

"My mom was a dental hygienist, so she was livid when she caught me, and told me my teeth would rot out of my head. I didn't care, though. I loved butter and sugar — why not combine the two?"

"Amen, sister." Leo held out a fist in solidarity, which made her smile.

"She bought me a Julia Child cookbook from Bart's Books, this really cool outdoor bookshop in Ojai, where we grew up. She said if I was going to use up all the butter and sugar, I needed to make something she and my sister could eat, too. Cooking together became a Sunday tradition. My mom worked a lot during the week, but on Sundays I always knew she and I would be in the kitchen. We didn't have a lot of money, but we'd make a recipe from the cookbook. If we couldn't afford an ingredient, we'd improvise and make our own special version. We'd spend all morning, and sometimes into the afternoon, perfecting a dish from Julia's cookbook. I fell in love with French cooking after that."

"Truly an unexpected journey you just took me on." His arms tightened around her.

And she liked the way his muscles pulsed gently — holding her, but not pressuring her, which made her feel like she was truly supported. She continued to rest against him, easily fitting in the space he'd made for her, a mildly disturbing realization.

"My love for cooking started in the kitchen with my mom. That became my favorite place in the world to be." She tried to bring her mind back to the story, and away from thinking about how easily her body fit against Leo's. "Sometimes I can still feel her next to me when I'm cooking."

She went quiet and so did he. Had she said too much?

"My dad comes back to me, too, especially when I'm at Vinny's. It's important to have those memories." He leaned down, and his lips brushed against her ear again. "How are you feeling? Any better?"

His espresso scent gave her an abrupt shot

of energy. "Better," she said.

"Ready to try standing on your own?"

No, I'm actually fine with you holding me up indefinitely. "Yes," she said.

His grip on her loosened enough so that she could push off him. Her legs weren't shaky anymore. She bent, then straightened her knees, trying them out.

She turned to face him and she had to bite the inside of her mouth. Because the way he looked at her . . . there was almost something like a heat burning in his eyes. Her cheeks flushed. She'd been resting against his half-naked body, felt his sweat on her . . .

"Hold on." His eyes roamed across her face.

Great. Had she accidentally drooled and left a mark?

His hand came next to her cheek as he brushed a piece of hair behind her ear. The lightness of his fingertips, paired with the cool air, sent a spark through her. She inhaled deeply and looked down.

"Thanks," she breathed out.

When she looked back, they locked eyes. Then Nina's gaze went to his lips. His mouth parted, as if noticing the attention.

She knew that if they were ever going to kiss, it should be now. They were framed by

215

the sunset at the top of a mountain. The cameraman was waiting. They couldn't have asked for a better time to be caught in the act.

She'd be able to lean in and nibble his bottom lip as easily as biting into a croissant.

"Tom's suggestion . . ." she began.

She couldn't finish the sentence, because this was still Leo. Yes, he was sexy, especially shirtless. But that didn't erase their history. Even if their careers were at stake, was kissing him really going to fix anything?

"If you're okay, I'm okay," he finally said.

He's okay *with kissing me,* she told herself. There wasn't anything passionate about someone feeling okay when it came to sharing a kiss. And that was totally, one-hundred-percent fine. The kiss didn't need to have any significance beyond being part of their job. This didn't have to mean anything.

So she nodded, and tilted her head up as a next step. One of his hands met her waist, while the other cupped the side of her face as he brought her in toward him.

"Okay?" he asked.

"Okay," she said firmly. But inside, her mind just raced with, *holy shit, holy shit, holy shit.*

Then he dipped his head, she closed her eyes and . . . he kissed her. So soft and tentative, as if he was afraid to hurt her. She wasn't even completely sure if she'd felt him there or had just imagined it. She instinctively reached a hand up to his shoulder and squeezed, which apparently was a signal for him to kiss her more deeply. The hand at her waist wrapped around her back as he pulled her in.

His lips were salty from the hike, and his stubble rubbed against the top of her mouth — two things she didn't know could be sexy, but absolutely were. A low hum came from deep within her, and the sound caused his grip on her to tighten.

They were locked together. And there wasn't a single piece of them that didn't fit like they were always meant to be doing exactly this. She tried to remind herself that they were essentially actors, playing roles. But his mouth pressed into hers, and she couldn't deny how good having all of him against her felt.

He abruptly pulled away, and muttered, "Sorry."

Sorry? What was he sorry for? And then she realized, with much dread, that he was sorry because he'd wanted the kiss to end. He obviously sensed that she wasn't pulling away fast enough, and so he was apologizing because he assumed she would've kept going. And maybe she would've, but still.

Could this date be any more humiliating? Sweating, nearly fainting and now . . .

His eyes darted behind her. "Mission accomplished," he whispered into her ear. The closeness of his lips to her skin sent a shiver down her spine.

He nodded over her shoulder. When she turned, the cameraman was snapping away.

The first man she'd kissed since her ex, Charlie, and it had been for her job. Maybe worse, he'd had to forcibly pry her off him. No, actually, the worst part was how incredible the kiss had been.

She'd been hypnotized by his stupid waffle-iron abs and deliciously salty mouth. But then he'd pulled away when all she'd wanted was for him to keep going. He probably thought she was pathetic.

"Can you make it back down?" Leo asked. "I could go grab some food and hike back up, if you're feeling light-headed."

She nodded, not wanting to meet his eyes. She had to get off this mountain and away from Leo. The dirt path ahead of them was clear but endless. Even without knowing where the path would lead, she knew there was nowhere to go but down.

GOOGLE NEWS SEARCH FOR NINA LYON AND LEO O'DONNELL

This On-Again, Off-Again Couple Is Definitely Back ON

Nina and Leo Rebound . . . With Each Other!

The Next Make-out Champs: Nina and Leo's Kissing Sesh

Get a Room: Nina and Leo Can't Keep Their Hands Off Each Other in Revealing New Pics

Leo O'Donnell's Workout Secrets: How to Get Six-Pack Abs Like His

Steal the Look: Nina's Surprisingly Affordable Workout Wardrobe

Nina and Leo Heat Up Outside of the Kitchen

POLL: Should Leo O'Donnell Remain Shirtless for All Time?

NINA'S TEXTS

Wednesday, October 12

Leo: Feeling better?

Nina: I'm never hiking again.

Leo: The only reason to hike is so you can eat a lot afterward.

Nina: I was only in it for the EDM.

Leo: Ever the artist . . .

Friday, October 14

Leo: Saw you posted a photo of a pumpkin tart on IG, cool if I comment?

Nina: No pie puns, please.

Leo: Why? Don't you crust me?

Nina: 👎

Leo: I'm filling awesome about my comment. Aren't you?

Nina: "Hap-pie Friday"???

Leo: you're welcome ☺

16

NINA

"Nina!" Cory and Dori singsonged her name as they opened the front door to their ancient but beautifully maintained Victorian home. They wore complementary fleece Patagonia pullovers and their heads tilted to the left at the same time. If Nina hadn't already met them and known this to be their normal MO, she might be a little freaked out by the synchronization.

"So great to see you both!" Nina hugged Dori, then Cory, and stepped into their life-size gingerbread house.

They spoke over each other as they led Nina through the front hall, across the living room rug and out into the backyard.

"Jasmine is setting the table," Cory said.

"Did you do something different with your hair?" Dori said.

"Oh, I love it!" Cory said.

"But have you ever tried bangs? With your

face shape —"

Cory interrupted her, "We're so glad you're here."

"Well, I *did* wash my hair last night," Nina finally said.

They both laughed. "You are too funny," they said at the same time.

From what Jasmine had told her, her parents had bought the 100-plus-year-old house not only to restore it to its former glory, but also because of the rare — for LA — two acres of land it sat on. Enough space to grow their own plants, raise chickens and build the greenhouse they'd always wanted. Their mini-oasis was impressive, and transported her to her own childhood, where she and Sophie had grown up in a small town, surrounded by farmland.

Nina made her way to the large wooden outdoor table, where Jasmine was setting plates and utensils.

"Thanks for coming," Jasmine said as they hugged.

"If you're cooking, I'm always coming." Nina grabbed the bundle of napkins from Jasmine and distributed them as they all sat down to brunch.

Jasmine had made shakshouka with eggs from the chickens and tomatoes from the garden. She'd also baked focaccia sprinkled with rosemary from her parents' herb garden. It seemed so natural that Jasmine had gone into food, especially growing up with all the fresh ingredients around her.

"Mini," her dad called, using his nickname for Jas, "the omelet is absolutely perfect. But the bread . . ."

"More salt?" Dori asked, finishing for him.

"Hmm . . . maybe that's it." Cory took another bite.

"I think you mean thank you for cooking us brunch?" Jasmine said as she passed her dad the salt.

A brief flicker of tension passed across the table, and Nina decided to dab it away. "The flavor of the bread is so nice and complex with the rosemary," Nina said. "We'll have to add this to the menu next week."

"I hadn't thought about it that way!" Dori looked at Jasmine. "Don't you just love how she talks about food?"

"I'm still going to add a little salt." Cory took the salt spoon and sprinkled some on his bread.

"Go for it, Dad." Jasmine rolled her eyes and took a large bite of her own bread.

"Did you show Nina the listing we sent you?" Dori asked.

Jasmine pointed to her mouth, which was still full of bread she was busy chewing.

"Oh, well, we sent Mini a listing for a sweet little bungalow that's for rent a block from here." Cory pulled up the listing on his phone and passed it to Nina. "That way she'd be closer to home, and there's a beautiful garden where the owner has gorgeous mature avocado trees. It's a really special place."

Jasmine smiled tightly through her mouthful of food.

"Jasmine's loft is such a great find," Nina said, filling in the silence. "And the kitchen is enormous. This bungalow wouldn't have the counter space she needs, right?" Nina held the phone up to Dori, who cocked her head as she eyed the listing photo.

"You know, you were really too good for that show, Nina. I'm so glad you left," Cory said.

"But now you're dating that Leo?" Dori frowned. "We have so many people from the arboretum we could set you up with. Nice, successful men."

Nina politely smiled. Hell, maybe being set up with someone else wasn't such a bad idea. After all, she needed to stop thinking about Leo, and how her hands had tangled in his hair. A distraction could be good for her. Though the thought of being on a date with someone else made her stomach clench.

"Mini never lets us set her up on dates," Dori said.

"I want to meet someone on my own, thank you." Jasmine straightened in her chair — or maybe she was fidgeting, Nina couldn't tell.

"Well, the people you meet aren't looking for long-term relationships. Nina, are you looking for a long-term partner?" Cory asked.

"Dad, I don't think Nina wants to talk about fertilizing techniques — no innuendo intended — with one of your coworkers." Jasmine dipped her bread into the tomato sauce.

"That's where you're wrong," Nina replied. "You know I keep meaning to grow my own herbs for the restaurant."

Dori kissed Nina on the forehead as she said, "See, Jasmine? At least someone appreciates my offers."

"Did she tell you?" Cory asked.

"No," Nina hesitantly replied, looking at Jasmine.

"Turns out we need a caterer for the benefit gala we're hosting," Dori said. "And we told Jasmine she should do it."

"You mean like, have Jasmine make the menu and hire the sous chefs?" Nina asked, to clarify. Because if *that* was what her best friend's parents were offering, it was a really big fucking deal. Especially because Nina knew that people with money would RSVP to Jas's parents. And money could mean connections for Jasmine that would help her open her own place.

"Yes, why not?" Cory said. "She's a chef. We need a chef."

"You know we love you, and Lyon," Dori clarified. "But she needs to build a name for herself like you have, Nina."

Jasmine scratched the back of her neck, like she'd just had a patch of hives spring up there. Her best friend didn't love being cornered — who did? — and she was sure the comparisons to her weren't helping anything.

"I wanted to build my own brand. It's not for everyone. But cooking for the gala could be a fun way to test out some recipes," Nina said, hedging.

Jasmine scowled at her. "What now?"

"Exactly!" Dori chimed in. "What's the harm? She'll make money. She'll cook. What could go wrong?"

"Cooking is not just turning on an oven, Mom." Jasmine parked her elbows on the table and leaned forward. "And cooking for hundreds of people is a job in itself. I already have a full-time job. Remember?"

"Well, Nina could help you," Cory said. "Couldn't you, Nina?"

"Um." Nina looked to Jasmine, who frantically shook her head. But her mom caught sight of the motion.

"Jasmine, if you don't work hard, you'll never build anything for yourself," Dori said, her voice overflowing with concern. "This is an opportunity."

"Mom, do you know how much work an event like this would be for me?" Jasmine pleaded. "And you don't always like my food."

"What are you talking about? We love your food."

Dori's puzzled expression seemed to fuel Jasmine, who leaned across the table and said, "What about the bread, Ma?"

"Mini, if your parents aren't going to annoy you, then who will?" her dad joked back, hugging her in close. She seemed to relent and relaxed against him.

Seeing their closeness made Nina ache for her mother. What she wouldn't give to be hugged by her in that moment. But she loved seeing Jasmine's connection with her parents and being included in their meal.

This was why she'd gotten into food — bringing people together around a table could be so healing and important.

"Do this as a favor for us," Dori said, trying again. "We never would ask you to do this if we didn't believe you could."

Jasmine looked up from under the crook of her dad's arm. She and her mother shared an unspoken moment as they stared at each other.

"I will think about it." Jasmine sat up straight and dabbed at her mouth with a napkin. Then her gaze turned to Nina. "Why don't you tell Nina what you've been dying to ask her?"

"Oh, is there something you need from me?" Nina sat forward.

"Well, we actually do need help with the auction . . ." Dori adjusted her glasses and looked to Nina.

"Like, um, you need someone to host the auction?" Nina had been asked to host several things since joining the world of TV. She hadn't committed to any due to her intense schedule. But she'd encouraged Jasmine to cater the event, so now she'd show up for her friend however she could.

"No, actually. We need items to auction off." Dori tucked her chin closer to her chest, like she didn't want to finish the thought and was hoping Nina would magically read her mind.

"You want to . . ." Nina began. "Auction me off?"

"Oh, good gravy, no!" Cory laughed. "But we *could* auction off cooking classes."

"Ah!" Nina patted her thighs, relieved. "That makes much more sense. Yes, I'm happy to donate my time for your worthy cause."

"Excellent!" Dori smiled. She pulled Nina in for a hug next to her.

Nina let herself lean in to Dori. She may not have her mother on this earth anymore, but she was glad to allow Dori to mother her a bit.

Cory pulled in Jasmine again. "Now if you could just talk some sense into our Mini . . ." he said.

Jasmine groaned. Nina smirked. You couldn't pick your family, but she was glad to be part of theirs. She needed all the love and support she could find, especially with the challenges — to put it mildly — that she had ahead.

17

LEO

Leo swiped. Swiped again. Then paused. A bob of intensely curly hair caught his eye. Dark skin and eyes with hipster glasses, like an edgy librarian.

"Finally found one," he said.

Gavin looked up from the dough he was rolling out by hand for lasagna noodles. Part of the monthly lunch feast they cooked as a family. Well, Gavin was the one who cooked while Leo and his mom ate. But he stopped cooking to wipe his hands on the apron, then came to the kitchen table to look over Leo's shoulder.

"Oh, hello, my future husband. I'm ready to worship."

"There's a potential deal-breaker, though . . ."

Leo scrolled down the page until he came to the most important photo. The guy on a couch, cuddled up with a massive poodle.

"Oh, shit, that won't do at all." A timer went off, and Gavin opened the oven to check on the eggplant parmigiana.

"To be fair, this is an app for people with dogs, and you have a cat. It doesn't feel like a situation where you can be picky." Leo had very limited experience with dating apps, though he'd been on Tinder before the show. There were even a few interesting dates that had come from it. But once he was picked to cohost, the network's publicity team advised that he keep his social media strictly to places like Facebook, Instagram and Twitter. Midwestern moms — the target demo — didn't want to think the host of their favorite cooking show could also be sending dick pics.

Helping his brother online-date had been a compromise. He still got the fun of swiping without any of the awkward first meet-ups.

"Yes, but I'd like to find someone who has a dog, so that when we move in together we can start an Instagram account about inter-species friendship. The dog can't over-shadow the cat, though."

Gavin put a plate of fried eggplant slices on the table, leftovers from the eggplant parm in the oven. Leo took a bite. The fried exterior crunched in his mouth, giving way to the soft, piping-hot eggplant inside — perfection.

"Well, what would be cuter than a giant poodle and a cross-eyed tabby?"

"Hmmm . . . interesting." Gavin took out a bowl filled with ricotta, Parmesan cheese, salt, pepper and shredded basil.

"Pizza, do you think you could chill with a dog ten times your size?" Gavin yelled out to the cat, who meowed back. "That's a maybe."

Their mom's sandals clip-clopped down the hall until she appeared in the kitchen, bundled up in a sweater dress and a comically long scarf. "You want a date? I can set you up."

"Ma, you don't exactly have the best track record," Leo responded. He'd made the mistake of trusting his mom's matchmaking skills himself a handful of times. While his mother meant well, she never really asked enough questions to properly vet the women she found.

"Remember when she set you up with the married woman who thought she was on a job interview?"

"She told me she was open and looking." Their mom shrugged back, as if she didn't see the problem.

"For a job, Ma." Gavin laughed.

"Why do you look tired?" His mom walked over to Leo, grabbed his chin in her palm and turned his head from side to side. She eyed the dark circles under his eyes, which he knew were more prominent than usual.

He'd brought the financials home with him and had stayed up most of the night studying what he already knew was happening. Another restaurant would need to close. Traffic at Vinny's had increased, but not enough to make a difference. He was cutting corners to try and avoid this closure. He'd give it another week of dating Nina to see if there was any significant pickup, but if business didn't change, he'd have to find a way to tell his mom and Gavin.

"Got up early for a morning run." He swatted away her hand. He didn't want his mom to worry about him, ever. She wasn't a sensitive person, really. But she'd also suffered enough when their dad passed. It felt necessary that he keep his mom and brother from knowing how much trouble they were in.

"You weren't up late with your girlfriend?" His mom winked.

"Ma!" Leo hadn't told his mom about his and Nina's . . . arrangement. Gavin knew the truth, but telling his mother — who loved to gossip — any kind of secret was a recipe for it no longer staying a secret.

"Your father and I couldn't keep our hands off each other, especially when we first met." She looked off, as if remembering something, then returned her focus to him. "Set up a dinner with her. I want to meet Nina, finally."

"Ma, come on —" He and Nina went out when there was an opportunity to be spotted together. Bringing her home for dinner would be . . . outside of their terms.

"No — no excuses. You've worked with her for years, now you're dating. She's coming for dinner."

He sighed. Trying to argue with his mother had never ended well for him, and he wasn't about to try and make up an excuse — she'd see right through it. He'd just have to ask Nina for a favor, somehow. "I'll see if she's free."

"Make sure you don't overcook the eggplant this time." Their mom pointed at Gavin accusingly. The food would be insanely good, and the kitchen already smelled like garlic and tomatoes. She knew there was nothing to worry about, but she also liked to keep Gavin on his toes — the way she had with their dad.

"Love you, Ma," Gavin and Leo said in

unison. She waved a dismissive hand as she left the room. While the boys cooked, she went for a massage — that was the tradition.

"I've been patient, monk-level respectful." Gavin made prayer hands in front of his chest for emphasis. "But you've gotta tell me — what's going on with Nina?"

Leo examined a nonexistent spot on the counter. There was no easy way to sum up what was happening between them. They'd hated each other a few weeks ago, but now they might actually be friends? He'd had multiple dates with someone he never thought he'd be alone in a room with. Maybe he was reading into the looks she gave him, or the way she'd kissed him back, but she didn't seem to hate him, either. He'd even sent her a random text that morning — a link to a fanfic story involving them and Willy Wonka's R-rated chocolate factory. He thought it would make her laugh. She'd sent the skull emoji back, so . . .

Kissing Nina was an entirely different situation. He'd seen Tom's suggestion, but he never thought she'd want anything beyond hand-holding. So when she'd brought up the idea . . . he was surprised. Then, when they actually kissed and they weren't sucked into a sinkhole, that was another shock. He wouldn't have ended it so soon, but he didn't want to seem desperate, either, like he was lingering when she was just trying to do her job. Still, he had a weird sense that she hadn't minded the kiss.

"Nothing's going on," he finally said.

What he had to keep reminding himself was that they were in a manufactured situation, because when he forgot, it was easy to imagine that he was on an actual date with Nina.

"Don't bullshit me. Any time I used to bring up Nina, you'd tell me what a massive snob she was. But you haven't said one bad word about her." Gavin took a rolling pin to the ball of dough on the counter. "Fuck, wait, do you . . . *like* her?"

Leo shook his head and gazed up at the ceiling. Why did he have to have such a nosy brother? And how was he supposed to answer that question? "So maybe I was wrong about her, okay? She's actually a nice person."

"She's a 'nice person'? Oh, bro, you are in *trou-u-u-u-uble.*" Gavin elongated the word *trouble* until he ran out of breath.

"She did me a big favor. It's nothing. Just work," he hedged. The kiss they'd shared had absolutely been for work, as fake as the homey kitchen set they used on the show. But her lips pressing back against his hadn't felt fake. Neither had the urge to pull her in close to him . . .

Gavin raised an eyebrow, then let out a "pshhhhh" as he cut the flat dough into neat lines. "How did I get the job involving manual labor, and you scored the job where you make out with people?"

Leo cracked his knuckles. He certainly hadn't sought out the spot as a celebrity cooking-show host. He ran a family business and had gotten an MBA — there was a clear path for him that didn't involve fame.

But a casting director reached out after seeing a profile story on him in the *Los Angeles Times.* Not all local restaurants became nationwide chains, after all. According to the casting director, he had valuable experience to pass on to the aspiring chefs.

And when the show began, the restaurants exploded. People loved coming in with the hope of seeing the wholesome and funny TV host. His TV persona reinforced the restaurant's image as a family-friendly haven. Even though being in front of the camera sent his anxiety through the roof, that really didn't matter. He had too many people relying on his success to go back now.

Vinny's wasn't profitable because of Leo. The food and family atmosphere his dad had established, and his brother had continued, were what brought people in the door. He often wondered why he was the one on-air and not his brother.

"When are you seeing her again?" Gavin leaned across the kitchen island. He had a grin on his face that Leo couldn't place.

"Sunday. We're going to the LA Food and Wine Festival." The daytime festival would bring foodies, chefs and sommeliers from around the city together in one place. The most celebrated restaurants would have booths present, with their chefs at the helm serving samples from their menu. Visitors who bought passes would be able to taste wine paired with the food at the event, and Nina and Leo would be VIP guests.

He'd done his homework this time and researched all of the chefs in attendance. He was going to arrive overprepared so he could avoid another disaster like the one at the Sunset Grande. He should've been thrilled for the second chance to be immersed in the food scene that Nina had promised to bring him into. Meeting twenty or more chefs within the span of a few hours would be a huge leap toward his goal of making connections, but he was genuinely nervous, and not about meeting the people he needed to impress. Because the overwhelming thought he kept having was that the only person he really wanted to impress was Nina.

18

NINA

Historically, Nina only wore heels during episode tapings. But today she'd put on a pair of slightly uncomfortable and chunky wedges, all in the name of the LA Food and Wine Festival.

And also, maybe, because she was feeling a little uneasy about seeing Leo again. Because if he thought she was a bad kisser, or whatever the hell had made him pull away, she at least wanted to look better than he did.

Not that she was trying to impress him, exactly, but she did want to feel as confident as possible. There were no winners or losers, but *if there were,* she wanted to be on the winning side. So, yes, she'd put in a bit more effort than was strictly necessary for their date, including base-level contouring and wearing a flared, forest-green pleather skirt.

"VIP badges just feel different, don't they?" Leo said as he fingered the lanyard-and-plastic pass around his neck. "Like, I am better than a significant amount of the people here."

"Keep telling yourself that." She laughed.

She eyed the tall concrete buildings around them. When people thought of LA, they pictured palm trees and wide streets, but that wasn't the case downtown, where the festival was. The skyscrapers made you feel like you were in New York or Chicago.

He handed her a lanyard and their fingers brushed. The little electric charge she felt from his touch was annoying, at best.

Okay, so they were kind of friends, which was a truly bizarre shift from sworn enemies, but she wasn't totally sure how to act around him. She'd thought holding hands had been a step too far, but now that she'd kissed him, how was she supposed to behave?

So she opted to stand a healthy two feet apart. She didn't want Leo to think she was desperate to be near him, especially since he'd made it abundantly clear that he wanted to move away from her the last time she'd gotten too close.

They walked through the gate, which opened to a wide street with two rows of booths on either side. And since they were VIP guests, they got early admission before the real crowds arrived and crushed their way through. Seemingly endless food being served by the city's top chefs was an incredible experience. This would be a dream date in any other scenario, but with Leo . . . she just felt unsure of what could happen.

As if reading her mind, he reached for her hand. "May I?"

"If you must . . ." She tried to play it cool, but her heart thudded extra hard. He wound his fingers through hers, as natural a fit as peanut butter and chocolate. Though she didn't want to dwell on how warm his hand felt against hers.

"Should we start light, and then move into the heavier dishes?" If she could focus on the food, that would take her mind off whether or not Leo was thinking about how her hand felt, too.

"I can go hard if you can." He smirked at her.

"Okay." She took the bait. "UOVO is one of my favorite small Italian restaurants in the city. They ship their pasta in from Bologna, and —"

"Bologna has the best pasta in all of Italy." He smiled. "I did my research this time. I know all about UOVO, and how they have actual Italian grandmothers making the pasta by hand in Bologna."

She assumed Leo would try hard to win over the chefs, but she hadn't expected him to study them. His attempt to make a good impression wasn't lost on her, though. She felt the urge to smile encouragingly, but instead she raised her eyebrows. "A pasta scholar!"

"You can call me Doctor Pasta, if you choose." When he looked at her, there was humor in his eyes, and they shared a moment before looking away.

They approached one of the white tents, where a display of fresh, uncooked pastas sat under a glass case. She spied Antonio, the bona fide Italian head chef at UOVO. He wore an UOVO baseball cap and smiled widely when he saw her.

"Nina! When I heard you were coming, I made a special plate for you."

On the table, there were small, recyclable plates of their killer cheese tortellini smothered in a thick Parmesan cheese sauce. But Antonio ducked behind the tent, then emerged with a much larger and more colorful plate.

"Oh, no." She laughed. She knew what this plate was. When she'd first gone to UOVO and sat at the counter with her sister, they'd ordered the ravioli, covered in a gorgeous tomato sauce. But she'd told Antonio he needed to pair that ravioli with a sweeter version. Salty and sweet, the way every meal should flow.

"Pumpkin ravioli for you, principessa! This is the pumpkin ravioli of your dreams, I promise you that." He handed her the plate with a fork. The dish smelled like nutmeg mixed with Parmesan. She wasn't going to last long at the food festival if she ate the whole thing on her own.

"If anyone can turn me into a believer, it's you, Antonio. And I'll need two forks." She looked up at Leo and squeezed his hand to signal this was his cue. The last time she'd introduced him to a chef, he'd choked. She hoped that this connection would be better. They both made Italian food, were both Italian.

"This is my boyfriend." Had she really just said *boyfriend*? Could she sound any more ridiculous? Though the word had swirled out as easily as pouring a glass of wine.

If Leo was fazed, he didn't show it.

"Leo O'Donnell," he added. "I'm thrilled to meet you. My work schedule has kept me from visiting the restaurant in person. I'm glad I get to taste the pasta everyone in the city raves about."

"I hope you enjoy! I'm a big fan of the show. I knew there was sexy tension between you two." Antonio pointed his finger accusingly at them. "Naughty Nina."

He probably wishes there was a wall between us, Nina thought.

Antonio handed Leo a fork. "It's all about the pasta with Italian food, no?"

"It really is." Leo smiled and relaxed.

This is going well. Even if he would never be comfortable with her again post-Kissgate, she still wanted to fulfill her promise. She owed him for all his efforts thus far.

"My brother makes our pasta by hand at the Pasadena location, but I'd love to hear more about where you're getting yours. We're always looking for ways to improve."

"Let's talk over pasta? Maybe there's some kind of partnership we can do. You come to my restaurant, I'll come to yours, huh?" Antonio leaned across the table, his eager smile genuine and warm.

"Let's do that." Leo looked enthused.

This was how she'd wanted Leo to be at the Sunset Grande, but the second time was apparently the charm.

Antonio took a card off the table and wrote his cell number on it before handing it over. "You call me anytime, yes?"

Then he turned to her. "And, Nina, you better tell me what you think of that ravioli!"

"By the smell of it, you've outdone yourself." The plate was warm in her palms. She couldn't wait to dig in.

"Prego!" Antonio nodded goodbye to them.

"Way to go, Doctor Pasta," she said to Leo as they walked away from the booth.

"That wasn't me — you made a great intro. And how cool that he cooked you a special pasta. But I'm sure that happens all the time."

"Thanks." She wasn't used to getting compliments from Leo, and she fought the urge to say something sarcastic back. "What did you think of Antonio?"

"I might have a man crush." Leo blushed so deeply it was almost charming. *Almost.* "Having him come to our restaurant would be next level. My dad would've flipped to meet another Italian chef."

She could see the gears in his head turning — the same expression she got when she was crafting up a new recipe and stumbled upon something original. She sensed his energy and genuinely felt happy for him.

They sat on plastic chairs at one of the outdoor tables and she handed him the plate. "Taste the food before you agree to anything."

He stabbed a forkful of ravioli and smelled it before taking a bite. He chewed slowly, then closed his eyes as the flavors hit him. She hadn't paid attention to Leo when he tasted the food on their show — she'd actively avoided looking at him most of the time — but now she took him in, all of him.

What would it be like to cook food that gave him that kind of a reaction? The better-than-sex-and-sleeping-in-afterward kind of look that only truly perfect food could give you?

"Well?" She leaned closer, as if that would bring her his answer faster.

"I think I understand the concept of heaven on earth?" He laughed and took another bite. Then passed her the plate. "You need to try this."

She took a bite of the ravioli and let the pillowy soft perfection of it flood her mouth. *Heaven on earth, indeed.* "That man knows how to cook pasta." She took another bite.

"I was really anxious to meet him, especially after how the last one went." Leo wrung his hands briefly, then shook them out. She couldn't help but notice that just talking about his nervousness seemed to make him . . . nervous. "With everything going on with Vinny's, these meetings have really gotten in my head."

His vulnerability surprised her. So she decided to throw him a bone, and was vulnerable right back.

"It's not the same, but I kind of know what you mean. Every time I see a chef now, I'm just constantly worried about whether they'll ask me how Lyon is doing. I don't want to lie, but if I say we're barely holding the walls together, word will spread, and I'll have an even harder time getting people through the door."

Leo nodded back, and she could tell he was listening and hearing the doubts she hadn't wanted to say out loud to anyone. But why had she mentioned them to Leo at all? She didn't want his pity or sympathy, but her deepest fears had just spilled out.

"I wish you weren't in the same situation that I am," he said. "I'll do whatever I can to help."

He squeezed her hand, the same way she'd squeezed his earlier, and a calm settled over her. He was the steadying force she needed to get through the day, and she had a feeling she was doing the same for him. How bizarre to know they were finally on the same page, after so many years of trying to sabotage each other. He may have started off as the guy who called her Nasty Nina, but the real Leo was nothing like what she'd anticipated.

And before she lingered too long on how cute the crinkles around his eyes were, she stood up, tossed out their plate and waved for him to follow.

There was butternut squash soup from Providence, crispy rice and sour-pork salad from Lum Ka Naad, prawns with black vinegar dressing from Kato, Wagyu beef prepared by n/naka, crispy fried chicken from Dulan's, duck tartare from Animal, barrio tacos from Teddy's and miniconchas from La Favorita Bakery that were so small and delicate that it was hard to just eat one . . . or six.

And in between each tasting, their hands had found each other. She'd fallen into a rhythm. Approach a booth, make small talk with the chef, introduce Leo, take the food sample, eat, then hold hands as they walked to the next station. Being next to him didn't feel forced. Though, perhaps that was in part because she'd known him for years — there was nothing like the comfort of familiarity.

An invigorating fall breeze shifted through the air, her belly was delightfully filled with the best food LA had to offer and her mind wasn't wandering to all of the work she had to do after this. She was having fun . . . and with Leo, of all people.

"I didn't know what to expect today," she said. "But I'm pretty sure all of these chefs like you more than me now."

"I'm not being smarmy?" He searched her eyes.

"No, you're just going to have to deal with the fact that you're a natural here. The devil has his ways." She raised up a hand in a what-can-you-do? sort of way.

"Thanks, I needed to hear that." He gave her an appreciative look.

"Just telling the truth, and you know I'm a terrible liar."

Then someone called her name. This was an event where she was bound to run into people she knew, which had initially given her apprehension — now that her business was floundering — but with Leo by her side, she'd gained confidence. They were in this together: she had his back, and it felt like he'd have hers, however bizarre that was to realize.

"Nina." The gravelly tone was clearer.

She frowned, because she definitely recognized the voice. And when she looked over her shoulder, she saw him. An inch shy of being a full six feet tall, straight black hair that fell just below his ears and a thick, well-manicured beard that Nina could still remember running her fingertips through. Broad and toned . . . everything. He made eye contact and she froze.

She'd imagined what it might be like to see her ex, Charlie, plenty of times. She just hadn't thought he'd look this good, or that he'd show up after she'd eaten so many carbs that her head was starting to spin.

"Charlie," she breathed.

Even though he owned Zest in Hollywood, one of the few Michelin-starred restaurants in LA, she never expected to see him at this event. Charlie was an idol in the foodie world, but this wasn't his scene. He was always above it all. His philosophy was to curate a select and wealthy clientele versus appealing to the masses.

Leo looked at her, then Charlie. He ended up introducing himself. "I'm Leo."

She was having an out-of-body experience, watching from above as her ex stood across from her fake boyfriend. Maybe she really had eaten too many carbs, and this was a sugar-induced hallucination.

Leo extended his hand to Charlie, but Charlie just stared back at Nina.

"It's been a while," Charlie said to her.

"Work has been keeping me busy." Her

pulse was rapid, signaling her to flee.

Charlie nodded tightly. "You didn't text me back the other night."

She looked to Leo, trying discreetly to mouth the word *help.*

Leo cocked his head, then licked his lips. "We were just about to head out," he said.

Charlie finally looked at Leo, like he was just registering that there was someone else in his vicinity.

"Yes, we should go." Nina mouthed a thank-you to Leo as she took his hand and led them quickly away.

That did not just happen. Oh, but it had. She was grateful she'd put in the extra effort to look cute, and that Leo was by her side and looking fine as hell, too. Not that she needed to make Charlie jealous — he was in the past — but she certainly didn't want to seem like she was still dwelling on their relationship.

"What was that all about?" Leo spoke from the side of his mouth.

She didn't realize she was shaking from the shock of seeing her ex until they'd walked away, a little vibration traveling across her shoulders. All she wanted was to get back to her car and drive to the nearest bar, order a stiff drink, or five, and try to forget what had just happened.

"Charlie is my ex," she said. They walked out of the entrance and back to the safety of the open street. At least this way if Charlie popped up again, she could take off her wedges and make a run for it.

She didn't know why she wanted to get away from him as quickly as she did. She'd broken up with him, after all. But she'd left that relationship so she'd never have to be in the same vicinity as Charlie. He was toxic and manipulative in the worst ways. She didn't need anyone like that in her life ever again.

"Nice that you get along with your exes so well," Leo joked. He put his hands in his pockets.

"We had a complicated relationship. He's not a good guy." But that was an oversimplification, really. Explaining how much damage Charlie had done to her self-esteem wasn't an easy story to share.

He made a big show of cracking his knuckles as he said, "I'm glad you're not with him, then."

She didn't think Leo was jealous, necessarily, but he seemed to be puffing his chest out in a way that suggested he was . . . protective? She wasn't exactly sure, but she wanted to return the gesture.

"You did me a huge favor back there. I

owe you."

Leo shifted from one foot to the other. He opened his mouth, then closed it.

"What? Why do you look like you just ate the last slice of pizza?" She thought she'd been the awkward one, and now here he was one-upping her.

"On that note, I have a favor to ask."

She shot him a look. She really did owe him for the save — she just hadn't thought he'd cash in on the ask so quickly. "Anything," she responded, curious to know what could possibly be in store for her.

19

LEO

Leo was a tidy person, the Marie Kondo of the single white male world, so he never had epic messes to clean. Still, he'd gone through an entire box of Clorox wipes in the last hour to ensure every surface of his house was spotless. This was Nina's first time seeing where he lived, and to his surprise, he cared about what she thought.

"I googled her ex, ya know," Gavin said from the kitchen.

The mention of Nina's ex stopped Leo cold. He'd told his brother about the food festival, and about who they'd run in to. He hadn't mentioned how unsettling it was to come face-to-face with someone Nina had actually dated.

Plus, Leo had also googled Charlie. As Leo discovered, Charlie was a Michelin-starred chef and as obsessed with food as Nina — they had real things in common.

There were also photos of the two of them together — lots of cozy, cutesy, clearly-in-love photos.

But the big difference was that what Nina and Charlie had had was genuine, whereas what Nina and Leo had was . . .

Ugh, he hated how confused he was. Because, really, he shouldn't have any question about the fact that theirs was a work relationship, nothing more. But he'd gone from thinking Nina was one of the most selfish people on the planet to waking up and immediately checking his texts to see if there was anything new from her.

Which is why googling her ex hadn't helped anything.

"Dude sports a topknot. He looks like someone I'd hate," Gavin said matter-of-factly.

Leo chuckled, but he was grateful to hear his brother badmouth the guy. Nina would be at his house any second, and he'd need all the help he could get to not feel like a total fraud standing next to her. Especially because his mother was an expert at sniffing out the truth.

The doorbell rang. He considered not opening it at all. He'd just say that he'd had to unexpectedly leave town, and a return plan was TBD.

But then the doorbell rang again, and his mom firmly said, "You're being rude."

Okay, this was happening — Nina was going to have dinner with his family. Nothing to worry about . . . except for everything.

"Hey," he said as he opened the door.

Words left him momentarily as he took her in. Her wavy hair fell across her shoulders. She wore a navy, long-sleeved sundress with a row of bright red buttons down the middle. His eyes drifted toward the sweetheart neckline, which revealed the top of her cleavage. Had her breasts always been this distractingly perky?

"I brought bread." She held out a bouquet of baguettes. "Much better than flowers, I think."

She handed over the baguette bouquet, and breezed past him. He turned to watch. The bigger problem, he realized, was that his mom was going to absolutely love her.

By the time he got to the living room, Nina was already introducing herself.

"I'm Nina," she said to Gavin.

He laughed. "I know. I'm Gavin, Leo's better-looking twin brother."

"You said it, not me."

"But you were thinking it, right?" Gavin winked at her.

Then his mother came into the room. She

was wrapped in a flowing, floor-length dress, and her silver hair was tied up in an ornate bun.

Nina smiled, and moved toward her. As they were about to shake hands, his mother said, "You're short."

Leo pursed his lips. Just like Nina, his mother could be blunt. And there was the added level of his mother's first language being Italian, not English, so her tone often got lost in translation.

Nina cocked her head. "That's true," she finally responded.

"You seem taller on TV." His mother crossed her arms over her chest.

"The heels."

"Ah!" His mother snapped her fingers, as if that was the answer she'd been trying to come up with.

"Mrs. O'Donnell —" Nina began.

But his mom interrupted her. "I loved my husband more than my own life, but I didn't take his last name. I would've been Donna O'Donnell. Way too cheesy, don't you think? You can call me Donna."

"Donna," Nina repeated with a smile. She looked over her shoulder and caught Leo's eye. She raised her eyebrows playfully, which he appreciated.

Not everyone could handle his mother.

He always found her lack of a filter enter-
taining, but she'd pissed off plenty of people
with her well-meaning honesty. Which, he
realized, wasn't dissimilar from how Nina
interacted with the world.

He scowled. Was he attracted to someone
who reminded him of his mother?

Then he scowled deeper. He wasn't allowed to be attracted to Nina.

"Nina brought us bread," he announced,
ignoring the thoughts he'd just had.

"Homemade baguettes," she corrected
him. "Italians know pasta, but the French
know their bread."

"I like her." Donna wrapped an arm
around Nina. "Don't you like her?"

Heat rose from his neck to his face. Leo
didn't say anything. He smirked for his
mom's benefit, but, yes, he realized, he *did*
like her.

Well, damn it. He'd been trying, and failing, to ignore his attraction to her. But *liking* Nina was a different problem entirely.
Now he'd have to figure out how to deal
with his feelings. He had a habit of falling
for unavailable women, so he wasn't completely shocked that his hopeless romantic
self had done it again.

"I am single as fu-u-uck," Gavin said
dramatically into the silence.

"Gavino, language!" their mother snapped.

Leo caught Nina's eye, and she smiled back. He'd been worried about what Nina would think of him, his house and, most importantly, his family. He wasn't sure if her expressions were all part of the act, but he couldn't help hoping that she was enjoying herself just as much as he was.

The house was a modern new-build, and the kitchen was all chrome with sleek granite countertops. His brother had laid out a board holding thinly sliced prosciutto and sweet chunks of melon on the kitchen island.

Nina took a piece of melon and topped it with prosciutto. He tried not to stare as she nibbled.

"Can I help with anything?" Nina offered as she chewed.

"No, Gavino and I will get the wine — you two eat." Donna squeezed Leo's shoulder.

Without saying a word, he knew what his mom was thinking. She loved Nina. Which, he realized with a sinking feeling, was actually not great news. If she hated Nina, dealing with their eventual fake "breakup" wouldn't be hard, but now that his mother liked Nina . . .

And then they were alone. She chewed. His foot nervously tapped the floor.

"Your house is cozy for being the place of eternal damnation," Nina said to him. "Didn't realize Satan liked shag rugs." She looked toward the living room.

"Even Beelzebub needs some creature comforts," he returned, playing along.

"Your mom is way cooler than you, by the way." She folded a slice of prosciutto into her mouth.

How had he never noticed that her lips curled up into a very cute little grin every time she made a playful jab at him?

"She doesn't know about our arrangement . . ." he began. Then stopped himself, as his mom came back into the room with a wine opener and a bottle of red.

"Make yourself useful." His mother handed both to Leo. "Now, Nina, don't you think it's odd that we've never met? Three years of working with my Leonardo. He never once invited me to set. Don't you find that odd?" his mom asked.

"I do." Nina nodded her head.

That's just fantastic. Now he had two strong women ready to gang up on him.

"Have you invited your mother to set?" his mom asked.

Leo saw Nina's mouth twitch, almost

imperceptibly. He'd been put in similar situations, where people who didn't know his story asked about his dad, and he'd had to explain that he'd passed away.

But Nina's mom's birthday had just come and gone. He imagined she was still reeling from the experience of having to open that wound at the dinner they'd had.

"Mom . . ." he began.

"It's okay." Nina pursed her lips at him, then she smiled at Donna. "My mom passed a few years back."

Donna put her hand on Nina's knee, and squeezed warmly. "Your mom and I would've gotten along. I feel that."

"She would've loved you," Nina said.

Leo wished he could've met her mother, too. Anyone who raised a woman as strong, talented and funny as Nina was worth meeting.

Even though Nina had done him a solid by agreeing to come to dinner, he'd made the situation infinitely more complicated. Because for the first time, he'd brought a woman home to meet his family and he could actually picture her being in their lives for longer than the expiration date on their relationship.

Leo washed dishes at the sink while Nina

sat at the kitchen island, polishing off a second helping of his brother's chocolate gelato. The meal had been special — Gavin insisted on cooking a feast for a fellow chef: braised rabbit stew, spaghetti squash with rainbow chard and homemade gelato.

"Thanks for inviting me over."

He turned. Her legs were crossed, and the hem of her dress slid up her thigh just enough that he had to look away to avoid staring.

"You did me a huge favor, and I owe you now."

"You don't owe me, I had fun," she insisted. She'd also stayed after his family left, so as not to make his mom suspicious. Nina was a lot more generous than he deserved or had ever given her credit for. "You and your family seem so effortless together."

"I don't know what's healthier — not telling your sibling every detail of your life or having them pretend to be you on dating apps. Which is what Gavin has me do, by the way."

"Cute?" Nina's nose crinkled.

"My mom calls it pathetic, so either way — not great."

"The last time I met someone's parents was with Charlie." She took a final spoonful of the gelato, after scraping the sides of the

264

dish to get every last bit. "We dated for two years, and I only met them once. He never asked me to spend the holidays with them or anything. But they eventually came to LA, so he couldn't keep hiding me."

He wiped his hands on a dish towel. Hiding her? Leo couldn't imagine a situation in which Nina would be with someone who was hiding her away. If he was dating her — which he wasn't — he'd tell actual strangers that Nina Lyon was dating him if they so much as asked for the time.

"Which is when I discovered that they didn't even know what I did for a living. He never talked about me to them, clearly." She finished the remaining sip in her wineglass.

She'd opened up to him again, now revealing something deep about her last real relationship. He felt lucky to be given the privilege of her trust.

"He's a moron," Leo blurted out, but he meant it. Charlie had to be a special breed of idiot to not realize how incredible Nina was. "I've never eaten at his restaurant, but he clearly has shit taste if he wasn't smart enough to know how lucky he was to have you."

Leo leaned across the kitchen island. He had an affogato for his dessert — espresso with a scoop of gelato — and he took a sip.

He was more than a little depressed over the fact that he hadn't met someone as special as Nina. Well, he'd met *Nina,* but he couldn't be with her.

He wanted more of her, but that wasn't on the kinda-friends menu they had in front of them. But friends *could* hang out late, after a boozy meal. They *could* let their eyes linger on how full each other's lips were. They *could* want to lick each other . . . right?

As if reading his mind, she smiled. She was really adorable when she smiled. *Ugh.* He had to stop noticing all of the quirks that made her even more appealing than she already was.

"What are you giddy about? Unexpected coven meeting?" He raised an eyebrow.

She gestured toward his mouth. "You have a little . . ." She licked her top lip, and he followed the line her tongue made. He wished he could lean farther across the countertop and taste her, the way he had on their hike.

He swiped his thumb across his lower lip. "Gone?"

She rolled her eyes, then stood up from the barstool and came around to him. "There are, like, dozens of rom-coms where people drink lattes and then get milk on their lips."

"Excuse me, this is not a latte, it's an affogato," he pointed out.

"Well, excuse me, but you look absolutely ridiculous drinking it."

Her gaze darted toward his mouth, which opened slightly at her touch, the same reaction he'd had when they'd first kissed. But this time they were alone. There wasn't a waiting cameraman, and no career incentive dangling like a carrot. He wanted to kiss her, not because it was part of an itinerary, but because his whole body leaned forward instead of away from her.

She took her index finger and traced it above his upper lip, wiping off the cream.

"Nina . . ." Her touch was sending flames through him. How was his entire body suddenly warmer?

And her index finger stopped and lingered at the corner of his mouth. She kept her gaze fixed on his lips, not daring to meet his eyes. If she looked up at him, he was sure the sound of his heart pounding heavily against the walls of his chest would be impossible to miss.

"Leo." She slowly pulled her hand away.

When she finally looked up, her long, fixed stare blazed at him. His gaze darted from her mouth back to her eyes.

Was it possible that Nina actually did feel something for him, too?

He could feel her warm and quick breaths against him. The back of his knuckles brushed the line of her cheekbone. She breathed out, and a shiver ran through her. His head dipped toward her, and she tilted up her chin to meet him.

"This okay?" he asked, their lips so close he almost breathed the words into her. He wasn't sure what *this* was, or what he'd done right in his life to be in a moment where Nina might actually want to kiss him, but he hoped she wanted this as much as he did.

She squeezed his bicep, then said, "Please."

His fingers found their way through her hair to the back of her neck, where he held her steady. He leaned down and into her, his lips brushing against hers softly at first. He tasted cinnamon and the chocolate from the gelato. All he wanted to do was nibble and lick indefinitely.

Kissing Nina pushed the anxious thoughts he'd had into the background until all he focused on was her. He hadn't been able to appreciate the warmth of her mouth, and the sweet way her tongue flicked against his, during their first kiss. He'd been too unsure of what to do or how to act around Nina. But she wasn't the woman he thought she was — cold, calculating, ruthless. He'd been so wrong about her. And the way her mouth pressed against his lips made his body light up.

He pulled her into him, and she arched her hips in to meet his hardness. They stayed together, and his hands held her steady as she scratched her way across his shoulder blades. His tongue explored her, and she explored him right back.

Eventually, she peeled back from him and said, "I should go." Her voice was throaty and her lips had bloomed from being pressed against his.

"Stay." He practically growled the word. He didn't want her to leave, not while his skin could still feel a burn from where she'd scratched across his back with her nails.

She opened her mouth, then closed it tightly. Her expression was pained as she stepped away from him. "I have an early morning."

Had he completely misread the situation? A minute earlier, he wasn't sure if there was anything that could pry him from her, but now there was enough room between them — physically and emotionally — to park a sedan.

She bit her lip, then walked out of the kitchen without so much as a "Hey, that was still some great kissing!" pity acknowledgment. He moved to follow, still drawn toward her like a moronic moth to the flame, but managed to stop himself. If she didn't want him, he couldn't chase after her. He'd tried to push the boundaries of what they had, and she wasn't interested. Now he had to completely close himself off to the possibility of anything more.

LEO'S TEXTS

Donna: You're gonna marry that woman.

Gavin: Ma, easy . . .

Donna: Don't mess this one up.

Gavin: You're scaring Leo. He's not even answering.

Donna: Leo?

Gavin: Maybe he's busy . . .

Donna: Use protection. I'm too young to be a grandma.

Gavin: MA.

20

NINA

Lately Nina's life felt like it'd become a series of times where she needed a distraction. But after dinner with Leo's family, she definitely required something to take her mind off of all the thoughts cluttering the pantry of her brain. She'd loved meeting his mom and brother — they were easy to talk to, adored good food and Donna was, well . . . She respected the hell out of any woman who spoke her mind. And then, when she was alone with Leo, he'd kissed her. Or she'd kissed him? Either way, those kisses led to feeling their way across each other's bodies and . . . making out. They'd made out. She hadn't made out with anyone and felt like she'd fallen into another dimension where only the other person existed in a very long time. But that was exactly what had happened. Leo pressing into her, and against her, had stopped time.

That sounded ridiculous, but she'd completely and utterly lost herself in his lips, and the smell of him, and the way his shadow of a beard scratched across her cheeks. How else to describe what had happened between them? Because she also had no concept of how long they'd been kissing. Not until the edge of the countertop bumped her in exactly the wrong place, snapping her out of make-out mode and back to reality. What were they doing? More importantly, what the hell was she doing in trusting him? She'd seen Leo, the *real* one, who'd gone out of his way to make her work life miserable.

Even if he was the most incredible kisser she'd ever encountered, she knew Leo too well to forget everything he'd done to her — not just calling her nasty, but every time he'd dismissed or intentionally hurt her. Treating him as anything other than part of her job would be a mistake.

So when she checked her phone and saw Jasmine's name instead of his, she was more than grateful.

Jasmine: I don't think I can do the gala. I just had to google "How to cater food for a big event"

273

Jasmine: This is not going well.

Jasmine: This is completely your fault.

Jasmine: HELLO??? What if I have to tell my parents they need to order Domino's because I can't get my shit together?

Nina: Was in the shower! You will be brilliant! Domino's is delicious, worst-case!

Jasmine: All I have written down on this notepad is: Food?

Nina: k, I'm coming over

Jasmine: Just added: make some?

Nina: Gimme 5

Jasmine was sitting in the wicker rocking chair on the front patio of her town house when Nina arrived. A yellow notepad and pen rested in her lap, and she slowly lowered her shades down the brim of her nose as Nina approached.

"Why did you tell my parents this was a good idea?" Jasmine asked.

"I don't know." Nina opened the patio gate, then closed it behind her. "They're so

274

encouraging. I fell under the spell of the Dori and Cory groupthink. And, honestly, it is an amazing opportunity."

"It is," Jasmine admitted. She rubbed her hands together and said, "But my parents paid for my private schooling, then cooking school and the rent on my first apartment while I found a job. Getting a spot at Lyon was the first thing I'd earned on my own. I just don't want to constantly feel indebted to them. I know this will be good for my career, but I wanted to earn something like this for myself."

Nina crossed her ankle over her opposite knee, then leaned forward. "Jas, you have earned this. Your parents wouldn't give you an opportunity to cater for hundreds of their rich donors if they didn't think you'd knock it out of the park. Yes, they're your parents, but who cares? If my mom had had any connections that would've made my life easier, I would've taken them. Why are you fighting this?"

She was having a hard time following Jasmine's hesitation. Fundamentally, she understood the importance of wanting to make your own way — Nina had done that her whole life. But Nina also would've taken any helping hands she'd been offered, if any had bothered to come.

"They keep trying to insert themselves into my life. And, like, I get it — I'm their only child. But I want to be able to figure my life out without them weighing in on every detail." Jasmine rubbed her temples so hard her head started to sway from side to side.

"I'm sorry." Nina sighed. "I realize I inserted myself, too, but then you got me back and volunteered me. So we're in this together, I'm afraid."

Nina sat down in the chair opposite Jasmine. The sky was a shade of gray that made it look like the world wanted to go back to bed. Her best friend lived in Frogtown, an area that had massive industrial buildings being converted into lofts. Jasmine's town house was one of those lofts, and she even had a view of the LA River.

"Do you think I want to stand on a stage and hope someone bids for me like a prize heifer?" Nina leaned forward and rested her elbows on her knees.

Jasmine shrugged. "I'd bid on you."

"You'll have to when no one else does." Nina eyed her nails, swallowing down the very real fear that no one would bid on a cooking class with her. "So still not sure you wanna do it, huh?"

"I'm leaning toward no. Just because I

can't come up with any ideas of what to cook." Jasmine slumped back into her chair.

Nina cocked her head to the side. She knew her best friend. And if she was trying to come up with ideas, then she was interested in the idea of cooking for the gala. She didn't need Nina's help or advice, but she could use a little backup.

"Come on." Nina stood up, then held out her hand to Jasmine to help her up, too. "Let's go cook."

Jasmine reluctantly took Nina's hand and stood up. They walked into the jewel-toned house, with walls painted a soft citrine and an emerald green couch in the middle of the open-concept living room. Plants dangled from the ceiling like stars, catching sun from the enormous windows that allowed natural light to seep in and across the two-story loft.

Nina followed Jasmine into the kitchen, pressing her palms into the island's cool granite countertop.

"I know you," Nina said. "You've been cooking. Testing things. You've probably got a fully stocked fridge. Want to show me what you've been working on?"

Jasmine crossed her arms. "Nothing has been good enough to show."

"You say that any time you make something that is almost perfect," Nina said. "So show me the not good."

"Fine, but I told you so." Jasmine opened her fridge and pulled out cauliflower, an onion, garlic, tomato paste, crushed tomatoes and molasses.

"Are plant people for or against eating the plants?" Nina asked.

"I sure hope they're pro, because vegetarian is what's calling to me."

Nina watched Jasmine bread and bake the cauliflower, mash tomatoes in a pot with the garlic, spices and onion, then pan-fry a homemade tortilla. She piled the baked cauliflower onto the tortilla shell, then drizzled a healthy amount of the homemade salsa across the top.

She passed the plate to Nina and the aroma of the flavors mixing together reminded her of being outside in summer. She wanted to live on that plate. Nina picked up the taco and folded it, admiring the colors of the ingredients as they blended together like new paint on a fresh canvas. She smiled at the food. "Hello, gorgeous."

Then she smelled the taco — spice and lime — before taking a bite. Not only was each part of the dish cooked perfectly, but it also practically melted in her mouth.

"It's missing something," Jasmine said.

Nina looked up to see Jas studying her. "I'm not your dad, I don't need you to add salt," Nina joked.

"But?" Jasmine persisted.

She took another bite and chewed, deciding if there was anything she'd add. The truth was that she knew Jasmine just needed reassurance and a second opinion, not advice. "If you wanted another texture, maybe a sprinkle of bread crumbs over the top?" Nina took another bite. "The baked cauliflower loses its bite in the oven. So maybe if you add more crispiness, you'll really kick it up. That's all I've got, and it's one of those notes you can take or leave."

"I'll try it." Jasmine tapped her index finger at her chin. "If I do this, I'm going to be stressed the fuck out."

"I know."

"And you're gonna have to listen to my crazy."

"Can I also taste-test the food while you go off? Because I'm happy to do that." Nina licked some of the spicy salsa that had dribbled down her finger. "Keep going. You're heading in the right direction with this menu."

"Thank you." Jasmine squeezed her hand. "Margarita?"

"And another taco? Yes, please." Nina

settled onto the barstool at the kitchen island.

While Jasmine went to the bar cart to grab the tequila, orange liqueur and simple syrup, she said over her shoulder, "Now that we're going to be drinking, it feels like the right time to ask you this."

"Uh-oh." Nina sat up straighter.

Jasmine carefully returned to the kitchen, glass bottles in hand. As she opened up the tequila bottle, she asked, "What was it like to kiss Leo?"

Nina was sure her mouth must have opened in surprise. She closed it.

"I mean, I know he's the scum of the earth, but . . . was he a good kisser?"

Nina was not someone who blushed, but she had no doubt that she was, judging by how hot her neck felt. Just the mention of kissing Leo immediately took her back to the feel of his hand gently tilting up her head to meet his mouth.

"To be totally honest, like, it was bizarre. I mean —" She cleared her throat, nearly choking on what she was going to say next. "It wasn't bad."

Jasmine nodded, like she was somehow picking up on more than what Nina had actually admitted. "Here I was worried you might be trying to shove him over that mountaintop, but for you to say the monster isn't a bad kisser is, well . . . that's something."

Ah, right. Jasmine was referring to their first kiss on the hike. Because Nina hadn't told anyone — nor did she plan to — about the impromptu kitchen make-out session. But was her friend right? What did it mean that Nina wasn't gagging at the mere thought of kissing Leo?

Of course, Nina knew what it meant. She'd had the trickle of thoughts enter, then leave, throughout the day: her opinion of Leo had changed. In fact, she almost felt something more than friendship for him.

"I don't remember the last time I caught a sunset," Nina said, trying to shift the discussion and her brain away from the actual kissing.

"Too bad it was with Leo." Jasmine squeezed fresh lime juice into a tumbler. "Sounds like a romantic date to me."

It was. Nina sighed and tried to ignore her inner monologue. "He's taking me out for Halloween."

Jasmine stopped squeezing the lime. "Come again? You're spending holidays with the man?"

"I just do what Tom tells me," Nina said. Though, actually, Leo had suggested the

Halloween date. And Nina hadn't told Tom about it yet, preferring to keep a small sliver of their relationship to herself. For now.

"Well, it's your favorite holiday. You know I'm coming over to get you all dolled up," Jasmine said and handed Nina a margarita.

"You don't have to do that." Nina clinked her glass against Jasmine's. She took a sip and savored the cool and salty drink.

"Oh, yes, I do! You don't know how to use highlighter, and I plan to drink a lot of that good wine you keep in your cute little wine fridge."

"Bottoms up." Nina smiled out of the corner of her mouth as she took another sip of her drink. She'd acquiesce to Jasmine because, really, did she have any other choice? And while she wouldn't tell her best friend, she wouldn't mind looking better than a freshly frosted cupcake for the next time she saw Leo.

21

NINA

Nina's hands shook, a tremor just noticeable enough that she stared at her right hand as she reached for another mini-Butterfinger.

"Sophie," Jasmine said toward the phone. "Please tell your sister to quit eating chocolate while I'm trying to put on her eyeliner."

"I'm about to hit that sweet spot of sugar overload where I start seeing double." Nina blinked rapidly, not by choice, which caused Jasmine to huff in irritation.

"I *just* got the eyeliner on, can you chill?" Jasmine exhaled sharply.

"Ni, are your hands shaking yet?" Her sister's stern voice came through the speakerphone.

"Maybe." They weren't even on FaceTime. Her sister knew her too well.

"You and I both know once you go past that point, there's no turning back. Remember eighth-grade Halloween? We had to dunk your head in the bobbing-for-apples bin to stop the room from spinning."

Truthfully, she barely remembered the event because she was on such a sugar high she'd nearly blacked out. Drugstore candy, Leo would be amused to find out, was irresistible to her. It was *finally* Halloween night — the holiday for which she'd been waiting all year — and stress eating was kind of her *thing.* So why not do it with the bowl of candy meant to be left out for trick-or-treaters?

On top of being worried about her business, her reputation and the livelihood of her employees, she was also at a loss for what to do about Leo. She liked him. Like . . . *like* liked him. She didn't know what he thought of her, or if he thought of her as anything more than someone to make out with, but what had become clear was that she had feelings for him. Confusing, messy, eat-an-entire-bowl-of-candy kind of feelings. But she would never tell him how she felt. In fact, she had to be better about reminding herself that he was human garbage, normally.

"Fine." She put the candy back into the bowl and whispered, "I'll see you later" to it.

"My next appointment just got here, and you better not stuff a Butterfinger in your bra for the road." Sophie hung up before Nina could say goodbye.

"Will you finally let me do my magic?"

Nina nodded in response. Jasmine lifted Nina's chin and continued to work on her face.

Tonight, Nina could use the confidence that a little added glam could provide. Jasmine and Sophie didn't know anything about her last date, where she'd met his family and ended the night with an extra helping of dessert, so to speak.

She couldn't tell Sophie this, because her sister's romantic goggles would fog up and then explode on her face. Jasmine was still under the impression that Nina despised Leo, so having to explain that she had not only met his mother, but had also left his house wanting more from him would be too complicated.

And besides, Nina didn't know what the hell was going on, either. Which was exactly why she'd stopped their kiss. Her business was her top priority, so where did having a make-out buddy fit into that?

"Your eyelashes are like spider legs."

Nina could almost see cartoon hearts

exploding out of Jasmine's eyes.

"I think that's a compliment, but you know it sounded weird, right?" She was itchy to see what was happening. Jasmine had been brushing and blotting and dabbing makeup onto her for the last forty-five minutes. All the while, Nina hadn't been allowed to peek.

"What I'm trying to tell you is that your face is a work of art."

"Hopefully not abstract."

Jasmine waved her off, then grabbed her shoulders and spun her around to face the mirror in her bathroom.

Nina's first instinct was to let her mouth hang open in shock. *What the hell?*

"What is that look?" The hearts in Jasmine's eyes disappeared. "Don't tell me you hate it."

Nina's lids glittered with a creamy, blush-colored powder, her cheekbones were sharpened with highlighter and her lips were coated in a strawberry-pink glaze. She was as tempting as an éclair — soft and delicious. "If I tell you how much I love it you might quit cooking, and I can't have that."

"You love it!" Jasmine squealed and clapped her hands together. She gently pushed Nina's chin to the side so she could admire her work. "Leo's gonna drop dead from how hot you look."

"I don't need him dead, necessarily," Nina said. She needed him alive to at least see the magic Jas had worked on her. Nina wasn't insecure, but she still wanted a little validation in the form of makeup and hair.

"Mmm-hmm" was all Jasmine said in response. But when her eyes locked with Nina's, a curious expression crossed her face.

She could've easily told Jasmine then about how one thing had led to another and they'd ended up making out. But she still didn't know what she and Leo were. And she didn't want to tell Jasmine, for fear that her best friend would commit her to an institution for suddenly finding the man who'd derailed her career attractive.

"So . . ." Nina was desperate to turn the spotlight onto someone else, that someone being Jasmine. "Are you catering the gala?"

Jasmine rubbed mousse on her palms, and then twisted pieces of Nina's hair. "Probably. My parents are going to be delighted to know that I'm finally listening to them."

"Are you delighted, too?" Nina asked.

"I just need to make sure they're clear that this is my area of expertise, not theirs. If they'll be micromanaging me the entire time, I can't handle that."

"Fair."

Jasmine washed her hands in the sink. "I've gotta head back before the sous chef starts to think she owns the place. We've got another packed dinner tonight."

"Are you sure you don't want me there?" Nina asked. Halloween night at the restaurant was always fun — the kitchen staff wore subtle costume bits, like cat ears. They had a special menu and Nina came out at the end of every meal with pumpkin truffles for each table. Leo would have understood — business was business — but at the same time, she'd also be disappointed to miss the night out with him. She'd been looking forward to it, shockingly enough.

"We will miss you, but we'll be fine. You're allowed a night off, and this is technically work for you. Keep it up, we need the customers." Jasmine packed up her makeup bag, which was actually a backpack stuffed to the top with supplies. "Text me if you need a rescue."

And then Nina was alone and waiting for Leo. If you'd told her last year that she'd be spending her favorite holiday with this man, she would've rolled her eyes so hard they'd be permanently in the back of her head. But now, all she wanted was to discover the big surprise he had in store for her. He hadn't given her any hints via text. All she knew was that he'd planned the date — no itinerary from Tom allowed.

The doorbell rang. Coincidence? Had he sensed that she was having a moment of weakness and chosen to strike just then? But then she saw the shape of the man standing behind the frosted glass.

Charlie.

She froze. It was too late for Nina to pretend she wasn't home. And, fuck it, because if there was ever a time to face him, it should be when she looked this good.

She opened the door wide, but kept one hand firmly planted on her hip. She looked him up and down, trying to channel her best who-the-hell-are-you? look. "What are you doing here?" She said it more as an accusation than a question. But her voice caught in her throat as she took in the full force of him.

Damn. He looked even better than he had at the outdoor festival. Too good.

To be fair, Charlie had always been the master of the rugged-and-handsome-without-having-to-try look, like a biker with a wardrobe budget. That old familiar smell of his — honey and mint — hit her instantly, and her body's only response was to sway. It was the same feeling she'd had the first time they'd met, an instant attraction that made her take a step closer instead of a step back.

And what he was wearing didn't help the situation. He'd always run hot, and despite the cooler air, he was in a short-sleeved green cotton shirt that left his chiseled arms exposed for Nina to goggle at. His broad shoulders only emphasized his tapered waist, and his dark-wash jeans just hit the tops of his motorcycle boots.

"I saw your car in the driveway," he said. His voice was thick, the way it always was, like he hadn't had coffee yet. "Where are you off to, looking like that?" His eyes roamed over her, taking all of her in.

Miss me much? Why shouldn't he be jealous? She looked sexy as hell, and he couldn't have her anymore.

"I've been saving this dress since we broke up, just hoping you'd show up," Nina finally said. She'd attempted a joke, but it sounded like she was still hurt, like she wasn't actually over him. And she *was* over him, wasn't she?

"I should've come sooner." Charlie closed the distance between them. He ran the back of his knuckles across her bare arm. "Can we talk?"

She shivered at his touch, which was irritating.

She could imagine a lot of things Charlie might want to discuss, and they all revolved around him. So he probably wanted to ask her a favor, or maybe he had an opinion about the state of her career — a topic he loved weighing in on.

"The last time you asked me if we could talk, you told me you couldn't be with someone who was . . . how did you phrase it? 'Inauthentic'?" Nina crossed her arms over her chest, fully aware that it would make her cleavage pop. That last conversation they'd had was exactly why she'd broken up with him. She didn't want to stand alongside a man who belittled her career and goals.

She wished Leo had come early to spare her from this confrontation. Or that she had one of those dogs that barked at evil men to warn her not to go near. And even though she could've easily walked back inside and waited for Leo, her history with Charlie kept her there.

She'd broken up with him because immediately after she'd signed on to do the show, his attitude toward her had turned from dismissive to rude. He didn't agree with her choice to go mainstream, and he'd started making passive-aggressive, then just plain aggressive, remarks about how she was ruining her career.

He wasn't entirely wrong. When she'd opened up a third restaurant, it meant that the quality control she'd had over the food coming out of each kitchen diminished. He knew she wanted to be recognized with a Michelin star, and he'd argued the best way to do that would be to focus on one spot at a time. After all, Charlie was a chef, too, and his restaurant *did* have a Michelin star — two of them.

She hadn't listened to his advice. She'd gone for a big impact, and she'd never gotten a star. What she *had* been given was a spot on a show with a man who'd given her a reputation problem, even if he'd done so by accident. So who was right in the end?

Rather than stay, try to resolve their issues, or even hear him out, she'd left. And they hadn't had a long, on-again, off-again breakup. When she ended a relationship, she was done. So maybe he wanted closure, or something else entirely — she could at least hear what he had to say.

"I've missed you a lot." He was many things, but open with his feelings was not one of them. The man hadn't even cried when she'd made him watch *Steel Magnolias* with her. Him saying he missed her was the equivalent of getting down on one knee. "You and I need to talk, and I'm not leaving until we do."

Nina could tell he meant business by the way his legs were firmly planted. Still, she didn't care — he had no right showing up at her doorstep. She was just glad he'd picked the day that she looked edible from head to toe.

"You have one minute and then I'm going inside to wait for my *date*." She emphasized the last word.

"He doesn't exactly seem like your type." Charlie's eyebrows furrowed as he searched her face for a response.

"Thirty seconds." She wasn't going to just hang out while Charlie took swipes at Leo. If he had anything to say, then he needed to spit it out. She just had to stand there for a few more seconds and . . .

. . . And then Charlie was kissing her. His lips were on hers, hungry and pressing into her with a need so desperate she was nearly knocked off balance. But when she righted herself, she found she was steadied by his hands, which were wrapped around her back and pulling her into his own warm chest. Her body hadn't forgotten what it felt like to kiss Charlie, and how easily they fit together. Even though they pushed each other's buttons, that fire often fueled their desire, too.

Kissing Charlie was also so different from kissing Leo. Charlie was a wolf, and he wanted to devour her whole. Whereas when she was with Leo, she felt like she was being worshipped by the way his mouth and body rose to meet her.

And then thinking about Leo made kissing Charlie seem . . . wrong. Completely and totally off. She pulled away.

"Stop," she said forcefully, both to herself and Charlie. She tasted him on her lips and she wanted to wash her mouth out.

She stepped back from Charlie, realizing that the only man she wanted to be kissing was Leo.

"Nina?" Leo called out to her.

She turned to see him in her driveway. She didn't know how long he'd been there, or what he'd seen, but judging by the confused — and hurt — look on his face, he'd seen enough.

22

LEO

How much more time do I have with Nina? Leo wondered as he drove to her house. *And why can't I think about anything else?*

He'd asked himself these questions every day, multiple times a day, since they started "dating." Initially, it was a countdown he was eager to have end, but now? After their last date, where she'd raked her hands through his hair as they kissed . . .

But then she'd pulled away — no, ran from him. And he just couldn't figure out what Nina wanted from their relationship. He wasn't the kind of person who dealt well with uncertainty. His anxiety couldn't handle the stress of constantly guessing where they were headed.

So he was going to talk to her about what was going on with them tonight. Even knowing that she likely wanted to keep things professional, he had to tell her how he felt. Though just the thought of her potential negative reaction was making his palms itch.

He was a few minutes early to pick her up. Nervous about traffic on Halloween night and, honestly, overeager to see her. Her single-story Craftsman home, with California desert landscaping out front and shutters painted a brilliant red, stood out among the new-build designs and modern architecture of her neighborhood.

Outside on the large front porch lined with stone pillars, he caught a glimpse of her. But his view was partially obscured by a wall of a man with long hair and shoulders that looked like they'd spent most of their life in the gym. Nina looked . . . concerned. Worried? Either way, Leo didn't like it.

He parked, got out of the car and made his way up the driveway.

As he hurried toward her, he saw the man reach for Nina. *Oh, shit.* This was clearly a stalker, someone trying to hurt her. Leo began to sprint, keeping his eyes trained on Nina. He was about to call out and try to scare the guy off, but then she leaned into her assailant.

Leo stopped running — he stopped moving altogether — as he watched Nina kiss another man. What *was* the sensation brewing deep in his gut? His fists bunched together. He felt sick to his stomach with . . . jealousy? Not that he had any right to be jealous. She wasn't his actual girlfriend.

Nina pulled away from the man, and her face contorted into an unreadable expression.

"Nina?" His voice sounded much more wounded than he'd anticipated.

She slowly looked toward him and their eyes locked — a kind of apology seemed to lurk on her face. Even though his insides had shriveled and died from what he'd just seen, he couldn't help shrugging an "it's okay" back her way.

What the hell was wrong with him?

Then the man turned to face him and . . . Charlie, her ex, stared back.

"Cool outfit," Charlie said.

Leo looked down and remembered that he'd worn his part of the Halloween costume: devil horns, black suit with a red tie and a pointed tail. Nina's witch hat and broom were in the car.

She smiled at Leo, and he instinctively began to walk toward her.

But then Charlie reached for Nina's hand. She pulled away.

"I gave you a minute, and as we tell contestants on the show . . . your time is up." Nina glared at Charlie.

Leo almost felt sorry for the guy. He'd been on the receiving end of that withering stare more times than he could count. But, then again, Charlie *had* just made fun of his Halloween costume and kissed Nina. Not okay.

She closed the door firmly, brushed past Charlie and walked toward Leo. When she grabbed his hand, a sense of relief flooded through him. She'd chosen him. He didn't know why she'd been kissing Charlie at all, but she was leaving with Leo.

Whatever was going through her head, he'd ask later. He could tell by the pleading look she shot him that she needed out of this situation. What he really wanted to know was if she was *with* Charlie. But he couldn't ask that, because he had no right to.

She didn't owe him an explanation. Still, seeing her with someone else was gutting.

He couldn't talk to her about whether or not she had feelings for him or how she viewed him — not now. So instead of saying anything, he opened the passenger-side door for Nina, then got in the car himself and they drove away.

His house was a twenty-minute drive from

Nina's. As they drove, the sun dipped behind the mountains and turned the sky a fiery orange before settling into a murkier blue.

Trick-or-treaters filled the sidewalks, and he was glad he'd left massive bowls of candy outside the house. He parked in the garage.

Nina still hadn't said a word. She continued to stare out the side window as the garage door closed behind them. He wanted to respect her need to just process what she was feeling, but . . .

"You haven't even mentioned my pointy horns," he joked.

If she heard him, she was ignoring his comment. "I didn't know he was going to show up like that." She stared down at her hands, rubbing at a scar on her thumb.

Was she mad that Charlie had come to her house? Or was she mad that Leo had caught them kissing? "He seems to have a knack for surprising you," he offered.

"Unwanted surprises, yes."

Unwanted. Now there was a word Leo could live with. He could handle the mental image of her locking lips with a human Ken doll so long as she hadn't actually wanted that to happen.

"Wait, did he force himself on you?"

"He didn't give me an option or ask my

permission, if that's what you mean."

So Charlie was no longer a guy he was jealous of. He was now a guy he'd plan to punch in the face if he ever ran into him again.

She took in a deep breath, then another.

Leo recognized that kind of breathing — he'd had several occasions where he'd attempted steadying breaths to calm himself down.

"Three deep belly breaths have been scientifically proven to ease anxiety," he said.

She cocked an eyebrow at him. "Did you learn that in a self-help workshop?"

"I get panic attacks." Why did he go and tell her that? No one knew about his . . . issue, let alone the woman who had brought him to the brink of a public panic attack by storming off set many weeks ago. Now she was going to think less of him, or judge him, the way he'd worried anyone would when they found out about his condition. The last thing he wanted was for Nina to view him as weak.

"Used to get them, anyway," he lied.

She nodded with a slight frown, then looked ahead, and around . . . "Wait, why are we in a garage?"

While Nina investigated the bar cart in his living room, Leo took a bottle of white from the wine fridge and poured them two glasses.

Then he opened up Postmates and found his favorite dumpling spot. He couldn't cook, but judging by what she'd frequently ordered at craft services, he knew she loved just about every kind of steamed bun and dumpling she met.

He glanced at Nina. Why did the mere thought of Charlie touching her make his throat burn? The whole scenario was ridiculous. This was Nina, a woman who was embarrassed to be seen out in public with him, until she had no other choice.

But the truth was that Leo liked Nina; he'd developed feelings for her. Now he had to learn how to manage those feelings.

"Voulez-vous vino?" Leo asked as he handed her a glass of wine. "I didn't know the French word for wine, so you got a bit of both there."

"It's vin." She snorted and took a sip of the wine, then scowled. "Is this . . . ?"

The wine was the same bottle they'd had at the Sunset Grande weeks ago. He'd liked it so much he went and bought a bottle for himself. It had never occurred to him that he'd be sharing it with Nina — not at the time, at least.

"Yes, okay? You have excellent taste in wine and terrible taste in men, are you happy?" He took a long sip.

He was surprised when he looked over and saw her smiling.

"I do have great taste in wine, you're right." She took another, longer sip. "Where were we supposed to be going tonight?"

"I figured you wouldn't be up for a bunch of photo ops after . . ." He didn't want to finish the sentence. *After your ex kissed you.*

"Yeah." She took another sip of wine.

"We were going to go to the Haunted Hayride." He sat on the couch and glanced up at her. He'd been so excited to take her to the yearly festival — haunted houses, candy apples, the works. Anyone who loved Halloween would love the date he'd planned.

"Are you kidding me? The haunted houses are legit scary." She angrily flopped onto the couch next to him. "Ugh, Charlie."

He was secretly pleased she was mad at Charlie.

"Tom is going to be livid that we don't

have anything to post." She gnawed on her lip.

"I have a solution for that." He leaned forward. Then reached his hand down toward her bare foot. "May I?"

She cringed. "Whatever you're about to do, please don't."

But she also didn't protest when he gently lifted both her feet until they were resting firmly on the white coffee table in front of them. Then he placed his leather loafers next to hers. They were so close they were almost on the same couch cushion, and he didn't move to correct that. "Hold up your wineglass and give me your phone."

"I'm too tired to argue."

He positioned the camera lens so it captured their clinking glasses and the way their legs touched. The gas fireplace was on in the background, and *Hocus Pocus* was on the big screen. The staged photo created the impression of a perfectly cozy night in, which was exactly what a real couple might be doing.

"You really do have striking feet," Leo said. He opened her Instagram and added the photo. "The fetish porn site I'm uploading this to is going to have a field day."

"I know you're joking. Well, I think you're joking."

Leo gave a half grin back. She raised an eyebrow as she took another sip of wine. He'd been treading lightly around her all night, but now they seemed back to the place they'd left off before he-who-shall-not-be-named showed up.

He typed the caption: Wine, takeout, and a virgin lighting the black flame candle. Photo @LeoODonnell. Then turned the phone to show Nina. She grabbed it, deleted his caption, then typed her own.

I put a spell on you. Photo @LeoODonnell. She turned the phone back to him, and he saw she'd posted the photo. She had no idea how accurate of a caption she'd written.

He pulled out his own phone and began to type a comment: Because I'm yours . . . His finger hovered over the send button, and he realized his comment was just as truthful as her caption. It seemed ridiculous that the way he was revealing his true feelings was through an Instagram post. But, then again, it felt easier to couch them in the safety of his phone screen. He hit Post.

"Now, let's eat Chinese food and watch Bette Midler deliver the performance of a lifetime. How does that sound?" He turned to face her. This wasn't the night he'd originally planned, but hanging out at home with Nina didn't feel disappointing, not in the slightest.

She studied him, twirling the stem of the glass in her hand. Then she licked her lips, shook her head and said, "I've never wanted anything more."

He lingered too much on her words, spinning them around in his mind, hoping there was substance to them. If nothing else, she wanted the same thing he did, at least for the night. Which might be all he ever got from her, and it would have to be enough.

23

NINA

Jasmine: Are you at Leo's?????? It's alllllll over IG. What is happening?????

Sophie: What? You're at his house?

Sophie: omg, just saw the photo

Sophie: he's hot. You're hot. Just DO IT.

Jasmine: No, no, no nonononononono-nono

Nina turned off her phone. She didn't feel like explaining that this wasn't actually the first time she'd been to his house, or that she and Leo were watching the greatest Halloween movie of all time with her favorite takeout food, or that Charlie had shown up at her door. The whole situation felt complicated, and what she wanted was to pretend like she didn't have to figure out what this meant. Not yet, at least.

Especially because for the first time in a really long time, she felt relaxed. She was curled up on one end of the couch with her feet skimming the side of Leo's pants, while he was sipping wine and grinning at the TV. It was all bizarrely . . . normal. Like something she used to do with Charlie.

But then again, if she'd been doing this with Charlie, he'd want to be watching an indie film. And takeout food would never happen — he hated the thought of all that packaging and eating nonorganic ingredients. He would have insisted on cooking.

Being with Charlie had never been easy, the way that Leo had made their night easy. Charlie viewed Nina as a kind of project. Like trying to perfect how to cook the best scrambled eggs — she was always too runny, too soft, overdone. Over their two-year relationship, he'd tried to mold her into the kind of chef he was: admired, singular and award-winning. When she deviated from his expectations of her, they fought. But then they'd make up, and the making-up part was why they worked for as long as they had. So being on Leo's couch was the best thing for her — a reminder that she didn't have to be miserable. Even if she actively had to ignore that espresso smell of his, and how it made her want to nuzzle her nose against his neck to get more. The last hour of eating, drinking and watching the best movie had felt like biting into a freshly baked cookie — warm and indulgent. Except for the dress, which was way too tight and getting tighter with every bite of food.

"You look . . . pained. There are more dumplings, no need to despair."

Were his eyes always this shade of Scotch brown? *Gah,* she really did have to stop noticing how cute he was, especially when he talked about food.

"I want more noodles, actually, but this dress . . ." She stood up and tried to pull down the bottom to see if that would give her a bit more wiggle room, which only made her outfit tighter.

She caught him staring at her, but then he nodded with fake empathy. *Jerk,* she thought, but she smiled, too.

"I imagine you sleep in head-to-toe black lace curled up in your cauldron, but if you want to give pajamas a try, I do have a spare pair," he said while spooning more noodles onto her plate. "Or there's always the witch hat."

He was still wearing his costume, after all.

She considered her options: continue to be squeezed into her sausage casing of a dress, or change into the undoubtedly Hugh Hefner–esque pajama set from Leo.

"Fine, I'll do it if you do it." She placed her hands on her hips, trying to seem put out by his gesture. "But I get the silk and you get the bunny ears."

"Kinky." He waggled his eyebrows.

She rolled her eyes. So, okay, she *was* in an alternate universe where she and Leo were having a movie night and she was about to wear his pajamas. Fine, her life had taken an odd turn, but could the day get any weirder?

"Little bats or cutesy pumpkins?" Leo held up two pairs of pajama bottoms, each with their own Halloween-themed animal motifs.

Yes, it had actually managed to get weirder.

"Bats, obviously." She grabbed the black-and-white pants from Leo, along with a cotton shirt. Their hands brushed briefly, and a snap of static electricity shot through them. Or at least that's what she assumed the spark was. She frowned at him, and he cocked his head in response.

She quickly walked through Leo's bed-room, went into the bathroom and closed the door, taking a deep breath. She was in Leo's bathroom, at his house, about to put on his pajamas. Their relationship now couldn't be more different from how they'd actively avoided each other on set. Maybe because she'd entered this arrangement with absolutely no intention of impressing Leo, getting close to him was easier than she'd anticipated. She hadn't felt the need to act a certain way around him. She'd just decided to be herself — he could take or leave her.

And as it turned out, he didn't appear to mind who she was — all the qualities Charlie had made her hide, Leo seemed to accept.

She turned toward the sink and began to investigate the products there — electric toothbrush, toothpaste, a dopp kit. She wondered what he might be hiding in his above-the-sink cabinet. For sure, there had to be beard oil — he seemed the type. There was a 50-50 shot that he owned bronzer, because no one had cheekbones that defined without a little help. And probably a weird surprise — human teeth?

She quietly opened the cabinet and took a quick glance. Band-Aids, moisturizer, a variety of combs and a full prescription bottle for Prozac.

Leo had casually mentioned panic attacks, but he'd said he used to have them. She shouldn't be snooping. His personal life wasn't any of her business. Yes, they'd shared things about themselves, but that didn't mean she had a right to keep asking questions.

She closed the cabinet and cringed when it made a loud bang. She clenched her teeth and waited to see if he'd heard. When she was greeted by silence, she started changing into the pajamas. Only, she realized there was an impossible-to-reach zipper on her dress.

She huffed out a sigh — *this* was how she'd die someday. Trapped in a designer dress, unable to tear it off, until it cut off her circulation and she collapsed.

But she had Leo nearby, so today wasn't going to be her time. She opened the bathroom door to call for help, but before she could say a word her breath caught in her throat. Leo was just outside the door, and he was shirtless. His arm flexed against the sleek white top of his dresser as he stared into the open drawer. He was clearly searching for a shirt, as his devil suit had mysteriously vanished.

And she just went ahead and stared at his arms, chest, shoulders and back, because that's what she wanted to do — especially after the last glass of wine she'd had. She'd seen him shirtless once before, on their hike, so the sight of him shouldn't have felt so new, but it was like seeing him for the first time all over again. She let her gaze linger over how the muscles between his shoulder blades emphasized his strong back, and the tricep that flexed as he straightened his arm. A small, parched noise escaped her lips, and he looked up.

She coughed, trying to cover the sound.

Leo turned. "You're supposed to be in pajamas."

You're not supposed to look this fucking good.

"The problem is the dress. Not built for food or unzipping. I was wondering if you could, um . . ." She turned and motioned toward her back, where the zipper was.

When Leo stepped forward, his bare torso briefly brushed against her back. His skin was warm in contrast to the cool air, and goose bumps erupted across her arms in response. She hoped he wouldn't notice her body's reaction to being so close to him. At least he couldn't see that her gaze was fixed straight ahead, on the pesky bed nearby . . .

His fingers grasped the top of the zipper, and he pulled on it just enough that she stumbled back and against his chest. She muttered an apology under her breath as he slowly lowered the zipper down her back. His knuckle grazed the track of her spine, and his hand stopped at the bottom, just above her ass. She wondered if his eyes were roaming over her exposed skin. And he didn't move his fingers from the zipper right away, which made her feel like he wanted the back of his knuckle to stay exactly where it was. Neither of them moved. She was afraid that if she did, she'd break the fantasy of Leo examining her — of him potentially wanting more of her.

Eventually he leaned down, and the shadow of his beard scraped against her ear as he said, "All done."

If she wanted more to happen between them, she sensed that all she'd need to do was say the word, because his mouth still hovered just next to her ear, and his hand was still on that zipper.

Her hand moved from her side, and trailed behind her to find the spot where his hand was. She skimmed her fingertips along his palm until he caught her hand in his and turned her to face him. She looked up and her eyes searched his as her chest practically heaved against him.

Was she really going to take this next step?

313

If they crossed the more-than-make-out-buddies line, they wouldn't be able to go back. And she knew Leo wasn't a relationship guy; he just didn't seem the type.

Then his thumb brushed across her cheekbone — so featherlight that it made her breath catch — and any doubt she'd had about doing more with Leo vanished.

"Last time, you stopped me and said . . ." he trailed off.

"Fuck what I said," she murmured. "Devil."

"Witch," he replied.

And without thinking of the consequences, or what their relationship was, or how Leo might view her afterward, she crushed her lips against his.

He didn't miss a beat. He took her face in his hands and pressed more urgently into her. His tongue meeting hers. His legs walking her back so she was pressed firmly against his bedroom wall.

Nina waited to hear the warning sirens in her head blaring to remind her that this was a bad idea, but there was nothing but Leo's hungry growl as she nibbled on his bottom lip.

She trailed her hands down his back, and was delighted to feel not only muscle, but also softness. She wanted to thank him for having what felt like a healthy body, and one that she was now getting to enjoy, but she didn't want to disentangle her mouth from his. Instead, she pulled him closer, letting the warmth of him turn her into melted caramel.

He'd shown her more of himself, and she wanted to return the gesture. While she was rarely self-conscious about her curves — she'd eaten so many delicious meals to get them — she couldn't help but feel apprehensive as she tugged slightly on the straps of her dress so that they fell away. Was Leo going to like what he saw, just as much as she'd liked him?

Leo pulled back to watch as she stepped out of it. His fingertips traced a line along his jaw, and he licked his lips like she was a ripe fig that he wanted to bite into. The strain against his pants confirmed what his longing expression told her, too.

"Nina . . ." he began.

Before he could make some ridiculous joke and ruin the moment, she interrupted with, "You're wearing pumpkin pajamas."

Well, that wasn't any better, was it?

"That's what really sent you over the edge, isn't it? The sight of these round, luscious —"

"You really do need to shut up," she

315

laughed.

"Keep telling me what to do. I'm into it." He pressed closer and traced a finger between her breasts. His gaze darted from her lips back to her eyes. "I can stop," he said.

This was the moment. If she wanted things to end, she could just say so. She knew he didn't care to stop, and she didn't want him to either. As inexplicable as the situation was — she and Leo almost naked in front of each other — she craved more of him.

"Not to sound dramatic, but if you stop, I might actually die." Her hands tightened around his triceps, and they pulsed back against her grip.

"We can't have that." A relieved smile crossed his face. Was he relieved that she wanted to hook up with him? Did he think that just because she was half-naked in his bedroom that this was going to be a regular thing? And would that actually be so bad?

Whatever, she wasn't going to overthink the situation. Obviously, they were attracted to each other. She knew not to mix business with pleasure, but she wasn't technically in business with Leo. They were helping each other's careers — and occasionally hooking up, apparently.

So she wouldn't allow herself to get in too

deep, which is why she needed to say, "I'm not looking for anything serious."

As she said the words, she realized that part of her hoped that it did mean something — that she meant something — to him. She wasn't exactly sure why, but she didn't want to feel discarded by him.

He hesitated, then said, "Okay."

A little hard spot formed in her chest, but she nodded back. *Okay.* Definitely a word that didn't suggest he was fighting her on it. He was attracted to her, but nothing more. She'd asked for the answer, and she had no right to be offended by it.

They locked eyes. She could do this. She wanted more of him around her, inside her, all over her. She and Leo would be friends with benefits. Or at least that's how she decided to justify what this was.

She unclasped her bra and removed it. As she did, his pupils dilated. The buzz of anticipation rocketed through her.

His palm wrapped around the back of her neck, and he pulled her against him. Her nipples stiffened against the soft scrape of his chest hair. "I'd always suspected you had absolutely perfect breasts. I do like being right."

Perfect they were not — her right one was noticeably larger than her left — but she wasn't about to correct him on calling something on her body "perfect." She had heavy and impressive breasts, something many men had loved about her body. And while finding the correctly sized bra, or trying to work out, in general, had proven to be trickier because of her cup size, she always loved seeing a man's reaction to them.

He circled her nipple lightly with the tip of his finger. "Do you want this?" he asked.

She nodded, feeling the brush of his chin just above her head. He pinched and tugged the bud between his thumb and index finger, just hard enough that a little hiss escaped her. He cupped her breast in his palm so that her nipple pointed up toward him, and he lowered his mouth to her. He gently pressed her shoulder into the wall as he sucked so sharply on her nipple that she gasped.

As he bit and nibbled, warmth coursed down and through her until she turned damp and slick. As ridiculous as his pajama pants were, she pressed her wetness against him and felt his erection throb back against her.

He took her need as a cue, kneeling in front of her while keeping a hand on her nipple to tug and pinch. His other hand found its way to her panties, and he lightly traced his finger along the edge of them, teasing.

She could feel his hot breath against her inner thigh as his fingers inched her panties down her legs. As he slid his palm over the top of her mound, she arched toward him so he could feel just how excited she was.

"Nina . . ." He breathed. "You are so fucking wet."

"You made me so fucking wet," she panted back.

The situation didn't seem real — not him, not the strength of his hands, not the way her body melted like butter in a skillet for him. Because this couldn't be happening with Leo. But it was.

In one smooth motion, he lifted her leg and wrapped it over his shoulder. The angle opened her up to him, and he breathed out and across her bare thighs as he made his way to her center. He started by parting her with his fingers and flicking her clit with his tongue. Her head fell back and against the wall. She'd never been eaten out while standing, but being able to watch Leo from above was undeniably sexy. He began to lick her clit, gently circling with his tongue and applying more pressure whenever he found the tip of her bud.

Her leg tightened against his back in response, but he kept her firmly planted with his heavy palm against her hip. Then his tongue dipped down and delved into her, filling her entirely.

He spread her open with his free hand and nestled one, then two of his long fingers inside of her, dipping them in and out as he circled her clit with his tongue. He sucked her into his mouth, then lapped at her as softly as the tip of a finger stroking her. She rode his face, moving against the rhythm of his fingers as they fucked her.

"Please . . ." She was barely able to get the word out. Her legs began to tremble. The one wrapped around Leo tightened, then released as the pressure continued to build. She raked her hands through his hair, urging his mouth to bring her to the point where she had to erupt . . . and she did. She let out a series of moans as pleasure surged through her, her core throbbing as Leo held her in place until she'd finished.

When she came back to her senses, her hands were still in Leo's hair. She removed them and leaned harder against the wall. Her limbs were light as cotton candy. When she looked down, Leo's normally soft brown eyes were nearly jet-black. He looked up at her, leaning his cheek against the leg he'd propped up, and gave a small smirk. She wasn't sure what his expression meant, but she was eyeing his still prominent length . . .

He stopped her. "It's okay," he said. "Tonight is all about you. Watching you was enough for me."

She squinted at him. Was he trying to tell her he didn't want her touching him? She was certain that, judging by his very obvious erection, that wasn't the case.

"Maybe it wasn't enough for me," she said.

He tried to hide the smile crossing his face. "Next time," he said reassuringly.

After this, there was no turning back, and Nina wasn't sure how to even move forward. She liked Leo, that was a fact, but she had to make sure her feelings didn't get confused with the boundaries she'd set and he agreed to — a physical relationship.

And in the moment, she wanted more of him, too. She didn't care what they were, or where they were headed. She wasn't interested in stopping what they were doing. And whenever he wanted her, she planned to make him come just as hard as she had.

24

LEO

Leo woke up to a thud. He blinked awake, then sat up. The light trickling in through the curtains suggested it was early enough that not even the sun had fully risen. Once his eyes adjusted to the room, he saw Nina bending over to pick up the shoe she'd dropped. Her hair was brushed, the makeup was gone and she'd managed to put the dress back on without his zipper assistance.

This wasn't the first time he'd invited a woman home only to have her leave early the next morning. Serial dating over the years inevitably led to some casual encounters. This was, however, the first time he'd been unnerved by the move. Was she actually planning to just sneak out? He'd agreed to her request that last night wouldn't mean anything — just sex — but still.

She turned to look at him with the cautious speed of a bank robber who wasn't sure if she'd just tripped the alarm. She cringed when he waved.

"Cinderella left her shoe behind, and things turned out all right for her," Leo said. A worried knot formed in his throat. Had he done something wrong to make her want to flee his house? Had she completely regretted everything that had happened?

Just the thought of last night, of how she'd moaned then tightened around his fingers . . . He was hard again. He bunched a bit of blanket around his erection.

"But if anything, you'd be the wicked stepmother." She smirked, clearly proud of her joke.

He was relieved to hear her banter with him. He could work with that. "If I'm the stepmother, that makes what we did quite unorthodox."

He'd barely slept. He'd closed his eyes to act like he was asleep, but he was just reliving every moment that had happened. After making her come, all he wanted to do was cuddle with her in bed. But they were just having sex, per her request. Still, he'd caught himself reaching for her more than once, and had to stop himself.

So, of course, the minute he'd managed to *actually* fall asleep, she'd taken that as her opportunity to leave.

If this had been a normal date with anyone else, he'd have no problem suggesting they spend the morning going for another round. But this was Nina, and she wasn't just anyone. They needed each other if they wanted to make it through the fiscal year, but he also *liked* her in a way he knew she didn't reciprocate. If she did, she wouldn't be searching for the exit.

Then there was the deeper, fun-house part of his brain that stowed away the darkest of his humiliated thoughts — maybe she was thinking about the model/chef trying to win her back. Leo had done his best to distract her from any thoughts of *him,* but maybe it hadn't worked. What if all he'd done was remind her of how great she used to have it? Unintentionally driving Nina back to Charlie.

His stomach churned. He had no right to dictate how she viewed him, but he also couldn't ignore the heaviness that settled over him.

"What's wrong? You look like you ripped a hole in your cashmere," Nina joked.

He must have looked as bad as he felt. But he wasn't sure how to hide the fact that he had a crush on the woman he was fake dating and for-real sleeping with.

He changed the subject. "How were you

planning to get home, exactly? You know I drove you here."

She squinted, thinking about that. "I was going to borrow your car?" She wasn't asking him a question so much as searching for an answer.

"That would be stealing my car," he said, "since you didn't ask for permission to borrow it."

"That's not true. I left you a note in red lipstick on your bathroom mirror." She pointed toward the closed bathroom door.

He forced a smile. "I'll drive you home. Just give me a few minutes to drink some coffee and get us breakfast. I get a little hangry if I don't eat right away." This was true.

"You don't cook," Nina said, tilting her head in a devastating oh-you-sweet-little-thing kind of way.

"I paid a very expensive personal chef to teach me how to make smoothies that taste like a milkshake. It's my thing."

He waited for her to protest. She looked toward the door, then back at him. She eyed her nails before responding. "Better be a chocolate milkshake, then."

As he walked into the kitchen, he quickly checked his phone. There were lots and lots of texts from his publicist, agent, mother and brother.

Gavin: Ma is going to start planning your wedding if you're not careful! You know she follows you on IG.

Leo would have to deal with his family later. There was a more pressing text that caught his eye.

Tom: You did NOT run this sleepover by me. I've sent a photographer to the house. Look presentable and IN LOVE.

"Did you see this text from Tom?" he called out to Nina.
"Shit, I better call him," he heard her say.

Gavin: Don't leave me hanging. What's going on??

Leo: Don't you have to be at work in an hour?

Gavin: My boss seems to be taking the day off, so maybe I will too . . . !

Leo rolled his eyes, then stretched his stiff back. He did need to go into the restaurant to update the inventory, come up with an agenda for the next staff meeting and check

in on details of the staff Christmas party —
all part of his running to-do list. But right
now, all of those responsibilities were the
furthest thing from his mind, because he
was walking toward Nina with the greatest
smoothie she'd ever taste . . . he hoped.

"Tom? I'm going now. I have not lost my
mind. Okay, I will, 'bye." She looked at the
smoothie, then at him with suspicion.

He took a big gulp from his own cup,
licked his lips, then smiled with the confidence of an actor getting paid to sell a
product. "Worst-case scenario, you'll have
another thing to make fun of me for."

She cautiously accepted the glass,
scrunched her nose, then took a sip. She
smacked her lips, then slowly looked back
at him. "That's actually edible. No way you
made this. Did you Postmates it?"

"Yes, and I left an extra-large tip." Leo
took another sip and so did she, which he
counted as a victory. His hand reached to
touch her arm, but he stopped himself. The
last thing he wanted was to scare her away
completely. So he decided to treat this the
way she wanted it, as business. "So what's
the plan?"

"Tom is sending a car. You'll walk me out.
We'll . . . kiss," she said hesitantly. "It'll be
another twenty minutes before the car is

here," she said, a little too quickly. "Any ideas of how we can fill the time?" She lowered her lips to the straw in her smoothie, keeping her eyes locked on him as she sucked on the straw. Then her gaze flicked to his dick, which was . . . alert.

Holy sex eyes. Nina wasn't just flirting with him, she was laying it on thick as syrup.

"Are you . . . ?" He hadn't had enough coffee to finish that sentence.

Nina put down her smoothie. "Am I . . . ?" She took the few short steps to him to close the distance between them. She put her hands on his shoulders, and walked him backward to the leather chair in his living room. She sat him down and stood over him. "Are you okay if I touch you?"

Her fingertips left his shoulders and trailed their way down his arms, over his forearms and down toward the sweatpants he'd tugged on. She hovered above his cock, and looked at him for confirmation. His lips opened, then closed. He had to make sure she wanted this just as much as he did.

"I'm okay, if you are?"

She nodded. She took her hands and tugged down his pants, and he moved slightly to help. She pulled at the corners of his boxers, and he used his thumbs to help slide them off. His cock popped out at full attention and just the right height for her mouth, which opened slightly as she looked at him.

She ran her nails up and through the hair on his thighs, guiding her hands toward his waiting dick. When she reached him, she started with one hand gently running over the tip, then down his shaft. He sucked in a breath as she tightened her grip around him. When her hand reached the base of him, she opened her mouth and her tongue flicked his head, over and over, while she slowly worked his shaft with her hand.

Then she ran her tongue along the underside of his shaft, licking him in one smooth motion. When she trailed her tongue back up, she stopped at his tip and popped it into her mouth, sucking him into her with tight pressure. His hands went for her hair, gripping her as she brought her mouth down the length of him, sucking firmly as she went up and down his cock.

He needed her. He needed more of her. He reached down and brought her up, releasing her mouth's hold on his dick.

"We're going in the bedroom," he said. "I need to taste you."

He kissed her mouth, tasting her and himself, as they slowly made their way to the bed.

Her dress was tight, but he smoothly lifted the dress up her thighs and around her hips until he could see her panties. He pulled them down, and she was wet and hot for him. He moved onto the bed, lying on his back, then motioned for her to join. As she crawled toward him, he said, "Turn around. I want you to come in my mouth."

"Are we about to . . . sixty-nine?" Nina asked.

He hesitated before replying, "Like it's twenty sixty-nine."

She laughed, then positioned herself over him, the wisps of her hair teasing him. Before he could taste her, he felt her mouth meet his cock again. His hips arched up to her, and she took in the full length of him until he was buried deep in her mouth.

"That's so fucking good," he said. But he didn't linger long; he had to taste her. He reached his hands up to grab her ass, and he gently pressed her down until her pussy was directly over his mouth. His tongue reached for her clit, and he drew her bud in. He nibbled at the tip of her and felt her buck against him. He could tell she liked the pressure, so he took her in again and again. Rolling his tongue over and around her clit in playful circles while sucking her into his mouth.

Her hips began to rock as she bobbed her mouth up and down his cock and rode his mouth with her pussy. He squeezed her ass as he focused on her clit, not releasing her or letting up on the pressure he could tell she was responding to.

"Leo, I'm so close," she said. Then returned her mouth to his cock. He squeezed her ass harder and sucked her into his mouth again. He rolled his tongue as he sucked more on her clit. She stilled over him, and her legs tightened. "Fuck, oh fuck," she choked out. He held her still so he could continue to pleasure her as she moaned and finished on him.

With his free hand, he reached down and rubbed the shaft of his throbbing cock. As he felt her come, he tightened as well. He pointed his cock away, letting his load come on the top of his sheets.

They stayed like that, the only sound their heavy breathing. Until Nina's phone pinged. She reached for it, then said, "Car's here." In one swift move she swung her leg around him and was off the bed. He sat up on his elbow and watched her wipe herself with a Kleenex, pull her panties back on and smooth out her dress.

"Tom said I need to channel Julia Roberts post-makeover in *Pretty Woman,* versus the hooker that I clearly am — his words, not mine." She smoothed her dress, ran a hand through her hair and shifted from one heeled foot to the other. "How do I look?"

Like the most beautiful woman I've ever seen.

"Perfect. I credit the smoothie." His brain wouldn't allow him to say anything genuine to her, because if he did, he was sure he'd be rejected. She'd looked incredible last night. But he wanted to tell her that she looked even more beautiful now — hair still a little mussed from the bed, her lips their natural flushed hue rather than bright pink.

"Let me add one more thing," he said.

He got out of bed and pulled on his sweats, along with a T-shirt. She had little goose bumps trailing up her arms. At this time of morning, it would be quite chilly outside. His jacket from last night was hanging in the closet. He grabbed it and wrapped it around her shoulders. His fingertips skimmed her bare shoulders and he saw her shiver slightly at his touch. Maybe she'd sensed the little jolt he had, too . . .

"Thanks," she said quickly. "Shall we?" She held out her hand, and he took it. He drew closer as they walked out the front door to the waiting car. His thumb rubbed the top of her hand, and she didn't stop him.

"Do you want to talk about any of what happened?" he asked, hedging.

She bit her lip and shook her head. "We'll just keep it casual, right?" she asked.

He nodded in reply, but his stomach turned at the thought of it.

"You have to kiss me before I go." She was on her tiptoes as she whispered the words into his ear.

He closed his eyes and savored the feel of her lips against his skin. He was overwhelmed with the thought that this could be their last kiss. She could go home, decide to call off the whole thing and run back to her ex.

So when he leaned down to kiss her, he let his true emotions escape through his lips. He pulled her in so their bodies were flush. If this was goodbye, he wanted her last memory of him to be a good one. His hands found their way through her hair. She wrapped her arms around his back and he felt the familiar tug of her nails digging into him.

When he pulled away, her cheeks were flushed. She showed him a small grin, and that gave him a renewed sense that he could get through the loss of her. Because even if he'd managed to make her happy just this once, that could be enough to carry him the rest of the way through their arrangement.

He opened her car door, and she got in without saying a word. As the car drove away, he thought he saw her turn in her seat to look straight at him.

25

NINA

Nina knew that joining Jasmine at the arboretum to talk to her parents about the gala wasn't necessary. But Jasmine had mentioned she was going. Then Sophie texted that she could join. And Nina said she'd come, too, because she didn't want to be left out.

So now Nina and Sophie were driving up together in the safety of a four-door car, while Jasmine cruised there on her motorcycle, which had zero doors.

"Have you heard anything about whether spicy foods actually help you go into labor?" Sophie asked.

Nina raised an eyebrow. If she didn't already know that her sister was asking for a client, she'd be concerned. "Assuming this is a work question?"

"Yeah." Sophie gave a small laugh. "One of my clients is almost a week past her due date, and she's itching for some at-home remedies."

"Your massages aren't doing the trick?" Nina asked.

Sophie specialized in pre- and postnatal massage. Which was weirdly not a service that was widely offered or done correctly. She'd found a rewarding niche helping women who needed relief from the constant ache in their backs, feet and . . . well, everything. Not to mention the effects that birth wreaked on their bodies afterward. Sophie had told her so many stories in the last year about women who'd come to her after being injured by a masseuse at a spa who wasn't properly trained. She was glad her sister could provide a much-needed service.

"She's got a little mole who doesn't want to come out, I'm afraid." Sophie sipped at a matcha she'd brought with her. "And my induction pressure points don't seem to be helping, either."

"At least she has you to help with the aches. I don't know anything about the spicy food trick. But Jitlada makes the spiciest Thai food in town, if she wants to cry while eating."

"I'll let her know," Sophie said. "Also, if you get any more of that fancy olive oil in, I want to give it a try. One of my new moms has a C-section scar that's causing her a lot of pain. I want to show her how to massage it before bed every night, but she's very into natural oils. I remember Mom putting that Ojai olive oil on any cuts we got to minimize the scars."

"I actually did get some in last week. I'll give you a bottle when we get back." Nina gave her sister a quick glance, then refocused on the road. "I think it's really cool that you can help other women this way. We need someone looking out for us. Mom always said she hated being pregnant. I bet if she'd had someone like you in her life, she wouldn't have minded as much."

"You help women, too, ya know." Sophie squeezed her shoulder. "Your kitchen is mostly women."

"I could be doing more. I'd like to help the way you're helping." She felt fulfillment from hiring women to help her run the kitchen, but she'd always sensed she could do more to lift up other women.

"Maybe we can brainstorm some ways to do that," Sophie said.

Nina briefly smiled at her sister. "That would be awesome, Soph, thanks."

They parked and walked to the ticket gate, where Jasmine was rocking from one foot to the other. She seemed on edge, which made sense. She hadn't ever told her parents how their needling made her feel. This would be a first for her.

"Tickets?" a teenaged boy in a wheelchair said from behind the booth.

"They should be under Jasmine Miles," Jasmine said into the microphone piece.

"Oh, yeah, got you in the VIP pass box here," he said. "Can I see your IDs, please?"

They all shuffled to grab their IDs. Only, Nina couldn't find hers. "Shit," she said.

"What?" Sophie asked.

"I switched purses." Nina continued to rifle through her bag, as if that would change what she already knew. "I must've left my ID at home."

"These are VIP passes," he said. "You can't come in without ID."

"Uh . . ." Nina said as she went through her purse. "I have credit cards. Would that work?"

He took a card from her. He looked at her name on it, then back at her. He leaned against the armrest of his chair and nodded.

"Nina Lyon. You're that cooking lady, right? My moms think you're hot." He said it as if he was commenting on the weather.

"Oh, that's . . ." Nina frowned. What was

she supposed to say?

"I get it," he added. Then licked his teeth.

"Oka-a-a-ay." Jasmine grabbed the tickets from him. "Thank you for those."

"Did he just call you old?" Sophie asked.

"I think he called you hot," Jasmine said.

"Oh, and remember to stand five to ten feet away from the peacocks!" he called out to them.

"The peacocks?" Nina asked.

Jasmine nodded. "There are a lot of them on the grounds here. They're pretty harmless. But, ya know, they are big birds."

Nina gave Sophie a look, as if to say, "Why did I come with you again?"

But then they made their way through the entrance and into the gardens. The cool, breezy air snapped with electricity. They stood surrounded by enormous, dense trees that had gold-and-pink flowering pods at the tips of their branches. Nina reached up to touch a pod and felt the silky-smooth exterior between her fingers. Like rubbing a freshly shelled bean.

"That's a Koelreuteria, commonly called the golden raintree. It's native to Asia." Jasmine shrugged. "Pretty, isn't it?"

"How do you have so much brain space, and how do I make room for more in mine?" Nina asked. She touched a finger to

Jasmine's forehead and it was swatted away.

A loud squawking sound split the air. Then another, filling the space with piercing shrieks.

"What is that?" Sophie said. "A velociraptor? A rabid monkey?"

Jasmine shook her head. "Remember the ten-feet warning? The peacocks like to impress the peahens."

"What is a peahen?" Nina asked. What kind of a name was that for anything?

"Peacocks are the male birds with those big plumes," Jasmine explained. "Peahens are the females."

"Why do the men get the pretty feathers?" Sophie asked.

"Like most things, I blame the patriarchy." Jasmine smiled.

Nina guffawed, then held up her hand for a high five, which Jasmine gladly returned.

"Okay, Cory and Dori's offices are right up there." Jasmine pointed to two windows on the top floor of a khaki-colored building. "So they'll be down any second."

"We'll be here if you need us," Nina said.

"Great. I'll text you when we're done?"

"We're not going to go too far, right?" Sophie asked as they walked off to give Jas some privacy. "Like, we can still eavesdrop and stuff?"

"Oh, absolutely," Nina said. They found a nearby golden raintree with a trunk thick enough that they could hide behind, close enough that they could overhear Jasmine and her parents. They huddled together and waited to hear the family discussion unfold.

"Is this wrong? Should we leave them?" Sophie asked. She kicked at the fallen yellow pods that covered the ground.

"I don't think so. She told us to stay close." Nina leaned her back against the tree and looked up to see an older couple holding hands and making their way into the gardens. Their shoulders were pressed so tightly together that Nina was sure she couldn't so much as fit a thin slice of prosciutto between them. The woman pointed to a flowering plant, and her husband stopped walking. She leaned down to smell the blooming purple flower, and her husband smiled back, the most loving and earnest grin Nina had ever seen.

Would she ever be able to find someone who looked at her the way this older man had at his wife? She hoped so.

"Hey, Mom," Jasmine said. "Hey, Dad."

Nina turned back around and pressed herself against the tree. She stared at Sophie, who held a finger to her lips to signal they had to be quiet in order to hear.

341

"Aren't you cold? You should wear a sweater on a day like today," Cory said.

"Or a scarf, at least! You have to keep your neck warm," Dori added.

"I'm fine. I came on the bike, and I'm all warmed up from the engine."

"Have you eaten? Your wrists look thin," Dori said.

"Why don't we get you a nice veggie burger from the café? And some cocoa to warm you up?" Cory asked.

"She'll want coffee, but after noon it's really not good for anyone," Dori said.

"Okay, you two just need to take a beat," Jasmine said. "I want to talk to you about the gala."

"Okay," Cory and Dori said simultaneously.

"First of all, I love you. But there's really no easy way to say this, so here it goes — you both need to back off."

"Back off?" Cory repeated.

"Yes, Dad. I haven't officially accepted the job, but you send me a minimum of two emails a day with suggestions for the menu. I'm the chef — I'm the one who sets the menu."

"Well, don't you want our thoughts?" Dori asked.

"No, Mom, because what you're sending

me aren't thoughts. They are requests. But cooking is personal, and it needs to be a reflection of me, as I've tried to tell you both. You've been trying to control me my whole life. When I didn't go into horticulture, I know that hurt you. You thought we'd work side-by-side, the way you two do. And I'm sorry that we can't be together all the time. I will take this opportunity you're giving me, because it's amazing, and will be good for my career, as we all know. But from now on, I need you to trust me. I need you to believe that I know what's best for me."

Nina looked at Sophie, who looked back at her. "Did they say anything?" Nina whispered.

"What?" Sophie whispered back.

"Did they say anything?" Nina said.

But before Sophie could answer, Jasmine spoke again. "And stay out of my dating life. No more setups with people from the arboretum."

"They are nice people. What's so wrong with the arboretum?" Cory asked.

"Nothing is wrong," Jasmine said. "But let me make my own choices. I've never said all this to you before because I didn't want to hurt your feelings. But you've hurt mine by constantly making me feel like I'm not doing enough, or I'm doing the wrong things. Just please believe me when I say that I'm capable of making decisions without your input."

Nina tried to lean closer — not that she actually could, seeing as she was pressed up against a tree — but all she heard was Sophie's heavy breathing. "Do you think they passed out?" Sophie joked.

"Okay," Cory and Dori finally said in unison.

"Okay?" Jasmine asked.

"We will do our best to email less," Dori offered.

"I just need you to not micromanage me," Jasmine clarified.

"We don't micromanage," Cory said.

"Cory . . ." Dori said with a hint of warning. "I'm glad you'll be catering the event. And we will do everything we can to treat you the same as anyone else we'd hire."

"But you might have to tell us if we're being too . . ."

"Annoying?" Jasmine said, finishing the thought for her dad.

A shrill cry broke through Nina's concentration. The peacocks had seemed so far away before, but now they sounded like they were standing next to her. She turned and froze. There was a massive peacock directly in front of them. Its green, turquoise, indigo and burnt orange plumes fanned and high — taller than Nina and her sister.

"Sophie," Nina said quietly.

Sophie turned, saw the bird and scrambled to press herself flush against Nina.

"Oh, holy night terrors." Sophie clutched Nina's arm, her fingernails digging in with the force of a lobster cracker.

The peacock's plumes seemed to gain a few inches at the mere sight of Sophie. And, bizarrely, he also seemed to be staring right at her sister. Nina looked from the peacock to Sophie, then back again.

Nina tried to position herself in front of Sophie. The peacock, though, took the move as a sign of aggression. He only had eyes for Sophie. And when Nina stood in front of her, he howled.

"What does it want from me?" Sophie whispered.

"To mate?" Nina said instinctively. In her experience, male aggression typically had something to do with a bruised ego.

"What?" Sophie's voice was now panicked.

"You're his peahen." Nina was about to explode with laughter, but she didn't want to piss off her sister — or her peacock suitor — more than she already had.

The peacock raised one spindly leg and raked its footed claws through the dirt, like he was a bull getting ready to charge. It occurred to Nina that to get stampeded by a peacock would be an absurd way to die. The potential headlines alone were fuel to try and stay alive.

Nasty Nina Goes Plume-to-Plume with a Peacock and Loses!

Feathered Hero Takes Nasty Nina Down, Finally!

Nina Lyon Killed By a Horny Peacock — We Can't Make This Shit Up

So Nina turned to her sister and said, urgently, "Go find Jasmine!" then turned back to the peacock, who was still sizing her up. Sophie moved from behind her and dashed toward where Jasmine, Cory and Dori were standing. The peacock's feathers vibrated with wild and angry energy.

"Go ahead!" Nina shouted at the bird. She raised her arms above her head to get as tall as possible, though she was somehow still smaller than the bird. She took a big gulp, then added, "You're not the biggest asshole I've ever dealt with!"

That honor used to be reserved for Leo. But now? Maybe it would be this randy peacock.

"I told you to stay five to ten feet away!" The teenager from the ticket booth appeared on the path that led to the tree she was standing under. He looked at the peacock. "Reginald, heel!"

The bird paused its rhythmic, intimidating dance, and turned to face the kid.

"Reginald . . ." the teenager warned again.

Ever so slowly, the peacock's plumes began to lower, lower, lower, until they were flat on the ground.

"Good boy," the teen said. He threw a handful of raspberries on the ground, and Reginald happily pecked at the fruit. It was then that she understood that the real power the boy had was in his snacks, which she could respect on a deep and personal level. The key to her heart was food, after all.

Nina stared openmouthed at the bird. And Reginald looked up calmly, like he hadn't just tried to murder her moments earlier.

"Nina!" Cory and Dori said. "Are you all right?"

Nina turned and saw the group approaching. Cory and Dori held hands. Jasmine and Sophie clung to each other. And Nina was slightly shaking from the rush of adrenaline that came after having an actual altercation with a peacock named Reginald.

Jasmine gave Nina a thumbs-up. Nina tilted her head back, trying to convey that she wanted to know how Jasmine felt about the conversation with her parents. Jasmine shrugged, but there was a glimmer of a smile that told Nina they'd smoothed things over.

"Do they sell alcohol here?" Nina asked. If ever there was a time for a drink, it was now.

"Yes," Cory said.

"But you should get the chardonnay, not the mixed drinks. Our bartender isn't exactly first-class," Dori whispered. She put a hand on Nina's back and started to lead them toward the café in the building.

A shrill cry erupted from behind them, and Nina jumped. She turned to see Reginald staring her down.

As it turned out, if there wasn't one man out to get her, another would always find his place.

26

NINA

Nina jumped slightly as the kitchen door swung open. She hadn't quite recovered from the confrontation with Reginald the peacock.

Hadi, the pastry chef, walked in balancing an enormous baking sheet in his hands. It was lined with delicate pink macarons topped with gold leaf. As he set the tray down on a countertop, he wiped his forehead with the back of his sleeve.

"I'm terrified of tripping and spilling these every single night. I have nightmares about it." He turned to Nina and said, "Chef, how are you not sweating? Do you get Botox in your forehead? I saw that on an episode of *Real Housewives.*"

Nina shook her head with a half smirk. "I do sweat. Just not in the kitchen." She'd been covered in sweat after her hike with Leo, for instance. And also after their session in his bedroom . . .

But she didn't have time to think about him, because she had to crack pepper over the plate of Nicoise pasta she was finishing. The fresh spaghetti was plated onto a rich nest of heavy cream, basil, garlic and Parmesan cheese. Transcendence on a plate, the most satisfying thing . . . outside of Leo's head between her thighs.

"Order's up." She carefully placed the pasta on the pass — the long, flat counter space where chefs placed finished dishes for servers to come and grab.

"Soigné!" Jasmine said.

Nina grinned. Her dish was elegant, wasn't it? They were halfway through the evening with another booked dining room. She was grateful for the distraction of the kitchen and the food. Whenever she had a spare moment to think, her mind went to Leo. Which was ridiculous, considering how much time she'd spent perfecting the art of ignoring him.

"Maeve, what do we have on deck?" She quickly snapped herself out of the Leo spiral.

"Four scallop, two steak and one pasta, on order," Maeve said, reading from the hanging order tickets. Nina was on pasta duty, Jasmine was handling seafood and

Maeve, the sous chef, was overseeing the red meat.

Nina nodded. She hadn't been in sync with her kitchen staff for the last few weeks. She was used to balancing her restaurants with filming the show, constantly working to meet her goals. Adding in a fake relationship on top of all that was just as exhausting as she had worried it would be.

But tonight, she'd brought her A game to work — no distractions. She was zoned in on the smells, the texture of the ingredients and the rhythm of the kitchen. The outside world, including Leo, was beginning to fade into the background.

"Chef?" One of the servers popped her head up above the pass. "A VIP is finishing up their main. Table four."

Nina nodded and took off her apron. She checked in toward the end of every patron's meal, the same way her mother would always ask if they'd liked their dinner. She wanted people to see the hands that cooked their meal. For Nina, she never viewed her restaurant as simply serving up a menu. Food created memories, and she wanted to elicit conversations through the pieces she cooked. The meal they were having wasn't really about her, but the experience of coming to Lyon was something she hoped they'd remember forever.

And now that her business was on the verge of being flambéed, it was necessary to do everything possible to get repeat customers. Even if every question she was asked wasn't about the food, or if the only people who came in were journalists — she didn't care. She was going to throw herself into keeping her staff employed and her career relevant.

As she made her way through the dining room, she stopped short. Table four was a two-top in a corner tucked under a stained-glass window, usually reserved for couples celebrating an important date — anniversary, birthday — but there was only one person at the table.

Leo brought a forkful of her pasta to his mouth. As he chewed, he shut his eyes then swallowed. And she swore she heard a groan of pleasure come from him, not dissimilar from the noises she'd brought out of him the other day. He was in her restaurant and eating a dish she'd made. She inhaled sharply, pleased at his response.

And, of *course,* the server hadn't disclosed who the VIP was. As far as most people were concerned, Nina was dating Leo. The server probably assumed Nina knew about the visit, even though she definitely hadn't.

When he looked up and caught her eye, he smiled widely. His hair was in an impeccable, Disney-prince swoop. The cerulean sweater he wore complemented his dark eyes. He'd rolled up the sleeves, which revealed the way his forearms flexed against the table.

She'd spent so much of her day staying as busy as possible so she wouldn't think about Leo, but now she had no choice — every gorgeous inch of him was in front of her.

Then he stood. She couldn't tell if it was because he happened to be tall, or if it was just the mere presence of him that made everything else in the room appear smaller. And when he slowly began to clap, she felt like it was just the two of them in her restaurant.

But he pointedly nodded behind her, because many customers had stopped eating and were watching the Nina and Leo show. A few of them even awkwardly joined the clapping.

She grinned without having to fake anything, relieved to see him and a little more than flattered at the solo standing ovation. Even if he was just doing it for the crowd, the gesture felt like it was solely meant for her.

"Brava, chef!" He grabbed her hand and

kissed the top of it. The heat that rushed to her face was annoyingly truthful.

"I didn't know you were coming." Her body vibrated from the proximity. Being in the kitchen made her satisfied, but being next to Leo . . . *That* also did something to her.

He frowned. "Tom told me to come. He thought it would look supportive. He said you knew."

"Oh." Okay, so this *wasn't* some special surprise visit from Leo — it was a planned one from Tom. The one day she turned her phone off also happened to be the day when Tom decided to add in an impromptu date. Because, *of course.*

"Well, surprise!" He smiled. "Apparently I've ruined your night. But I don't think I've had a meal this good since . . . ever. Unless you count that takeout we had."

Just the mention of their night together made her legs clench firmly closed. She was warm from the kitchen, but even warmer from standing next to him.

"I'll take that as a compliment," she said.

"I am legally not allowed to say any pasta is better than my dad's, but that pasta was . . ." He made elaborate hand gestures to indicate explosions.

But no amount of hand fireworks could

fix the fact that she felt a bit deflated. He wasn't here for her — he was here because of Tom. She removed her hand from his. She couldn't indulge whatever feelings she had for Leo, not when they were so clearly one-sided. Even if it was her fault for setting the terms.

"I think your title of Supportive Boyfriend is officially secured."

He scratched the back of his neck. His arm lifted, and so did his shirt, revealing a sliver of his flat stomach, and the small hairs she remembered running her fingers along. Her mouth opened slightly. She wanted to lick him.

"Can't argue there," he said.

"Thanks for coming." She remembered his expression as he took a bite of her pasta, like it was lighting up his soul. Even if the encounter had been staged, his reaction was real.

He leaned down and whispered in her ear. "Tom said we need to post another photo. Should I come over after work is done?"

She licked her lips, nearly able to taste his espresso scent. But she had to control herself and focus on Lyon. Still, part of improving traffic meant posing for photos with Leo, and she'd made a promise to do whatever she needed to succeed.

"I'll text when I'm leaving," she finally said.

She wanted to look at him — to search his eyes for confirmation that he cared about her in some way. But she stopped herself. If she saw how little he really did think of her, she'd lose her nerve or change her mind. Instead, she walked back to the kitchen.

She couldn't believe she'd agreed for him to come over. She had a whole night of work ahead of her. But what other choice did she have? She needed him just as much as he needed her.

And there was no getting around the fact that he was . . . talented. She'd been thinking about how talented he was all day. So if inviting him over also meant she'd get another round, then so be it.

She could do this. She could have no-strings-attached sex with Leo and not get confused about what it meant. *Just casual sex.* She'd set the original boundaries with him, and now she needed to abide by her own rules. She wasn't usually a casual person, but using Leo would be cathartic. After all, hadn't he used her on the show to boost his own career? Now she'd get to use him to release some much-needed tension.

When Nina came back into the kitchen,

and her station, shallots, butter, garlic and freshly cut basil all stared up at her.

"Two pastas, on order."

She nodded.

"Did they enjoy the meal?" Jasmine asked, keeping her eyes trained on the scallops she was plating.

"Rave reviews." Nina didn't want to tell Jasmine who the VIP at table four was. She'd come in ready to focus on work, and she would get back to exactly that.

Because the emotions she had for Leo weren't real. Lust and great sex were clouding her mind. Since she knew he didn't feel anything for her, she just had to guard her heart.

27

Leo

He unbuttoned his pants, then buttoned them back. He let out a frustrated sigh.

Why had he gone and finished off the entire tray of desserts? He'd been served a tower of raspberry mille-feuilles, éclairs, pistachio profiteroles, crème brûlée tartlets and macarons so light and fluffy he didn't feel guilty when he popped the fifth one in his mouth.

But now his pants were impossibly tight and his throat burned from sugar overload. Leo was being self-conscious in a ridiculous way. She'd already seen him naked, but still, he wanted to impress her. And collapsing into a sugar coma wasn't going to win him any points.

The problem was he hadn't actually planned on coming back to her place after the dinner at Lyon. Tom hadn't requested a photo, and he hadn't told Leo to go to the restaurant . . . Leo had made it all up as an excuse to see Nina. And watching her work in a surprisingly sexy chef's apron turned out to be an added bonus. He wasn't willing to leave dinner and not see her afterward. So he'd gone out on a limb and, to his delight, she'd agreed.

He didn't care if they hooked up again, he just wanted to have another night with her.

Then she opened the door in a gray, silk robe that clung to her breasts, hips and thighs, showing off all of the round, full curves he'd seen the other night. Her hair was wet, fresh out of the shower, and her skin glowed pink from the hot water. He was suddenly very awake . . . everywhere.

"Can I be honest with you?" She planted a hand on her hip. "I've been on my feet all day. I'm exhausted."

He'd been so busy admiring her that he hadn't noticed that her eyes were a little heavy. Now he felt bad, because she'd had a long day at work, and here he was trying to stretch it out even longer.

"I can leave, no worries." He placed his hands in his pockets to try and match her aloofness. He wished he could channel a more nonchalant look, but he'd been excited to spend time with her. Catching feelings was a problem he'd had in almost every relationship — apparently, even the fake ones.

"No, no, I'll make us cappuccinos." She yawned. "If I'm going to be selfie-ready, I should look awake."

"Tom would probably suggest that, yes," he said.

He was relieved to be invited inside. He'd never been to her house, but assumed it was meticulously curated, much like her restaurant — French, tasteful and chic.

So he was surprised to see that her entryway had a table stacked high with unopened mail. In the living room there were sweaters and shoes in messy clumps, and a coffee table covered with old dishes. Nina hadn't known he was coming over, and maybe her cleaning person had the week off . . . ?

He heard a machine hum to life in the kitchen as he stood in her living room. He rocked back and forth on his heels. He took in the space, which was midcentury modern, if you were able to see under the piles of . . . stuff. He didn't love messiness. Just seeing the clutter gave him a ping of panic. And he'd have to do something about that.

He started by shoving all her clothes in one corner, then sorted the mail into bills, junk and personal. He then took a cloth and wiped down the coffee table.

The work kept him busy, for how long he wasn't sure. But a low cough interrupted him. When he turned, Nina was there, carrying two cappuccinos.

He put down the cloth and tried to seem like less of a neat freak than he clearly was. "Think of me as one of those topless-maid services, but still wearing my top."

She smirked. "I've never had a man clean my coffee table before." She put down the cups.

"Just wait until you see what I can do with a Swiffer." He took a long sip of the coffee. There was a hint of cinnamon, which reminded him of the smell of her hair.

She sat on the couch and sipped from her cup. He'd never been all that comfortable with silences, so he was surprised that he wasn't trying to fill this one.

"Ugh, I just remembered we'll need to take a photo." She rubbed her temple with her free hand. "I'm going to have to put actual clothes on."

"We can take the photo tomorrow morning, if you want." He took another sip from his mug before looking up to see her reaction. She stared back at him, curious.

"Are you saying you're not done cleaning?" she asked playfully.

He rubbed his lips to hide a smile. "I

really want that five-star Yelp review," he said. "I'll do anything to get it."

She shrugged her shoulder so the fabric of her robe slipped. He hadn't known the power of an exposed shoulder until he saw hers.

He raised an eyebrow. "I love working overtime."

"Is that so?" Nina stood and guided him to sit. She straddled his lap, her core directly above his arousal. "If you do a good job, I'll post before-and-after photos."

"Not sure that's at all appropriate," he said. He tucked a strand of damp, wavy hair off her face and behind her ear, exposing more of the long line of her neck. He dipped his head and skimmed across her still-warm-from-the-shower throat with his tongue.

"I'm giving you five stars," she muttered. "Do you have a condom?"

"Nina, we don't have to . . ." he began. Though it was impossible not to be excited at the idea of completely filling her until she peaked.

"Oh, I think he wants to." She nodded at his cock, which strained against the fabric of his jeans.

He wasn't going to let his first time inside her be on the couch. He needed a space where he could see all of her. Where he could stretch her out and watch the look on her face when he pushed all the way inside of her.

Picking her up wasn't hard. He cradled her ass, made sure her legs wrapped tightly around him, and walked her into the kitchen. He saw a long, thick wood table, and he sat her on top of it.

Her legs stayed around his waist as he grabbed a condom out of his wallet. "If those Nina and Leo fanfic writers could see us now," she said.

She grabbed the bottom of his shirt, and he helped her raise it up and over his head. "Oh, I'm pretty sure I read a few that involved a kitchen . . ." His hands pulled her in and he kissed her as his bare chest met the fabric of her robe.

Her hands found the button of his jeans, and then glided his zipper down. She wasted no time in seizing his cock with her hand, stroking him up and down as he pulled down his pants, then his boxers. He stopped her only so he could sheathe himself. And when he looked back up, she'd removed her robe, which fell around her in waves like drizzled icing.

As he did, she began to guide his cock to her entrance, stroking her clit with the tip of him. He was already so fucking hard, and he hadn't even sunk into her yet.

"Ready?" she breathed into his ear.

He nodded, and his hands found her hips. His fingertips dug into her as he eased himself inside her, so slowly he could barely breathe, and they both moaned as she cradled him with her pussy. She braced her hands against the table as he slid farther, burying himself deep inside her.

Fuck. How did Nina feel so good? They both paused, him filling her. She stretched and tightened against him. He hadn't even begun to fuck her the way he planned to, but she already felt better than anything he could've imagined.

He rocked into her, hitting her core deeper, and her head rolled back as a moan escaped. She fit around him in such a silky way that he already knew he'd want every waking moment to be inside her. She moved back and forth on his dick, his hands steadying her hips. He wanted to make sure that every time he pumped into her, she felt all of him. He was going to delve into her so deeply that she'd have no other choice but to come all over him. He needed to feel her heat pulsing against him.

Her breathing quickened, and she said, "I need you."

All he wanted was to hear this woman moan so loudly that he'd be able to hear it whenever he closed his eyes.

So when he slid his cock back inside her, he made sure to push until he was all the way in. She arched her back in response, and he slowly pulled out, then pumped back in.

Their moans, their thighs meeting and the slap of his balls against her ass were the only sounds in the room. He reached toward her heavy breasts and pinched one nipple tightly as he continued to fill her.

"I'm . . ." She couldn't get the words out, but he knew what she was trying to say. She was going to come. He moved the hand that pinched her nipple down to her clit and gently rubbed.

"I'm almost there," she said.

He grunted in approval and pushed into her slower, bringing his length almost fully out, then plunging back in. She tightened around him. As her groans reached a crescendo, he knew he was going to erupt as well. He thrust hard and deep until his aching cock came.

They held on to each other for several moments until their breathing returned to normal. And he knew that whatever this arrangement was . . . he didn't want it to end.

■ ■ ■ ■

Leo woke up much earlier than Nina. So he showered, brewed coffee and then drank all of it while waiting for her to wake up.

Leo: How late do chefs need to sleep?

Gavin: Why?

Leo: Just tell me.

Gavin: I get home around one, sleep till 10.

Gavin: Is this about Nina?

Leo:

So he sat on her deck, checked emails and made more coffee. When he heard her stir, he brought a cup into Nina's room. Her eyes went wide when she saw him.

"There is not enough caffeine in the world to process this." Her voice was adorably throaty as she sat up. She eagerly took the mug from him. "You're already dressed?"

"You became an escape artist the last time we had a sleepover, so I figured I needed to get ahead of whatever route you might have planned this time. Do you have the day off?" He'd had so much caffeine his foot was now jiggling.

"I do." She swallowed a gulp of coffee and closed her eyes.

He hadn't had the pleasure of watching her wake up when she'd stayed at his place. But he noticed how extra-big her hair was from sleep, and the little pillow indent on her cheek.

"I do, too." He didn't actually have the time off, but he was taking it off because he wanted more time with Nina, if she'd let him. They hadn't had a proper date, just the two of them with no photographers, so he hoped he could convince her to come with him.

She raised her eyebrows.

"How would you feel about a little road trip to get that photo for social?" he asked.

"I'd feel like I just woke up, and you're suggesting a road trip?" Her mouth opened in a very displeased kind of way, like the words *road* and *trip* tasted bad on her tongue.

"What if I told you there were freshly baked donuts involved?" He tapped the side of his mug.

She took a beat to answer, her eyes narrowing at him. "Give me fifteen minutes."

She threw off the quilt and stood up, sipping from her coffee as she walked toward the bathroom.

"And bring a coat," he called out. "It's going to be chilly."

She stopped and turned to look at him with a curious expression. "Where are we going, exactly?"

The drive out to Oak Glen took a little over an hour. They wove through a scenic loop of apple farms and fruit orchards. When they arrived, it felt more like a cozy town than a stretch of road, with plenty of restaurants and local stores serving up seasonal treats like cocoa and peppermint fudge.

But Leo remembered Oak Glen as the place he and his brother went every autumn for apple picking when they were kids. He hadn't been back since high school, but he'd always wanted to return when he had a family of his own. Nina wasn't family, but he'd still felt the urge to bring her.

When they parked at the apple farm, the fall foliage was rampant, with trees covered in bright red and orange leaves dotting the hillside in front of them.

"I'm still waking up," Nina said as they walked toward the gated entry. "But does that sign say 'hot cider and donuts'?"

There was a hand-printed sign resting against the frame of the gate that listed the entry fee for the orchard, the price of hot cider and the cost of a bag of donuts.

"Indeed it does." He smirked.

She raised her hand, as if volunteering. "Well, I hope you brought cash because I'm going to need one of each."

He grabbed paper cups of hot apple cider and a bag of freshly baked donuts covered in powdered sugar. Nina stood at the opening of the orchard, with rows of apple trees to the left, and chestnut trees to the right. Her wild hair blew in the wind, and when she turned to grab a cup of cider, a few wisps landed in front of her eyes. He used his free hand to brush them back behind her ear.

She looked down and her face flushed, the way it had when they'd first kissed on the hike. His mouth twitched just remembering the cinnamon taste of her.

She pulled out her phone. "Are you willing to take a photo without hair and makeup being here?"

He grabbed the phone from her and positioned it for a selfie of the two of them. "Just promise me you'll use a flattering filter." He took a few shots before she pocketed it.

"I've never been apple picking," she said, looking back up. "Growing up in Ojai, we picked tangerines."

"Picking something orange in the fall seems festive to me," he said.

They started to walk through the maze of the orchard. She reached for his hand, and he wrapped his fingers around hers. The gesture was so effortless that he didn't stop to wonder what it could mean. He just let their fingers find and hold each other.

"We came here every year as kids," he said. "But they run out of the baking apples right away, so you just end up bringing home twenty pounds of normal apples. Can you imagine?"

"No, I can't imagine being forced to eat a regular apple, knowing that it could've been baked into a pie." She took a bite from the donut, powdered sugar dusting her chin. "What a terrible childhood."

"Exactly." He brushed the sugar off her chin with his thumb. "My parents were monsters."

They stopped in front of a tree that was mostly bare except for a few gloriously ripe red apples at the very top. She took a sip from the cider and tilted her head back to look up at the whole of it. He admired the length of her neck as she did.

"If you brought me here to pick apples, I think we're a bit too late," she said.

She squinted, but he could still spot the amber flecks in her eyes and his words caught in his throat. She was looking at him, and he looked back, and he knew that something had truly shifted between them. But he wasn't sure how or if he should put that thought into words, so he continued, "I know your menu is seasonal. I thought a new environment might spark some ideas for you."

"Ah, so you *do* care about my snobby, pretentious menu?" Her mouth quirked up.

"After tasting the food last night, I care very deeply, yes." He was already holding her hand, but he wanted to be closer. He stepped behind her and wrapped his arms around her. He leaned down and buried his nose against her neck, taking in the sweet scent of her. Then he said into her ear, "Maybe something new will come to you."

It took a moment, but her feet shifted, her shoulders loosened and she eventually relaxed against him. They stood there, taking in the rolling hills covered in apple trees. He breathed in and out, feeling more at ease than he could remember. He was always so tense from work, but being here with Nina made him feel like he could finally stop his anxious thoughts from spinning.

She exhaled a long and satisfied breath, then turned to face him.

She hung her arms around his neck, standing on her tiptoes. She glanced around. There was a lightness in her that he hadn't seen before. "Do you think we're the only ones here?"

"When I called, they told me no one comes up on Mondays. It's just us." His gaze flitted from her mouth, back to her eyes.

Her hands traveled down the front of his shirt. A dare. "So we're all alone?"

Her mouth smelled like apples and cinnamon, and when he kissed her, she tasted like the cider they'd been drinking. He backed her up and against the tree, cradling her head as he continued to press his lips into hers.

As her fingers slinked their way around his neck and into his hair, he knew he couldn't just be friends with benefits. Not anymore. And now he'd just have to find a way to tell her that.

28

NINA

Nina was at a booth in the restaurant, folding napkins by making crisp, satisfying and easy-to-understand lines.

She needed a simple task she could manage, since her last date with Leo had her head absolutely spinning. Their impromptu sex on her kitchen table was one thing, but then, in the middle of the night, she'd surprised herself by waking Leo up for another round by trailing her tongue along his inner thigh. And then there was their apple-picking date, which sounded wholesome, until she remembered that he'd fucked her against a tree . . .

She had no idea that she was someone who liked sex in public, but, apparently, she really did. Because the sound of Leo's groans as he thrust into her would not leave her head. And she suspected the scratches from tree bark meeting her arms weren't about to vanish any time soon, either.

The words *Leo* and *best sex* did not belong in the same sentence. Logically, she knew this. But then again, neither did the words *feelings* and *Leo*. That hadn't stopped her from developing them for him, though.

"A table last night ordered this beautiful 2000 Bordeaux and only drank half." Jasmine sat across from Nina, the bottle and two wineglasses in her hands. "Can you imagine being so heartless?" She removed the cork with a flick of her thumb and poured them both a glass that nearly hit the rim.

"It's, like, ten a.m.," Nina replied. But she still took the glass, swirled, sipped, then took another sip because, fuck it — the world was upside down. She *liked* Leo. He might *like* her. Drinking was necessary to sort through all those new feelings.

Jasmine reached across the table and held on to Nina's free hand. "We need to go over finances. So drink up. Meet me in your office when you're done."

Nina squeezed her friend's hand and Jasmine left. She'd told Jasmine everything. Well, close to everything. Jasmine knew they were in a "relationship," emphasis on the air quotes. And that they'd hooked up on Halloween. But Nina hadn't given her the newest updates — that she couldn't stop thinking about Leo, and they'd slept together . . . a lot. She also hadn't spilled that they'd gone on a date, just for fun. And that he'd been texting her, and she'd kept him on read for the last day.

Leo: You haven't insulted me today. Everything all right?

Leo: I'd assume something was wrong, but it's very hard to injure a banshee.

Leo: That was a joke. I know you're more witch than anything else.

Leo: You might be shocked to hear that I actually do love talking to myself. I'm quite good company.

And then:

Leo: Are you . . . ghosting me? Is this what ghosting is?

What was she supposed to say? She wanted to be the cool, casual woman who could enjoy sex and carry on, but she just wasn't. She was developing very real feelings for Leo that she didn't have time to dissect. She had enough unknowns in her life, especially with her restaurant, and she didn't want Leo to become another puzzle she had to solve. Even if that puzzle cracked dad jokes that made her laugh, brought her apple picking and fucked her against trees. Hating each other was so simple and clean compared to whatever this was.

Her phone pinged and her fingers stopped folding. That was another new side effect of sleeping with Leo — she was checking her phone *a lot,* and if it wasn't him then she felt . . . disappointed.

Charlie: We still need to talk.

Well, a text from her ex could *also* make her feel disappointed. How about that. Charlie wasn't the type to grovel or beg. And yet, here he was, blowing up her messages.

Apparently, all the men in her life had been simmering on the stove up until this very moment, and now they were threatening to boil over. Leo wanted to know that she wasn't avoiding him — she was and she wasn't. And Charlie wasn't used to being turned down. The shock of not having Nina crawling back was probably the only reason he'd even bothered to text again. He needed her to acknowledge him and stroke his ego, the way he always had. But hadn't she done enough of that during their two-year relationship?

She needed to cut Charlie out of her life. The sooner she was rid of him, the sooner she could focus on keeping her restaurant afloat.

Only bad shit happens when we're in the same room, Nina texted back to Charlie.

"Nina?" Jasmine shouted from down the hall.

Nina ran a hand through her hair. She'd deal with a response to Leo later. She silenced her phone, took a sip of the wine and walked toward Jasmine. Her office seemed small, because she'd crammed it full of bookshelves with recipes and hanging potted herbs. There was also one shelf dedicated to framed photos — three of Nina and Jasmine from cooking school, and one solitary picture with her mom and sister taken at the opening of Lyon. She thought of Vinny's, and how the entrance was lined with photos of Leo and his family.

She smiled, remembering the dinner with his mom and brother. And when she looked back at her sister and mom, she smiled, too, which was new. Usually, when she looked at that photo, there was an undercurrent of grief. But her perspective had shifted from her talks with Leo, and now she was able to see the happiness in the memories of her mom.

"You want the good or the bad news first?" Jasmine still had the bottle of wine, and she poured the remainder into Nina's glass.

There was also a plate of croissants on the desk, and Nina took one as she sat in the vintage leather office chair. "If you've got wine *and* croissants, then I think I need the good first." She took a bite of the flaky perfection, willing it to act as a salve to the eventual bad news she'd hear.

"Business *is* better." Jasmine leaned across the desk and opened a manila folder she'd spread out. "Our reservations are up. On nights when you're here, people tweet about it and that brings in more buzz."

There were charts and cash-flow numbers pinned on a graph. Lines spiraled downward and turned red, so without even studying the numbers, she knew that part signified the loss of sales. But there was a slight uptick in the last few weeks. Nina's strength had never been the business end — that was all Jasmine — but her stomach tightened in an anxious knot.

Jasmine sighed. "We're still recovering from the first half of the year. If reservations continue as they are, we can pull out from some of the debt, but not all of it."

Nina rubbed her temples. Why had she thought everything wrong with her business could be fixed in a few weeks, and with a silly PR stunt? Her efforts had barely made a dent. "Is this fixable, or are you telling me it's game over?"

"With you and me it's never over. I wouldn't allow us to go down easy." Jasmine's expression was cool and measured.

"What do we need to do? Actually . . ." Nina finished off the wine — she might as well. "What do I need to do? This so isn't your problem. And you have to keep focusing on the menu for the gala."

"Don't forget that I work here, too." Jasmine took an enormous bite of her croissant, closed her eyes as she chewed and thought. Then she exhaled sharply as she said, "Leo. The answer is Leo."

Nina could trace all the bad career moments in her life back to Leo. Being coupled up with him apparently hadn't solved anything, either. So how could he continue to be the answer?

"When you're steady with him, the restaurant is, too. A trending hashtag means we're booked solid for a week. Hell, even your cookbook sales shot up over the last month.

We're just riding this up-and-down wave, and it's all based on whether or not your fans think you're in a good place with him." Jasmine perched on a corner of the desk and shrugged, as if to say, "I don't like this either, friend-o, but here we are."

"I mean, what am I supposed to do? Marry the guy?" Nina's voice trembled, because she knew there was no future for them. Leo would never see her as anything other than a hookup.

"Look, I'm your business partner, best friend and I have incredible style — these are all facts. The other fact I know is that these numbers don't lie. When you're with Leo, our business looks salvageable."

Jasmine hugged her. Nina didn't realize her shoulders had been so tense until she felt her best friend's arms wrapped around her. She hugged Jasmine back. They were in this together.

"This is just one thought I had," Jasmine added. "You need to do what's best for you, and I'll support whatever decision you make. You know I've got your back."

Then Jasmine left, closing the door behind her.

Nina's foot shook nervously as she weighed her options. Cut things off with Leo to spare her own feelings and let her business and best friend's career tumble into oblivion . . . or keep on seeing him and risk falling even harder for him.

The choice was simple — she'd keep seeing Leo. But she'd have to set clear boundaries, because if she was in the same room with him, who knew what her instincts and body would choose to do.

She pulled out her phone — now was the time to finally respond to Leo. She'd set a date for them to meet and lay out new ground rules. Having to fake a relationship with a person she wanted a real connection with would be awful, but she needed to do what was best for her business, and her friend's livelihood.

She had a new notification: a text from Leo.

Leo: Right.

Right? What was right? Was this a passive-aggressive way of reminding her she hadn't responded? Which . . . was fair.

She opened their chat, ready to reread everything he'd said. Which is when she saw it: the text she'd sent to Charlie. Except it wasn't to Charlie; she'd sent it to Leo. It was marked as delivered. She must have opened the wrong chat and sent it by accident. Her mouth went dry as she read what she'd sent: Only bad shit happens when we're in the same room.

And then he'd responded with "Right."

"Fuck!" she shouted, to no one but herself. She was a complete idiot. Jasmine had just told her how to save herself and everything she'd worked so hard to build. And without even knowing, she'd blown up her only chance in a single text.

Not only that, but now Leo also thought that she didn't want to be in the same room as him, which couldn't be further from the truth. If anything, all she wanted to do was be around him. The realization hit her like a ton of flour. She wanted to be with Leo, like, really wanted to be with him. She furiously texted back.

Nina: Please ignore — meant to send that to someone else!

Nina: Really sorry. Huge misunderstanding.

Nina: And I'm sorry I didn't respond to your earlier texts. Work has been crazy . . .

Nina: Are you seeing these?

She looked at the messages, which weren't actually marked as delivered. Had he turned off his phone? Fuck it, she wasn't going to wait. She called him, but immediately got his voice mail. Okay, so his phone was *definitely* off. She gritted her teeth. If she hoped to smooth over his hurt feelings, she'd just have to go to him in person and show Leo that she was sincerely sorry.

She grabbed her phone and bag and made her way toward the front. Nina straightened as her mind cleared. She and Leo would talk about a way to move forward. Maybe this accidental tension would be a good thing after all.

"I'm going to talk to Leo."

Jasmine stuck her head out of the kitchen window. "Take the day and think about your options. I don't want you making any rash —"

A gentle knock at the front door made both of their heads turn. The unmistakable, hulking frame of Charlie was just outside. He looked through the glass and nodded to Nina, a cocky smirk on his face.

"He knows we have very sharp knives in this kitchen, doesn't he?" Jasmine held one up for emphasis.

Nina closed her eyes and took a deep breath, fully aware that she'd have to deal

with this mess before making things right
with Leo.

29

LEO

Leo's thighs strained, each muscle tightening then relaxing, only to firm right back up. He'd only been running for a few minutes, but each step was like trying to kick at a wall of sand. He squinted through beads of sweat. The air was stiff with heat — one of those unseasonably warm November LA days — making the run feel irritatingly like punishment.

To be fair, he deserved the torture. He hadn't had time to work out at his usual clip while playing fake boyfriend to Nina, and it wasn't just that he was out of practice. He'd been distracted, waiting for Nina to text him back, and wondering if they would ever get to . . .

Boom, boom, boom. He kept his feet thudding across the pavement, needing to push through his anxiety. So she hadn't responded to any of his very witty and carefully crafted texts. So what? And when she did finally respond, she'd called off their relationship.

Big deal. That's exactly how they had operated before. He'd lived a passive-aggressive existence with her not so long ago, so he could do the same again, right?

The shittiest part was that even though she'd indicated how much she didn't want to be with him, he was still attracted to her. She'd laid eggs in his brain and quietly crafted a web without him noticing.

As long as he didn't go back home, he was safe, because then he'd be reminded of all of the places they'd hung out in his house, or he might pick up a pillow from his bed and smell it to capture just a hint of her cinnamon scent. Not that he'd been pathetic enough to try that . . . more than a few times.

Vinny's was just five miles from his house, which would put him five miles away from thinking about her. His phone was off, and he planned to keep it that way for the rest of the day. He'd push through the physical pain and make his way there, however slowly.

"See, when you show up like this — all sweaty but still looking better than me —

that's a problem." Gavin stood in the doorway of the restaurant, his apron already spattered tomato-red from prepping the sauce for the lunch rush. He waved Leo inside. "Rami Malek has a twin brother."

"Does he? And is his twin as irritating as you?" Leo skillfully dodged a shoulder punch from his brother.

"You need to tone down the brooding, smoldering thing." Gavin stood taller, crossed his arms and glared. "I'm not going to be Rami's forgotten twin. I refuse."

"I did ask if you wanted to join me on the run, did I not?"

"Do you know how much work it's taken to get a body this dense? I've had to channel Dad's carb-loading for years. Becoming the human equivalent of garlic bread hasn't been an easy journey for me."

"I can only imagine." Leo had hoped being with Gavin in the restaurant would take his mind off Nina, but he just kept wondering if she'd even bothered to read his response. He wasn't about to check his phone to find out. He wasn't that desperate . . . was he?

"Okay, you're not even laughing at my jokes now? Unacceptable. Sit down." Gavin placed a hand on his brother's shoulder and led him to a four-top, forcefully sitting him in a chair. "I know you don't like talking about your feelings."

"That's not true. I just don't talk about them with you."

"I'm going to cut through the bullshit — is this about Nina?"

Yes, I'm losing my mind. "Yes." Leo surprised himself by telling his brother the truth. He clenched, then unclenched his fists. He'd been sweating when he came in, and now his body started to shiver from the combination of sweat and the AC. "She just . . . she doesn't want to see me anymore."

"Tell me exactly what she said." Gavin sat across from him, his forearms on the table, ready to listen.

And the whole story spilled out, without any further prodding needed. He told Gavin about their dates, about Nina opening up to him, how they'd kissed, then slept together. He couldn't even stop himself from telling Gavin that he was head over heels in deep feels for her.

"You have a crush on a sexy, strong business owner — worse things have happened," Gavin said.

"It's more complicated than that." What he had wasn't a crush. His reaction to Nina was . . . alarming. His throat went dry when he thought about her, a burning that tightened and made it nearly impossible to swallow. He drank water, took deep breaths and at one point had even popped an allergy pill in a moment of desperation. But he wasn't allergic to her, obviously. So, no, he didn't have a crush — he had a reliance, and he went through withdrawal whenever they weren't together.

"All I know is that this is the first time you've ever talked to me about someone you're dating. So Nina must be different if you actually want my advice."

Had Leo really never talked about his relationships with Gavin? He tried to remember the last time they'd had a chat that went beyond the business. Leo had always put his mom, brother and Vinny's first, and any of his needs came after those. But now that he was with Nina, his priorities had shifted. What they had felt more real to Leo than any other relationship he'd been in.

"Yeah, she is different," Leo admitted.

She'd given him hope that his issues weren't a deal-breaker. When she'd opened up to him, he felt safe opening up right back to her. So maybe that had caused a little emotional avalanche, and he was now able to talk to his brother in a more truthful way.

"I know what will make this better."

Gavin's knowing look made Leo nervous. "I'm getting you The Usual."

"Gavin, not now." He rubbed his eyebrows with his palms. The Usual would not fix anything.

Gavin held up a finger, then headed into the kitchen. Leo heard the pizza-oven door open, and he smelled melted cheese and bread just as quickly.

Gavin returned, carrying out an extra-large pizza, topped with ricotta, pepperoni and hot peppers. The way his dad used to make The Usual for them if life hadn't gone the way they'd hoped. "Take a bite of The Usual and you'll forget the unusual," his dad would tell them.

"You said you didn't need The Usual, but a brother knows." His brother set down the pizza, then leaned across the table to study Leo. Gavin reached a finger out and tapped Leo's cheek, then withdrew it. "Oh, dude, you are sweating like a motherfucker. See? This is why I don't run."

Leo *was* sweating, and his head throbbed. Maybe the run had been too much, too fast. He took one deep belly breath to steady himself. He decided to change the subject.

"The numbers are still down, right?" If he brought his focus back to the business, he'd be able to get through the rest of the day.

"Why do you think I had The Usual ready to go?" Gavin helped himself to a slice and folded it in half before taking a bite.

"Has Ma said anything?"

"Well, she hasn't said the words, but she's doing that thing where she chews on her lips a lot. I saw her go through a whole tube of ChapStick the other day. She's got eyes — she sees how we're doing."

He nodded to himself, because he already knew what the answer was — he had to close a location. Looking at the numbers again wouldn't help. He'd squeezed, scraped and funneled as much as he could to buy them all some time, but now he had no choice.

Working with Nina hadn't solved his problem, and neither had her connections. And now he had the even bigger problem of being in serious like with someone who'd told him to leave her alone.

He grabbed a slice of pizza and chewed. The cheese and bread and meat filled his mouth, and his brain stopped spinning for a few moments. He swallowed a massive stress bite, then stood and cracked his neck. It was going to be a long morning. "I'll be in the office for a while."

"I'll eat the rest of this out of respect for

you," Gavin said through a mouthful of food.

"Someone has to." He tried to force a smile as he walked toward the back, where he had a small, neat office, to handle the bookkeeping.

He sat at his desk chair, the same old worn leather one his dad had used, and that Leo had been too sentimental to give up. He turned on his computer. For the rest of the day, he'd focus on a strategy to close another Vinny's location. He could salvage the mess he'd made, and to do that, he had to stop thinking about *her.*

When he opened his email, in addition to all the work emails he planned to sift through, there was one from Tiffany. The subject line read, "Nina hasn't signed on . . ." As in, Nina hadn't signed on to go back for another season of the show. Of course, he already knew that, and knew she never would. But he'd hoped that Tiffany and the producers would've changed their mind and allowed Leo to return on his own. He didn't open her email. Instead, he clicked on the Google news alert he'd set up to monitor mentions of his own name. Yes, he knew it was more than a little vain to be constantly surrounded by news about . . . himself. But he was a brand in many respects, so he had to keep tabs on how people viewed him in the press. Morbid curiosity made him open the email, but what he saw made his stomach drop.

The first article was titled, Three's a Crowd: Does Leo Know About Nina's Rendezvous? If he'd been a bigger person, he'd ignore the link, but he was petty, and a glutton for punishment. So when he opened up the article and saw photos of Nina getting into Charlie's car, then of the two of them walking into the exclusive Soho House lobby . . .

He wasn't surprised, exactly. Why should he be shocked that Nina wanted to go back to her ex? Even though she'd said he wasn't a good guy, as a fellow chef, Charlie would understand Nina better than Leo ever could have.

Was this why she'd tried to end things with him, and over a text, no less? She'd sent Leo the quick dismissal, then hopped in the car with Charlie. Did she really care for him so little?

A sickening trickle of sweat formed across the top of his forehead. Nina had used him. She was having one final fling before returning to the man she actually had feelings for. Everything he'd experienced with her was a lie. Why had he thought their relationship would be any different in this arrangement than it was on the show?

His jaw clenched as he remembered their last few dates. Where he'd sensed their connection deepening. He'd thought someone — Nina — was finally starting to see who he really was. The women he'd dated before Nina had all judged him, he thought. But she was different, like his brother said. She'd accepted him. So what was he missing? How had she not felt what he had? Apparently, she'd had the opposite experience. Being with Leo brought her clarity — that she should go back to being with Charlie instead.

He started to feel light-headed, and he gripped the arms of his chair. *Three deep belly breaths.* He took them in, and the air rattled in his throat as he tried to catch it. He had so many problems to fix, and a panic attack couldn't be one of them.

He was having a hard time slowing his thoughts. The room spun as he took in ragged gulps of air. His head throbbed. He could control this; all he had to do was find his breath.

Then there was nothing but blackness.

30

NINA

Choosing the bathroom as a hideout was not her brightest idea. She couldn't stay in there forever — eventually she'd need food, water and to not hear toilet sounds.

The inside of a locked stall was, however, an excellent spot to check her phone. More specifically, to see if Leo had called or read her texts, which he hadn't. And based on the last flurry she'd fired off, she wasn't sure she could — or should — send another.

Nina: Whoops, meant to send that to someone else! haha

Nina: Put down the kale salad and call me back!

Nina: I know I was rude, but you're also being rude now.

Nina: Ruder than usual.

Nina: Fine . . . I'll go hiking again if you call me back.

Nina: Please call me back . . .

He couldn't stay angry with her, not over something as silly as a text. Even if her text had suggested he was bad for her, it was a harmless accident. He had to understand that, right? Pissing him off used to be the highlight of her day, but now her stomach churned.

Or maybe her stomach was in knots because she'd come to a restaurant with Charlie and he was waiting at a table for her. How had this become her life? Stuck in a love triangle with her ex-boyfriend and a man she was fake dating. Maybe staying in this stall could be a long-term solution.

She took three deep belly breaths the way Leo had taught her.

Breathe.

Leo said to breathe.

Ahhh, Leo.

I'm losing my mind.

She shook out her shoulders, willing herself to stop obsessing, then left the stall and washed her hands. She told herself that he would call or text at some point. Yes, she'd fucked up, but eventually he'd have to acknowledge her. He had to. And if he didn't, she'd go to him and make him understand. As soon as she dealt with Charlie.

She left the bathroom and returned to the main lobby at Soho House, which was a members-only restaurant and bar known more for celebrity sightings. It surprised Nina that Charlie had chosen to bring them here instead of some hipster-owned farm-to-table place. But, then again, he'd been full of surprises lately. Showing up at her house, then her restaurant, and now . . .

What she did enjoy about Soho was the outdoor patio with floor-to-ceiling windows that gave a seemingly limitless view of Los Angeles. The sky was overcast, with puffy gray clouds blocking the sun. She would normally relish a view like this, but Charlie happened to be framed in it.

"Ordered a bottle of Tempranillo," he blurted out before she'd even had a chance to sit down. "*Your* favorite." He poured her a glass, but she gently pushed the drink back toward him.

Clarifying to Charlie that she actually preferred white to the full-bodied and spicy red wasn't worth the waste of oxygen.

Neither was explaining to him that when they dated, she was a different person — not herself. She'd been so riddled with insecurities that she never shared what her real preferences were. Going along with whatever his whims were seemed easier, at the time, but she wasn't about to get in to their history. She needed him to say whatever he needed to say so she could go fix her relationship with Leo.

"I was hoping to clear the air around how we left things . . ." He wouldn't meet her eyes, probably because the last words he'd said to her involved how he was embarrassed to be dating a reality star, and then she'd promptly told him to fuck off and that they were over. Yeah . . . not the best terms.

"If this is about kissing me the other day without my consent, you're not forgiven. But I will forget it." Whatever she had with Leo had proven that she was capable of moving on, physically and emotionally.

She didn't feel the tether that had always kept her tied to Charlie anymore. He shifted in his seat and their knees touched. He used to set her on fire just with a look, but now there was no spark where his leg met hers.

"Can you blame me? When you go walking around looking like . . ." Charlie licked his lips, but she got the sense he'd rather be licking her. He reached across the table, wrapping his hand around the tips of her fingers.

She decided to squeeze his hand back. Then she focused on him and pouted as she said, "What about you? You come over, looking like . . ." She narrowed her eyes at him. "Someone who doesn't seem to be able to take the hint that I'm no longer interested." She released his hand, sat back in her chair and crossed her arms. "Now, why did you bring me here?"

"Had to take my shot, what can I say?" He shook his head and avoided her eyes as he said, "I wanted to tell you that I'm sorry. When we were together, I was still figuring out who I was. I didn't treat you the way you deserved to be treated. I sincerely hope you can forgive me for that."

Was it possible that all he wanted was to clear his conscience?

And while she didn't owe him any kind of neat ending with a cherry on top, part of her wondered if forgiving him would help her, too. The mere idea of ever seeing him again had always filled her with dread. What would she say? Would she crumble in his presence? What would he think of her?

So maybe she could be the bigger person, for both of their sakes. "What happened is in the past," she said. Not forgiveness, exactly, but she was willing to start there.

"Okay." He sipped the wine, not breaking eye contact. "How are things going with what's-his-name?" So they were exes who talked about their new relationships now?

"You mean Leo? Don't act like you don't know his name." He could be *such* a guy sometimes. She'd forgotten that side of him.

He winked knowingly.

When she was first cast on the show, she'd told Charlie that her cohost would be Leo O'Donnell. He'd said, "Who?" And she'd laughed because . . . exactly. She thought she had the advantage of being the prestige chef, so the show would be more hers than Leo's. But it turned out they'd shared the spotlight equally, and she'd underestimated Leo's charm, enthusiasm and talent — a miscalculation she wished she could take back.

"How is Leo?" he asked, trying again.

"He's great." He really *was* great. Extraordinary. He was more than she was willing to say out loud to Charlie, because he was the kind of person who would want to see Leo fail. She owed Leo some respect after everything he'd done to try and save her business, to save her. Though, she was tempted to tell her ex just how hard Leo was able to make her come . . .

"Never thought you'd be calling the endless-breadsticks king 'great.' " He eyed his nails, but she knew he was deeply bothered by her compliment of Leo.

"Ah, so you *are* familiar with Vinny's?" If Charlie was jealous, and she was certain he was judging from his passive-aggressive comments, he'd never admit to those feelings. Part of her relished how uncomfortable he was, but another part just wanted this lunch to be over with so she could focus on winning back Leo.

"I have to go before service starts." She wasn't there to make small talk with her ex or stand by while he tried to make himself seem like a big man by cutting down Leo. He'd apologized, and she wasn't interested in staying a moment longer. "Are we done?"

Charlie smoothed his hand across the linen tablecloth and gave her a curious look, then said, "Part of me was hoping we could work things out. That would make this next part easier."

She checked the time on her phone, hoping to send the signal that he should speed things up.

"I was approached about taking the open spot on *The Next Cooking Champ!* Your old spot," he said.

401

She rolled her eyes so hard it actually hurt. *Here we go.* Now he was just being childish by making up a story to try and bait her into a fight. She wasn't going to walk into his trap. "I already know how much you hate the show."

"No, I'm serious." He scratched his chin absentmindedly. "I had a call with Tiffany last week."

How did he know Tiffany's name? He would've been too lazy to do the grunt work of googling the show and memorizing the producers. He could be an asshole, but he wouldn't put in that much of an effort to mess with her.

"They want you to be the new host?" She squinted at him.

He tilted his head in a smug way — which she didn't even know was possible, but Charlie managed to make it work. "They're looking to reboot now that you've quit, give it a fresh spin."

Her face was hot. She knew that at some point there would be new hosts on the show. One of those hosts would most certainly be a chef, but it had never occurred to her that Charlie could take her spot.

And, worst of all, he probably loved watching her be the last to know this information. He'd always viewed himself as smarter and more talented. So here she was, a lobster slowly boiling alive from humiliation.

"They want to elevate the brand," he added. He had the knife out now, and she could feel the blade pierce her skin. He let her blood trickle down as easily as spilled wine.

"Elevate it?" She knew exactly what he meant, though. He was suggesting that the show had been lowbrow because *she* had been the chef behind it, and by him taking over, everything would be different. "Why are you telling me this?" she asked.

"I wanted you to be the first to know." Charlie reached for her hand. She was in such a daze that she didn't immediately pull away.

"Are you saying you're going to take the job?" Her voice rose to a level she didn't expect. He pulled back his hand.

"We're still working out the details." He looked off into the distance, like she wasn't even there.

What she wanted to do was take a rolling pin and knock him over the head with it. Flip the table so she didn't have to look at his pompous expression. Instead, she grasped the tablecloth with both hands and leveled him with her most withering gaze.

He shrunk back in his chair.

"You told me not to do the show, do you remember that? You said taking the job would ruin my career," she hissed.

She couldn't believe this was happening. Was it possible that when she was first offered the job, he'd actually been jealous? And maybe all this time, he wasn't judging her, he was just waiting for her to fail? She hated to think that someone she'd once loved would harbor those kinds of feelings, but how else could she explain what he was doing to her now?

"I didn't say that." He caught a waiter's eye and made the signal for the check. "You're misremembering."

"Don't." She shook her head to keep from shaking him. "Your last words to me were that you were embarrassed to be dating someone on reality TV. And now you plan to take my old job?"

He was quiet, and so was the restaurant, which was odd, considering how full the room was.

"People are staring," he finally said. "And besides, this isn't about you. Not everything revolves around you."

"Nothing revolved around me when we were together. So why should I expect you to take my feelings into consideration now that we're apart?" She vibrated with rage. She was mad at herself for trusting Charlie enough to come to lunch with him, and at Charlie himself for . . . everything.

"I didn't think you'd react this way. I mean, you're the one who quit the show." He looked at her like he was truly dumbfounded, like he couldn't imagine how she could take any of this personally. And she shouldn't have been surprised — he hadn't changed at all.

But she had changed, thanks to Leo. She was a better version of herself — she'd become a more attentive friend to Jasmine and sister to Sophie. What she wanted was to be respected and adored by someone, the way Leo had made her feel. And Leo had helped her to see how powerful she was, so she wasn't about to just sit there and let Charlie walk all over her the way he had throughout their entire relationship.

"You clearly think you still have the power to hurt me, but you don't, Charlie. I'm done talking to you. I don't know why I gave you the opportunity to be in the same room as me. Let's make a promise to never speak again." She pushed away from the table, causing Charlie's wineglass to sway, then tip over, sending a wave of red toward his lap, a tiny tidal wave of her fury.

"Nina, what the fuck? These are linen!" He clambered to his feet, his cream-colored pants completely soaked in red wine.

"Can't wait to see how you *elevate* the show." She raised an eyebrow before turning to walk away.

By the time she reached the elevators there was a ringing in her ears — a buzz so loud she felt queasy. She didn't regret a word she'd said to Charlie, so why did she feel sick? And then she realized the true uneasiness she had wasn't from Charlie.

She liked Leo . . . no, *loved* Leo. She never imagined those words would cross her mind, but they were true — she had to talk to him.

And then she started to shiver, the kind of uncontrollable shaking that came with shock, because even though she was ready to commit to Leo, she would probably never have him. Especially not after blowing him off through her accidental text.

Her phone buzzed and she saw Leo's name on the screen. Well, his nickname — DEVIL. He'd called back, he was calling her back. A little pulse of hope started in her chest as she hit the button to answer. Just hearing his voice would give her some sense of whether she could tell him her true feelings.

"Hey, Nina?" The voice on the line wasn't Leo's, though.

His name was on the screen. Who was this? "Where's Leo?" she demanded.

"It's Gavin. We're in the ER. I just brought him to the hospital."

And then time seemed to stop, but for all the wrong reasons, as she listened for more.

31

LEO

Leo took a sip from his juice box. He'd asked for something stronger, and the nurse had simply laughed at him. But what he wouldn't give for one of Nina's cappuccinos — or Nina, in general.

Not that he would ever have her, or her ridiculously strong coffee drinks again. After all, she'd left him for another man. But he would, apparently, be doomed to think of her for all eternity. Because every little thing reminded him of her.

Like his hospital sheets, for example, which were stale and thin, unlike Nina's plush and cinnamon-scented sheets. Or the slow and steady beep of his heart monitor, which sounded uncannily like, well . . . it didn't sound *like* Nina, but he thought of her all the same. Would he just have to live the rest of his life knowing that she'd cross his mind roughly every few minutes?

Fucking hell. He'd brought this shitty situation on himself. He was always so desperate to fall in love that now he'd fallen hard for the only woman whom he knew would never love him back.

He rolled out one shoulder at a time, trying not to obsess again. Because the thought of truly losing Nina was what had sent him spiraling into a panic attack in the first place. He'd been consumed by thoughts of her right before he'd passed out. And when he woke up, Gavin was splashing water on his face. He knew what had happened. He'd been unable to catch his breath, had blurred vision, felt like his heart might explode, with a tightening in his throat and feeling cold and sweaty at the same time — all symptoms he'd experienced before. He'd never blacked out from a panic attack — so this one was much worse than the others — but still, the hospital's ER wasn't the answer. What he needed was to sit in a dark room, hydrate and eat something salty.

But Gavin insisted they make sure it wasn't more serious. What he didn't say, but Leo knew he was thinking, was *heart attack.* Their dad had died from one — he'd only been fifty-eight years old. Gavin had been in the kitchen with him when he fell onto the floor. And the symptoms of a heart attack were virtually indistinguishable from those of a panic attack.

Leo felt bad for worrying his brother, and worse for never telling Gavin about his panic attacks in the first place. But plenty of people dealt with anxiety on their own every day. How would burdening his family help anyone other than himself? But now that he'd been hospitalized, he knew he'd have to come clean. So not only had he opened up to Gavin about Nina, but now he'd also have to admit to having mental health issues. This was going to be a fun day for his brother.

The curtain opened, and the doctor who'd admitted Leo popped in. He was tall with an angular nose and glasses. "Good news — you didn't have a heart attack."

"I believe I told you that when I came in." He sat up as best he could, trying to seem sturdier than he felt.

"Yes, I do love an opinionated patient." He rocked on his heels. "Bad news is that panic attacks are more likely to happen again once you've had one."

"I see." Of course, he already knew that, since he'd researched panic attacks after the first had happened when he was twenty-one. It was finals week, and he'd curled up in a ball on the floor of the library to keep the room from spinning. So after the school physician diagnosed him with a panic attack, he hadn't been surprised at the second episode, or third, or seventh, in this case.

"Any panic attacks you've had in the past?" He held out a pen, ready to take notes.

The only other person who was aware of his history was Nina, he realized. The fact that she knew was a big deal to him, because he hadn't opened up to anyone about his mental health — he hadn't felt comfortable enough with anyone else.

"This isn't my first," he finally said.

"Okay, then you probably know to take it easy the rest of the day. Go have a bath, dim the lights and eat some chocolate."

"What kind of medical school did you attend that you're prescribing me chocolate?" He attempted a sly grin, but the effort just made him more tired.

The doctor stared blankly back. "Stanford."

"Harvard wouldn't have you, then?" He couldn't help himself.

The doctor adjusted his glasses, but Leo didn't miss the roll of his eyes behind them. "If you feel another attack coming on, there are a few options — try stretching while taking in deep breaths, and sometimes going

411

for a gentle walk can help, too. There's also medication."

"I'll keep that in mind." He didn't mention that he'd never taken the medication he'd already been prescribed, because his preferred method of treatment was to ignore what was happening, lock himself in a room and let it blow over. Hadn't worked this time, unfortunately.

"The nurse will be in shortly to have you sign some discharge papers. Any other questions I can answer?"

"Yes." Gavin came in through the curtain and tossed Leo a bag of M&M's. "How does your vending machine have Flamin' Hot Cheetos but no Takis?"

"Nice meeting you both." The doctor turned to leave.

"If you're ever near the Vinny's in Pasadena, come in and we'll hook you up." Gavin was smiling in a flirty, trying-too-hard way Leo had seen before.

The doctor, however, was unfazed as he left the room.

"Didn't expect to meet my future hubby in an emergency room, but here we are." Gavin sat on the side of Leo's bed, stealing the bag of candy and popping a few in his mouth. "Are you gonna tell Ma about this?"

"No," Leo said quickly. "This isn't a big

deal. A panic attack is nothing."

"You looked like you were about to keel over, and then you did. You scared the hell out of me."

Leo could see the worry written all over the lines in his brother's forehead.

"I'm fine." Leo tried to sound reassuring. He shoveled a handful of candy into his mouth. "I just don't want Ma to blow this out of proportion. You know how she gets."

"Okay, I won't tell her, but that shit was scary. You should do a follow-up with your doctor."

A nurse popped his head through the curtain and interrupted. "You have a visitor."

Leo looked past the nurse and saw a swirl of wavy hair just behind him — Nina.

His shoulders tensed. *Wait.* How did she even know Leo was in the hospital? Who told her?

Gavin sheepishly patted his brother on the back and whispered, "You're welcome." He then turned to the nurse and asked, "There are discharge forms to fill out, right?"

Without waiting for the answer, Gavin followed the nurse, leaving Leo alone with Nina.

They didn't speak. He rubbed at the ID bracelet dangling from his wrist, then

413

glanced up and thought he saw something like sympathy in her eyes. Which he hated, because he didn't want her to see him look so helpless, especially after she'd spent the last few hours with a man who probably owned a bench press and used it to double as a bed. If they were about to end their arrangement, the least she could do was allow him to shower and brush his teeth so they weren't candy-coated.

Especially because as soon as she came into the room it filled with light, like a god-damn sunbeam was shooting out from her head. She ran a hand through her hair, and it looked tousled, the way it did when she woke up in the morning. And she wore jeans and a T-shirt that, while simple, hugged the curves he loved touching.

"Your brother called me." Her voice was warm and gentle. He fought the urge to beckon her over and use her body as a human pillow.

He wished Gavin had at least mentioned this to him, but if he had, the odds were high that Leo would've found a way to undo the IV and escape through the nearest exit. He shouldn't have told his brother about Nina, because now he was clearly trying to play matchmaker when he had no idea that she'd already moved on.

"Was it a panic attack?" She wrung her hands as she approached the bed. "I thought you said you *used* to have them."

"I lied," he said.

"You? Too proud?"

She eyed his hand with the IV tube like she wanted to hold it. Part of him wished she would, because feeling the weight of her hand would be a much better option than the itchy hospital sheets.

"You didn't have to come," he offered. "No one knows I'm here, so there's no publicity angle we need to play."

"Come on, don't be like that. I wanted to come," she said cautiously. She sat on the bed and reached tentatively for his hand, but he didn't reach back. "Also, you turned your phone off, apparently. I tried to reach you. I called. I texted. So now I'm here. I want to apologize —"

But he didn't want to be broken up with while he sat in a hospital bed. He was too tired and drained from realizing she wasn't into him. So before she went on a tangent about how it wasn't him, it was her, or explained that she'd never really gotten over Charlie, or took the time to remind him that they were just friends, nothing more, he decided to make things easy.

"This isn't working," he interrupted her,

415

ripping off the Band-Aid. "We should call it off."

She looked surprised, but he was dubious. Why was she suddenly scowling? Shouldn't she be doing a victory dance that she'd finally be rid of him?

"Call it off?" she repeated.

"Don't act like you aren't relieved. I know you've been counting down the days. And this situation hasn't exactly been easy on me." He didn't want to get into the specifics, like the fact that seeing a photo of Nina and Charlie together had essentially sent him to the ER. Details like that would definitely affirm that he'd fallen for her, and he already knew she didn't reciprocate.

"I know I messed up today . . ." She stood and began to pace the short length in front of the bed. "But it was a silly text. I don't want to call it off because of that."

She stopped in front of the bed and swallowed hard. "Do you really want to end this?" Her voice had turned soft. He didn't say a word in response. But, no, he didn't. He wanted to wrap her in his arms and feel her wavy hair falling around his face, the cinnamon scent of her overpowering him. He would forever give up watching rom-coms if it meant he could leave this room, take her home and disappear into his bedroom for the next week. He wished he could erase the image of her with Charlie.

"I was coming here to explain that the text you saw was a mistake," she continued. "I feel terrible that you saw that. I meant to send it to Charlie. He wouldn't leave me alone —"

"But you were just with Charlie," he said, cutting her off.

Her jaw twitched. "I wasn't *with* him. He told me he'd leave me alone if we went to lunch. He just wanted to talk."

"It seems to me like any time Charlie shows up, you do whatever he says. He's on your porch, you kiss him. He asks you to lunch, you go." Leo was hurt. He knew he was taking out his frustration on Nina, but he didn't know how else to react, or what she wanted from him. "You won't even respond to my texts, but you're willing to spend the afternoon with your ex?"

"How can you say that to me?" she said.

"I can say that to you because I thought we had something." The words felt hot and rancid in his mouth. He wanted to take them back, because here he was, being vulnerable in front of Nina, when he knew she'd played him. But he couldn't stop himself.

"And my ex practically stalking me

417

changes that?" She was shouting the words. "If you are looking for an out, that's fine. I know all you wanted was something casual."

"What do you mean by that?" he quickly demanded.

But she waved him off. "Just don't throw this back on me and make me feel like shit."

"You made *me* feel like shit, Nina," he shouted back. "One minute you're all over me, and the next you're with this other guy. So go ahead and run back to Charlie. I guess you tend to run when things get tough, huh? Like with the show."

Her eyes narrowed at him. "When things get 'tough'? You have no idea what being hated by millions of people is like. The role I was forced to play wasn't just 'tough,' Leo. It was unfair and doing damage to my mental health. I had to take care of myself, because no one else would. If anyone should be able to understand that, it's you. Except I guess you wouldn't understand. You're so in denial that you put yourself in the damn hospital."

"I opened up to you!" His throat burned. He swallowed a big knot of tension. "Do you know how hard that is for me to do?"

"Opened up to me? Is this your version of opening up? Getting caught in a lie about how bad your anxiety is?" She threw up her hands, then placed them on the railing of his hospital bed. "And what do you think — that I just go around telling people about my mom? Or how hurt I am by the online comments I get? I opened up to you, too, Leo. I haven't been with anyone since Charlie. He seriously fucked me up. I didn't want to be with him today, but I needed him out of my life for good. And you know what? You're just like him — blaming me for everything. Trying to bring me down. I can't believe I thought you were . . ."

She trailed off and shook her head. Her fingers rubbed at her temples as she eyed the floor.

He was reeling from her words. Was she actually comparing him to Charlie? But he had to know. "You thought I was what?"

She looked up at him then, her expression as disappointed as he'd ever seen. "I thought that you were different from the rest of them."

"You think I'm as bad as Charlie?" he asked. Was she serious?

Nina looked away and shrugged.

Well, that confirmed that. His thoughts stopped spinning as he realized that at least part of what she said was right. Here he was, projecting his hurt onto her. Blaming her for a situation he'd had more than a

419

part in creating. Maybe he wasn't all that different from the other men who'd tried to put their needs before hers. He'd brought up Charlie to wound her when he knew damn well the guy had never deserved to know her name. He'd mentioned her nickname on-air because he was trying to one-up her. How was he any better than all the awful, egotistical bros she'd had to work with? Or date, in Charlie's case.

"I didn't come here to fight with you," she said. "I would never intentionally hurt you."

"I didn't mean to hurt you, either," he said, echoing her words. And he meant it.

"What are we supposed to do now?" she asked quietly.

He swallowed. The truth was, he was in love with her. Hopelessly, ridiculously and profoundly consumed with love for Nina. But he also knew he wasn't good enough for her, especially after she'd pointed out that he was just like Charlie. He wasn't going to be another man who destroyed her. He wouldn't let himself ruin her any more than he already had. The only thing he could do would be to let her leave. That way, at least, she'd be free of him.

He never should've agreed to be her fake boyfriend in the first place, but he hadn't been able to help himself. When it came to Nina, it turned out that he would do anything she asked, even if it broke him.

"I'm not supposed to be getting worked up, panic attack and all," he said. If he was going to get through the loss of her, then she needed to leave. If she stayed any longer, he'd end up changing his mind and begging forgiveness — she deserved so much better than he'd been able to offer her. "You should go."

"If that's what you think." She stood taller, seeming to steel herself as she waited for him to respond. But he didn't, and he couldn't. He didn't want her to leave, but he did need her to, for both of their sakes.

She gave him a fleeting glance, then said, "I can't believe I actually fell for you."

He almost stopped her. He pushed himself forward in the bed, and began to swing his legs to the side, but then she walked out of the room. And when she'd passed through the hospital curtain, he stilled, realizing that what was best for her would mean heartbreak for him.

His heart monitor beeped faster and louder. He took three deep belly breaths as the nurse popped his head in. "Everything okay?" the nurse asked.

No, everything was not okay. He wanted

to go home and replay everything he and Nina had said. He took another deep breath. "False alarm." Leo forced himself to smile back.

"I'll check on you in a few." The nurse pursed his lips and left just as Gavin came back in.

"What the hell, dude," he said. "I leave you alone with snacks and a queen, and she leaves in tears?"

Tears? "Tears?" he asked.

They'd both said things they probably wanted to take back. But if anything, he should be the one curled up in a ball with a pint of ice cream and a box of tissues.

Gavin sighed, and reached into his pocket. He looked away from Leo and started to crack his knuckles as he looked at his phone.

"Ohhhhh," Gavin said from the corner of the room. "Oh, shit."

"I just had a panic attack, so choose your words carefully," Leo warned.

"You don't want to know about this." Gavin gnawed on the side of his thumb while eyeing the phone.

"Okay, well now you have to tell me."

"That asshat Charlie is the new host of the show. Is that why Nina was so upset?"

"The new host of what show?" Leo was

confused. Nina had been crying, and Charlie was getting a show?

"Your show, bro." Gavin handed over his phone, and a headline glared back: Charlie Gauthier Confirms He's New Host of *The Next Cooking Champ!*

Leo inhaled sharply. Her ex was taking over the show? He quickly skimmed the article, which featured an interview with Charlie where he confirmed Nina would officially *not* be returning, and neither would Leo.

He realized that he hadn't even bothered to ask what Charlie had said at their lunch. Suddenly, the hurt she'd been feeling became justified, and his response to that hurt sounded incredibly selfish.

He'd completely fucked up, once again, and hadn't given Nina enough credit. Of course, she wouldn't be getting back together with Charlie; she'd said herself what a terrible guy he was. Leo's own insecurity had talked him into thinking otherwise, and into believing she would never find Leo good enough for her.

The beeping of his heart monitor ticked up until it blared loudly. The nurse reappeared in the room. "I was just about to take these off so you could go home. Did the thought of freedom get you that worked up?" The nurse spoke as he eyed the screens and wrapped a blood-pressure monitor around Leo's arm.

"No, this is — this is not what you think it is," Leo tried to explain. "I just saw something on my phone."

"Didn't I tell you to keep that away from him until tomorrow?" the nurse asked Gavin pointedly.

"Sorry," Gavin sheepishly replied. "He tricked me!"

"Well, thankfully, you're still at the hospital." The nurse swiped the phone off the side of the bed and pocketed it. "I'm going to keep this for your own good. And I'm getting the doctor back in here."

"We'd love to see him again. And please tell him I said that," Gavin replied.

"No, that's not necessary." Leo started to sit up, but the nurse planted a hand firmly on his shoulder and pushed him back onto the bed.

"You have a family history of heart disease, so you're not going anywhere until the doctor checks on you."

"Is it legal for you to take my phone? That's my property." Leo's mind raced. He hadn't known about Charlie's new role on the show. If he'd known that before seeing Nina, he would've handled everything differently. He needed to call her and explain the situation.

"Actually, you took my phone." Gavin reached into his other pocket and handed the nurse Leo's phone, taking back his own. "Don't worry, I'll stay six feet from him so he can't so much as lunge to open an app."

"Gavin . . ." Leo began.

But the monitor on his heart rate unleashed a wild siren of a noise as a warning.

The nurse pointed to the screen. "No phone. Nurse's orders."

He didn't know how, but the first moment he could do something to help Nina, he would. He wanted to prove to her that he wasn't just another guy trying to tear her down before she wrote him off completely. His stomach sank at the realization that she had possibly already written him off.

32

NINA

"Harder," Nina said into the pillow. She was facedown with her body pressed against the firm surface. Her world was spinning and she needed to feel anchored to something, even if it was her sister's portable massage table.

"If I go any harder you'll leave here in a cast," Sophie replied. She'd been working on Nina's back for the last half hour, trying to ease the stress knot that was giving Nina a splitting headache.

"Do what you have to do." She was numb emotionally; why not physically as well?

All men, apparently, were the worst. She still hadn't been able to understand Leo's indifference about their relationship ending. Even if he didn't want to be with her, weren't they friends, at the very least? Yes, the text she'd sent had been shitty, but she'd also followed up to explain her mistake. Did she really deserve the cold response he'd given her at the hospital?

The simple answer was that he didn't care about her the same way she cared about him. She was just thrown by how much he'd changed. She really thought she'd seen a whole new Leo, when it turned out the old one had just been waiting to make a comeback.

"I'm stopping. My hand feels like it might fall off."

Nina lifted herself up and wrapped the sheet around her. "But my ex stole my job and Leo hates me."

"You quit the job. And, reminder, Leo never said he hates you."

No, he didn't say he hated her, but he didn't have to, either. His good-guy act tricked her into thinking there might be potential between them, but her feelings were all in her head. She wasn't going to see him again, and *that* was what left her feeling as exposed as a plucked chicken.

She touched her face and felt pillow indents.

"Now get dressed. We're gonna go get drunk." Sophie left the room without another word.

Nina blinked after her.

■ ■ ■ ■

Escaping LA had been necessary. Which is why they'd driven a little over an hour away to Ojai, where they'd grown up. While it was a massive tourist destination because of its vineyards, spas and gorgeous blush-pink sunsets, it was also a small town. Many of the residents owned farms, and the sisters had driven behind an actual tractor once they turned off the highway toward the Ojai Valley Inn.

Going back to their childhood town seemed like the perfect way to escape from thoughts of Leo and Charlie. She felt bad — and frustrated — at leaving Jasmine to deal with the restaurant for the night, but she couldn't face the journalists who would fill the tables. The same ones who'd apparently followed her from lunch with Charlie to the hospital with Leo and captured her breaking down in tears after she left Leo, which had then gone viral on Twitter.

She shouldn't have been surprised to see people latching on to her crying. She'd been called "emotional" so many times online that she'd created a filter so she wouldn't see those mentions. Fans labeled her as "moody" and "aggressive" whenever she so much as raised an eyebrow, so she could only imagine what her comments looked like now that there was evidence of her shedding actual tears. Which is why the second Sophie got in her car, she decided to avoid her apps. She'd spend the night with Sophie at the hotel, recharge in Ojai and then go back to LA.

The bar Sophie brought them to was a true dive, with lighting so low they could barely see each other and every cheap, disgusting beer imaginable on tap. But they had a beautiful selection of whiskey lining the top shelf — wine wouldn't do — and she needed a stronger option. The burn would remove all the bad she'd experienced that day.

She sat on a cracked leather swivel chair right at the counter and ordered an old-fashioned from a bartender with a vibrant pink pixie cut.

Sophie peeled the label off her sweating craft beer. "Must've been really weird to be in the same room with Charlie again."

"He hasn't changed. Like, at all." He looked exactly the same and he'd disrespected her exactly the same. It had taken a relationship with Leo to understand how she deserved to be treated, and how much

429

of Charlie's bullshit she'd let herself tolerate.

"So still a massive asshole, then?" Sophie leaned across the bar and nodded to the bartender for a refill. "I never liked that guy. He was too weak to handle someone as strong as you."

"You did warn me." Even though Sophie was overly romantic about most everything, she had never indulged her whimsy with Charlie. She'd said repeatedly that he was toxic, manipulative and just plain bad, but Nina hadn't fully listened. She wanted things to work with him, because at the time she thought that if someone like him wanted *her,* then it was a sign she was actually worthwhile.

"Maybe I should be a contestant on the show. Then I can 'accidentally' stab him with a knife." Her sister gave a full grin that revealed the little overlap of her bottom teeth, making her seem extra mischievous.

"Awww, always so thoughtful," Nina joked back.

"Seemed like Leo turned out to be an okay guy, weirdly." Sophie raised the beer to her lips and waggled her eyebrows as she took a sip.

"Better than Charlie? Not exactly a high bar." She wasn't being fair, though, because

Leo was objectively a better man than Charlie. And they'd had a much easier time opening up to each other than she ever imagined they would.

"It's your life — do what you want — but you seemed really happy this last month. More yourself than you've been in a while."

A plate of wings with dipping sauce was placed in front of them. Nina wanted to bury her face in the food and not acknowledge what Sophie had just pointed out, mostly because she was right. She didn't want to think about how he'd brought out the best in her because, in the end, he'd also fucked her over.

"He definitely surprised me," Nina eventually said. She took a wing and dipped it in barbecue sauce. "But he also lied to me."

Lies of omission counted, and he'd kept his severe anxiety a secret from her. What she couldn't understand was *why*. After everything they'd been through together, did he really not trust her the way she trusted him?

"Leo's anxiety has nothing to do with you." Sophie swallowed a bite of chicken. "It's his and his alone to deal with. Sounds like he has a hard time opening up, and him sharing this — even if it wasn't a full truth — was probably a massive deal for him. And

431

for you to assume he owes an explanation is, well . . . it's a little selfish."

Nina curled her bottom lip into her mouth and nibbled. Maybe Sophie had a point, but still, wasn't his omission a sign of him not trusting her?

"I can see that your wheels are spinning, so let me put it this way — his mental health is personal and important. The same way that you don't owe him a full gynecological report just because you've let him in your vagina. Or how I don't go around telling every single guy I date that I have a literal hole in my heart. That's my health problem, and I'm sensitive about how people will react to it."

"If someone ever judges you, I will rip a hole in *their* heart."

"See? If you understand why I wouldn't share that info, then why are you mad at Leo for doing the same thing? He was probably trying to decide how much he could trust you," Sophie said. "Sorry, I'm not saying he *didn't* trust you."

"No, it's okay. Maybe he didn't." Nina raised her glass to salute the truth.

"I know you're not big on second chances." Sophie tilted her beer bottle toward Nina. "But maybe you need to get some closure."

"Let's change the subject." Nina took a sip of whiskey. It wasn't that Nina wasn't big on second chances, it was that she'd made the mistake of giving Charlie multiple chances. A mistake she didn't want to repeat with Leo. Once someone showed their true colors, that was all the proof needed to know who they really were. "Did I mention that massage was probably the best one I've ever had in my life? Your clients are very lucky."

"I know you don't give compliments easily, so I appreciate that one." Sophie licked her lips and twirled the beer bottle on the counter. "I like what I'm doing, and the flexibility of the hours. It's giving me more time to write."

"What about the novel, then? Can I read it yet?"

Sophie's mouth quirked up in a little grin. "It's coming along. And I've seen the feedback you give contestants on the show . . . No offense, but there's no way you're going to be reading one of my rough drafts."

"I only have strong opinions on food," Nina said. "I'll love anything you write."

Sophie had always been a writer. When they were younger, she'd write stories and read them aloud to Nina at bedtime. The problem was that she'd gotten a few rejections on the first novel she'd ever written and hadn't been able to bounce back. She'd taken the rejections as a sign that writing wasn't meant to be her job, so she'd tried about a dozen careers after high school to see what else would stick. Waitress, math tutor, dog walker — name a profession and she either attempted or had researched it extensively. So she was happy to hear that Sophie had found a job she finally seemed to enjoy.

"I know what we need to do." Sophie craned her head toward the stage, where a man in his seventies tipped his cowboy hat as he sang a very off-key rendition of a Johnny Cash song. "We have to sing it out."

"Why do you love karaoke so much? Neither of us can sing."

"That's not true. If you drink more you'll hear that my voice is a dead ringer for Adele's."

Nina laughed, maybe for the first time all day. She needed more of that and less of the terrible she'd experienced in the last week, so she'd follow Sophie's lead.

Her sister made a gesture for Nina to pour her drink down the hatch, and she did. She hadn't gotten good and properly drunk in some time, but she could tell by the feel of her mouth, and the way her sister swayed just slightly despite them sitting still, that tomorrow would be rough.

"Can we request a song?" Nina asked the bartender.

"Yes, thank the goddess for you. I love Johnny Cash, but this is that guy's fifth in a row."

"Lady Gaga?" Sophie asked her sister. " 'Shallow'? I'll even be Bradley."

"Fine, but only because you gave me that massage for free."

"Yes, yes, yes!" her sister squealed. "You're not going to regret this, trust me."

Ouch was the first fully formed thought that came to mind as Nina woke up the next morning. The hangover was not helped by the amount of light that poured in through the hotel-room window and onto the couch, where Nina was desperately trying to stay asleep. Aside from the bright sun, there was also the dull ache in her head, the sour taste of alcohol still in her mouth and the clothes from last night she hadn't managed to change out of — not one of her finest moments.

When she'd blinked enough to feel awake, the brown eyes of an overly plump squirrel stared back at her from the balcony.

"Don't start with me." Her voice cracked from dehydration.

The squirrel's tail fluffed ever so slightly in response.

She carefully sat up. Her sister was asleep in the hotel bed, on top of the covers and wearing a robe. She could get up and order them lots of room-service options to help cure their hangovers. She'd let Sophie sleep.

As she padded across the hardwood floor toward the bathroom to investigate the likely mess that was her face, hair and teeth, she spotted her iPhone charging on a coffee table.

All of the bad things that could happen already had — she didn't need Twitter, IG and news notifications to confirm that — but she'd have to tune back into reality at some point.

Plus, there could be a text or voice mail from Jasmine about the restaurant . . . or from Leo. She missed him. She didn't want to, but she did. The karaoke, drinking and wings hadn't distracted her the way she'd hoped. And now that she was alone with her thoughts again, he'd crept right on in.

So she looked at her phone and saw the missed calls from Leo. Just two of them. One at midnight, when Nina and Sophie had already fallen asleep, and another just seven minutes later at 12:07 a.m. No voice mails. She licked her dry and cracked lips. Of course, he didn't have to leave a message, because there wasn't really anything to say. He'd lied, she'd ignored him — both things that really didn't matter because they didn't owe each other anything.

While she wondered what Leo was thinking, her phone began to ring: Tom.

She cautiously answered, keeping her voice low so as not to wake Sophie. "I should warn you that I'm hungover, so if you start to yell I'll have to hang up."

"I don't yell. I speak sternly, like when I tell you that I've been emailing, texting and calling for the last ten hours to try and reach you. I would say that in a stern way so you know I'm not happy about it." He paused, then added, "Where are you?"

"I'm with my sister. I had to get out of the city. I've been trying to ignore my phone." Nina examined her face in the mirror. Her eyes were bloodshot, and some residual makeup had caked in certain spots.

"Lucky you. Some of us can't avoid calls because all of the outlets want to talk to their client, and said client is nowhere to be found."

"I don't have anything to say about Charlie." More like she was too hurt to say anything, really. She understood why journalists would want a comment from her, but she wasn't about to give Charlie the satisfaction.

"I'm not calling about the show. I'm calling about Leo."

Leo? Had the fans figured out their relationship was one big fat, phony lie? "So, the jig is up, then?"

"You haven't seen his IG post." Tom sounded concerned, which made Nina even more so.

"Looking now." She put Tom on speaker and opened Instagram, where a new post from Leo popped up at the top of her feed.

The post was a photo of them — a selfie from their hike when they'd shared a first kiss. She was laughing at a ridiculous pun he'd made — *these views are unbe-leaf-able* — and he was looking at her like she was the only person who mattered. She hadn't seen this photo. He must've kept it for himself until now.

There was a long caption. "Can I call you back?"

"Just remember that I know where you are, so I will drive up there if I don't hear from you."

"I'll keep my phone on, promise." Then she ended the call and began to read.

LEO'S INSTAGRAM POST

Nina Lyon, first of all I am so deeply sorry. Even though fans of our show have viewed me as the nice guy, we both know I'm anything but. Behind the cameras I went out of my way to be mean and make you feel like an outsider on your own show. I was insecure, jealous and, worst of all, I had feelings for you that I didn't know how to deal with.

So instead of treating you as a valued coworker, I tried to one-up you. Instead of coming to your defense whenever a critic wrote a piece about our show and called you words like ruthless, bossy and harsh — thinly veiled sexist remarks — I looked the other way. I could've used my social platform to fight back when some "fan" in the comments attacked you, blamed you, or accused you of being a "diversity hire," as one person put it, but I didn't. I've compared your Instagram and Twitter mentions to my own, and there's no comparison — I want you to know that I see the hate, body shaming and worse . . . I can't forgive myself for not looking sooner.

Our fans know you for your tough exterior, but the truth is that they don't know you at all. I've been lucky enough to be next to you for the last few years on the show, and the last few weeks as . . . something more. You've brought out a different side of me. I'm my best self when you're around, and all I want is for you to find the happiness, respect and love you're owed. I can honestly say that I don't deserve you. The fans of the show would be lucky to see more of you. But most of all, I want you to be truly happy. Here's hoping you know that . . .

I will always think of you.

I never disliked you.

And I never deserved a minute of your time.

33

NINA

Nina was back home and . . . cleaning. As soon as she'd walked through the door, she started to notice all the clutter lying around her house. Evidence of how checked out she'd been from her own life.

That, and she needed to avoid her phone. So she cleaned the living room, her bedroom and the office space she used to store more piles of shit she didn't need. Ten trash bags overflowed in her garage by the time she was done.

The trip to Ojai with Sophie had been long overdue; she just wished it hadn't been overshadowed by the fallout with Leo. Or that she hadn't had to spend the car ride home analyzing every line he'd written her.

After all the cleaning, her back ached intensely and she'd drawn a scalding hot bath, added in many handfuls of Epsom salt, lit a citrus-scented candle, dimmed the lights, poured a glass of wine that anyone would call generous and sunk herself deep into the water. Her hair was pulled up and out of her face. But that didn't stop the steam and heat from making her sweat.

What the hell was going on with her life? When she'd been good with Leo, she'd felt as light and airy as meringue, but now that they were in The Bad Place and she was simmering in the bath, she felt more like sweaty cheese. Things didn't look or feel good for her, despite the comfort of the water.

And she didn't really like the silence, either. She had friends for a reason. So she called Jasmine and turned on the speaker-phone.

"She lives!" Jasmine called out.

"Where are you?" The clatter of metal pots banging combined with the faint sound of '70s rock in the background.

"Practice run for the gala. I know we're three months out, but I like to be prepared. And I finally feel like I'm finding a rhythm here."

"That's amazing. At least someone is doing well," Nina said.

"Which means you're not, huh? What's up?" Jasmine asked.

"I don't want to be one of those women

442

who can't talk about anything except their crumbling love life." Nina leaned her head back against the cool porcelain of the tub.

"We all need some guilty pleasure. Your reality show dating is mine. Go on, spill."

Nina's lashes lowered as she stared into the water and said, "I don't know what to do about Leo's post on Instagram."

"Oh, *that,*" Jasmine said. "You don't have to do anything."

"But it feels like he wants me to respond," Nina hedged.

"As you know, I am not a member of the Leo fan club. He hurt you, and therefore I won't ever forgive him unless you do first."

"For being rude and sexist to me?"

"You know it."

Nina shook her head. She wasn't going to hold it against him, and she'd forgotten it. But she wasn't about to forgive what he'd done — that wasn't her job. "I'm not going to forgive him for that. He has to live with that."

"What's the *but* you aren't telling me here?" Jasmine asked. "I feel like you've got something on your mind, since you clearly want to respond to him."

"We slept together. It meant something to me. *He* means something to me." Nina said the last part quietly.

Jasmine hesitated before replying. "Okay."

"Okay?" Was that really all that her best friend was going to say?

"Look, you called me — not your sister. You know if you called your sister, she'd tell you to go running back to him. But you called me, so do you want to hear what I think?"

Nina wasn't sure, but to Jasmine's point, she hadn't dialed Sophie. Almost subconsciously, she had reached out to Jasmine. So now she'd have to at least hear her out. "Yes."

"You don't give second chances," Jasmine said. "Why would Leo be any different?"

Nina blinked. Of course, her friend was right. Her mom had always reinforced that when someone shows you who they are, that's exactly who they are. There's no changing another human being. No point in giving them another chance to right their wrongs. Because, in the end, they'd just revert to the person they'd always been from the beginning.

So why was she still holding on to Leo, if she already knew who he was, and had known for years?

"You're right," she said to Jasmine.

"Good, now I've got to go before my rhubarb burns."

"Happy cooking," Nina said before Jasmine hung up.

She slid farther into the water, letting it rise around her shoulders until just her head was above the surface. Even though she agreed with Jasmine, part of her wondered if she should chase after him. But she'd been broken before and beat down enough from her last relationship that the urge to pursue him felt impossible. She wasn't ready to be rejected, not by the man she loved most.

34

LEO

"Why do you own so many onesies?" Leo asked Gavin.

They were in Gavin's bedroom, and he'd laid out five different options on the dresser: a unicorn onesie, cat-eared onesie, T-rex onesie, panda onesie and shark onesie. They were having an emergency womb-mates sleepover.

"Dude, why don't you own any onesies? That's the better question." Gavin was already wearing his choice — a Batman onesie, complete with a flowing black cape in the back. "They're cute and cozy as hell."

Leo sighed and grabbed the T-rex onesie. Admittedly, the scale details across the arms were cool.

"Wise decision." He slapped Leo on the back as he walked out of the room. "Grabbing the snacks!"

The sleepover was Gavin's form of an

intervention. The hospital stint had been one thing, but then Leo's subsequent verbal diarrhea on IG and the pit of despair he'd sunken into had tipped things over the edge. Which just meant that Leo was going to sleep over at Gavin's so his brother could keep an eye on him. All Leo wanted to do was find a dark room and keep refreshing his messages to see if Nina had commented.

He knew that Nina didn't owe him any kind of response. And the whole point of posting to IG had been so that Nina could finally be free of him. He'd done the right thing for her, and he wanted to respect her silence. But that silence also clawed at his insides like a rake in the sandpit of his heart.

When Leo had left the hospital, #Ban-Nina was trending. The announcement about Charlie had come out, and the fans blamed Nina for Leo being ousted as well, since Charlie was her ex. Then she'd been seen with Charlie on multiple occasions, so the public had assumed Nina had arranged for Charlie to be the new host. They believed that on top of dumping Leo, she'd also had a hand in Leo being dumped from the show.

The fans turned against her: memes were made of her crying face, and her IG comment section filled up with snake emojis. The shift in loving Nina to vilifying her again had been so swift that Leo had almost missed the transition. Maybe they'd blamed her because it was easier to point the finger at a woman they'd been trained to hate and told was the "evil" one on the show. Either way, sexism was clearly alive and very real on the internet.

Leo had never paid much attention to Nina's comment feed in the past, but now that he'd seen what she was up against, he regretted not intervening sooner.

So he'd published his breakup IG post and taken responsibility for being the *real* bad guy of the show. He'd released her, because it was the right thing to do, and he owed her an out.

He knew no one could love her as deeply as he could, but he had to keep his distance so he could do right by her.

Gavin sat on the couch. "Okay, so we're going to watch a sappy movie, and I'll have the tissues ready for when you want to cry it out." An array of snacks were on the coffee table — popcorn, Brie, chocolate malt balls and lots of beer.

"You don't have to do this." His brother hated rom-coms, and all Leo wanted to do was go to bed and stay there until he forgot Nina's name. So forever, basically. "I'm fine, really."

"Would you just accept help when it's given? Have you learned nothing from your visit to the emergency room?" Gavin looked at him like he was a fucking moron, and he absolutely was, but still.

"I don't deserve help," Leo said softly.

Gavin fanned the bat cape behind him as he leaned back into the couch. He cracked his knuckles, then looked at Leo. "We're not doing that. We're not going to feel sorry for ourselves tonight. That's not what I'm going to let you do. Here's what I will allow — if you want to acknowledge that you were a rude, straight-dude prick to a strong woman who did nothing but work her ass off to get where she got, then we can do that."

Gavin's lips pursed as he looked at Leo. Leo blinked, and he could only imagine the tight little grimace his face was making at the truth to his brother's words.

"Would you like to say out loud that you were a douchebag to Nina, even though you already wrote it out in your sad little Instagram post?" Gavin added.

Leo crossed his arms and sunk farther into the couch. He felt more than a little reprimanded. "You're very mean."

"You made me take my clip-on earrings off." Gavin mimed removing earrings. "You can't change what you did to Nina. You called her a sexist name on live TV. That's shitty, bro."

"I know."

"Good. But you aren't a bad person. You've taken care of me and Ma and made sure we didn't run Dad's business into the ground. You've given us enough money that I could retire tomorrow if I wanted to. We wouldn't be what we are today without you. And you've been so busy worrying about everyone else, that you haven't stopped to worry about yourself. I know you're sad to lose Nina. I'm sad, too. She would've been a great sister-in-law for me to brag to people about. But maybe this is a gift. To quote RuPaul, 'If you don't love yourself, how in the hell you gonna love somebody else?' "

"You watch *Drag Race?*" His brother mainly kept to dramas, sci-fi and fantasy, or so Leo thought.

"The guy I'm seeing is crazy about the *All Stars* spin-off. I'm watching for him."

"Excuse me, the guy you're seeing?" Leo placed his feet up on the couch. This was news to him.

"It's not a big deal. We've just been on a couple of dates." Gavin popped a fistful of popcorn into his mouth.

"When did this start?"

Gavin swallowed. "Three months ago."

Leo paused. "What?"

"Calm down. I didn't want to tell you until I knew it was serious. And now it is. I've asked him to be exclusive."

"Three months is serious, Gavin. Why didn't you tell me sooner?" Leo snagged the bowl of popcorn from his brother, a small and childish punishment, but he did it nonetheless.

"Says the dude who can't keep a fake girlfriend." Gavin cupped his hand around his mouth and made an *ohhhhh* noise. Then paused. "Too soon?"

"Just a bit, yeah." He felt like at any moment a record would scratch to a halt, and the dramatic movie voice-over of his life would start. *I bet you're wondering how I got here . . .* Because he'd been on a TV show with someone who hated him, only to then fall in love with that person, and subsequently push them away. And now? He was in a onesie, about to binge-eat malt balls and cry his eyes out to *Bridget Jones's Diary.*

"I'm not sure watching this movie will actually help you get over Nina." Gavin had paused the movie on the opening credits, which Leo knew all too well.

The movie may not help him forget Nina, but watching it would tap into the emotions he kept carefully locked away. He'd definitely cry when Bridget caught Daniel Cleaver cheating on her, and then at the sappy happily-ever-after.

He needed this movie. And his brother. And all the snacks and beer. He realized that even though he'd lost Nina, at least he had his family, and they were extraordinary.

"Just hit Play," he finally said.

And so Gavin did. Leo settled into the couch next to him. Happy to have his womb-mate by his side to get him through the heartache. But with each romantic gesture they watched — big and small — Leo wondered if there might ever be a world where he'd get a second chance, too, the way Mark and Bridget had.

NINA'S TEXTS

Nina: Thank you for the Instagram post.

Leo: Can we please talk? There's been a misunderstanding.

Nina: I think everything we need to say has been said, right?

Leo: No, it hasn't.

Nina: It's gotten too complicated. And I don't have the energy to handle the restaurant and try to navigate . . . whatever this is.

Leo: Okay

Nina: Okay?

Leo: Yes, I'll respect whatever you want.

Leo: Nina?

Nina: Yes?

Leo: I'm so sorry.

Nina: Me, too.

■ ■ ■ ■

THREE MONTHS LATER

■ ■ ■ ■

35

LEO

Leo's fingers *tap-tap-tapped* against the arm of the leather chair. There was an open window, and he could smell lavender from the bushes outside. He rubbed his shoes against the plush, powder-blue carpet. Across the room, he focused on an antique clock that ticked away the minutes and seconds. When he licked his lips, he could still taste the espresso he'd had on the ride over.

"Have you located your five senses?" his therapist, Meredith, asked.

"Yes." Leo turned to face her. "I smelled the lavender, touched the carpet, heard the clock, tasted espresso and am staring at you. I'm officially grounded."

His therapist let out a pity chuckle. "Excellent."

Being in the present was difficult for Leo, according to Meredith. So their sessions started with a grounding exercise to try and silence the cacophony of thoughts that swirled around his skull.

Nina.

Pick up the dry cleaning. They keep texting.

Nina's mouth.

Brainstorm new ways to market Vinny's. Seriously, "Will You Be My Vinny-tine?" for Valentine's Day is cute, but you can do better.

Can't ever order anything with cinnamon. Ever.

Stop thinking about Nina, you unbelievable jackass.

"How are you feeling today?" Meredith sat across from Leo in a matching leather chair, a notepad in her lap. Leo often had the urge to stand up and see if his therapist actually took notes or just made doodles.

"Good." *A lie.* "Just trying to focus on work." *Truth, but cannot focus because of Nina.*

"Have you been having a hard time doing that?" Meredith asked blandly.

Leo made an angry little fist. Of course, he'd had a hard time. He was seeing a therapist, wasn't he? What kind of a question was that?

"I see you're tense, let's talk about why," Meredith continued.

He was tense because he was ready to

move on from Nina, but he couldn't. This was his sixth session, and so far he'd successfully avoided mentioning her. He'd talked about his brother, his mom and his people-pleasing problem. He briefly brought up losing his dad, but then shepherded them to the safer topic of Vinny's, in general. And, of course, the reason he was here in the first place — his panic attacks.

"Something is clearly on your mind," Meredith said, interrupting his thoughts. "These sessions are confidential. You don't have to talk to me, but with the amount you're paying for this hour, you might as well."

Maybe discussing Nina *was* worth it. After all, she was the person who had encouraged him to be more open and honest with who he was. He wanted to be better for himself and for Nina, even if she'd never witness the transformation. He would try. For her.

But he wasn't going to talk about her today — his feelings were still too raw — though he did have another item on his mind. "I'm a little anxious about my mom coming." Leo pursed his lips.

"That's understandable. Family sessions can be difficult," Meredith said.

One thing that *had* been helpful through

459

therapy was getting to the root of his triggers. Being overworked was top of the list, and he needed to discuss a new way forward with his mom if he had any chance of helping himself. So Meredith had suggested they bring Donna in for a family session. She could act as mediator and guide Leo through the process of finally setting boundaries with his mom.

A knock at Meredith's office door signaled Donna's arrival. Leo straightened in his chair and sipped from the water bottle at his side.

"Ready?" Meredith asked Leo.

"I am," he said. Though he wasn't sure he was.

"Hello," Donna said as she came in the room. "This is all very strange for me. I hope you understand?"

"Of course." Meredith motioned for Donna to sit. "Is this your first time speaking to a therapist?"

"Yes, unless you count Leonardo." Donna smiled at him.

He smiled back. He was nervous that in being honest with his mother, he might accidentally hurt her — something he actively tried to avoid.

"Where would you like to start?" Meredith asked him.

But before he could answer, Donna piped up. "What is it? Just tell me. Are you dying?"

"No, Ma —" He tried to assuage her.

"Do you have a secret love child?" He sensed the dread in her voice. Not that he'd have a child, but that he was hiding something from her. Which, he was.

"No." He laughed a bit, he couldn't help it.

"What is it? Tell me what's so wrong that you'd bring me here to this room with a stranger."

"Leo, are you ready to tell your mom why you wanted her to come?" Meredith asked, trying to guide him.

He blinked. He'd brought Donna here, and he owed her an explanation. "Ma, I asked you to come here so we could talk about my anxiety."

"The panic attacks, yes?"

"Yes, those, and more," he hedged.

"I'm listening." She sat forward, elbows on her knees, and looked at him so intensely he felt as if he was half his height and in a time-out chair.

He'd avoided the subject of his mental health to spare his mom's feelings. But in doing so, he may have hurt her more by keeping this from her. He just hoped she'd understand.

"When Dad died, I felt like I had to take over for him." Leo exhaled. This wasn't going to be an easy discussion. "Not just handling the business, but being the glue holding all of us together. Dad was our rock. And he'd always told me that since I was the oldest, I had to take care of Gavin. And I've done that. But I stopped making time to take care of myself. And I decided that to be like him, I had to do as much as possible. I tried to stay busy so I wouldn't have to think about losing Dad. Or how sad you seemed."

"We were all sad, Leonardo."

"Of course," he said. "I know that."

"We all had to take care of each other," his mom added.

"Let's try to remember that Leo is here to talk about the present," Meredith reminded them.

"Come ti pare," Donna said, sounding irritated.

But Leo had to keep pushing through the conversation if he ever wanted to change things. So he did. "Ma, the thing is that I tried not to show how sad I was about Dad. I buried myself in work to try to hide my emotions. And because of that, I've had a lot of anxiety just building up."

"And that is why you have the panic attacks?" his mom asked, genuinely curious.

"That's part of what causes them. And I've been taking on too much at work — trying to save the business we've built."

Donna leaned back into her chair. She crossed her legs and smoothed out the skirt of her dress. "When you were little, your dad always called you The Thinker," she said. "You'd watch a movie, or read a book with a sad ending, and you would be thinking about it for weeks. Sometimes months, in the case of *Bambi.*"

"His mom died, right in front of him," Leo said defensively. "How could they do that?"

"You have always felt deeply and with your whole heart," she continued. "I'm so sorry you've been grieving your father's loss alone. I should've checked in with you more."

"You were handling your own grief, Donna," Meredith offered. "I can't imagine how difficult it was to process your husband's death and remain strong for your sons."

"It was very hard," his mom said. "But I worried most about the boys. When Leonardo wasn't mentioning his father, I assumed it's because he didn't want to discuss him."

"I thought you didn't want to talk about him," Leo said.

"Of course, I did." His mom began to sniffle. She grabbed a tissue from the box on the coffee table and dabbed at her eyes. "He was the love of my life, the father of my children. Every day without him is a reminder of what's missing."

"I'm sorry, Mom." He reached out and grabbed her hand. She squeezed back.

"We're here for the present, just as a reminder," Meredith said. "We can't change the past, but we can move forward and be better to each other in the future."

"Yes!" Donna said with more enthusiasm than he could have imagined. "You need to take the time to go find what it is that makes you happy. The way your father made me happy. The way you seemed to be happy with Nina."

He stiffened at the mention of her name out loud. He tried to look anywhere but at his mom and Meredith. He was afraid that if he caught either of their eyes, they'd know immediately that losing Nina was a bigger issue than he was willing to admit.

"You're fired," his mom said.

He laughed. "You can't fire me, Mom."

The idea of taking time off from work seemed impossible to him. What would he even do if he wasn't going into the restaurant?

"I have a controlling stake in the company — fifty-one percent!" She balled up the tissue and threw it into the trash can. "Your father made sure of it so I could be the deciding vote if any issues arose. He didn't want you and Gavin fighting. So, yes, I can fire you. And you are fired."

His mouth fell open. He frowned. He hadn't wanted to be *fired* necessarily.

"Should I leave you two?" Meredith cautiously asked.

"No, I will leave." Donna stood, her purse already slung over her shoulder. "Thank you for telling me your truth."

"My truth?" he asked.

"I know it's a saying. I hear people in the restaurant say it all the time!"

"What will I do if I'm not at the restaurant?"

"I don't know." She kissed Leo on the head. "But you'll figure it out. And remember what I've told you in the past — be bold."

The words repeated in his mind and, as they did, so did the memory of being by

Nina's side. *Be bold.* Maybe that was the answer.

36

NINA

Nina walked into what was left of the dining room. The tables and chairs had been sold, as had the flatware, utensils, napkins and anything else someone could physically pick up and carry out.

Her restaurant, the one she'd built so many years ago and that was like an extension of herself, was unrecognizable. As of midnight, she'd hand over the keys to the new owners.

"I don't know how you can do this sober." Jasmine leaned an elbow on Nina's shoulder and carefully balanced an open bottle of white wine with her free hand. "I'm going to either cry or vomit pretty soon."

"We don't have any trash cans or tissues left, so save it for the car ride home." Nina wrapped an arm around Jasmine's waist and pulled her in for a tight hug. They held each other while the hum of midafternoon traffic rattled by outside. Normally, at this time of day, the space would be filled with the sound of clanging pans, knives meeting cutting boards and the kitchen staff catching up on gossip. The silence was eerie but calming.

Deciding to close Lyon was simple — there was no other option. She'd done everything she physically could to bring people back to her food, but no amount of PDA, trending hashtags, or blind gossip items could save her restaurant. She had to close the place she thought of as her real home. She'd promised her mom she'd keep the doors open, but she wasn't going to make good on her word.

She'd thought of Jasmine, the waitstaff, kitchen crew — all the people who got their paychecks from her business. She'd saved up enough to give them a month's severance. She'd been preparing for this possibility, and she hoped that a month would be enough for them to find new employment.

Her career was over. She was heartbroken to be closing Lyon. And ever since making the closure official, she felt like she'd placed the part of herself that loved cooking in the back of a deep cupboard and she wasn't sure how to retrieve it.

Having everything that defined her for the

last few years stripped away had meant that she could really look at herself. With no distractions, she realized that she'd lost her focus on Lyon and the food. Her world had become more about damage control than the art of cooking, which had brought her there in the first place. She needed to get back her spark, but she hadn't figured out how.

And she couldn't deny that she was still gutted from her breakup with Leo, if she could even have called it that. She felt robbed of any kind of label — boyfriend, breakup. Did she have any right to be upset over someone who had never been hers to begin with?

A sharp knock on the front door signaled that the reporter had arrived. Nina had agreed to one final interview with a journalist who'd been trying to do a profile on Nina for years. Her coverage of the show, and Nina, had always been fair. She'd steered clear of tabloid pieces and wrote thoughtful takes on women and representation in the food world. If she was going to announce the closing of Lyon, she wanted to give that story to someone who would handle it with respect.

"I'll be in your offic-c-e," Jasmine said, slurring the last word.

"One sip for courage." Nina took the open bottle. She wasn't nervous, exactly, but she was about to close a chapter of her life, and she had no idea what was waiting on the other side.

The reporter, Shay, wasn't bubbly or nervous. She had a bob of tight curls, a recorder and her phone. Nina walked her around the empty space.

"So it must be a little satisfying to know that your ex, Charlie Gauthier, will no longer be on your old show?" Shay asked.

Nina tried to hide whatever surprised expression crossed her face, because this information was news to her. She just didn't want her response to become a headline in itself. Was the reporter just trying to get a clickbait article, like everyone else?

"Ah," Shay said. "Is this the first you're hearing of it? Don't worry, we're off-the-record now. I haven't started recording. I couldn't give two fucks about him. He's always seemed like an asshole."

Nina exhaled and nodded. "You hit the bull's-eye there."

"Apparently he didn't test well with audiences." Shay raised a conspiratorial eyebrow.

"I am shocked," Nina said in her best deadpan voice.

"Ha!" Shay said and laughed. Nina liked her already.

"Would you like to sit?" Nina pointed to the two-top table in front of the picture window.

"I'll start recording now," Shay said. She placed the recorder on the table and hit the big red button. Nina licked her lips, ready to talk. There had been rumors circulating after Nina had covered the windows in paper and moving trucks were seen coming and going, but she'd never confirmed that Lyon was closing. As they sat in the picture window, Nina admitted the truth. The space had sold, and Lyon was done.

"You brought up losing focus once you started on the show. Can you talk a bit more about that? I don't think it's a secret that people treated you like shit online."

Nina laughed. She appreciated that someone other than herself had noticed.

Ever since Leo's Instagram post, where he called out the sexism she'd experienced, reporters had actually gone back and started to examine it. Think pieces were published, and some old comments were retweeted and discussed by Twitter users with verified checkmarks. A whole shift happened with the conversation around her leaving the show because, apparently, it hadn't occurred to anyone that she could've left for her own mental health, versus personally ruining their TV viewing lives.

In many ways, Leo's post had freed her from being the villain she'd been cast as. He forced their fans to reflect on their own behavior and take accountability for what they'd created. But they'd also taken stock of who Leo was, and now their fans thought he was the bad guy.

She hadn't been sure how to bridge that gap. There were no real villains on the show. She and he were just people on TV, trying to further their own careers. Their actions didn't make them evil — all they'd done was their jobs. Which was what she'd wanted to tell their fans — she just hadn't been sure how until Shay called.

"I want to answer your question by talking about the relationship Leo and I had after I left the show."

She was going to tell Shay the truth about her relationship with Leo and confess that being with him for publicity had been her team's idea. She'd used him.

Their feelings for each other hadn't all been fake, though — not for her — but she would keep that to herself. She wanted to help Leo, not create more headlines.

"The first thing you need to know is that

Leo and I hated each other pretty much every day that we were on set of *The Next Cooking Champ!*" Nina said. "But that changed."

She would tell this reporter the real story, the one her team had worked so carefully to keep under wraps. And she was ready to repay the favor Leo had done for her. Maybe if she could clear his name, he'd be able to put her — and his villain status — in the past. However painful officially losing him would be, she knew it was best for him.

GOOGLE NEWS SEARCH OF NINA LYON AND LEO O'DONNELL

Nina Defends Leo in Desperate Attempt to Save Their Relationship

A Fake Relationship and Failing Career — Nina Lyon Comes Clean

"Leo Tried to Save My Business" — Nina Tells All

Nina and Leo: Was It a Romance or Showmance?

14 Celebs Who Faked Relationships and Will Make You Question Whether Love Is Real

QUIZ: Which Reality Star Should You Fake Date?

@LeoODonnell's Twitter Mentions

@**justice4nina** you weren't dating Nina?? It was all fake?? How could you???

@**doughbro12** they kissed a LOT. Wasn't all fake . . . !

@**leoluvmeplx** Leo ur so hot. I would never do a tell all interview about you. DM me, please!!!

@**le0snumber1** Said it before . . . #Nasty-Nina strikes again

@**nuts4nina** he still was shitty to her behind the scenes, why are you always defending Leo??

@**le0snumber1** have you not seen my username?

@**nuts4nina** c mine?

@**le0snumber1** #NastyNina strikes again . . .

@**LeoODonnell** use this hashtag again and I will block you. Do you understand?

@le0snumber1 omfg

@le0snumber1 omfg yes, I mean. NEVER AGAIN.

@bakeryboxbod9 LOL

@bbqbrother LEO IS READING THIS

@rollingpindiva **@LeoODonnell** I AM SINGLE, COME TO ME

37

LEO

Leo held the binder tight to his chest, his fingers so firmly wrapped around the sides that his knuckles ached. He'd been preparing for this moment — the handoff — but the reality of letting go was only hitting him now. Could he actually step away from Vinny's?

"Yo, do you need a towel or something?" Gavin sounded concerned. He handed Leo a napkin. "You're sweating."

"I'm fine." He dabbed the napkin across his forehead.

They sat in a booth at Vinny's. He was seated across from his brother and Elisa — the new associate who would be helping him oversee the business.

He placed the binder on the table and pushed it hesitantly toward her. It was stacked with papers he'd put together on daily, weekly, monthly and yearly checklists, important phone numbers, passwords, latest sales figures, a mission statement and end-of-year goals. He'd worked tirelessly to put all of the knowledge he had about his dad's business into one place, and was surprised it all fit in a binder.

"If you get any questions, you have my cell. Anything I can answer right now?" He swallowed. He wanted an excuse to stay. Surely they needed him . . . right?

"Dude, we've gone over this how many times?" Gavin scratched the back of his head. He looked around the room, like he wanted out of the conversation. "There are no more questions, just get a life."

To be fair, his brother was right. Leo's daily check-ins with Elisa and Gavin had been extensive and maybe excessive. He'd been in charge of growing the business for so long that it had inadvertently become his life.

"I'll text you if anything urgent pops up." Elisa smiled warmly. She was the daughter of a woman his mom knew from church and had graduated cum laude from UCLA. Overseeing Vinny's day-to-day spending would be a massive opportunity, and Leo just had to hand over the keys, so to speak.

"Okay, then." Leo stood from the table. His knees wobbled slightly. He could do this. *He. Had. To. Do. This.*

A song started to play. He looked over and saw Gavin hold up his cell — 98 Degrees's "I Do (Cherish You)" blasted out of the phone's speakers.

"This is your exit song," Gavin explained. "Get out, but just know, I do . . . cherish you."

Leo chuckled. "How long have you been planning that?"

"Take a hint, bro, get out of here!" Gavin stood. He hugged Leo and then, rather forcefully, led him to the front door of the restaurant.

He held the door handle and didn't open it. "What would Dad think?"

"He'd think you don't really have a choice. You've literally never taken a vacation. It's time for you to have a break." Gavin smirked.

He couldn't argue with that logic. Leo suffered from extreme burnout, according to his therapist. Working constantly since high school, coupled with the stress of losing his father and taking on the emotional burden of his family, had triggered his first panic attack. His family and the business had continued to be a catalyst for the subsequent ones.

So he had to find a work-life balance and

retrain his brain so he could prioritize his mental health. He'd spent most of his adulthood trying to be perfect so that his mom and brother would have one less thing to worry about, but that had just led him to being a human hamster on a constant spinning wheel of doom.

"Seriously, though, Dad wouldn't want you to feel bad about this," Gavin said. He gave Leo's shoulder a squeeze. "I mean, all Dad ever did was pursue his passion. He loved Italian food and made a job out of cooking. His whole *thing* was about doing what made you feel good. Obviously, running the restaurant is making you feel like shit. You need to take time off so you can feel happy to come into work again instead of stressed."

Leo had to stop himself from countering, because Gavin was right.

"How will Vinny's survive without my crowd-pleasing bone structure?" Leo finally said.

"They'll just have to learn to love my dad bod." Gavin opened the door for Leo. "I'll come over tonight with The Usual."

Leo turned, walked out the door and couldn't bring himself to look back as he made his way to the parking lot.

The drive home was quiet. The sky was a cloudless, crisp blue, which matched the cooler February temperatures. Vinny's was located in downtown Pasadena, and his house was a five-minute drive away, but he wasn't ready to go home, so he continued to drive.

As he came to a bend where he could turn around and head toward the highway, a billboard caught his eye.

The Next Cooking Champ! was emblazoned in a fiery scroll. Two hosts, who were most definitely not him or Nina, smiled back. One held a dramatically long match that was lit at the tip, while the other extended a plate of perfectly cooked ribs toward passing drivers.

Leo nearly ran into the car in front of his. He pulled over and parked. His grip on the steering wheel loosened. He leaned forward and allowed himself to stare.

Had Nina seen this? Did she find it as unsettling as he did to know they would just carry on as if the last three seasons had never happened?

He pulled out his phone and snapped a photo. There was only one other person in the entire world who could understand what he was going through.

So maybe casually reaching out would be okay. He wasn't asking for anything. Just acknowledging that this part of their career had ended. Letting her know she wasn't alone, if she did want to talk to someone. Not that it had to be him. He wasn't expecting anything in return.

So he went into his texts, typed in Nina's name and uploaded the photo.

We are much better looking, he texted.

Then immediately deleted the text, and the photo.

He ran a finger across his bottom lip as he stared at the screen. He wanted to reach out, but he'd promised himself he'd do better by her. His mother's words came back to him. *Be bold.* And he would.

38

NINA

Nina spun in a slow circle. Her eyes widened with wonder at the bright new kitchen. Stainless-steel prep counters, a row of gleaming ovens, a gas range with multiple burners and an expansive steam table. All shiny and new. Her version of Candy Land.

"There's also a walk-in fridge and freezer just behind that door." The real-estate agent gestured to the back corner of the kitchen.

"What's behind door number three? A brand-new car?" Nina laughed at her own joke. The agent did not. "Sorry, bad joke."

Leo would've loved that joke, she thought. Then immediately tried to forget him again.

She turned to check on Jasmine.

But Jasmine's mouth was almost in a frown. Even her gorgeous high bun sagged, and her right foot jiggled so aggressively it started to shake her shoulders as well.

"Can we have a moment to discuss?" Nina

asked the Realtor, who smiled politely and left the room.

Nina placed her hands on the cool, stainless-steel countertop that sat in the middle of the kitchen. She remembered what it was like to look at potential spots for her first restaurant, how that decision had seemed like it was the most important one she'd ever make. She didn't want to minimize that for Jasmine, but . . . the space was ideal.

"How are you feeling?" Nina asked gently.

"I could fit a boat in here." Jasmine sighed. "I don't own a boat. This is enormous."

Nina laughed. "And cheap! An amazing deal for the money. But we're just browsing spaces. So what are you nervous about?"

"I love this one too much. What if I fail? It's going to break my heart." Jasmine rubbed at a spot on the chrome counter. Her chin began to quiver as she fought back tears. "Look what happened to Lyon."

Nina believed in Jasmine. From the moment they met, she knew her friend would open a restaurant. Whatever she created would feel uniquely *her,* and standing out in a massive foodie city like LA was crucial. So much of Lyon's success was because of having Jasmine in the kitchen right alongside her. Now it was her friend's turn to shine.

Lyon closing was a gift in this regard, because no more Lyon meant that Jasmine had to find a new job. If she'd learned anything from Leo, it was that family was vitally important. And to Nina, Jasmine was more than her best friend — she was part of her family. So she was going to do everything in her power to help her family succeed.

"You won't fail." Nina moved to Jasmine and wrapped an arm around her shoulder. "Come on, we both know you've always been the better cook."

Jasmine snorted.

"I'm the worst liar, as you know, so this is an absolute truth." Nina meant the compliment — Jasmine was a fantastic chef. "I'm not worried. You shouldn't be, either."

"I'm not worried." Jasmine wiped her nose with the back of her hand.

"Good."

"I'm terrified."

Nina leveled her with a look. "You love the space. The location is perfect. Let's just see who wants to invest after the gala tomorrow. Save the tears for when you're working eighty-hour weeks."

Jasmine laughed, then wiped under her

eyes. She exhaled sharply as she took in the kitchen. "Okay, so everything rests on tomorrow. No pressure."

"You're gonna have so many offers you'll have to wade through them." Nina's smile widened. She wanted this for Jasmine. Even though it would mean she wouldn't have her best friend next to her in the kitchen, she had a feeling watching Jasmine build something for herself would be just as satisfying.

"If this all goes to shit, you better have a spot for me on the new show."

After Leo's Instagram post, the other unexpected thing to happen was the overflow of emails and DMs she'd gotten from female chefs. So many women had come forward to tell her about sexism they'd experienced in the industry, the same way she had. Many had left cooking altogether because of how bad the environment was for women. Over the last few months, she'd slowly been working her way through the Twitter and Instagram messages, trying to respond thoughtfully to each one. But with every story of trauma she read, it brought back memories of her own that she wanted to forget. So she had to take big mental health breaks from being online. She wanted to find a way to help the women who were messaging her, and after some brainstorming with Sophie, she'd come up with an idea on how.

She'd worked with Tom on a pitch for a new series inspired by the women she'd spoken to. *Second Chance Kitchen* was picked up by Netflix, and it was going to be a cooking show that helped women who'd left the culinary world return to it. Nina would host, and each episode would focus on a different chef. Filming was set to start the following month. And the last episode of the season would focus on Nina looking for a restaurant space . . . so long as she could figure out what story she wanted to tell next as a chef. She hadn't found the inspiration yet, but she was hopeful.

Her phone vibrated. She pulled it out and blinked at the screen. Tom had texted her.

It wasn't that she'd been hoping for a text from Leo. But she'd been starting to see the new billboards and commercials for the next season of their show. Every time she did, she thought of him, and wondered if he ever thought of her, too.

She'd tried to keep loose, non-stalking tabs on him through the occasional — weekly — Googling session. But he'd stopped posting to social media. The only thing she saw were the rare Leo-sighting tweets, where fans acted as amateur sleuths and took photos of him out in the wild. He still looked good. He always had, though.

Jasmine bounced on the balls of her feet and clapped her hands. "I can see this working. I really can."

"I'm telling you, you'll be opening this restaurant very soon," Nina said.

But Jasmine caught something. "What's wrong? Don't tell me you think there's a rat infestation in one of these walls. I knew this was too good to be true."

Nina sighed. For a moment she'd been sad; a miserable, lonely, lost version of herself. And not just because of Lyon. Closing Lyon had only been part of her grief, because losing Leo still hurt. "Just tired," she said, shaking it off. "Come on, we should both go rest up. Tomorrow's a big day."

Jasmine nodded. As they walked toward the door, Nina pulled out her phone and opened a text to Leo. She typed I miss you. Then deleted the text. She turned the ringer up as high as it would go, on the off chance he texted.

39

LEO

Leo had meditated. Gone for a run. Taken a shower so hot he was certain he'd lost a layer of skin. Opted for tea instead of coffee so he wouldn't be too jittery. And then there was the masturbating . . . twice in one afternoon. None of that had done a goddamn thing to stop the small tremor in his hands. Or the sweaty palms.

He hadn't seen Nina in months. So the prospect of being in the same room with her was intimidating. What would he say? What would she say?

The uncertainty wound him up, so when the valet opened his car door, he didn't immediately move to get out.

"Are you here for the gala, sir?" the attendant asked.

Leo looked up at him and took a deep breath. *Be bold.* He was distracted, wondering if she was already inside the event, or if he'd see her on the way in. Which might have been why he went ahead and said, "I'm here to see about a woman."

Well, he hadn't meant to say *that* out loud.

"Uh, okay . . ." The attendant looked away, as if embarrassed for Leo.

"Sorry." Leo handed over his keys, along with a generous tip. "I have anxiety. It's a thing I'm working on."

"Oh, hey, that's cool." The attendant pocketed the cash. "My vision board this year involves a lot of self-care. You have to be good to yourself, right?"

The valet tipped an imaginary hat his way, then got into Leo's car and drove off. Which left Leo alone to stare at the entrance to the gala. Was he really ready to face Nina?

40

NINA

Nina had been to many fundraisers — all formal, mostly stuffy. So she'd assumed the gala for the botanical gardens would be much the same. Which is why she was surprised to see all of the waitstaff wearing I Dig Horticulture shirts under their formal blazers. Cheeky plant humor wasn't something she'd expected.

"Do you want the pomegranate-cranberry sangria or the raspberry-basil gin smash?" Sophie read the cocktails off the small, printed menu at the bar. "Wow, they really left no plant unturned here."

"You are such a good plus-one. I'll have the sangria." Nina wasn't sure she'd like either option, but sangria felt like a safe choice.

Sophie nodded and ordered for them. As she did, Nina turned just in time to see Cory and Dori approaching. They both opened their arms wide for a hug from Nina, and she ended up in a parent sandwich.

"Nina, isn't this just fabulous?" Dori asked.

"Have you found your table yet?" Cory added.

"We put you at the You Make My Heart Skip a Beet table. Beet with two e's. Can you stand it?" Dori laughed.

"I had no idea that people who gardened were so cutesy," Sophie said as she came up next to Nina, two drinks in hand. "I'm really into it!"

"Sophie, of course, we are!" Cory said. "Haven't you ever heard of the genus ranunculus, common name buttercup flowers? I mean, what's cuter than the word *buttercup*?"

"I honestly can't think of anything." Sophie smiled a pure and genuine grin that made Nina even more thankful she had an optimist in her life.

Nina took the sangria and wrapped her arm around Sophie's waist. "I'm glad you're here with me."

"Me, too." Her sister hip-bumped her.

Nina looked up and around the pristine white tent, where massive chandeliers and dangling lights lit the room in a soft yellow glow. The tent had been erected around large bushes of daffodils, eucalyptus trees and hearty magnolias. So the event felt more like being in a well-lit garden than an actual tent.

And Nina knew the run of show for the night. Dinner would be served. Then, during the dessert course, the auction for donations would begin. She wasn't the only item up for bid, as it were. But she was the only person. Everything else revolved around tree dedications, private tours of the gardens — things that made sense for horticulturists to bid on. Would anyone here actually spend money on cooking classes with her? Could she still call herself a chef if she didn't have a restaurant to cook in?

"Nina, I've been wanting to introduce you to Joseph, one of the arboretum's generous benefactors," Cory said.

She turned to see a very tall and very handsome Black man with tortoiseshell glasses and a smooth bald head. He extended his hand to her.

"Cory has told me so much about you." His voice was as sweet as the drink in her hand.

"Has he?" Sophie chimed in. She pointedly eyed Nina.

Nina subtly elbowed her, then shook Joseph's hand. His grip was firm and steady, instantly putting her at ease.

"Nice to meet you, Joseph, and this is my sister." Nina turned to introduce Sophie, only to see her quickly walking away. Nina licked her lips and turned back to the man. "Well, that *was* my sister."

"Is she your date tonight?" he asked.

"Yes. Finding a last-minute date for Valentine's Day isn't all that easy." She rubbed the back of her neck, feeling a bit of sudden tension there. A few months ago she'd been coupled up with someone she loved, but now? She wasn't even sure she liked the sangria all that much.

"Well, lucky for me." He raised his glass to hers, and she blinked. Was Joseph flirting with her?

A chorus of chimes sounded, and the people in the room began heading to their tables. "I hope to see you after dinner." His eyes met hers.

"Me, too," she replied. She turned to find her table and swallowed the lump in her throat. She wasn't ready to be hit on, not yet. Who knew when that day would come, but Joseph had unintentionally reminded her that someday she'd need to try and move on.

Nina and Sophie were seated at a large

round table settled under the branches of a blooming magnolia. The rich scent of the flowers mixed with the incredible food Jasmine and her team had whipped up had built an almost intoxicating aroma. They started off with sesame Halloumi and sweet potato tahini mash, followed by butternut squash and sage risotto, then there were hearty mushroom steaks with a side of roasted eggplant and miso salsa as their main. As they ate, she tasted the flavors from the earth, celebrating the gardens and passionate people around them. Her friend had harnessed the surroundings and created a rich culinary experience for the event. The other guests at their table barely spoke throughout dinner, focusing on tasting the food and washing it down with the perfectly paired wine offerings. Always a good sign that people were enjoying the meal.

"No offense, but this might be the best meal of my life," Sophie said through a mouthful of mushroom.

"Believe me, I get it." Nina dipped a bite of the scallion bread from the table into the remaining salsa on her plate.

Then she heard the uncanny voices of Cory and Dori from the small stage in front of the room. They stood tall and together, as if they were the proud parents of everyone in attendance. "Welcome." Dori tapped the mic, then coughed. "Welcome to the LA Arboretum, or as Cory and I like to think of it, our second home."

Dori smiled warmly at her husband, and he bent forward to speak. "We're in a part of the gardens called Meadowbrook, because as you can see and smell, the magnolias and daffodils are just spectacular this time of year."

"We feel so fortunate to be here with you on Valentine's Day. A time that is all about love. Isn't that beautiful? A whole holiday devoted to celebrating shared feelings," Dori said, then grabbed Cory's hand.

Nina and Sophie had never had a loving marriage modeled by their mother. Their lives had always just been the three of them. But she had to acknowledge that the sight of her friend's parents together made her hopeful that she could have that someday, too.

"Speaking of expressing our feelings, can we all give a round of applause for the beautiful meal tonight?" Dori clapped and the crowd joined her. "Chef Jasmine Miles, would you be so kind as to come out and take a bow?"

When Jasmine came out from behind the stage, she self-consciously ran her hands down her sides. Nina smiled widely and stood up from her seat to continue clapping. Sophie followed suit, then put two fingers in her mouth and whistled so loudly that Nina had to clamp a hand over her ringing ear.

Jasmine met their eyes and grinned. Nina gave a small wave. Sophie did a fist pump in the air.

"Thank you, Chef Miles." Cory smiled at his daughter as she walked back toward the kitchen.

"You have no idea how many couples get engaged on our grounds. How many others have their first kisses here under the bloom of a tree. How many weddings we've held. And the number of little babies that come from those unions, who love to run and play in our gardens." Dori shook her head wistfully. "So we think of this as a space for people to be inspired. To fall in love. To commune with their families. And we're delighted to be able to share this magical evening with you all tonight."

"We want to continue the memories made here at the arboretum. And in the spirit of giving back, we'd like to start our auction." Cory held up a blow horn. "Couldn't find the gavel we use every year."

"The man would lose his head if it wasn't

attached," Dori added.

The crowd gave a gracious laugh at the joke.

"So we hope you don't mind this substitution." Cory hit the blow horn, and the screech of the thing pierced through the air.

Nina gasped unexpectedly. Most people in the audience jumped. A few chuckled at their own reactions. Cory had nearly tripped backward and fallen off the stage. But Dori helped to right him, and he reapproached the mic.

"I'll use this wisely, then." He impishly waved it.

"Everyone, please grab your auction paddles!" Dori announced. "No ferns were harmed in the making of these, we assure you."

There was a container of "paddles" deposited in the center of each table — fern leaves with numbers attached to their sides. Before Nina could grab one herself, she heard her name loud and clear.

"Nina Lyon, would you come up to the stage?" Dori said enthusiastically. "Let's get started off with a little Hollywood glitz! Everyone, please give Nina a round of applause."

The audience began to politely clap as Nina stood up.

"You'll bid on me, right?" she asked her sister.

"Of course, but I'm basically a penniless sitar player and you're Satine, so I have about five bucks in my bag." Sophie squeezed her hand.

Nina inhaled sharply as she turned to head toward the stage. She'd been on camera hundreds of times, but for some reason walking toward the stage had her feeling extremely self-conscious. She was in a room filled with people she didn't know, and while she was used to being judged, she was also in the delicate position of currently having extremely low self-worth. If she got no bids, she might have to use her fern paddle to dig herself a hole.

"Thank you, Nina!" Cory awkwardly high-fived her as she came to stand next to him. "Now, remember, this is an award-winning chef, coming to teach you how to cook a five-course meal. A private lesson with a celebrity! Should we start the opening bid at five hundred dollars?"

She tried not to wince at the word *celebrity,* because now she was a celebrity more for her dating life than her food. But, blessedly, Sophie raised her fern paddle to signal she was placing the opening bid.

You owe me, Sophie mouthed to her.

Thank you, Nina mouthed then blew her a kiss back.

"Very good. Could I get six hundred?" Dori said.

Another paddle went up. Nina's eyes zeroed in on the table, and the handsome man sitting there staring back at her. Joseph had placed the next bid.

"Six hundred to the man at the Plant One On Me table."

She smiled politely at him. She was grateful for a bidder who wasn't related to her.

"Seven hundred?"

"I'd like to bid one thousand," a loud voice called out.

"One thousand, to the man at the . . . Oh, my." Dori stopped talking as her eyes landed on the person who'd bid.

Nina searched the crowd for the man who'd spoken, because she knew that low and confident voice. She spotted his swoop of dark hair first, which was oddly plastered to his head. And he wore a three-piece suit with the top buttons open just enough to see the hint of his toned chest. Leo looked back at her, a grin so earnest and toothy it nearly knocked her off the stage.

41

LEO

Leo didn't know if he was allowed to bid higher than what had been asked, but he'd seen it happen in movies, and money was money, so . . . it was probably okay?

He also realized that almost the entire crowd had turned to see him. He was standing at the entrance to the tent. It had begun to rain outside, and his hair was damp. He shook his shoulders slightly and walked toward the stage. He grabbed a fern paddle off a nearby table and waved it in the air.

"One thousand?" the auctioneer confirmed.

"One thousand," he shouted louder.

"Two thousand!" a stern voice said.

Leo turned to see the same guy who'd bid on her before. And this time, the guy had stood up and faced Leo.

Leo straightened his shoulders, then raised his fern. "Three thousand."

"Four thousand," the man called back.

The air horn pierced through the room. When Leo looked to the stage, the older man holding it sheepishly grinned. His counterpart, who looked almost identical to him, tapped the mic.

"Gentleman, please," the woman said into the mic. "I only get to do this once a year. I like the bidding to feel . . . civilized. Just like a lily of the valley."

"Okay," Leo called back to her. "But what do I need to bid to get this guy to stop bidding? Because whatever that number is, I bid that." He could sell his car. It was used, but worth a couple of thousand. Who needed a car in LA with all the traffic, anyway? He could walk. Or beg Gavin for rides.

"Are you two back together?" A man with floppy gray hair, wearing a shirt that read, You Grow, Girl! asked. He pointed to Nina, then Leo.

"No," Nina said sharply from the stage.

The room went quiet. Leo glanced to his right, then left, clocking a woman with a massive smile who could only be Nina's sister. Then he focused in on Nina, walking toward her as he spoke.

"Nina, I realize this might be a little weird," he hedged. Admittedly, he hadn't entirely thought this plan through. He wanted to do right by Nina and be bold. And when he saw the article saying she'd be auctioning off her time for charity, he thought . . . maybe he could put his money where his mouth was. "But if you're passionate about the arboretum, then I want to support that. I wanted to show up for you. And I plan to donate this cooking class to our first head female chef. Amanda works out of our Vegas location. She's looking for mentorship. So why not learn from the best chef in the world?"

"She doesn't even have a restaurant," a faceless voice from the crowd called out.

"Excuse me, whoever said that," Leo shouted back. "Nina Lyon is a James Beard Award–winning chef, so you can just shove this fern —"

The air horn cut him off. He looked at Nina again.

"Despite our differences," he continued, "that woman onstage is the most brilliant person I've ever met. And she is the only person I ever want to be around."

"Five thousand!" the original bidder called out.

"Six!" he practically screamed back.

"Haven't you hurt her enough?" another random voice from the room shouted.

Leo frowned. He looked back to Nina, whose lashes had fallen. She stood with her hands at her sides and wiped her palms across the front of her dress. He watched her rock back on her heels, then look up and at him. His mouth moved as they locked eyes, but no sound came out. She was the most beautiful thing he'd ever seen, and the idea that he was hurting her all over again was more than he could bear.

He'd meant to make this grand gesture of support to try and show that there were no hard feelings. Because maybe if she saw that they could be in the same room together, she'd be more open to the idea of giving him another chance. But as he looked at her, and how her shoulders tensed and her cheeks flushed, he wasn't sure they ever *could* be in the same place again.

"Nina?" Leo asked. He wanted her to say whether or not he should go. If she didn't want him here, he'd leave.

But she didn't respond.

Leo licked his lips and swallowed down all the hope he'd had walking into this place. He gave Nina one last look, wishing with all his heart that he could take back everything he'd ever done to hurt her. And then he turned away and headed for the exit, grateful for the rain that would be waiting to wash away the memory of what had just happened.

42

NINA

When she could no longer spot Leo in the room, something in Nina snapped, bringing her back to the present. His dramatic entrance had caused her to freeze to the spot where she stood. Seeing him after all their time apart felt surreal. Had she fainted from the pressure and was now hallucinating this scenario?

But he had been there. He'd made a big gesture, and an even bigger bid. And he looked . . . so good. Better than she remembered. She wanted to curl up against him. Without even being close to him, she could already smell his espresso scent.

Unfortunately, she hadn't snapped out of her state in time to stop him. He'd walked out of the tent, and back out of her life. And there she was, just standing like a deer about to be run over by reality's headlights.

"Nina Lyon." Her sister's voice cut

through her thoughts. She looked out into the crowd to see Sophie, standing and shouting at her. "It is Valentine's Day, and the man you love just left."

"Yeah," Nina said back. "He did." Breathing felt hard. Her chest grew heavy. What had she done?

"Get off the stage and go get him!" Sophie shouted. She held up her hands like she was trying to reason with a ficus.

"Ditto everything Sophie said!" Jasmine shouted, her head poking out from the kitchen door.

"Shit" was all Nina said before finding the stairs and running, as fast as her wedges would carry her, toward the door.

As soon as she got outside, the rain pelted against her, and she held a hand up to shield her eyes. She looked across the lawn, where tea lights in glass bowls lit a path back to the valet stand. She saw him walking quickly toward the lines of cars.

"Leo," she called.

But he kept walking, ever faster and farther from her. "Leo!" She cupped her hands to her mouth. "Stop walking with your fast legs, you giant!" she shouted again.

He stopped moving. Had he heard her?

"Devil!" she shouted.

He turned. When she reached him, their

bodies were just a few inches apart and she felt him, like a furnace, warming her. She blinked away water, and he smoothed his fingertips above her brow to wipe the rain away.

She'd almost let him leave. Watching him walk away would've been easy. All she had to do was stand and wait until his figure disappeared into the dark night. Eventually, she'd be able to bring herself to go back inside, collapse into a heap on the ground and get up when someone forced her to.

But she couldn't live with herself if she just let him go. Every day she'd wonder if there was more she could've done, or said, to make him stay.

"Don't go, please." Her eyebrows made a concerned crease. "I'm not sure where to start, but I need to just say that I can't stop thinking about you. I've tried very hard not to, but it's impossible. I'm sorry if I messed everything up by shutting you out. But I'm here now, and I miss you. I love you so much it hurts, actually."

Nina wasn't a romantic person. She didn't believe in soul mates. Or meeting someone you were meant to be with. At least that's what she'd told herself in every relationship she'd been in where she didn't feel that connection so many people claimed to.

But she was in love with Leo, and her feelings for him were more intense than anything she'd ever felt. She wanted to be with him. Not for publicity or sex. She wanted a relationship.

And judging by the romantic gesture of bidding for her time, she thought he might want exactly the same thing. So she grabbed the back of his head and pulled him toward her. Their lips met.

A surge went through her, breaking her open and easing the tension that had built in her since the day she said goodbye to him. He stepped forward and wrapped his arms around her waist. His lips were warm and invited her in, and she let herself delve back into them. How had she lived without this, and without him?

"Nina . . ." he began. His brow furrowed, and he took her face in his hands. "I can't just be friends with you, or whatever we used to be. It would hurt too much to want to be with you, and not be able to. So if we're going to do this —"

"We were never friends," she said. She pulled him back to her mouth. She wanted to show him just how much she wanted to be with him, too.

When they pulled apart, her voice trembled slightly. "Are we going to do this? For real this time?"

"I'm not going anywhere ever again, unless it's with you." He smoothed his thumb across her cheekbone.

"Could we go somewhere that's inside and not raining?" she asked. She kissed him again and tasted espresso.

"I have a place like that in mind." He gently pulled her hair as she bit his lower lip.

"And I have an idea of how to warm you up." She rubbed her thumb against the back of his neck.

"Don't tell me you have those nifty hand warmers." His hands spread across her rain-soaked back, and then slid down, down, down until they rested at the curve of her ass.

"What I have in mind will warm up more than just your hands," she eventually said.

"A heated blanket? I do love those."

A piercing shriek sounded through the air. Then another. Nina immediately knew what the source was.

She turned to look behind her, and there was Reginald, his mighty plumes spread so wide that all she could see was him. But his beady peacock eyes weren't looking at her. No, his sights were set on the man she loved.

"Reginald, back off!" she shouted at the peacock. "He's mine!"

Reginald hesitated momentarily. His wings quivered as if he might launch into his shimmying mating dance. But then he seemed to think better of it. Just as quickly as he appeared, he turned on his heel and fluttered off toward the tent to find another option.

"Are you on a first-name basis with all peacocks, or just that one?" Leo asked.

She turned back to him and exhaled. "What can I say? No one's going to try and steal my man without a fight."

He scooped her up and she wrapped her legs around his waist. He carried her toward the valet stand.

"I never hated you," he whispered into her ear.

She sunk her nails into the back of his neck, and whispered, "I did hate you."

He laughed.

"But you grew on me, like a barnacle. Or a zit. Or . . ."

"Or a pair of devil horns?" Leo's fingers brushed against her neck, and along her shoulders.

As they stood together in the rain, their lips meeting again was the realest thing she'd ever felt.

EPILOGUE

Eight months later . . .

Leo poured a bag of full-size candy bars into a plastic pumpkin bowl.

"Should I save you a Snickers, Reese's, or Twix?" he asked.

Nina walked over and plucked one of each out of the bowl. "You can't make me choose. It's Halloween. I need an assortment."

Leo clucked at her. "What about the children?"

"You're right. Let's turn out all the lights and keep the bowl for ourselves." She opened the Twix. "We don't want a mutiny to start on this cul-de-sac."

"You really are a witch." He handed her the black, pointy witch hat he'd gotten for her the year before.

"Did you order from Pink Metal yet?" Nina asked. "Jasmine told me she's got a new vegan chocolate pie on the menu. Can you make sure to add that?"

"I will never tire of your best friend being a chef," he said.

"Uh, you forget that your girlfriend is also a chef."

Girlfriend. Nina was his girlfriend. He never got sick of hearing or saying it. "Yes, but my girlfriend has been busy getting ready to open a new restaurant and spending so much time at work that she hasn't been able to cook me a proper meal."

"Excuse me? I always bring you leftovers from what I'm testing for Ensemble." Nina had decided to name her new restaurant Ensemble because she said it would be a marriage of cuisines — meaningful dishes, flavors and recipes, creating a whole. And tinkering with this new menu had made her feel energized again. The same way Nina made him feel — like he was complete.

She put on the hat and glanced in the hall mirror. "Honestly, this is a good look for me."

"And what about me? How's my costume?" Leo's hand shook slightly as he carefully put the devil horns on his head.

He breathed in, then out, as measured as he could. He should've waited for the takeout to arrive. He was always shaky on an empty stomach, and he wanted to be present for this moment. But he couldn't wait any longer to start the rest of their lives. At least, he hoped that's how this would go.

"Is it a costume if they're a natural extension of your head?" She smiled in the very specific way that always sent a jolt of pure adrenaline through him, then reached to bring him in for a kiss.

"Wait, wait, wait." He grabbed her hands before they found his neck. He steadied her there and took a deep breath, then said, "Notice anything different?"

He smiled so widely he was sure he looked like the creepy pumpkin they'd carved weeks ago. Not the look he'd been going for when he planned this out with Gavin and his ma.

"Uh." Nina scanned his outfit. Her nose wrinkled. "Is there a pointy tail I'm not aware of? Should we strip you down so I can have a better look?"

"Well, maybe you can strip me down later. Scratch that, you can definitely strip me down later, but . . ." He would try again. "You really don't see anything *different*. Something that catches your eye . . . ?"

"Are you okay?" She sounded genuinely concerned. "Did you have one too many of the Kit Kat bars? Do I need to send you for a run to burn off the energy?"

He rolled his eyes. Even though Nina was

his girlfriend, some things never changed — like her ability to knock him down a peg. Only now, he liked it. "My horns. Look at my horns."

Her eyebrows raised as she stepped closer. "Can you bend a bit? I'm not that short, but you've got a few inches . . ."

Her voice trailed off as he bent toward her. "Oh," she breathed. He was sure she could see the engagement ring he'd slipped over the tip of one horn.

"You got a Bedazzler, I see," she finally said. She wrapped her arms around his neck, and a wide smile crossed her lips.

He grinned. When they'd allowed themselves to be in a real relationship, he'd fallen in love with Nina all over again. And even though he'd moved too fast in past relationships, he knew this time was different. He wanted to marry her. He needed to wake up next to her each morning and do everything he could to remind her of how much he loved her. The best thing that ever happened to him was fucking up with Nina so badly that he'd had to work hard to show her he never would again. And he was lucky to be able to prove his worth to her, because Nina was worth every effort. He couldn't wait to start on a new journey as her husband. If she'd let him . . .

He carefully removed the devil horns, and then he got down on one knee.

"Nina Lyon," he began.

She slowly bit into the Twix bar as she watched him. "Don't worry, I'm listening," she said.

His mouth opened, then closed. "Can I assume you're stress eating?"

She nodded.

"Great, because I'm stress sweating." He wiped his hands on his pants. She laughed. They smiled at each other, and the look she gave him was so encouraging and pure — even through a mouthful of chocolate — that he had to go on. "I've been waiting to ask these words my whole adult life. And I'm so lucky that I get to say them to you. Nina, will you —"

The doorbell rang.

They both turned.

Nina bit her lip to stifle a laugh.

"It wouldn't be us if everything went smoothly," she said. She plucked the ring off the horns and put it on her own hand.

Leo stood up and held her hand in his.

"Will you —"

The doorbell rang again.

"See? We should've turned the lights off!" She squeezed his hand playfully.

"I couldn't, because there's actually one

more thing I wanted to show you," he said.

He moved to the door. When he opened it, Sophie and Jasmine shouted "Trick-or-treat!" in unison.

"What are you both doing here?" Nina said, as she moved to hug them.

"We're here to celebrate!" Sophie squealed.

"Not me — word on this cul-de-sac is that you're handing out full-size candy bars." Jasmine scanned the room until she found the candy bowl, then plucked out a Snickers.

"She hasn't actually said 'yes' yet," Leo told them. He looked at Nina, who crossed her arms.

"Well, I was going to, but I was told there was something more to see. Was this what you wanted to show me?" she asked him.

"Oh, hello, sparkly friend!" Sophie grabbed her hand to admire the ring.

"They are not the surprise." He raised an eyebrow at her. "Though they are here to take photos and drink a lot of good wine with us afterward."

"You forgot that I also brought too much food." Jasmine winked and held up takeout bags from Pink Metal.

"It's a *really* good surprise," Sophie said to Nina with a smile.

He reached for Nina's hand, liking the weight of the ring on her finger, and brought her to the doorframe. He pointed across the street to the actual surprise.

Getting a blow-up slide on Halloween night was harder than he anticipated, but he'd found one, nonetheless. It wasn't the exact same one they'd gone down on their first date, but he liked that this slide was witch-themed. An enormous, inflated black witch hat was perched at the top of the slide, with big black heels poking out at the very bottom. A recreation of the Wicked Witch being crushed, but this time by a slide.

He'd had the slide inflated in the neighbors' yard across the street, in exchange for a generous fee. The man operating the slide was dressed as a scarecrow. He waved at them.

When Leo looked back at her, her mouth was hanging open.

"You might be shocked to hear, but we can go down the slide as much as you'd like this time. I'll even go face-first." He waited for her to respond, but she just kept her mouth open as if she was stuck that way, so he carried on talking. "I won't go face-first every time, but at least once."

"Leo," she finally said. Her wide-open

mouth had turned into an incredible grin. He would never tire of how being in the same room with her and that smile could render him speechless.

"You are outrageous. This is absolutely ridiculous." She shook her head. If he wasn't mistaken, there appeared to be the beginnings of tears in her eyes. "I don't know how to tell you, but I like this more than the ring."

He laughed. She put her hands on his shoulders and then he realized that she was crying, just a bit, but from pure joy. "I love you." She kissed him, pressing her body tight against his. He wrapped his arms around her waist, feeling his way down her round curves and wishing he hadn't invited over her sister and best friend until the next day so he could continue to explore her with his hands.

"Delighted to hear it," he finally replied. "So, will you marry me?"

"Yeah, sure." She waved away his question with a flick of her hand.

"Nina!" Sophie guffawed.

"Don't worry, that was a *yes*," Jasmine said to him.

"Did you hear that everyone?" Leo shouted for dramatic effect. "She said, 'Sure'!"

Nina smirked. "I actually said, 'Yeah, sure.' Before we make it Instagram official, we have to go down the slide. We just have to."

"You're right. We have to," he said.

"Last one there goes face-first." Nina caught her bottom lip with her teeth before she ran past him and toward the slide, just like their first official date at the pumpkin patch. He immediately followed, because he didn't plan to let her out of his sight ever again.

ACKNOWLEDGMENTS

When I was asked to write acknowledgments for this book, I immediately thought of Travis Birkenstock from *Clueless* and his iconic acceptance speech. Because writing a book is not something you can do all on your own. Many, many people contributed to my book.

Starting with my husband, Eoghan, who gave me time, space, energy, support, and a lot of bowls of ice cream while I wrote, then rewrote. He was also the first person to read my pages, and has always been my biggest cheerleader. I love him very much.

Jeanne De Vita, who I met through the wonderful bookstore The Ripped Bodice, was extremely encouraging, a great early reader and mentor, and I am forever grateful for her friendship and early feedback.

My fabulous, thoughtful, no-nonsense — I mean this as a deep compliment — agent, Jessica Errera, believed in my book, saw potential in me, and provided fantastic revision notes that helped us to sell *For Butter or Worse.* Thank you, Tom DeTrinis, for introducing us!

Brittany Lavery at HQN Books has been an absolute dream editor. She not only makes my writing sharper and more interesting with her impeccable notes, but she's been a total champion of this book.

Deep thanks are owed to my friends, who've kept me sane and inspired while I've gone on this journey (shout-out to my book club babes and the Cute Jeans chat in particular). And my pre-order pals, Patrice Beecroft, Elisa Atwell, Trey Callaway, Floramae Yap, Amy Dickman, Dakotea McAffee, Jessie Rosen, Lindsey Allen, Amanda Strickland Henderson, and Rayna Schwartz Pinson — you have no idea how much the support means! Thank you.

And my parents, who are deeply funny natural storytellers, and who shaped my work ethic and drive so that I felt compelled to finish this book. Thank you for being so supportive, and I am sorry that your friends will probably bring up the sex scenes in the book.

Apologies and thanks also need to be sent to my cousin, Mela Lee, who is a fantastic audiobook narrator, and who I asked to narrate the book. She did! And now she's read my sex scenes out loud, but I do not know how to repay this favor!

And last, but not least, the wonderful crew at Donut Friend, for spending hours making those delicious, addictive donuts, without which I might never have finished this book!

ABOUT THE AUTHOR

Erin La Rosa is the author of *For Butter or Worse,* and on her way to writing romance, she's also published two humorous nonfiction books, *Womanskills* and *The Big Redhead Book.* She lives in Los Angeles with her husband and four daughters (two humans, two felines). Find her on Twitter and Instagram @erinlarosalit and on TikTok @erinlarosawrites.